The Fallen

R.D. Shah spent his formative years in the north west of England before attending Rugby School in Warwickshire. At seventeen he attained his private pilot's licence in Florida and shortly after attended the University of Miami where he studied motion picture & psychology before returning to the UK to work in television & leisure. He has travelled extensively throughout Europe, Russia and the Americas. R.D. holds a scuba diving licence, which he gained along the shores of the Hawaiian island of Kauai. All this experience has prepared him for a career in writing. He lives in Wiltshire with his wife and young daughter.

Also by R.D. Shah

The Harker Chronicles

Relics
The 4th Secret
The Last Judgement
The Dark Temple
The Shadow Conspiracy

The Disavowed

Project Icarus
The Fallen

R.D. SHAH
THE FALLEN

CANELO

First published in the United Kingdom in 2022 by

Canelo
Unit 9, 5th Floor
Cargo Works, 1–2 Hatfields
London, SE1 9PG
United Kingdom

A CIP catalogue record for this book is available from the British Library.

Print ISBN 978 1 80436 063 7
Ebook ISBN 978 1 80436 062 0

Look for more great books at www.canelo.co

Printed and bound in Great Britain by Clays Ltd, Elcograf S.p.A.

To Mum and Dad,

the cause and solution to all my problems.

Love you both

Chapter 1

'Burn everything. Leave nothing,' Howard Getz yelled from the upstairs window like a man possessed at the two security guards wearing blue jeans, T-shirts and coyote-brown assault vests who were shovelling handfuls of tanned folders brimming with paperwork into an incinerator, located on the patio below.

'Last load,' one of the men shouted back, and this received an impatient grunt from Getz, who closed the window and began briskly making his way to the front entrance of his expensive one-and-a-half-million-pound home on Alexandrea Road on the edge of Bristol city. At any other time, he would have been happy, even proud to tell those he wined and dined of the wealthy neighbourhood he lived in... but not today. Today he just wanted out, and the sooner he got away from here the better.

Getz flung open the front door and passed his briefcase and laptop to the security guard, who was wearing the same brown assault vest as the boys out back, waiting on the doorstep. 'Put it in my car and let's go,' he ordered as the guard took off running and quickly placed the items in the back of the black BMW 750 before rushing to the front passenger side as Getz hurled himself into the back seat.

'Drive, drive.' The BMW screeched off down the street as a black Porsche Cayenne filled with four more security guards tore off after it. 'How the hell did you miss it?' Getz yelled as the BMW continued at high speed, blaring its horn at anyone crossing the road.

'Our contact in Interpol's gone dark, you're lucky we got any advanced warning at all, sir.'

'*Lucky!* I pay you idiots, so luck never comes into the equation. What kind of Mickey Mouse bullshit is this?'

The guard looked unfazed by the insult and looked back past his headrest. 'You don't pay us, sir, but regardless, we'll get you to the plane and you'll be out of the country before anyone catches up.'

Getz ignored the retort and grabbed hold of the central armrest as the BMW swerved around the tight corners that would lead them out of the city. He could feel his temper getting the better of him and he settled back into his seat as best he could and took a few deep, calming breaths.

At thirty-five, Howard Getz was a highflyer within the financial system. He'd risen through the ranks of one of the largest firms in the world, eventually making the switch to investment banking, and from there to an influential hedge fund where he'd clawed his way to one of the top managerial positions in the company. He took great pride in the nickname bestowed upon him – 'The Machine' – for his ability to spot economic trends, and with a mathematical mind such as his, no one could touch him. His gift had earned him millions, and if anyone thought they were going to take that away from him now, just because he had dabbled in a bit of harmless Mexican narco money laundering, they could forget it. All the institutions did it on some level, but while these financial behemoths were too big to face reprisal from the powers that be, he was an easy target to single out. Hadn't that been the way since the beginning of time? The rich got richer and, when you made enough money, mammoth amounts akin to the gross national output of some small countries, that very fact brought absolution in the eyes of the world. Your money could be as crooked as a dog's leg, but make enough and you came out smelling like roses on the other side. He, unfortunately, was not quite there yet.

'Is the jet ready to go?' Getz asked, his anger tempering. The breathing had helped, but the answer he got had his blood boiling once again.

'I'm afraid the jet's a no-go, sir,' the guard replied as Getz's face began to flush red.

'What?'

'They know about your jet, sir. It's too much of a risk, but we've made alternative plans.'

As Getz waited for these alternative plans to be explained he found himself sitting in total silence, apart from the roar of the BMW's engine. 'Well! Davies, you prick, are you going to explain them or not?'

Davies was used to the man's temper, and given the circumstances he wasn't surprised, so he calmly turned back once again. 'We've secured another plane at a local airstrip. It'll be a bumpy take-off, but it will get us over to France and from there you'll transfer to a jet. It's all arranged.'

The details appeared to calm Getz once more, and as the nervous twitching in his shoulders began to subside, the financier settled back into his seat. Once airborne he could go anywhere. There were immutable dangers that went side by side in his chosen profession but with the money he made, finding a safe house and country was not one of them.

'Good, then get me in the air.'

Davies offered a respectful grunt and he gripped the dashboard hard as the BMW jerked to one side, just missing a teenager riding a green mountain bike who forcefully thrust his middle finger in the air at them as the car sped by.

Getz glanced back at the ill-mannered teenager and his lips curled downwards in disdain. Even though he'd been happy to be based out of Bristol for some years, it had often crossed his mind to make a move to greener pastures. Bristol wasn't London or New York and he was happy to be leaving, although he had never envisaged it happening under such undesirable circumstances. His company had offices in most of the main Western capitals, but after this debacle he would have to relocate further afield until the authorities could be handled.

'What's our ETA to the airport?'

'It's an airfield, and we're only seven minutes out,' Davies replied, his response serving to ease Getz's nerves further. So much so that he smiled smugly. 'UK police…' he sneered, letting out an arrogant snort, 'useless bastards.'

He had barely finished his insult when the entire back of the BMW was lit up in a barrage of red and blue flashing lights, and Getz looked back to see two BMW 335 police cars zip past the Porsche Cayenne and fall in right behind him.

'Shit.' As he turned, his eyes widened as he caught sight of Davies, who was already pulling out a semi-automatic short stock Bushmaster Parabellum from his footwell. 'Jesus, put that away. No guns.'

Davies looked surprised, Getz wasn't known to be bashful at the sight of blood, especially that of the police.

He lowered the weapon back to the floor and picked up a walkie-talkie while he watched Getz duck down from the back window, fearing any police cameras. 'Strike team two. No engagement. Keep your firearms shadowed.'

'Acknowledged. Orders?' came the crackled reply from the Porsche two cars back.

'Do it the old-fashioned way,' was all Davies had to say as the Cayenne now pulled out and sped closer until it was parallel with the police car on the right, and then slammed into it using the bull bar as the tip.

The aim was perfect, the force crumpling the front passenger-side door inwards and in turn sending the car lurching to the left and into the other police car. Their tyres connected, ripping the corner panel into pieces, and with one heavier shunt both police cars screeched through the barrier and down a grass embankment, spinning out of control as the BMW continued to accelerate, followed closely by the Porsche SUV. The timing had been flawless and although the police cars' passengers would have a few cuts and bruises, there would be no fatalities, just as Getz wanted. And therein lay the problem.

Getz was getting soft. Perhaps too soft.

Davies eyed his would-be employer as Getz fidgeted nervously, staring back at the two police cars tangled up against one another, with quiet unease.

Was the man becoming a liability? Had the years taken their toll and whittled his nerves away to the rind?

Davies sat back in his seat and gazed forwards as they put more distance between themselves and the police cars, and he found himself mulling over the question. Panic and nervousness led to only one thing, so far as he knew... squealing. He would have a word with the men that paid him on the trip over because, if that was the consensus, then it was very likely Getz wouldn't be making his connection in France.

The rest of the five-minute high-speed trip was uneventful and by the time they pulled onto the grassy turf of New Farm Airfield Getz had regained his composure. They swiftly approached the Pilatus PC-12 aircraft that was waiting for them, its propellers rotating and ready to go at a moment's notice. The strip was nothing more than a levelled field with a small hangar off to the side, but it was all that was needed to get them in the air and on their way to a private tarmacked airstrip near Brest on the north-eastern tip of France, no more than a stone's throw from the English Channel.

Davies was already out of the vehicle before it had come to a stop and he raced around and pulled open the back passenger door to see Getz fiddling with his seatbelt. 'Sweaty hands, sir?' was all he said, and he reached inside and calmly unclicked it.

For the first time since the trip had begun Getz appeared to notice his protector's unease and he swallowed hard and straightened his suit before exiting. 'I'm fine. Just a rocky start to my morning is all.'

Davies nodded dutifully and took a moment to retrieve the briefcase and laptop from the BMW's boot before proceeding with Getz as the stair hatch was lowered by an attractive pilot wearing a white shirt with gold stripes and a blue hat.

'Welcome aboard,' was all she said before disappearing back inside, allowing the two men to talk.

'You'll be met on arrival by a detail of my men, sir. They'll transport you to the waiting jet.'

The plans had Getz squinting. 'You're not coming with me?'

Davies replied with a shake of his head, motioning to the Cayenne. 'We won't all fit in. I'll be going with them by boat. But we'll catch up with you. We still have some clean-up to attend to.'

It was a reasonable answer but surprisingly Getz still looked hesitant. 'Do you have time for that? The authorities already know where we are.'

Davies shoved him up the stairs and thrust the briefcase and laptop against Getz's chest. 'We will if you get your arse out of here now, sir.'

Getz pondered the response momentarily and then, with a nod, he retreated inside. The pilot pulled up the hatch and the propellers began to rotate faster as the aircraft started to sluggishly pick up speed.

Getz took a seat with his back to the cockpit so he was able to watch from the portal window as Davies got back into the BMW, and even before the Pilatus had lifted off the ground the two-car procession was back on the main road and speeding away.

Getz watched until they were out of view and then he sat back in the comfy white leather chair and placed both his hands on the table in front of him. There was no trembling in his fingers and he took a measured breath and tried to relax. He had surprised himself with his nervousness during the short car chase, and he now focused on settling in for the trip.

'We don't have much in the way of drinks, sir, but I can offer a gin and tonic.'

Getz looked up to see the attractive pilot who had greeted him at the hatchway, who was now beaming warmly.

'Do you have Bombay Sapphire?' he asked, deliberately staring at her ample chest.

'I'm afraid not,' the pilot replied, ignoring the leering attention of her passenger. 'Will Gordon's do?'

Getz finally looked her in the eyes and nodded. 'It will have to.'

The pilot turned and began to rummage around in a small cupboard, all the time watched by Getz. She retrieved a small plastic glass and began to mix his drink.

'I don't think I've had a female pilot before. Certainly not one so attractive. Would you care to join me?' he said as she added the Indian tonic water and placed the cup on the table before him. 'That's very kind, sir, but I don't think we have enough alcohol on the plane for me to consider that.'

Getz's smile evaporated almost immediately as the pilot turned tail and headed back to the cockpit, closing the door gently behind her. Getz was left alone in the cabin with just his drink and his bruised ego.

'Bitch,' he murmured to himself, and with a shrug he turned his attention to the drink, which he took a generous slug of before pulling his Samsung from his pocket and checking his emails. He'd barely begun when he heard the sound of the cockpit opening once more. 'Changed your mind, have you?'

A solid punch to his cheek knocked him back into his seat. His vision blurred as someone sat down in the seat opposite him.

'Hello, Howard.'

Getz pulled away his hand and stretched his jaw, noting the 9mm Beretta poking over the top of the table at him. 'Who the hell are you?'

Ethan Munroe, dressed in a pilot's uniform, minus the hat, stared at him with piercing blue eyes and smiled. 'You're a tough man to find, Mr Getz.'

Getz said nothing, remaining motionless in his seat like a rabbit caught in the headlights.

'I just missed you in Berlin last month, and Marrakesh before that, but of all the places I expected you to turn up, I'll admit, the UK was not one of them.'

Getz was obviously more concerned about the gun pointing at him than with what he was hearing, and Munroe sensed it, placing the weapon squarely on the table before him.

'Is that better?'

Getz offered no reply, fixing his gaze upon the weapon.

'You wouldn't get to it even if you tried,' Munroe stated as he clasped his hands and rested them on the edge of the table. 'It took a lot of effort to get you here and time is of the essence, so let me get straight to the point. In the eyes of civil society you are a hedge-fund manager responsible for hundreds of millions of dollars of investors' capital. A man at the top of his game whose position is coveted by many in the legitimate world of finance.'

Getz appeared to regain some of his confidence and he raised his chin proudly. 'And what of it?'

Munroe smiled playfully and tapped his finger on the table. 'But in reality, you launder money for some of the most vicious organisations the world has to offer. The Mexican cartel, the Russian mafia and numerous high-profile terrorist affiliations in the Middle East. Word has it that you even rub shoulders with the highest members of the Iranian regime, and impressively none of your… customers,' Munroe raised his fingers momentarily in air quotes, 'appear to know about the others. They believe you are solely owned by them.'

Getz's looked unimpressed and slouched in his seat. 'Anyone who read my recent Interpol arrest warrant could have figured that out.'

'Oh, you mean the arrest warrant we faked in order to flush you out?'

Munroe smiled knowingly, though there was menace in his eyes, and his comment drew silence from the financial fraudster. 'We managed to track your jet's location late last night and after some gentle persuasion of your real pilot, and the threat of hefty jail time, we were able to get the contact number for your security detail. Mr Davies, I believe. It only took a phone call to alert him to your compromised position and a new flight was set up off the mainland for you. Your own panic did the rest.'

Getz was now breathing heavily, more from fear than anger this time, and a few beads of sweat began to appear on his forehead. His lips tightened and his nostrils flared. 'I asked who the hell you are.'

Munroe reached over and picked up Getz's gin and tonic before draining it in one long swig and then dropping the plastic cup to the floor. 'I'm your salvation, Howard. But not from your friends in organised crime who would have you capped in a moment if they knew you'd been arrested... No. I'm talking about who you really are. The man beneath the facade.'

Getz was already shaking his head in confusion. 'And who is it you think I am?'

Munroe slowly raised his hand and pointed towards the man's right arm. 'You, Howard Getz, are the revolting sum of that recent tattoo you received on the underside of your right arm.'

The mention of it had Getz reeling in realisation of who the man sitting before him was, and he spoke in little more than a whisper. 'DSV.'

Munroe's eyes widened comically, and he offered a slow clap with his hands. 'And you are Daedalus to the core, you repulsive prick, and one of their top sleeper agents. A financier with access to enough illegal money to send the Bank of England itself into financial turmoil.'

Getz said nothing but his stare was unyielding as Munroe continued.

'So, now you know who I am – and we certainly know who you are – I want to extend you an offer, an offer with two outcomes. One, you come with us and offer up everything you know. Perhaps, if your information is worthy enough, you won't end up in a military court that sentences you to the end of a rope… we're a bit old school like that, we like a bit of tradition.' Munroe gave a sarcastic wink. 'Or two, we arrange to have this plane end up at the bottom of the Atlantic never to be seen again. I think your mobster pals would call it "sleeping with the fishes".'

Both men sat silently as the sound of the aircraft's engine hummed in the background, and after what must have been a full sixty seconds Getz's face sagged as he realised his life of opulence and splendour was now gone forever. Whatever his choice.

'It's not much of an option, is it, Mr Munroe?'

'Of course it is, Howard. But when you play tough you should expect to get treated roughly.' Munroe picked up the gun from the table and held it lazily in his right hand. 'But most bullies I've met tend to be abject cowards when their own life is on the line. Believe me, I'd happily put a bullet in your head and send you to the briny depths. But I leave that decision to you.'

It was clear to Munroe that Getz had already made up his mind, and the odious little man gave a shaky nod of his head. No sooner had he done so than the cockpit door opened and the pilot appeared, holding three parachutes. She strode over and pulled Getz to his feet before roughly strapping one of them to his back.

'Thank you, Jax,' Munroe said, as Captain Jaqueline Sloan passed over his own 'chute and then began slipping on hers.

'Hold on, can't we just land the plane?' Getz protested, looking evermore nervous as Jax tightened the straps around his chest.

'In ten minutes this plane will succumb to engine failure and plummet into the Atlantic never to be seen again. Anyone who is interested in the pathetic tale of Howard Getz will believe he went down with it, including your Daedalus cronies.'

Getz already had his mouth open wide in complaint as Jax delivered a hard slap across his face. 'Shut up,' she growled, before dragging the man towards the exit hatch. 'The transponder's inoperative so there's no way to track where we are. They'll never find the plane and at this height the depressurisation will be bearable. The plane can cope with the drag of the open hatch, so no problem there.'

Munroe nodded and fastened the last buckle of his own 'chute as Sloan pushed Getz back towards him. He grabbed the man around the shoulders and grasped the sturdy handle protruding from the cabin's ceiling. Munroe knew the aircraft had been specifically modified for just such a jump but still, things go wrong.

'Your parachute is tuned to its altimeter,' Jax said, pointing to the round plastic gauge attached to the 'chute. 'When you reach a certain height it will open automatically. Our people will meet you on the ground. We'll be landing near Dartmouth National Park, so enjoy the view on the way down.'

Before Getz could complain, she grabbed the handle near the cockpit to hold her secure and then pushed a button on the wall and the entire aircraft door exploded outwards as the cabin was flooded with high winds, almost pulling them off their feet. It took only seconds for the air to equalise as Munroe pushed Getz towards the door, the wind tearing at their bodies.

'I'm not jumping out of this plane,' Getz yelled, his voice barely audible above the hissing of wind.

'Fair enough,' Munroe replied, and kicked the man squarely in the back, sending him tumbling out head over heels, his screaming quickly fading into the distance.

'Enjoy the view!' Munroe shouted as Sloan steadied herself at the open hatchway, and she looked over at him with squinted eyes due to the blinding wind.

'Briny depths...'

Munroe managed a smile. 'Too much?'

'Too dramatic,' Sloan yelled, and then she disappeared out of the hatch.

Munroe edged towards the opening and took one last look around the plane so as to savour the moment. It wasn't every day one got to do this, and with a satisfied smile he jumped. Above him, the Pilatus continuing its course over the coast and towards the Atlantic.

All in all, not a bad day's work.

Chapter 2

'Welcome to Cape Wrath, sir.'

Sergeant Caffey was precisely what you'd expect of a career officer in the British Army. Polite, honest, straight to the point but with a looming presence and tone that said 'if you don't do as I say I'll tear your balls off and pound you to a pulp'. Munroe liked him immediately.

Upon delivering Howard Getz into the waiting hands of DSV, he'd been offered a night of R and R, which he took without hesitation. The operation tracking down the Daedalus financier had taken over a month and he'd maxed no more than a couple of hours sleep each night. A push by anyone's standard.

Jax had also taken off for the night, which she'd said was to sort out some personal business, but Munroe was fairly sure it would be a late-night drinking binge at some local dive. Everyone relaxed in their own way. When he awoke after a lousy night's sleep to an urgent call from John McCitrick, his boss at DSV, he wished he hadn't answered it.

'I need you, Ethan, quick as you can. Catch the first available flight to Inverness. I'll have someone meet you.'

This, as he was only now getting used to, was the usual vague instruction he received during a call from McCitrick. He was always briefed intricately upon arrival – DSV had no secrets between themselves – but McCitrick was a man who always kept his cards close to his chest until the moment he absolutely needed to show his hand.

The flight had only taken a few hours, and then a further two-and-a-half-hour drive with his chauffeur, Sergeant Caffey. The serviceman had been unwilling to disclose their destination, but as they drove further north, the air smelling ever stronger of salt, Munroe knew they were headed for the coast. And, as they drove up the winding dirt road with the green rocky Highland hills surrounding them, the only thing he could guess for sure was that they were in the middle of nowhere. It was only now that Caffey was happy to speak about their current location.

'There's not a lot to see out here, sir. Mainly bird-watchers and hikers are the backbone of this countryside, but the coastal views are beautiful… bloody freezing though.'

'It's MOD land, isn't it?' Munroe asked, nodding towards the mountainous grassland before them.

'That's correct, sir. The Ministry of Defence owns most of it, primarily for ordinance testing on the rocky islands close to shore, but the Americans and our NATO allies have access as well.'

Munroe let out a deep breath. 'Sounds like a real holiday destination.'

Caffey offered a wry smile as the green military Land Rover passed the crest of an incline and Munroe found himself staring down at vast open grassland leading to the rocky coastline and the expanse of the North Sea beyond.

A few hundred metres ahead stood a series of single-storey concrete offices surrounded by barbwire fencing. By MOD standards it was hardly an impressive base. It wasn't the layout, though, that had Munroe looking puzzled, but rather the tarmac and the white-painted helipad landing marker that sat off to one side. 'Couldn't we have flown here?'

Caffey chuckled. 'That's for the important people, sir. Not us squaddies who work for a living.'

It was hard to argue with that, and Munroe now turned his attention to the manned entrance they were approaching. The 'base', if you could call it that, was nothing to write home about, and apart from the single military provost guard protecting the gate, in a somewhat lacklustre attempt at security, it appeared to be a regular MOD operation.

Caffey brought the Land Rover to a stop and as the SMPG guard leant into the driver's side window, he flashed his ID card. Without a single word uttered the gate swung open and in they drove, parking up next to the nearest building. Caffey was out first, followed by Munroe, and in response to a directing nod Munroe followed the sergeant into the first building to find what looked like a planning room. There was a man leaning over its central table with his back to the door.

'It's been a pleasure, sir,' was all Caffey said, and after a grateful nod from Munroe he disappeared back the way he'd come, closing the door behind him.

The man before him obviously knew Munroe was waiting patiently but he continued to stoop over the table until the sound of Caffey's footsteps were out of earshot, before turning around.

'Nice to see you, Ethan.'

Colonel Jacques Remus shot Munroe a wide smile and both men stepped towards each other and shook hands. The tall Frenchman had an iron-firm grip and he clasped his free hand on top warmly. 'Good job with Getz,' he said, his accent gruff and very French, 'well executed too.' Remus raised his iPhone up to Munroe's face, displaying the headline.

AIRCRAFT LOST AT SEA. WEALTHY HEDGE-FUND MANAGER AMONG THE MISSING. PRESUMED DEAD.

With a satisfied grin, he slipped the phone into his pocket. 'I've wanted to put a face to the name of that little shit stain for a long time.'

Munroe returned the grin. 'Well I can assure you there was more than a shit stain in his pants by the time we got him to the ground. He was not a happy camper.'

Remus's grin widened. 'Good. And the intel we'll get out of him will be crucial in joining the dots.'

Munroe nodded and then glanced around the empty room. 'Where's McCitrick?'

'Ah, yes,' Remus said, walking to the back of the room towards a steel door, which he pulled open to reveal the cage bar of an elevator. 'Let's go see him, shall we?'

The elevator was no surprise to Munroe. He'd already suspected that the reason for the Cape Wrath base being here was not in plain sight, and he joined Remus inside and pulled the cage closed as the colonel slipped a key into the single lock. With a turn, they began to descend.

Munroe guessed they'd dropped about fifty metres before the elevator came to an abrupt stop. Remus pulled back the cage protector and pushed open the door to reveal a reception area.

'Welcome to the Rogues Gallery,' he said, ushering Munroe out before slamming the door shut behind them and locking it securely with the same key.

The room was large, with a receptionist standing behind a sealed booth with a large bulletproof window separating them from an array of handguns and semi-automatic machine guns hung from a gun rack behind. Dressed in a navy jumper and black trousers, the woman slid a clipboard through a small opening in the panel and tapped the piece of paper with her forefinger. 'Signatures, please, gentlemen, and you'll have to check in your weapons.'

In silence Remus took his turn, followed by Munroe, after which they were given two red clip-on security passes. There was no official MOD symbol on them, or any symbol for that matter. The passes read only 'GUEST' with a square barcode underneath.

'Please wear these at all times when in the facility. Failure to return them on departure will be considered a violation of British law.'

Munroe clipped the pass to his shirt, as did Remus. 'Good to know.'

The receptionist gave him a polite smile before pointing down the corridor. 'Colonel McCitrick is already waiting for you.'

Remus took the lead down the long corridor, its walls bare steel, its panels secured with rivets, the same as in the reception area. There were four separate wings all leading off the main room, each secured with steel-bar doors with bulletproof glass covering both sides. The only openings were the keyholes, and a retinal scanner had been allocated to each door. The lights above were set into the concrete ceiling with sliding panels that could be retracted securely, preventing the smashing of the Perspex coverings if a situation were to develop.

'Good, you're here. I was about to send someone out to look for you.' John McCitrick strode towards them both and grasped Munroe's outstretched hand. 'Any problems?'

'None except the long drive.'

McCitrick raised his eyebrows and nodded. 'Can't be helped, I'm afraid. Remus and myself have to do the same. Helicopters require flight plans and as you've probably already guessed, this is not a place we like to draw attention to.'

'And where exactly is that, sir. The Rogues Gallery?'

McCitrick shot Remus an unamused look. 'Thank you, Remus,' he said as the colonel gave a thin smile. 'Its official designation is S3, but suffice to say it doesn't exist so far as the outside world is concerned. This, Ethan, is a holding facility with only one purpose. The housing and temporary detention of a certain type of prisoner.'

'Daedalus.'

'Correct. It's used for the debriefing of combatants until they are either found guilty in those secret military courts I once told you about, or passed on to the French or Americans for further intel extraction. Your boy Getz is already in residence. Not happy though. For a sleeper agent he sure is a lively one.'

'I'm surprised there aren't more guards, given the people you have down here.' The observation had McCitrick shaking his head.

'One of the buildings up top houses a six-man fire team, and that's in addition to the guards we have down here. Regardless, our secrecy is for the most part our security.'

Munroe knew how these places worked, and although he had been told about it, this was the first time he'd seen the operation with his own eyes. 'I thought you said we didn't utilise torture, John.'

His comment was met with a fiery glare from McCitrick, his lips pursed. 'And we don't. I told you, I would never lie to you and that's the truth. We can drop them at the end of a rope or put them in front of a firing squad for their crimes, but torture is never authorised. When the men and women enter this place they are given a choice. Work with us and possibly gain some element of freedom in the future, or refuse and face a military court. It's their choice. Are we clear?'

'Crystal. I'm just surprised they're on British soil.'

'Well, technically they're not,' Remus chimed in. 'We have sister facilities in France and America, all designated as embassies.'

'Embassies? Whose?'

McCitrick couldn't help but smile. 'Egypt's. Which means that technically we're on Egyptian soil. It's a deal we made with their authorities some decades ago in return for something they wanted. It's all legal... technically.'

Munroe was surprised, but not shocked. The threat of Daedalus to the West and world at large was not something to be taken lightly. 'What did they ask for?'

'We leave that to the politicians,' McCitrick said with a raised eyebrow, clearly desiring to shut down the conversation there and then. 'Now, let's get to it, shall we?'

Sparing no time, McCitrick led them both to the opposite cage door and pressed his eye to the retinal scanner. Within seconds the metallic sound of a heavy-duty lock could be heard releasing and McCitrick pulled away and slid a key into the lock below. With a click the door swung open and Munroe found himself in a wide, lime-green painted corridor with rows of cells on either side. Each cell was similar in nature to the entrance, with steel cage doors covered on both sides with solid Perspex, with the only difference being that within the cell stood another cage door. The set-up allowed someone to enter but still had the added security of a second barrier between them and the occupant, and Munroe could see all the prisoners as he passed by. The cells were larger than an ordinary prison's, with shielded toilets and showers. The beds and tables were constructed of seamless concrete, like shelves jutting out of the wall. Suicide proof, Munroe noted. Many of the prisoners were sat at their concrete stools and wearing white boiler suits. Most barely glanced up at the passing visitors. Munroe recognised none of them.

'We used to house between ten and fifteen "guests" at one time, but the number has gone up in the past few months.'

Munroe knew that all too well. Since taking down Daedalus's Blackstar HQ in Texas, the intel gained from the site had provided more leads and captures in a few months than in the past decade combined. It was strong progress, but still only a minor in-road into the huge scope of the Daedalus organisation. One thing was for sure though, they would be needing more cells. 'So, do you want to tell me why I'm here, or is it just for the tour?'

McCitrick remained silent as they passed a guard room on their right with three armed military personnel, each with handguns at their sides, hunched over the screens of numerous surveillance cameras. They all offered a respectful nod before resuming their duties and it wasn't until McCitrick reached a door marked 'Interrogation Room' that he brought them to a stop.

'In the four months we've had him he's hardly said a word, that is until last night when he made a request. One I've granted.'

'Someone wants a chat,' Munroe replied, and McCitrick nodded.

'I didn't want to tell you until you arrived. I need your mind in the moment, Captain.'

The reference of his rank had Munroe stiffening slightly. 'Well the moment is here, sir,' he replied as Remus gave him a light pat on the back.

'Never forget, for these people, bullshit is the primary language. Just hear what he has to say. We'll be watching from next door.'

McCitrick unlocked the slide bolt and pressed his palm on the silver handle before looking back at Munroe uncompromisingly. 'Despite the name on this door you're just here to listen. I need your professionalism, Ethan. Now more than ever.'

His comment was cryptic, but Munroe replied with a curt nod. 'Always.'

With that, McCitrick pushed open the door to reveal a small room with painted white walls. On the right, a large one-way mirrored viewing window had been imbedded into the wall, and at the room's centre a grey plastic table had been bolted to the floor. On opposite sides of the table were positioned black plastic chairs, and it was from the far one that a man in a yellow boiler suit glanced over to the door and smiled shrewdly. 'Ethan Munroe. What an expected pleasure.'

Hans Bauer, great-grandson of the Nazi war criminal Reinhard Heydrich, sat casually in his seat with his chained wrists resting upon his thighs, and greeted his guest with a thin smile. The highest member of Daedalus ever captured by DSV, and the man who had ordered the murder of Munroe's wife and child, now stared at him arrogantly, despite his current predicament.

As Munroe stood there, motionless, the battle that had led to the capture of Hans Bauer came flooding back. In the six months that had passed, Munroe had barely thought back over the events that had brought him to this moment, and the man behind them. Or even the discovery that he himself had been a product of Project Icarus, the culmination of decades of work to perfect not only the world's first super soldier, but generations of bio-engineered people with the perfect traits to become the next leaders of the world. Natural-born traits and skills that allowed them to successfully infiltrate the political apparatus of the West.

It was a project as impressive as it was terrible, using data to accomplish the task based on the misery of human experiments beginning in the concentration camps of Nazi Germany back in the forties. A serial killer known as Icarus, a direct product of the experiments, had led Munroe directly to Bauer and his band of powerful misfits.

If someone had told Munroe a year ago that he would be engaged in taking down Daedalus, a group of neo-Nazis, directly descended from famous war criminals, engaged in an effort to create a Fourth Reich, he would have said they were crazy. Yet here he was, working for the Disavowed, or DSV as it was known, and fighting an enduring war that only a select few inside Western governments even knew was transpiring. A shadowy, secret world where black and white descended into ever changing shades of grey.

As Munroe stared down at the prisoner, he began to feel a building fury. He had forgotten how much he despised this man.

'Please, have a seat,' Bauer said with a smile, holding out a hand to the empty seat opposite him.

Munroe felt his chest tighten, but he subdued the anger and calmly walked over to the empty chair and placed his hands on its back as the interrogation room door closed behind him. He then stared at the killer for a few moments blankly before taking his seat. 'Well, if it isn't my favourite Nazi,' he began, even managing a chuckle as he settled into his chair. 'I had a lovely meal and some drinks last night in the outside world. A rack of succulent BBQ spare ribs. If I'd known what a crappy place you were living in it would have tasted juicier.'

Munroe slumped back in his seat and rested his arm on the table. 'How's the accommodation, Hans?'

The annoying smile on Bauer's lips remained steadfast. 'Better than you'd think. Three square meals and a comfy hotel room. Bed's a bit hard, but I've no complaints.'

'Then it sounds as if you're exactly where you should be. I'm happy to be of service in putting you here. It really was my pleasure.'

A flicker of anger shot across Bauer's face, but it quickly vanished as the man resumed his smug demeanour. 'As it was a pleasure to have your family butchered. So, it would seem, we are both content.'

Munroe barely shrugged at the comment. Goading was all this narcissistic psychopath had and he wasn't about to give the man one ounce of satisfaction. Anyway, Munroe knew how to hit the man where it hurt. His pride. 'You know I really should thank you, Hans. Because of your incompetence we're taking down Daedalus one slice at a time. Your lazy bookkeeping back at Blackstar has given us more of your Brown Shirts than we could have possibly hoped for. As the saying goes, a chain is only as strong as its weakest link, and your link was pretty loose. Some might say inept. Honestly, I expected more from the master race. Your attempt at a resurgent Fourth Reich is crumbling fast, and I'm happy to say it's all down to you.' Munroe leant forwards and casually placed his hands on the table. 'I can't imagine how painful it must be,' he said in a hushed tone, 'to see a plan that, after clawing itself from the ashes of the Second World War, taking over seventy years to put into action, is now in the shithole, and all because of your arrogance. A pathetic delusion that the liquid that courses through your veins allows you the wisdom and intelligence of a god.'

Bauer gazed at him with cold eyes. He didn't look angry, upset or smug, but somehow disinterested, and Munroe tapped his fist on the table lightly.

'If you just wanted to reminisce, Hans, you could have saved me the journey and asked for a telephone call. I hear the concierge here is excellent.'

Munroe was already shifting in his chair, preparing to stand up, when Bauer opened his mouth.

'I didn't call you here to reminisce, Ethan, but there is a matter I wish to discuss.'

Munroe paused and glanced at his watch. 'Then get it out, man, because I have dinner reservations in London tonight and I don't want to be late just because I was wasting time talking to you.'

Truth be told the only dinner he would be having was perhaps a pack of peanuts on the flight back, if he was lucky, but as he stared down Bauer he sensed the man had something of importance to say.

'I am well aware that there is no way I will ever get out of this prison. Your powers that be would never allow it. But,' Bauer cocked his head to one side, 'I would like that time to be as comfortable as possible. And with the information I can provide you, it seems like a small ask.'

Munroe only sat there motionless before offering a light shrug as Bauer continued, his tone of voice becoming irate. 'If you think Howard Getz is going to get you anywhere, you're wrong.'

The name had Munroe tensing slightly, and Bauer noticed it.

'He was brought in yesterday, he passed my cell on the way. Deliberately so, I'm sure.'

'I hear he's a talker,' Munroe replied, raising his eyebrow. 'Whatever he knows is going to pour right out of him.'

'True, true. But it's *what* pours out that matters at the end of the day. Howard is a low-level catch. He's a finance man. Now, if you want to seize funds from the Mexican cartel or throw in with the Russian mafia then he will suit your needs just fine. But if its Daedalus secrets you desire, then I am the spoon of medicine that can take care of that particular craving.'

His words were met with contempt from Munroe. 'What, you're suddenly not the Daedalus believer and fanatic to the cause?'

'On the contrary, Ethan. I have no doubt that my dreams will be realised yet, and when that time comes, and my brothers and sisters are in power, they will release me and hunt you and your DSV cronies down like dogs. But, until that day arrives, maybe years from now, I would like to be, as I said, as comfortable as possible.'

Bauer looked over at the one-way glass and with fluttering eyelids sang, 'Mirror, mirror on the wall, who is the shittiest Frenchman of all? Hello, Remus, the guards here have loud mouths and I have no doubt that clot McCitrick is with you. Say, boys, what would you give to have the name of the mole in DSV. A Daedalus agent who slipped through your...' Bauer waved both hands in the air sarcastically, 'lucky dip of a selection process.'

The blue-eyed Nazi now had Munroe's full attention, although his poker face never slipped. 'And who would that be? More importantly, why would you give up such a key asset?'

Munroe's question was met with a scoff. 'Give me a break, Ethan, the rag-tag band of idiots you call DSV are not that important in the grand scheme of things, no matter what your little heart tells you, and, as for the asset, her worth has more than been depleted by now.'

Munroe was sure that both Remus and McCitrick would be in deep conversation behind the mirror, evaluating the worth of this information. Both section heads suspected DSV had been infiltrated by Daedalus, but what price would they be willing to pay for that knowledge? It could be just another ruse to cause them problems, the kind of move Bauer, despite being silent since his capture, was known to love playing.

'OK, let's say I believe you. What do you want?'

The smug smile was back, and Bauer slouched in his chair, expelling a deep satisfied sigh. 'I will provide you with the name and then, once you've confirmed that I have given you gold dust, I would be willing to offer up a further three names – and these little beauties are embedded within not only the UK government, but the French and US as well. Once our little transaction is

27

complete I want out of this prison to a small estate in any of the DSV's three nations. I expect to be guarded for the rest of my time, but I want access to all the amenities I am used to. Food, clothes, entertainment. Just the usual things that make life worth living.'

Munroe was dubious to say the least. The man was a bullshit artist whose lies rolled off his tongue like running water, but he also knew there were only a few things that Bauer held sacrosanct and one of those was his personal wellbeing. 'Why would you give these people up? Especially if you think Daedalus are on a winning streak.'

'That's easy,' Bauer replied flippantly. 'Life is a chess game, Ethan. And there are always pawns to be sacrificed. Some are just less important than others.'

There was little faith on Munroe's part, but the man's self-assuredness and arrogance could be the chink in his armour, and Munroe slowly nodded his head. 'OK, but if you expect us to trust you then you'll have to trust us.'

'Meaning?'

'You give us the name of the DSV mole, as well as the others, and we'll see what can be done. No signed contracts, though. They wouldn't mean anything anyway. Ever since your capture – you don't exist.'

Munroe considered it while chewing at his bottom lip. That McCitrick had not entered the room yet meant he was almost certainly considering the proposal. Whether they stuck to the deal was another thing entirely.

'Very well, I will take a chance and hope that the supposed virtues that DSV claim to be imbued with are genuine – such as that of honour. The name of the mole in DSV is… and you're going to have a hard time accepting the truth of this, believe me, but it's the truth and I will prove it… Your mole is Colonel Anne Sinclair.

The American section head of DSV, or should I say the Disavowed.' Bauer smiled and he snorted a chuckle to himself. 'Of which she will now most certainly be.'

'Bullshit,' Munroe replied, shaking his head. 'Sinclair? That's just a name you've plucked from a hat.'

Bauer was now staring at him with wide eyes. 'Really. Well then, if that's the case then you won't find a secured computer hard drive in a hidden safe beneath her bed, code 2472, at her London address. And neither will the code "DETERMINATION040317" open the encrypted said hard drive.'

Munroe was already tapping the information into his iPhone and when finished he got up out of his chair only to pause. 'You could have given this information to anyone here, Bauer. Why did you need to see me?'

Bauer looked as if he'd been waiting to be asked the question all along and he raised his finger and flicked it towards himself as Munroe put his phone back in his pocket and, resting his hands on the table, he leant closer.

'Try anything and I'll snap that finger off, ram it down your throat and choke you with it.'

Bauer now wagged the offending digit from side to side and then retrieved his hand. 'Now why would I do that? We're almost becoming friends.'

'Not in this lifetime, Hans. Spit it out.'

Bauer took a deep swallow and then he began to examine Munroe's face as if he were a piece of art. 'When we met back in Texas I was barely able to spend any time with you. Just to talk, to admire the job we did.'

Munroe could feel his fists tightening instinctively, but still he maintained a close distance to Bauer's face. 'Whatever you think you did, you failed.'

'But we're the same, you and me.' Bauer's face scrunched up as he realised his poor choice of words. 'Obviously not by blood, but we are joined nonetheless. We gave you your strong bones, healthy cheeks and warrior DNA. I just wanted to see it up close again and admire the workmanship.'

Bauer was only making a pathetic attempt to wind him up, but it was something Munroe had thought about over the past four months. It wasn't easy to discover one was grown in a test tube by a degenerate bunch of Nazis, but all in all it didn't matter to him. Should one ever blame the sins of the father on the son? And besides, who gets to choose their parents, it was just a roll of the dice anyway.

'Well you screwed that up. Really piss poor job. Must irk you to know that the one you created to protect you ended up being the one who destroyed you.' Munroe took his hands off the table and headed for the door. 'And if I find out you're just screwing around with us then expect a more informal visit next time.'

'Not at all, Ethan.' Bauer smiled smugly. 'I expect this to be the start of a good relationship. And it will begin with you eating your words.'

'If I find out you're lying, you'll be eating more than your words, Hans. That I promise you.'

Chapter 3

The day was drawing to a close as Munroe drove his black BMW 330e along the busy roads of Primrose Hill. In the distance behind him, pockets of tourists were making their way off the lush green parkland as the restaurants began gearing up for evening trade and the many revellers and tourists who would soon crowd the streets. In the passenger seat beside Munroe McCitrick sat quietly, his fingers tapping upon his thigh the only clue to his unease. To say that Bauer's revelation had stunned both section heads was an understatement, but McCitrick had struggled with it more than Remus. He and Sinclair's relationship went further back than anyone's, long before she had been invited to join DSV, and even the possibility that she had betrayed him for so long was a bitter pill for the man to swallow. Remus on the other hand had taken it in his stride. Shocked? Sure. But Remus's hardened and natural regimented disposition had only been reinforced by years of military operations, and his only concern was to find out if what Bauer had admitted was true, and it was with this sole question that they approached Sinclair's London residence.

At that time of day there were still free parking spaces in what would soon become a crammed street of vehicles as shoppers left for their evening plans and before the Hill's residents came back from work. Munroe pulled up to the kerb and turned off the engine. Both men sat silently, staring up at the house they would shortly be knocking at. Seeing the top window open was a solid indicator that her office had been correct in telling them she had worked from home that day. There would be no security detail to contend with as all DSV section heads never sought to bring undue attention upon themselves. Given their anonymity was assured there was no need. Of course, if Bauer was telling the truth then Daedalus had known every member of DSV for some time, which would have to be addressed.

But not right now.

'Let me do the talking. I need to be sure this is on the level,' McCitrick stated bluntly.

'And if it is?' Munroe replied, glancing up at the house.

McCitrick unbuttoned the strap on his side holster. 'Then we take her in and put her on a one-way trip to Cape Wrath for debriefing.'

Munroe offered a stern nod and both men now exited the car and made their way up to the front door.

Back in Wrath, Remus and McCitrick had been adamant that no outside agencies be involved. This was to be kept 'in the family', as they had put it, and there was no need for any judicial complications that might arise. Taking an American colonel into custody was a delicate matter, and anyway, there was nothing they could tell anyone. They were the only ones who knew about Daedalus and, even given the treasonous nature of the arrest, such omissions would only serve to leave DSV exposed. That couldn't happen.

McCitrick pressed the bronze buzzer and they waited until the intercom crackled into life.

'John, what are you doing here?' Sinclair's tone was calm yet curious.

McCitrick gave a quick wave towards the small camera lens. 'I've got business at the Foreign Office, but I need to have a word. You free to talk? I have Munroe with me, it concerns him too.'

There was a short pause and then the door lock buzzed open. 'C'mon up. I'll get some glasses ready.'

Followed by Munroe, McCitrick led them up a short flight of green carpeted stairs and onto the first floor where Sinclair poked her head out from the nearest door. 'This is a pleasant surprise, John. And you saved me a phone call, Ethan. Good job on Getz but I have some questions. Come on in.'

Her head disappeared and they both followed into a spacious yet minimally decorated front room. The dark wood flooring was complemented by heavy green curtains pulled back from the windows with white rope holders. A black leather sofa was the only seating apart from a grey mesh-backed office chair pushed underneath a two-tier glass desktop with an iMac displaying a landscape shot of Nevada. A wooden coffee table with a small drinks cabinet set into its centre sat beneath a sixty-inch flat-screen TV embedded into the wall. The white walls were bare, with only a floral divider running below the plaster ceiling.

Sinclair pulled out three crystal tumblers from the cabinet and placed them on the side of the coffee table. 'So, what information has our latest guest, Mr Getz, unloaded to warrant a social call, John?' Sinclair asked, retrieving a bottle of Johnnie Walker Red Label from where the glasses had come from. 'That is why you're here, isn't it?'

'Actually, no, Anne, it's Bauer. He's decided to cooperate.'

Sinclair paused for a moment, and then smiled and uncorked the bottle. 'It's about time. I was beginning to think that odious little shit actually had principles. What's he told you?'

'He wouldn't talk to me. It was Ethan he spoke to, and what he told us, if true, is a bit of a game changer. He says he knows who the mole in DSV is.'

Sinclair's arm went limp, dropping the bottle to her thigh, and she raised her chin upwards curiously. 'Who?'

McCitrick paused for a moment, examining her expression and then he let out a light sigh. 'He says it's Remus.'

If Sinclair was feeling any relief she never showed it. 'Remus! And you believed him? That's as unlikely as if he said it was you.'

'That's what I said… initially. But since then we've uncovered some things that can't be ignored.'

Sinclair stood motionless for a moment, her mouth hanging open slightly and then she turned her attention back to the glasses. 'You better have some solid evidence, John,' she said, pouring two drinks and looking over at Munroe. 'Whisky good for you, Ethan?'

'Straight up, please, Colonel. But would you mind if I use the restroom first? It was a long flight down.'

'Of course. Out the door and down the corridor to the right.'

As Sinclair passed McCitrick his drink Munroe exited the room and headed down the hallway, but when he reached the bathroom instead of going inside he opened the door, flicked on the light to activate the sound of a fan whirring overhead, and then closed it before entering the opposite doorway.

Munroe had taken a look at the plans of Sinclair's house on the flight down to London and so there was no surprise when he found himself in the colonel's bedroom. It was clean and tidy with the minimal furniture angled uniformly. Everything one would expect from the private room of the anally retentive colonel.

Munroe carefully closed the door behind him before going straight for the silver bed frame. He knelt down and very slowly pushed it back to one side.

The frame slid easily on the green carpet and he kept pushing until he saw the vague outline of a square set within the carpet.

Munroe pulled out a retractable, finger-grooved knife with a wooden handle and unfolded it before gently slipping it between the thin cut in the carpet and then probing deeper until its tip struck something solid. With a gentle nudge it gave way and a metal lid slowly opened on its springs, revealing a black miniature safe with a digital lock embedded into its face. So far Bauer had been right on the money and as Munroe lightly tapped in the code he genuinely hoped it wouldn't let him in. Sinclair was already a legend within DSV and to think they had been infiltrated from the top would not only have far reaching consequences for the security but the morale of every single officer.

2472.

With each press a beeping sound was emitted and then his worst fears were realised, and he felt a sickening feeling in the pit of his stomach as the safe lid unclicked and popped open.

'Shit.' He paused and listened intently for the sound of any approaching footsteps but upon hearing only the murmured conversation continuing next door he pulled back the lid. There were bundles of various currencies – dollars, euros, yen – and a small stack of passports of different colours held together with a rubber band, which he took a moment to flick through. Each one contained a photo of Colonel Anne Sinclair but all with different aliases. Finally, there at the bottom of the safe, was a small hard drive, just as Bauer had disclosed.

Munroe pulled it out and then stared at it for a moment with disdain. He had no idea what was on it, but the very fact Bauer had the access codes, plus what was obviously an escape kit with documentation and finance, was more than he needed to see to warrant a confrontation.

Munroe retrieved the stack of passports as well, then got to his feet and made his way back to the hallway where he could hear McCitrick still deep in his bogus revelation of Remus being the mole. McCitrick's hope of garnering a slip of Sinclair's nerves upon mentioning the mole had not materialised and Munroe had to admit she had played it well, her reaction perfect.

Did he really expect anything else from a deep-cover mole who could have been undercover for decades? Christ, who knew for how long.

'Ahh, Ethan. Your drink,' Sinclair said, seeing Munroe appear at the doorway. She strode over stiffly and placed the drink in his hand. 'I'm still not buying this. Especially coming from Bauer. He'd like nothing more than to have us all turn on one another… but, if what John's telling me turns out to be true then we have a serious problem. This not only compromises every officer in DSV but the political protection as well. The Three Kings will be as vulnerable as anyone.'

She headed back to the coffee table. McCitrick glanced over at Munroe and Munroe gave a simple nod of his head, confirming the sections head's worst fears. Sinclair sat down on the leather sofa and took a large sip of her drink while McCitrick walked over to the desk, pulled out the chair and sat down.

'When we first met – what was it, fifteen years ago? – I remember thinking how impressed I was by you. Your sharp mind, your blunt attitude to the facts of anything presented to you and the confidence and skill to carry them out no matter the mess it would cause. Truth was sacrosanct and although you never compromised, you never forged ahead, solely blinkered by the facts. Your strong common sense kept you grounded... always.'

McCitrick didn't sound sad, even though the tone of his voice was soft, but he appeared disappointed and let out a deep sigh.

'What are you getting at, John?'

'What am I getting at? I suppose it's just a question.'

Sinclair could sense something was up and for the first time Munroe saw a chink in her demeanour as she gulped lightly. She brought her drink up to her mouth in an attempt to hide the automatic response, but the timing was off and Munroe saw it.

'My question, Anne, is to do with the tragedy of your predecessor whose demise created the opening for you to join DSV.'

Sinclair finished her sip and stared at him in puzzlement. 'What has that got to do with anything, John?'

McCitrick raised his hand placatingly. 'His death was due to a failure of intelligence. When on DSV business his convoy was caught in a rocket attack in Libya and the blame was placed on radical insurgents and a captain of the Islamic Wave, Captain Mustaffa Salem. At the time I didn't see the connection because the intelligence report had been buried. In fact, it had been buried so well I never found it. But after the conversation with Bauer I thought it prudent to go over old ground.'

Sinclair's breathing was now becoming shallow and drawn out. She slouched back into the leather chair as McCitrick continued.

'It turns out that Salem was an intelligence asset back in 2012 after the Gaddafi regime fell, and you wouldn't believe who his handler was.'

Sinclair looked up at Munroe, her eyes heavy in their sockets. 'Bauer. He didn't tell you the mole was Remus, did he? He told you it was me.'

Munroe gave nothing away and instead allowed McCitrick to finish the point that everyone in the room already knew.

'That handler was you, Anne. Not a full colonel yet and embedded in military intelligence. A position you had openly coveted for many years before getting. You had your predecessor killed, Anne, and in doing so secured his job for yourself.'

McCitrick finished off his drink in one swig and placed the crystal tumbler down on the table gently as Munroe pulled out the small stack of passports he had found and threw them over to the coffee table, where they landed with an unceremonious thud. He then held the hard drive up before him. 'Just where Bauer said it would be. Password and all.'

'It's over, Anne,' McCitrick said, glaring at her. 'Tell me one thing though. When did Daedalus turn you? Or were you born into it from the start?'

The last question had a switch effect, possibly due to some previous conditioning, and Sinclair suddenly looked furious. 'Of all the people I thought had my back, John, you were number one.'

'Yeah, and you played on that, didn't you?' McCitrick replied, now standing up as Sinclair joined him, her face full of betrayal.

'Mustaffa Salem was one of hundreds of informants we had on the ground in Libya. Hell, I never even met the man. I didn't even remember his name until you brought it up just then. And as for these—' she picked up the stack of passports and flicked through them '—I've never seen these before. Where did you even get them? And what is that you're holding?'

'This is the hard drive from the safe under your bed, the code for which we were given by Bauer. I'd bet my life that his password for this—' he gave the hard drive a gentle shake '—will unlock it.'

'He named you as the mole, Anne. He considers you expendable.' McCitrick glared at her once more. 'I didn't want to believe it… Christ! How long have we known each other? Fifteen years?'

Sinclair still looked defiant and her lips curled in anger. 'You think I'm the mole? That's the most preposterous thing I've ever heard. I've never seen that hard drive before and I didn't even know there was a safe under my bed.'

'Well that's odd because the passports have your picture in them, with aliases, of course.'

Sinclair was clearly not ready to give it up yet and she slammed her drink down hard onto the coffee table.

'Bauer's conning you. I only spend three months of the year in this house, total. Anyone could have broken in, installed that safe, and planted that evidence.'

'That would be difficult, Colonel,' Munroe stated coldly. 'Your house is always monitored by our security cameras when you're away. We'd know about it if someone just knocked on your door.'

Sinclair stared at them in disbelief and as if giving into their accusations she swayed slightly before moving towards her desk, perching on the corner.

Her movement had McCitrick pulling out his weapon and with it pointed at her he moved back towards the door cautiously where Munroe was still standing. 'We're taking you in, Anne. Once we're at the Cape we can have a proper chat, but right now I need you to slip these on.' He pulled out a pair of handcuffs and tossed them over to her.

In most other situations Munroe would have cuffed her himself but he understood why McCitrick was being cautious. Sinclair wasn't your average detainee. She was a hardened Iraq veteran – she had gained her Silver Eagle. A colonel with every form of unarmed combat training under her belt. She was not someone to take chances with.

Sinclair seemed to fade out for a second, deep in thought, and then she looked up and nodded. 'Fine.' She slipped the handcuffs behind her back and began rummaging around behind her before slowly walking towards them both. 'You're making a big mistake, John.' She said as she approached them, her eyes dull.

'That's not what the hard drive says, Anne,' McCitrick replied, still aiming his weapon at her chest.

'That's not the mistake I meant.'

As she came within two feet of McCitrick's barrel, Munroe got a glimpse of the glass desk behind her and that's when he saw the pair of handcuffs lying on its surface.

'The mistake of thinking I'd ever come quietly.' Sinclair pulled her hands from behind her back to reveal the live grenades in each palm.

Instinctively, Munroe grabbed McCitrick by the scruff of the neck and jerked him back through the doorway so the hallway wall was between them and Sinclair.

'Heil to the glorious approach of the Fourth Reich,' Sinclair bellowed, as if she had wanted to yell it out loud for years, and in one fluid motion Munroe flung McCitrick against the banister, flipping them both head over heels over the edge and down the stairs below, just as the grenades blew.

The explosion was thunderous and they both tumbled down the stairs and onto the tiled porch entranceway as plaster and sections of banister piled down upon them.

Then everything was silent except for the sound of bricks clattering to the floor.

A few seconds or maybe minutes had passed by the time Munroe awoke, his ears ringing. He wiped the thick layer of powder from his face and coughed as his lungs expelled the dust he had inhaled. He was alive at least, and apart from the section of banister that had landed on him he could feel all his limbs. Better still, McCitrick – who although still unconscious was breathing steadily – appeared to be OK, apart from a few scratches to the face. They had escaped the worst of the blast and no doubt they would find Sinclair still on the first floor. Pieces of her, anyway, and at the very least it put to bed the question of her being the mole. But as Munroe took a moment to catch his breath he considered the possibilities surrounding Sinclair's suicide, and the conclusion he came to made his stomach wrench. He wasn't sure why, but his gut told him they'd just been played by the psychopath back at the Cape. He sucked in a deep breath and growled a single name.

Bauer!

Chapter 4

'Prisoner transfer.' The man wearing a grey puffer jacket slipped a tan document through the small opening in the Perspex panel. The receptionist picked it up and took a few moments to sift through the orders.

'Welcome to Camp Wrath, Mr Gaskin.'

Now satisfied, she nodded and reached back to her desk, retrieving a single sheet of printed paper, which she passed over to the new visitor.

'I'll need your signatures,' she said, looking over the man's shoulder to the other two arrivals behind him, 'and from you two as well.'

Dressed in near identical clothes, the two other men said nothing, but once Gaskin had left his mark the others came forwards and did likewise.

'You'll need to check in your firearms,' the receptionist stated, passing through three red guest passes. 'Please wear these at all times when in the facility, failure to return them on departure will be considered a violation of British law.'

'I know the drill,' Gaskin said courteously, and then all three men unholstered their 9mm Glocks and passed them to the receptionist who placed them in a metal drawer under her desk.

'Thank you, gentlemen. Follow the corridor to your left and I'll have a guard meet you in the waiting room.'

Gaskin said nothing and headed down to the waiting room with the other two men following closely as the receptionist made a call to the guard room.

It was here the trio waited for a few minutes in silence until a guard appeared and unlocked the Perspex-covered cage door and swung it open. 'Mr Gaskin, the guest is in his cell. If you'll follow me.'

The reference to 'the guest' had Gaskin smiling. This facility was not designated as a prison and as such held no prisoners, only detainees and guests. 'I hope your *guest* has enjoyed his stay.'

The guard offered a dry smile and then closed the gate behind them once all the men were through. 'Legalities, legalities,' he replied, amused, and then marched off along the corridor with the three men close behind.

The cells they passed were mostly filled and the occupants barely gave the visitors a second glance as the group passed by.

'I have to say, I'm surprised he's being moved,' the guard said as they passed the break room. 'I thought we'd have him here for much longer.'

'The intel he provided has caused concern for his safety and that of others,' Gaskin replied blankly, not prepared to give too much away. 'There are a lot of powerful people who know he's here and we're here to take away any temptation that they may have to silence him.'

The guard raised his eyebrows and nodded. 'Should we be on alert?'

'My friend, this is a top-secret facility housing some of the most dangerous prisoners the world has to offer. You should be on alert every moment you're on duty.' The stiffening of the guard's shoulders had Gaskin relaxing his demeanour slightly. 'Look, Sergeant Caffey is aware of the concerns and once we get him out of here and rehoused, those concerns will be nullified. Believe me, where this guy is going no one's going to find him, not even the tax man... and those bastards find everyone.'

Gaskin's reply put the guard back at ease as they turned a corner, the corridor now opening up into a much larger space, much like a common prison but with only cells lining the right side of the room. The middle of it was used as a rec room of sorts, with plastic tables bolted to the floor in a single row, not unlike a school dinner hall.

'I'm surprised you let your guests mix,' Gaskin noted, motioning to the tables, and the comment brought the guard to a halt, out of earshot of the cells.

'The whole area is bugged with listening devices. You'd be surprised how much intel can be gleaned from eaves-dropping on their personal conversations.'

Gaskin nodded, understanding. It made perfect sense, although knowing the type of men and women housed here he doubted they would be naive enough to ever speak that loosely.

'C'mon, he's in the last cell. Your timing's perfect. Each guest has an hour a day in the exercise habitat. Your boy just finished his.'

Within a few steps, Gaskin's line of sight offered him his first view of the man they were here to collect, and he came to a stop as the guard began to unlock the cell door through a keyhole in the Perspex panel before swinging the door open.

'Mr Bauer, I'm here to take you to a new location. Please, come with us.'

Hans Bauer placed the book he was reading down on his concrete work table and gazed up at them inquisitively. 'And why would that be, pray tell?'

The guard stood back, and Gaskin grabbed Bauer by the arm and forcefully pulled him from his seat. 'I wouldn't know, Mr Bauer, I'm just your ride along, to make sure you get there.'

'Just a taxi driver, then,' Bauer replied as one of Gaskin's men placed Bauer's hands behind his back and slapped on a pair of handcuffs. 'Three men just for me! You must consider me a dangerous fellow.'

The comment had Gaskin pushing Bauer face forwards against the wall and holding the handcuff chain connector in his palm tightly. 'I don't want to hear a squeak out of you, understand?'

Gaskin now leant closer to Bauer's ear. 'And if you give me any trouble I'll have my lads work you over.'

The guard eyed Gaskin uneasily but he said nothing as Gaskin now frogmarched his 'guest' back the way they came.

'I doubt your superiors would be best pleased to receive a bloody prisoner when you hand me over.'

'My orders are to get you to where you're going,' Gaskin snarled, 'it never said what shape you had to be in.'

'Such bravado. This should make for an interesting trip.'

Gaskin ignored Bauer's quip, but he paused upon noticing what all the other cellmates were doing. The entire row of men and women wearing their white boiler suits were now standing to attention and staring at Bauer with reverence. It made for an eerie sight, and Bauer returned the gesture with his palm raised in a Nazi salute.

'Be strong. Your only weakness would be a failure of loyalty. You shall not be forgotten.'

'Get going,' Gaskin growled uncaringly, pushing him forwards. 'Enjoy it, Bauer. You won't get any of that respect where you're going.'

In silence, Bauer was pushed all the way back to the reception area, more 'guests' standing as he passed by like some military parade. With each salute Gaskin's expression only hardened.

'Passes, gentlemen,' the receptionist instructed as Gaskin passed over Bauer to one of his men and then collected their passes, which he dropped back through the gap into her waiting hands. He was repaid in kind with their firearms, which were quickly holstered by the three men and with a turn of the key the elevator door opened and Bauer was roughly pushed inside, whereupon he was joined by the others.

'Say goodbye, Bauer. You won't see this place again,' Gaskin growled, and he was already sliding the cage door closed when inside the receptionist's cubicle the phone rang and she picked up the receiver. As the elevator doors began sliding shut, Gaskin saw the woman's eyes widen and she dropped the phone.

'Wait!' was all she managed before the doors closed fully and the elevator began ascending.

Gaskin shot his men a concerned glance and it was at this point that the sound of sirens began to wail up above them.

All three men immediately unholstered their Glocks and faced the doors in readiness.

'Spot of trouble?' Bauer remarked caustically. He was ignored by all three men as they pointed their firearms forwards stiffly. With a sharp bump the elevator came to a stop and the doors slid open.

The sound of sporadic gunfire filled the air and upon checking the room beyond was clear, Gaskin pulled Bauer from the elevator and thrust him down behind the table in front of him as the other two men took up position and crouched down by the windows on the far side of the room as the elevator doors closed.

'Don't move,' Gaskin yelled at Bauer, who appeared quite relaxed in his sedentary position, and then Gaskin ran to join one of his men by the window. He stole a glance to see the entire base squad of six uniformed soldiers in his line of sight, hunkering down twenty metres ahead and using one of the concrete buildings as cover. One of the soldiers had already taken a shot to the shoulder but, despite this, he and his teammates were returning fire against a group of men on the far side of the yard. It was difficult to tell how many were in the group assaulting the Cape, but from what Gaskin could tell the base squad were heavily outnumbered. Regardless, they were putting up one hell of a fight.

'They're pinned down out there,' Gaskin yelled to his men, flicking his finger at the window on the other side of the room, a blind spot for anyone outside. 'Exit there, and then I want you to circle round behind them. Keep me in your peripheral. On my signal open fire and we'll attack from the front. They'll be caught in the crossfire.'

Both men gave a sharp nod and then on their haunches crossed over to the opposite window and jumped out.

Gaskin pulled out a Motorola walkie-talkie from his coat pocket and pressed down on the receiver button. 'This is Gaskin, can anyone hear me?'

All he heard was static, and he took a moment to steal another glance from the edge of the window to see one of the squad guards take a 5.56mm bullet through his neck, propelling him backwards to the floor where he scrambled to apply pressure to the wound with his now blood-covered hands.

'Can anyone hear me?' Gaskin repeated, waiting in his position, his entire focus on the sound of static being emitted from the walkie-talkie.

'Yes, sir,' came a reply, finally.

'My men are approaching the enemy from behind, so for Christ's sake don't shoot them.'

'Acknowledged.' Gaskin glanced back towards the table to see Bauer poke his head over the surface. 'Get your head down,' he shouted, sending Bauer scuttling back behind the desk as quickly as he'd appeared. Gaskin now slid up the side of the wall to a standing position and brought his gun to bear over the shattered window.

He could just see his men in position, taking cover behind a stack of wooden crates. He brought his barrel down on the opposition force, and with his men poised and looking to him for the signal, he began firing. This was followed instantly by a barrage of gunshots from his men as they all proceeded to empty their firearms into the targets' backs, sending men dropping to the floor. The noise was deafening, but within seconds it fell silent. As Gaskin released his clip, sending it to the floor with a thud, he heard one of his men shout out.

'Clear.'

Gaskin expelled a sigh, his heartbeat already beginning to slow as the building's main door swung open and the face of one of his men appeared, offering a confirming nod of his head.

Gaskin looked relieved and he swiftly got to his feet only to hear the sound of the elevator door opening above the roar of the sirens.

Sergeant Caffey and three other guards appeared with M4 machine guns in their hands and exited swiftly as Gaskin and his man raised their guns in the air. 'We're clear. All pacified, sir,' he yelled, but even so Caffey and his men held their guns at the ready and, after momentarily glancing down at Bauer, who was still crouched behind the table, the sergeant led the guards warily towards the open door. 'Get that man back down into the holding cells until we have confirmation we're all clear.'

Gaskin immediately flicked his finger, ordering his man back so as to let the sergeant witness the carnage. 'We're clear, sir. Take a look for yourself.'

Caffey and his men paused, and he glanced back at Gaskin furiously. '*I* say when we're clear, Mr Gaskin. You spooks may carry weight out there in the real world but in this place I am God and my word is gospel. Understand?'

Gaskin kept his mouth shut and offered a submissive nod of his head as Caffey, flanked by his men, continued over to the open doorway before coming to an abrupt stop. 'What the—'

The sound of gunfire thundered around the room as Gaskin and his men pumped bullets into the backs of Caffey and the guards. None of them stood a chance, and even the last guard to get hit, who had managed to turn his M4 fully on the shooters, was only able to expel one shot into the side wall of the building's interior before tumbling to the ground in a heap.

Gaskin was immediately upon them and he raced over and stood above the only body still writhing, that of Sergeant Caffey, and stepped on the officer's hand with the heel of his boot, allowing him to pick up the machine gun next to Caffey and toss it off to the side.

'If it helps, you never stood a chance,' Gaskin said before raising his Glock and delivering a shot directly to the man's temple.

There was an instant, sharp groan and then Caffey's body went limp, his lifeless eyes staring up towards the ceiling at the flecks of blood from his murdered men that the assault had sent spattering high above.

Behind them, Hans Bauer rose to his feet with a resolute gaze and he made his way over to the pile of corpses.

'Did the helicopter take any hits?' he shouted as a couple of the tactical-vest-wearing intruders checked the aircraft's fuselage for bullet holes.

'We're good,' one of the men called back, coming to join them in the building. Sidestepping the still-bleeding bodies, Bauer managed a smile and he patted Gaskin on the shoulder.

'How many helicopters do we have?'

'Two, sir. There's one outside and then another parked up about half a click from here.'

Bauer said nothing, but instead took a step over to Caffey's sprawled legs and gave them a hard kick. 'Prick.' He was about to deliver a further swipe when a voice called out over the intercom next to the elevator.

'Can anyone hear me? Update requested.'

It was the voice of the receptionist down below and Gaskin immediately turned to the man wearing the tactical vest. 'Did you cut the surveillance cables?'

'Yes, sir. Just before the sirens went off.'

Gaskin now walked over to the intercom and pressed the button. 'We've suffered an incursion, but we're clear.'

'Understood. I've already tried contacting personnel, but the lines are down as are the security cameras.'

Gaskin shot Bauer a menacing grin before pressing the button once more. 'Keep trying, there's a lot of damage up here and we've got casualties, including Sergeant Caffey. I'm sending one of my men down to you. We need med packs. Anything you've got.'

The line went silent and Gaskin made his way back to Bauer, who glanced over to one of Gaskin's men and slid his finger across his own neck, motioning to the elevator. 'When you're done, join up with the other helicopter.'

The man took off and got into the elevator, his gun now holstered accordingly as Gaskin pulled up Bauer who was already navigating around the bodies to the cold air outside. 'Sir, we have enough room for many of the other prisoners. Should we load them up?'

'No,' Bauer replied, getting a nod from the other man as the elevator door closed behind him. 'They still have a role to play. Don't worry, we'll get to them at some point in the future.'

Gaskin only nodded and then he joined Bauer outside as he made his way over to the helicopter on the far landing pad. The firefight had taken place far enough away from it that it appeared to have taken no direct hits.

Bauer came to a stop at the aircraft and visually inspected the fuselage for any obvious bullet holes, and once satisfied he slid open the entrance door. He then climbed in, followed by Gaskin, as the rotors of the Airbus H115 began to turn.

'Did you make the call to the media?' Bauer asked as Gaskin passed him a clean, folded pair of black trousers, pale-blue shirt and a green tie.

'Yes, sir, just before the operation commenced. They'll be all over this place within the hour, I guarantee it. And the charges are already being set.'

'And they won't damage the facility below?'

'No, sir. But it will make a hell of a mess above ground.'

'Good. Then let it begin.'

Bauer unzipped the front of his boiler suit and then he paused. 'You mind?'

Gaskin stiffened in his seat and then turned away and faced backwards. 'Of course not, SS Reichsmarshal... of course not.'

Chapter 5

Black smoke billowed furiously from the front windows of Colonel Anne Sinclair's Primrose Hill residence as the fire crew doused the upper floor with water. High above, the cloud of gathering smoke hung in the still air like a dark warning to all those who approached. Down below, a medic attempted to tape McCitrick's arm in a sling.

'Easy,' McCitrick groaned as the temporary bandage was tightened securely around his neck, causing him to wince. 'Can you give us some space, please?'

The medic smiled curtly. 'You both have concussion. We'll need to take you back to the hospital for a check-up,' he said, before disappearing around the back of the ambulance, leaving them alone.

McCitrick was clearly pained, but mostly at having Sinclair slip through their fingers... even if it had been in pieces.

Munroe stood by the side of the ambulance and massaged his forearm. Ironically the fall down the stairs had caused more damage to them both than the grenades, the walls of Sinclair's flat absorbing most of the blast. If she'd made it a few steps into the hallway it would have been a different story altogether, and Munroe had hardly registered where the section of banister had landed on him. McCitrick, although receiving a possible fracture to his arm, had also escaped mostly unscathed. It was the attack itself though and not their injuries that had Munroe remaining uneasy, however. Why had Bauer been so willing to give up such a prize asset as the US section head of DSV? No wonder Daedalus had always had an uncanny way of staying one step ahead. With that kind of inside intel one could run circles around your enemy, and that brought Munroe to the question that had him most concerned. If Daedalus had access to that level of information on DSV, then how the hell was Hans Bauer ever allowed to be caught in the first place? That said, it had been Bauer who had come after Munroe, not the other way around, and after the attack on the British Parliament, security levels and restrictions had been raised to their highest levels. Any security discrepancies or outside communications would have courted swift attention upon Sinclair.

Munroe was still rolling such questions through his mind when he felt a firm nudge in his back and he glanced behind to see a friendly face.

'I got here as soon as I could, what the hell happened?'

Captain Jaqueline Sloan looked over at McCitrick with a concerned glance as the DSV head raised his unbandaged arm up at the smoking house and pointed. 'That happened. And how did you get here so quickly?'

'I was enjoying the last few hours of sleep from my R and R, sir. I was already in Central London when I got the call.' Sloane glanced up at the smouldering destruction of Sinclair's flat and let out a single breath. 'Jesus… So, like I said, what happened?'

'Sinclair blew herself up with a couple of grenades,' Munroe declared coldly, animating the explosion with his hands.

Sloan looked stunned. 'But why?'

Munroe glanced around for any eavesdroppers and then he leant in closer to her and whispered, 'Sinclair was the Daedalus mole.'

Sloan said nothing but her look of astonishment said it all.

'Bauer grassed her up, but when we confronted her she tried to take us along for the ride.'

Sloan was not usually a woman to be caught on the back foot, but with her mouth hanging open she looked completely blindsided.

'I'll be heading back to see our friend Bauer next. You coming?'

Sloan's mouth closed and she winced at the offer being made. 'That will be difficult, Ethan,' she said, before reaching into her back jeans pocket and pulling out her Galaxy widescreen phone. After a few taps she held it up so both men could see the display clearly.

Explosion at Cape Wrath military facility in Scotland. Many feared dead as emergency and police services race to isolated spot on the north coast of Great Britain.

McCitrick gasped silently as he pulled himself off the back of the ambulance and shook his head at Munroe's outstretched, steadying arm. 'We need to get ahead of this. Cape Wrath isn't even on the books.'

'We could head up there, sir. Do some damage control,' Sloan offered, but she was met with a stern shake of McCitrick's head.

'No, both of you stay well away. Last thing we need is the media delving into your backgrounds. I'll coordinate with the Ministry.' McCitrick ran his free hand through his hair roughly. 'Does the article mention anything about the guests we have holed up below ground?'

'Nothing yet,' Sloan replied, returning her mobile to her back pocket. 'I made a call after seeing the newsflash, but the lines are out.'

'As is Hans Bauer,' Munroe stated, shooting McCitrick a wide-eyed look that said *we just got screwed*. 'Whoever or whatever we find down there I'll bet you a bottle of Grey Goose that Bauer's nowhere to be found.'

Sloan and McCitrick stared at each other silently, neither prepared to take the bet as Munroe reached into his jacket pocket and pulled out the small hard drive he'd taken from Sinclair's safe. 'But we have some leads to where he's going.'

'I've got a laptop in my car,' Sloan said, pointing to the grey, muddy Audi ZZ parked further back up on the pavement.

'Go take a look,' McCitrick ordered, his tone firm, fighting back his obvious anger. 'I'll join you in a minute. I need to make a call.'

Without a reply Munroe and Sloan made their way over to the vehicle. McCitrick used his free hand to fiddle with his mobile while at the other end of the street the press cars were already arriving.

'Jesus… Sinclair!' Sloan said quietly.

'Yep,' Munroe uttered in disappointment. 'Daedalus knows everything about us. DSV is not only compromised but has been for years.'

The infiltration didn't bear thinking about and as they reached the car and slid into the front seats, Sloan turned her attention to the hard drive. 'Where did you get it?'

'Sinclair's private safe,' Munroe said, passing it over to Sloan, who reached back and picked up the Mac from behind her seat and inserted its cable as the computer buzzed into life. 'The password is "DETERMINA-TION040317".'

Sloan waited for the window to appear and then she tapped in the code and waited as the hard drive was accessed. 'How did you get the password?'

Munroe looked uncomfortable at the question. Of course, it still had to be determined, but he was almost certain that Bauer's admission to him had been nothing more than the precursor to his breakout. Even though no one could have guessed where it had all been leading, he couldn't shake the feeling that he'd been hoodwinked. 'Bauer gave it up, and, looking back on it, far too easily. I should have seen the angle.'

Sloan stared at him blankly and raised her left eyebrow. 'A favourite poet of mine once said "I never saw a wild thing look sorry for itself".'

A confident smile now grew across Munroe's lips. 'D. H. Lawrence.'

Sloan smiled back as the laptop brought up the hard drive's files. 'Yes, it was. So don't go getting all domestic-ated on me now, Munroe.'

They both turned their attention to the screen and began pouring over the reams of information contained within.

'We've got a list of bank accounts, Germany, Switzer-land. Sinclair's been shifting a fair amount of money around.'

'Payments… or a salary,' Munroe replied, hovering his finger over the transfers. 'Moving it around the world, clouding the paper trail.'

'Mmm. Either way, she's been busy.'

'Yeah, but doing what?' Munroe shifted his focus to one of the folders labelled 'Amen'. 'Open up that one.'

'Looks biblical,' Sloan remarked with a light smile, and she clicked it open to reveal what must have been fifty or so stored emails, each sent to the same email address.

Behind them the passenger-side door opened and McCitrick dropped into the seat with a hefty thud, the motion causing him a slight grunt of pain as his fractured arm bumped against his thigh. 'I've laid down some insulation between DSV and Cape Wrath but it's only temporary. If the media don't unearth what facility we've got down there then the Home Office and military will without a doubt. I've got a meeting with the secretary of defence in an hour to find solutions, but frankly I don't know if he's got the resolve to see it through, which is… worrying.'

Since the previous defence secretary, and Daedalus asset, Jacob Ryan, had been killed in a head-on car crash with an Aztec truck, courtesy of DSV, four months ago there had been some unresolved issues with his successor. MP Michael Jankins, now secretary of defence, had begun a rocky relationship with DSV since first being briefed about the covert organisation. The man was an idealist, which to McCitrick was a good thing, but the fact that his ideals extended to resisting any form of lying, when it came to the British public, had made things difficult. The new secretary had initially been near overcome upon hearing of Daedalus, formed from the ashes of the Third Reich to establish a new world authority, and it had taken calls from both his American and French counterparts to fully get him on board. That an intelligence apparatus such as DSV, with little if any oversight, had the power it did was considered by him initially to be as dangerous as any outside threat. But after being shown all the evidence and work that had been carried out on behalf of the main sphere of nations, he had reluctantly agreed to the oath he was expected to take. It didn't mean he liked it and with only four months under his belt there were many, including the other 'Three Kings', that saw him as a potential problem to ongoing investigations. Out of all the section heads, including Colonel Anne Sinclair, it had been McCitrick who felt most secure with the problem of Defence Secretary Jankins.

'We've had problems like this before,' McCitrick had reasoned. 'France in '99, the US in 2003. We even had a similar situation during the Blair government, but pressure and reasoning from the other nations' secretaries has always secured secrecy.'

The threat of breaking the Official Secrets Act and the long jail time incurred had always ensured any new political faces entering the fold saw sense. Jankins though was different. He was honest, but in the world of espionage and defence secrets he was too much so, and it was possible McCitrick was beginning to have second thoughts on the matter.

'I'm sure he'll come around to the bigger picture, but either way, this mess at Cape Wrath is a problem. So, what did you find?'

'Lots of money transfers we can track down—' Sloan began but was interrupted by Munroe who reached over and pulled up the most recent message in the folder.

'But it appears she had a meeting tomorrow in Russia, with someone named "Amen".'

'Amen?' McCitrick replied, unsure what to make of it. 'Where in Russia?'

'Just outside Moscow,' Sloan replied, taking a few moments to delve through the other recent emails. 'It's concerning something called Illuminate.'

'Illuminati?' McCitrick replied, shaking his head disbelievingly.

'No, sir, Illuminate, like a lightbulb.'

McCitrick expelled a disgruntled sigh and he rubbed both his ears. 'Damn ringing in my ears is still deafening. Thank Christ for that. That's a conspiracy rabbit hole I have no bloody interest getting sucked down. You could trace the email address back at the Ministry, get a real name, and in the meantime I'd suggest we send a new email. The IP address must be hard coded into the drive so this "Amen" can confirm it's from Sinclair and her only. We can use it to send a new email.'

Sloan nodded in agreement. 'We could do that. We could keep it from leaking that Sinclair is dead and that she received only minor wounds, but she's under tight surveillance due to security concerns. She could send someone in her place. Another Daedalus operative.'

McCitrick thought about it. They didn't want to scare off the contact, but a lot had been lost today, and when one's back was against the wall what could otherwise seem like reckless plans became solid and reasonable. 'OK. Ethan. You're it.'

Munroe nodded and considered his options as McCitrick turned his attention to Sloan.

'Nothing happens until every one of those emails has been studied thoroughly, then you can send ours. Keep the message consistent and select the meeting place close to where they've met before. Keep it on a familiar track and he'll be less likely to suspect anything, and remember he'll already have his hackles up after hearing about the grenades that went off.'

McCitrick now turned to face Munroe. 'Sloan has assets in Moscow who can offer you assistance.'

'Then why not Sloan?' Munroe asked, but McCitrick was already shaking his head.

'No, after she's dealt with this I've a task for her. She'll be busy for the next forty-eight hours and in less than half that I want you in Russia for the meet.'

It was fine by Munroe, and he already had an idea of who to contact. A bit of a wild card but someone he could trust when it boiled down to it. 'I have someone in mind.'

'Very well,' McCitrick said without skipping a beat, his faith in his team absolute. 'But I want due diligence on those files, agreed?'

'Agreed,' Munroe and Sloan said in unison, and with that McCitrick pushed open the passenger door and pulled himself out using the roof for support. 'Oh, and check her itinerary for tomorrow. I want to know what her excuse was for taking the trip to Russia. Once I speak with Secretary Jankins I'll be in touch. And, Captain Sloan? Get the media out of here ASAP and get in the Ministry of Defence support staff. I don't want anyone knowing Sinclair's dead. Not yet... and make it look good, will you.'

McCitrick slammed the car door shut and headed back to the grey government licensed Jaguar XJ and the assigned driver who was already opening the door for him.

Munroe and Sloan gazed at each other for a few seconds, each processing the enormity of what had just happened. Not only was DSV compromised at the highest level, and had been for years, but if the media or parts of the government found out what Cape Wrath's true purpose was it could blow everything out into the open.

'Maybe Daedalus is getting desperate. Maybe they're trying to drag us out into the light of day. Compromise us.'

Sloan was only slinging ideas, but regardless it didn't make any sense to Munroe. 'That would be bad for them. If the world finds out about DSV then it finds out about Daedalus and their hopes of a Fourth Reich. It might be painful for us, but it would be suicide for them.'

Munroe rubbed at his chin in deep thought, but he couldn't see the answer clearly. 'This is something else. It's a game. But to what end?'

The sound of Sloan slamming shut her laptop pulled him away from his thoughts and he turned back to see her unplugging the hard drive and dropping it into her pocket.

'Well, whatever it is, that's for you to worry about. I need to gain control of this whole Sinclair situation.' Sloan gazed up at the burnt building and shook her head slowly from side to side in disbelief. 'Christ, it's difficult to accept she was one of them. I've laughed, joked and taken orders from her over the past few years and I never even suspected what she was.'

For just a moment Sloan looked rattled, and it caught Munroe off guard, but then he smiled and gently slapped her on the arm with the back of his hand. 'You're not gonna get domesticated on *me* now, are you, Jax?'

'Fuck off, you cheeky bastard,' Sloan snapped at him, though she struggled to contain a smile. 'That's my line. Get your own bloody material.'

'Good, you're back,' Munroe said, laughing. 'I'm going to prepare my travel arrangements. Let me know what you find and where I'm meeting this "Amen" character, will you? Just make sure they know I'm coming alone.'

Sloan gave a nod as Munroe pushed open his car door.

'Who's your asset?' she asked, more curious about who rather than why he was using someone off the books.

'Yuri Drogan.'

The name made Sloan screw up her eyes in thought as she racked the name through her memory. 'Drogan… Drogan… hold on,' she said, looking incredulous, 'the Spetsnaz agent turned hitman?'

'Bingo,' Munroe replied, exiting the passenger seat before turning and bending down so he could see the distasteful look he knew Sloan would be displaying, 'but he's not a hitman per se.'

'Not what I've heard. Our world is a small place and it's our job to know all the players. Bad and worse. Wasn't he hung out to dry by the Kremlin after getting caught in Chechnya?'

'And he was held for eighteen months, tortured throughout. I'm impressed,' Munroe replied. He had not been expecting her to know who Drogan was. 'Afterwards he quit Spetsnaz and used his skills on another path. And for the record, Yuri only uses those skills within the criminal fraternity he signed up for.'

Sloan still looked unconvinced with Munroe's choice of partner, and noting this Munroe shook his head dismissively.

'DSV is compromised. We have no idea who else is and that includes our assets. One thing I know with certainty is that Yuri Drogan is someone I can trust.'

'Oh yeah, Ethan. And how can you be sure he wasn't turned by the Chechens? Don't ever forget that Daedalus has strong ties with many terrorist organisations. Maybe they let him go. How do we know he escaped without their help?'

Munroe smiled and began to close the door, uttering a final sentence before it slammed shut. 'Because it was me who broke him out.'

Chapter 6

Heavy beads of snow thudded lightly against the cottage's downstairs window as, inside, the silhouette of a man hunched over in the kitchen, next to a single brightly lit table lamp and table, placed an object into a black briefcase and gently closed the lid. He stood up and expelled a satisfied sigh before tenderly stroking the leather surface with his open palm. 'The first part is complete,' the man said with a smile, 'it's always the hardest bit.'

He now stood up straight and stretched his aching his arms outwards, revealing the heavy yellow sweat marks staining the armpits of his long-sleeved shirt, which had been rolled up to his elbows. 'Ready to go, just as I said it would be.'

On the other side of the room a man wearing a black suit and tie with a coat folded over his forearm was leaning against the side of a black, glass-panelled wood burner whose red embers flickered in cosy warmth. The man gave a single nod of his head. 'That you did, my friend, that you did.'

The suited man rocked himself upright and put on his knee-length brown overcoat before retrieving two shot glasses from the nearest sideboard with his fingers, grasping the opaque bottle of peach schnapps with his other hand. He made his way slowly over to the table, placing the two glasses down on its surface and unscrewing the cap.

'This is a great thing you have done for us, Dimitri,' the man said as he carefully filled both shot glasses, and after placing the bottle next to the backpack, he passed over a drink to Dimitri, who took a moment to wipe his brow before gratefully accepting it.

Both men stood there in silence for a moment, appreciating their achievement with mutual admiration. They then raised their shot glasses in unison.

'To success,' Dimitri said resolutely.

'And the calm before the storm,' the suited man added, and both men lightly nodded at one another before slugging the drinks in a single gulp and then slamming the glasses down on the table with a clink.

'What now?' Dimitri asked, his tone sounding less confident than his toast.

The suited man reached into his overcoat pocket and retrieved a silver pack of cigarettes before flipping its lid back and sliding two out, one of which he passed over. 'Now begins the real task,' the man said, raising a gold lighter, which was sparked into life with a single flick, and lighting Dimitri's cigarette. 'It is time to right the wrongs of the past.'

The suited man lit his own before sliding the pack and lighter back into his coat pocket and both men once more stood in silence, as smoke began to fill the kitchen. Outside, the sound of heavy rain was beginning to subside.

As Dimitri took another drag and blew it downwards to the floor, the smoke clinging to his shirt, a look of unease began to spread across his face, and although he had wiped his brow just moments earlier a fresh line of beaded sweat was already appearing across his forehead. It was clear he wanted to say something, but he bit at his lip, holding the words back as the suited man stared at him, his eyelids tightening, a smile beginning to play at the corners of his mouth.

'Do you wish to ask me something, Dimitri?'

The question was asked playfully but there was a hint of menace in the man's tone, and Dimitri gulped nervously as the man drew on his own cigarette and exhaled in Dimitri's direction.

The question hung in the air like the smoke, and after some fidgeting with his fingers Dimitri released a measured breath and cautiously looked up to stare the man directly in his cold black eyes. 'Now it's done... will you need me for anything else?'

The suited man reached down with his free hand and slid his fingers along the side of the kitchen table mindfully before dropping his half-spent cigarette and grinding it forcefully into the wooden floor with the sole of his shoe. 'No, Dimitri. You have kept your side of the bargain and I will do no less. A promise is a promise, and as you know, I'm a man who honours his agreements.'

The wave of relief that swept over Dimitri was visible; his shoulders relaxed as the suited man continued. 'But, if your services are ever required again I will expect you to answer my call without hesitation. Until then you will be under our protection.'

'Thank you, and of course. Whenever and wherever. You only have to ask.'

His answer was greeted with a look of approval and the suited man tapped him on the shoulder firmly. 'Good, Dimitri. Very good. You've taken a personal gamble in changing allegiances, but I assure you we protect our own.

No one would dare or be able to take us on so feel good about it, not just for you but for your family.'

Dimitri gave a relieved nod before taking one final drag on his cigarette and then walking over to the sink where he dropped it into the basin. He turned back and motioned to the briefcase. 'Do you wish me to deliver it?'

The suited man was already shaking his head. 'No, I will take it from here, my friend. Let us get you back home.'

Without another word, Dimitri briskly strode over to a wooden chair on the far side of the kitchen and picked up a shiny blue padded ski jacket. He slipped it on hurriedly before making his way to the main doorway. 'Thank you, I cannot wait to see my family again.'

'And you shall, Dimitri. You will see them very soon.'

Dimitri pulled open the door and was met by an icy gust of wind, which sent thick snowflakes swirling inside the room. Raising a hand to his eyes, he caught a reflection in the glass panel at the top of the door which caused him to spin around in shock.

The short black barrel of the Walther P99 was aimed directly at his face, and behind it the suited man offered a grim smile.

'Sorry, Dimitri, but it has to be this way. There is too much at stake.'

Dimitri froze as the man began to squeeze the trigger, but then something very strange happened. The suited man's whole body jolted slightly, like he had just received a small electric shock, and his arm slowly fell to his side along with the gun. His expression began to fade, and the whites of his eyes quickly turned crimson red until they were completely saturated by the colour, so much so that a tear of blood dripped down the man's cheek. His mouth fell open slightly before he collapsed to the floor.

Dimitri looked behind him to the man wearing jeans and a green jumper, holding the silenced pistol before him.

'Dimitri,' the man said, making a disapproving clicking sound with his mouth, 'I told you these people couldn't be trusted, did I not?'

Tears began to well up in Dimitri's eyes and he dropped to his knees, as behind him the high-pitched whine of the snow storm continued to whistle its ominous tune.

'I'm sorry, but they threatened my family. I had no choice.'

The gunman lowered his weapon and slowly shook his head. 'You always have a choice, you idiot. And anyway, they killed your whole family the moment after they turned you.'

The information had Dimitri hanging his head in despair. He burst into an outpouring of grief that was met with complete intolerance from the gunman. The man stepped over the dead body and slammed the butt of his gun across Dimitri's cheek, sending the bawling man to the floor, unconscious.

'I would love nothing more than to spend a few days slowly taking you apart, piece by piece,' the gunman said loudly as he grabbed the unconscious man's leg and dragged him outside into the snowfall, 'but I don't have time for it, so I will have to think of something else.'

Dimitri, of course, was out cold, but the gunman appeared to be enjoying his own running commentary and he grinned before heading back into the rundown cottage. He then disappeared through the nearest side door and re-emerged moments later with a red metal gas cannister. He knelt down and briefly rummaged in the dead man's pockets before proceeding to douse the kitchen walls generously, but cautiously. He turned his attention back to the corpse, drenching it with the remaining liquid. Once empty, he placed the cannister gently on the floor and with both hands picked up the briefcase and headed back towards the open doorway.

The pungent smell of kerosene filling the air had the man wrinkling his nose as he stepped over the lifeless body and made his way back into cold night air, allowing the feeling of refreshment to again wash over him. He then raised his palm upwards and, after noting the snowstorm was already beginning to subside, he smiled to himself and walked over to the silver 4x4 Range Rover parked up in the driveway. He opened the boot and placed the briefcase into a rack with belted straps. Once it was secured, the gunman strode back to Dimitri, flung him over his shoulder with a hefty grunt and then pulled a cigarette from the pack. With his free hand, he lit it with the same gold lighter he had picked up off the corpse.

He took a few moments to enjoy it, the red ember lighting up his face in the darkness outside, before blowing on the tip until it was a sharp glowing point, and then he tossed it inside through the open doorway, immediately sending the corpse into a swirl of yellow-blue flames. The man then headed back to the car and dumped Dimitri into the boot. After placing him in a pair of handcuffs, he closed the boot and checked on the fire to ensure it was spreading as he had intended. The man waited calmly, enjoying the comforting glow he had created, and only once he saw the kitchen window crack and shatter due to the intense heat did he get into the vehicle and slowly drive away into the night.

The flames from the cottage lit up the Range Rover's rear-view mirror and as the man drew further away, the flickering embers swirling into the night sky soon faded away entirely. He thought to himself how much he loved these precious moments. Things to be savoured. For all stories have a beginning and an end, but for him there was nothing more satisfying than the end of the beginning...

The calm before the storm.

Chapter 7

At just under four hours, the trip to Moscow had been uneventful, with Munroe using the time to go over his legend once more. What many people didn't know, because Munroe rarely told anyone, was that he had an almost photographic memory. 'Almost' because thankfully his recall wasn't total and for those who did possess the skill it was surely a curse. To never forget a thing, every good and terrible thing you've experienced emblazoned in chilling clarity, was not something that would have served Munroe well. Not in his line of business. For him, one look meant it was there if he needed it, with the added benefit that he could push things off to one side into the pitch-black recess of his mind and forget.

After Sloan had mopped up the aftermath – not quite literally – of the Sinclair episode she had taken the hard drive back to the Ministry of Defence. With speed of mind she had gone through the folders and extracted the necessary information, which had been passed on to Munroe immediately. In fact, only two hours after she'd arrived at the scene, the media had been given, and accepted, the story of a burst gas main causing the explosion. As had they reported on the stable condition of the house's owner, and by the time she had got around to calling Munroe, the news cycle had already moved on. Her intelligence training had served her well, and overall it was just another feather in her cap, another example of why McCitrick had recruited her to DSV in the first place.

As for McCitrick, he was having a far harder job of it on his end, with the explosion still a regular part of the day's news. There had been no mention of what lay below Cape Wrath, but the fact that so many soldiers had lost their lives in an undisclosed explosion had not only the media but the MOD and the Home Office weighing in as hard questions were being asked, both through official and unofficial channels. The power of the secretary of defence's national security order, 14-45/57, an order installed by Winston Churchill himself, was being questioned aggressively, especially given that the deaths occurred on Home Office territory. Politically speaking.

The good news was that no one had linked the two explosions, and with information balancing on an even keel it was with Munroe that the next stage of their investigation would reside.

'He's an Armenian, hence the codename "Amen", real name Davit Gasparyan,' Sloan had informed him. 'Emigrated to Russia in '65 at the age of two with his parents, who died when he was thirteen. Was adopted by the Soviet system, where his ability for physics and engineering was recognised and nurtured. He attended Moscow University as an undergraduate. It's here that his file trails off.'

The last, unfinished part of Gasparyan's history was, to Munroe, the most noteworthy. Back in the Soviet era the only reason for someone dropping off the radar like that was either because they were working on something top secret, or had been sent to the gulag as an undesirable. And the fact that the man was still alive told Munroe it was most likely the former. What his ties to Daedalus were, though, was yet to be determined. As Munroe approached the front desk of passport control at Sheremetyevo Airport in the north of Moscow, he couldn't shake the feeling he was being watched. And given the hundreds of passengers swarming the concourse, it was an odd feeling to have.

'Passport, please,' the attractive woman wearing an official airport, military-style uniform and *pilotka* requested, and Munroe passed it over. She studied it before glancing up at him and, once satisfied with the likeness, she stamped. 'Business or pleasure?'

'Pleasure,' Munroe replied, and the young woman gave him a seductive smile, clearly taken by his looks. 'Lucky girl,' she said, passing his passport back. 'Welcome to Moscow, Mr Munroe. I trust you will enjoy our city.'

'How could I not… Natasha,' Munroe replied, noting her name badge. 'It's beautiful.'

Natasha winked at him, and then having enjoyed his flirting Munroe headed on past the desk and towards the series of entrances leading outside when a voice called to him off to his left.

'You know she only feels sorry for you. A foreigner looking out of his depth.'

The thick, grating Russian accent made the sentence a challenge, but Munroe recognised it immediately. 'Better looking out of his depth than being up to his neck in shit, and you have a permanent watermark, Yuri.'

Munroe turned around to find Yuri Drogan beaming at him with blinding white teeth that screamed Hollywood. His buzzcut was so short it was difficult to tell how receding his hairline actually was, and he wore a brown Italian leather jacket with a silver shirt undone to the second button, with dark blue jeans, and heavy-duty hiking boots on his feet. At six foot, with wide shoulders and thick biceps that stretched the leather of his coat, Drogan, his eyes almost black in colour, was not someone a stranger would think twice about antagonising. Munroe, though, was no stranger.

With a smile, they hugged, and as Munroe pulled back he motioned to Drogan's teeth. 'Do they glow in the dark?'

'Fuck you,' Yuri grumbled, but his smile never let up, 'these cost me fifty-two thousand roubles.'

Anyone who didn't know Yuri Drogan could be forgiven for thinking the man was obsessed with his smile, and in some ways they would be correct. But not for the reasons they might expect. The Chechen uprising against the Russian Federation ended in 2009 officially, but many pockets remained in the mountain for years, something the Russian government could not forget about. A botched raid had led to all but Drogan being killed and the young soldier had been taken hostage. About a year later a British student, travelling before university and foolishly wanting to see the places many could not, had got his wish and was taken by the same group. Within a week intel had been obtained of the boy's location, and an unacknowledged SAS four-man patrol had been sent in for a recovery operation, with Munroe being chosen to lead. The mission had been a success, with all Chechens pacified and the student retrieved. They had also found a very thin and weary Yuri Drogan on death's door after months of abuse. Most of his teeth had been pulled out with pliers, one at a time. Although the Russian wasn't part of their assignment, Munroe had chosen to get the man out, and after a few weeks in a military hospital he was sent back to Russia, courtesy of the MOD. Unacknowledged, of course. The betrayal by Drogan's government in leaving him to rot may have set him on the path into the criminal underworld, but he and Munroe had remained firm friends ever since.

A debt of blood was not something military men of honour ever forgot, and Drago was no different even if it had been stained by his criminal activities in recent years.

'Come. Let's get to my car,' Drogan said, grabbing the Samsonite overnight case from Munroe's hand. 'The Soviet flag may not fly above this country any more but the culture of surveillance remains, eh?'

The two men made their way out to the vast series of car parks in silence, and it wasn't until they reached the white BMW 750 with extended wheelbase and expensive gold-coloured alloys that Munroe spoke. 'Nice, Yuri. I see you still appreciate the need to keep a low profile.'

Drogan clicked his key, opening the boot automatically, and dropped Munroe's bag inside. 'I've no need to hide from anyone these days, my old friend. The CCCP may be long gone but the art of corruption amongst officials still runs strong. Why, what do you drive these days?' Drogan asked, slamming the boot shut and heading for the driver's side. 'A Jaguar? The only car that comes with a guarantee... that it will break down.'

Munroe laughed at the inside joke, and shook his head as he opened the door. 'No, BMW 330e.'

'Ahh, so you've become an environmentalist. Good for you. The 330 is a nice little car but you could do better. You're on the wrong side of the justice scales, Ethan. My side pays more. A man with your skills could do very well in Russia. Almost as well as me.'

Munroe smiled and got into the front passenger seat as Drogan joined him in the car. Every time he met with the

Russian, the warhorse attempted to recruit him. 'Thanks, Yuri. But I'm good where I am. Besides, if I have to go I'd rather take one in the head than end up being fed to the lions at the Moscow Zoo.'

Drogan rested his fingers on the engine's start button and paused, looking offended. 'Hey, I don't do things like that. Besides, that hasn't happened in a long time.' He started up the 750, which purred away quietly. 'Well, not for a few months and it was nothing to do with me. Now, do you want my help, or did you fly all this way to ruffle the feathers of an old friend?'

Munroe took a moment to enjoy getting under Drogan's skin and then expelled an amused grunt. 'You're getting sensitive in your old age, Yuri. And I came to you because I need the best watching my back.'

Drogan let out a wide satisfied smile. 'And that you have.'

The 750 tore out of the car park and connected up with the M-11 motorway heading north-west. Drogan passed Munroe a black plastic case.

'Just as you asked for,' Drogan said, and Munroe unclicked the lid to reveal a black FNX-45 tactical handgun neatly stored within the grey foam bedding. Above it lay a long, sleek silencer attachment.

'I included the silencer so you have the option.'

Munroe pulled out the handgun and then the two metal clips, each filled with 10mm rounds. 'Appreciate the thought, Yuri, but if this meeting goes loud then I'm not going to have time for it. That's why I need your skills.'

Drogan nodded understandingly. 'Better to have it than not, though. The barrel's never been used so its unidentifiable. Unless you use it again.'

Munroe closed the case and placed it into the foot-well of the back passenger seat, before opening the glove compartment and putting the handgun inside for the journey. 'What do you know about this place?' he asked, closing the glove compartment with a click and settling back into his seat.

'New Jerusalem Monastery is exactly as it sounds, just expect a lot of turquoise. It's surrounded by a wall and looks like a religious fortress to me, but it's open, with many daily visitors, so I would say it's an acceptable place to meet.'

Munroe knew that by the term 'acceptable' Drogan meant defendable.

'Where will you be, Yuri?'

'You're meeting at the base of the main church in an open courtyard, so I'll take position upon the walls. There are turrets along it that are inaccessible to visitors, they will give me more than enough shadow from which to cover you.'

Munroe appeared happy with the information and it was Drogan who was now looking intrigued.

'So are you going to tell me who is on the books for this operation? Or what we're doing here?'

Munroe couldn't blame him for asking. The Russian had already organised the weapons and transport on nothing but a simple request, and Munroe felt he should at least throw his friend a bone. Even if it was a rotten one. 'It's a special services operation. As to why I'm here – the usual.'

Drogan glanced over at Munroe and they spoke in unison.

'None of your damn business.'

They both chuckled at the line as Drogan pulled out and passed a silver Mercedes Benz barely doing the speed limit, flicking the bird at the driver before focusing on the road once again. 'I thought you quit the SAS. Did you get tired of hostage negotiation?'

'No. And yes. I did quit, but when you get the call it's difficult to say no,' Munroe said, smiling dryly, but his response had Drogan shaking his head.

'I understand, Ethan, but if my old masters asked me for a favour I'd stuff those caviar blinis of theirs up their rectums.'

'It's asses, not rectums,' Munroe replied, always amused at Drogan's alternatives for Western slang words.

'No, I prefer rectums. It sounds more civilised.'

'Yuri, I don't think anyone could accuse you of being civilised. But you're a charmer, I give you that.'

Drogan grinned widely at the compliment, pointing to his gleaming teeth. 'It's true, my friend. And I have the Hollywood smile to prove it.'

The drive to Istra took forty-five minutes. As they pulled up at the top of the entrance road to the New Jerusalem Monastery Munroe could see what Drogan meant by a lot of turquoise. Nearly every turret and bulbous church steeple was an unsavoury turquoise colour, with only a few painted in gold, and as Munroe took in the lay of the land Drogan exited the car.

'You take it from here. There's a car park just before the wall entrance. Park there and I'll be watching you from the other side.'

Munroe slid over the BMW's central partition into the driver's seat and then reached over to the glove compartment and retrieved the FNX-45 handgun, which he snuggled in the holster at the back of his belt, covered by the tan-leather jacket he was wearing. 'Where's your weapon?'

Drogan gave him a look of surprise. 'Exactly where I left it last night. You expect me to just walk in there in broad daylight with a rifle under my arm?'

That wasn't what Munroe had meant, but he nodded anyway. 'And remember. Don't do anything unless I make the first move.'

'Of course, lover boy,' Drogan said, in his usual sarcastic tone, blowing a kiss, which Munroe pretended to catch.

'See you in there.' With that Munroe took off down the drive for two hundred metres and pulled up in the car park, fortuitously taking the last space there was.

Within minutes he was passing under the walled entrance and after some bustling with the packs of visitors Munroe entered the open-air inner sanctum of the monastery.

At its centre sat the church, from which a multitude of bulbed spires rose upwards. Apart from the unsavoury choice of paint, the place had a look of St Basil's Cathedral on the edge of Red Square in Moscow, as well as the many Orthodox churches that had survived the Soviet rewriting of history.

Surrounding the cathedral on all sides were smaller, less impressive buildings and cloisters, presumably where the monastery's inhabitants lived.

Munroe stood still as other guests flowed past him, and as he scanned the open area he noticed a man wearing a grey suit, with a heavy, navy-blue padded knee-length jacket over the top. Probably in his early forties, his jet-black hair sharply highlighted the thin sliver streak of white running past his ear. The man was seated on the bench opposite, and looked anything but intimidating.

There was an unnatural slouch to his shoulders, and that he was rubbing at his forearms to warm himself, suggested weak circulation, even if the time of year demanded some protection from the elements. Spring in Russia was a cold affair, and so Munroe took the opportunity to put on a pair of black leather gloves before heading towards the seated man, who now noticed him. Jax had attached a picture of Munroe to the email she sent from 'Sinclair', and as Munroe approached Gasparyan, the man stood up and raised his hand, delivering a single, short wave.

'Mr Hincker?' Gasparyan asked, offering his hand, which was shaken by Munroe, acknowledging the alias Sloan had come up with. 'I recognise you from your photograph.'

'As I do you, Mr Gasparyan. Our friend the colonel sends her apologies for not being here in person.'

Gasparyan retrieved his hand and nodded soberly, but he didn't say another word, merely raising his palm upwards subtly.

Munroe stood there staring into the man's eyes and perhaps a millisecond before the moment became uncomfortable, he realised what the man was waiting for. He mimicked the palm gesture and uttered quietly the magic words he guessed were appropriate. 'Heil Daedalus and the Fourth Reich.'

For a moment the man's blank expression had him wondering if he had said the wrong thing, but then a wry smile appeared on Gasparyan's lips. 'That is good to hear about the colonel, she is invaluable to us. But accidents do happen, Mr Hincker, and in our business, they are always cause for concern. How is she?'

'It could have been much worse. The gas main that took out her kitchen and living room should have killed her, but she got lucky. She's more than well enough to have made this trip but the extra scrutiny by her office would have made it... risky.'

'Oh, I agree,' Gasparyan said, taking Munroe by the arm and leading him along the white paved stone path around the side of the monastery. 'You know this place has been here since 1656, and although a huge restoration project has taken place in the past decade, neither the Soviets nor the German war machine in '43 could destroy its significance. You cannot destroy an idea by physical means. It must be a far more delicate method than that. It is for this reason that, if truth be told, I have never been a strong supporter of the journey we are embarking on.'

The calculated, wary look on Munroe's face had the man immediately seeking to explain his words.

'Don't misunderstand me, Mr Hincker. I am loyal to the cause. It's in my DNA. But to subjugate through fire and brimstone, I would say, does not provide long-lasting results.'

Munroe could only speculate on what they were talking about, but he played his part and nodded thought-fully. 'Perhaps, Mr Gasparyan, but sometimes we must put our faith in those we trust. Why, what part of the journey are you having second thoughts about?'

It was a leading question, but Gasparyan appeared unwilling to go into detail and he skipped over the last part. 'I know, I have faith, but it is one thing to justify beliefs to oneself, another to lie. That is a difficult thing for anyone to do.'

The short walk had taken them around the side of the monastery and Gasparyan, his arm still locked with Munroe's, began leading them towards the western entrance.

'Never mind, Mr Hincker, such things are out of our control, let us get to the business that brought you here. Come, I have a car waiting for us. It is a shame Sinclair cannot see it with her own eyes, but I've no doubt you will be able to relay it to her.'

'Of course,' Munroe replied, subtly glancing up at the turrets in search of Drogan who was nowhere to be seen. 'Lead the way.'

A black four-door Mercedes Benz, engine running with two suited men in the front seats, was waiting for them as they exited the arched stone wall of the western entrance to the monastery. Gasparyan unlocked his arm from Munroe's and entered the vehicle from the far passenger door with a gesture inviting his guest to do the same.

Munroe opened the door and took one last look around. It was now he saw Drogan, if only the top of his forehead and the barrel of his rifle, poking up over the ramparts above. Munroe pulled out his car keys and shrewdly tossed them into the nearest flower bed as he entered the Mercedes and then slammed the door behind him.

'It is only a three-minute drive,' Gasparyan explained as the vehicle pulled away, heading towards the centre of the town of Istra, 'but that's more than enough time to put everything in context for you.'

The blond man in the front passenger seat turned around and Munroe suddenly found himself staring down the barrel of a grey-tinted Desert Eagle pistol.

'It was foolish of you to think that we would not have known that Colonel Sinclair was already deceased, "Mr Hincker",' Gasparyan commented, shaking his head in disappointment. 'My name is not really Gasparyan, but you can call me that, although I think I will call you by your real name… Mr Munroe.'

Munroe glanced down to see the door handles had been removed, meaning he wasn't going anywhere. 'Forgive me, Mr Gasparyan, but I thought deception was the order of the day.'

His host snorted in amusement before pointing back to the monastery. 'And the friend you brought along will have to wait for you, I'm afraid.'

Gasparyan leant forwards, menacingly, and he licked his lips as an all-knowing smile formed across them. 'I could have you killed here and now but I believe you may be of some value to us.'

'Oh, I doubt that,' Munroe replied casually, as if he didn't have a care in the world, 'collaborating with Nazis is not something I would entertain. You're like scorpions.'

The analogy made Gasparyan grin. 'Because we remain out of sight but when we strike it is with a killing blow.'

'No,' Munroe replied, shaking his head, 'because you're small, nasty and unpleasant to be around.'

'Very good,' Gasparyan said, enjoying the insult, and he clasped his hands together tightly. 'But after you've heard what I have to say I think you'll change your mind.'

'I'm afraid not.'

'We'll see, Ethan Munroe, we will see.'

Chapter 8

The black Mercedes came to a loud stop on the weathered side road, its tyres crackling against the gravel on the edge of an open expanse of brown grassland ahead. The whole area was surrounded by forest, creating a circular opening at its centre. The opening for the side road behind them allowed a partial view of the small town of Istra, less than a couple of miles away in the distance, looking so near and yet so far, and making the open area of grassland feel even more isolated than it actually was. On one side stood a mishmash of what looked like metal generators, some on silver metal towers and others on the floor beneath, and although the structure was unlike anything Munroe had seen before it did appear to have been built with some purpose in mind.

It was in stark contrast to the small group of buildings on the other side of the clearing, which appeared to have been abandoned some time ago, and large surface cracks littered each of the buildings' walls. At the base of each one, vegetation had crept up many of the corners and in some cases all the way to the roof, and a spongy-looking green moss now occupied most of the visible grout between the bricks, adding to the feeling that the building was condemned.

'Welcome to the secret of Istra,' Gasparyan announced as Munroe was pulled roughly from the car by one of the suited chaperones while the other held the Desert Eagle to his head. 'Or at least it was until the Soviet Union collapsed. It's such a shame, things were so much easier back then. I was just a boy when the Berlin Wall fell, and Mother Russia's culture changed rapidly in the aftermath. Still, the mindset of the CCCP remained hardwired for those that believed.' Gasparyan raised his hand and swept it across the open area in front of them before coming to a stop on the towers of steel surrounded by rows of protruding vents and metal bars. The unknown devices rose twenty metres into the air at certain points, and the tangled mix of tubing and metal railing looked like a twisted piece of modern art. Frankly it looked like something out of a sci-fi movie, and as Munroe scanned the odd beast of heavy machinery he ended up focusing on a wide concrete square that had something protruding out of the ground at its centre.

'Unfortunately, this place only serves as a tombstone to the achievements made by that once glorious state.'

'And the twenty million dead in the gulags would surely be that tombstone's epitaph.'

Gasparyan now began walking towards the intertwined mass of metal as his henchman slapped a set of handcuffs around Munroe's wrists and took his holstered FNX-45 attached to the back of his belt. In any other situation Munroe would have seized the opportunity to disarm the man with the gun back in the Mercedes and pull his own, but he needed to know more about what Sinclair was involved in and what Bauer or Daedalus were planning. His willingness to go along with whatever was going on was also due to Gasparyan. As the Daedalus agent had suggested, Munroe wasn't being brought here to be killed, but to be made an offer. And that was worth a roll of the dice.

Gasparyan came to a stop at the ten-by-ten metre expanse of concrete flooring, the weight of which had secured it to the grass below, and then he walked to its centre and the white-painted pyramid protruding to waist height. 'I would say more than twenty million, but you are correct,' Gasparyan replied whimsically, only now referring to Munroe's previous insult. 'But extreme sacrifices must be made in the quest for utopia. Wouldn't you agree?'

Munroe tested his bound hands with a firm tug and then stared directly into Gasparyan's dark-brown eyes. 'Ahh, there's the little Nazi I've been looking for. I knew you were in there somewhere.'

Munroe now looked back at the two suited men and noted their blond hair and blue eyes. 'Courtesy of Project Icarus?'

'Yes, Ethan. As were you, before we kicked you out.'

The truth of Munroe's inception had little effect and he shrugged. 'Too many morals, unfortunately, for Daedalus. Killing innocent people… it's just not for me.'

Gasparyan laughed sarcastically. 'Oh, you've killed plenty.'

'Only the ones who deserved it.'

'Ahh, yes. But it's a fine line, morally speaking, isn't it? And it is that line you're going to have to cross. That is if you want to live past the next few minutes.'

Munroe remained silent as Gasparyan placed his hands in both pockets and raised his chin like a commander preparing to deliver an order. 'A few days from now, the beginning of an event we call Steel Thunder will take place, which will shift the balance of power in the West and then around the world. I tell you this because there is nothing you can do about it.' Gasparyan craned his head to one side. 'I know that is a difficult idea to swallow, but just as your Houses of Parliament were razed to the ground six months ago so will this next event happen. There is though one minor a hitch, a loose end we wish to tie up, and it is this loose end that Colonel Sinclair was going to take care of for us. With her now gone, I brought you here to ask you to take her place.'

Gasparyan, like Bauer, had a penchant for the dramatic, and even though Munroe had no intention of carrying out whatever deed was being asked of him, any intel he could gain was paramount. 'What's the job?'

'Oh, it will suit your skills perfectly, Ethan. You could say it is what you were built for. It does entail the retirement of a Daedalus contact, though.'

'No honour among thieves,' Munroe replied, but his comment had Gasparyan waving his hand dismissively and he leant in closer as the two guards stiffened in preparation for any attempted attack from Munroe.

'There is no honour in *betrayal*, Ethan. And it is a betrayal by this man that has warranted such an action. He has something of ours that he believes is benefitting his beloved Mother Russia, when in fact it is Daedalus he is serving. In truth this item is not the most important thing to us, but leaving it in his hands could possibly involve Russia, their government and military, and that is not something we wish to see happen. Eliminate the contact and retrieve the item and I will set you free to graze your pastures once more in the knowledge that our paths will undoubtedly cross once again.'

'Why me?'

'The question is not "why me" but "why not". We could accomplish the job ourselves, but it would draw attention to us, and that is something we would rather avoid at this moment in time. Colonel Sinclair was a perfect choice, she had the resources at her disposal to carry it out efficiently.'

'So you expect me to use DSV assets and intel to do this for you,' Munroe said, beginning to wonder if Drogan had managed to follow him to this place.

'Yes, I do.'

'And if I say no?' The question had Gasparyan looking entertained.

'If you say no then I will have no other option than to do this to you.'

Gasparyan clicked his fingers and one of the guards headed over to the nearest building, reappearing with a frail-looking man in his thirties. Handcuffed and hunched forwards like a broken soul, he was led to the pyramid and swiftly attached to a circular ring sticking out from the top of its point. The man looked petrified, and realising what was about to happen he started to beg for his life.

'Please, Mr Gasparyan, I beg of you. I can still be of great help.' The chaperone slapped his open fist across the man's face and then pulled out a grey piece of cloth from his pocket and used it to gag the man tightly.

'This undesirable little shit is Dimitri Pushkin. He was doing some valuable work for us, but then he decided to change sides, and all before he had completed his promise to aid in operation Steel Thunder.' Gasparyan flicked his finger in Munroe's direction. 'The man who convinced him to betray us initially is the same man I want you to dispose of. It's all become messier than I would usually allow for, but there it is.'

Gasparyan now moved close to Dimitri, who couldn't even look him in the eyes, instead staring at the ground, petrified. 'When I tracked this snivelling turd to his safe house yesterday evening his new friends were about to put a bullet in his head. Not sure why, because Dimitri here hadn't completed his work, but that doesn't matter. I have others who can continue where you left off, Dimitri. What matters is that I saved your life, and now, for your betrayal, I intend to take it. So I thought, why not kill two birds with one stone?'

As Pushkin collapsed into garbled tones of tear-strewn panic, his whole body quivering uncontrollably, Gasparyan moved back over to Munroe and whispered in his ear. 'Screw the stone. I've been wanting to try this for a while.'

Munroe's host held his arms upwards. 'This estate used to be a Soviet research and development facility.'

Munroe shot him a look of concern.

'Nothing like that. No weaponised viruses or nuclear fission was ever carried out here,' Gasparyan reassured him. 'Relatively low-level stuff that – how do you say? – went the way of the dodo when the Red Empire crumbled.'

'What kind of research?' Munroe asked. His question was met with a wide-eyed look of terror from Pushkin, and a dark stain appeared on the front of the man's trousers as he lost control of his bladder.

Gasparyan ignored him, and instead continued with his informational speech. 'Generator technology. This piece of technology is known as the Marx generator. Personally, I would have called it the Lenin generator. Sounds punchier.'

He now pointed to the wide-open countryside around them. 'Moscow is considered a warm part of Russia, and yet in the winter it can drop to minus ten, so when Mother Nature provides you with such a cold environment in which to live then energy technology is crucial. This facility has been deserted for decades, but it still works.'

Gasparyan clicked his fingers and, with him in the lead, Munroe was frogmarched between the chaperones into the same building Pushkin had been led out of and up some rusting metal steps that led to the upper floor of the Soviet-era building.

With the stairs creaking underneath him, Munroe made it to the top to find a dusty Soviet red star with hammer and sickle hanging on the grey painted wall, above what looked like the machinery of an airport control tower. An old grey control table took up most of the space and a large single piece of dirty glass provided an observation window, which looked over Dimitri Pushkin, who was visibly fighting with his bindings to no avail.

Gasparyan began to flick switches and the hum of electrical power filled the room as rows of lights flickered on, and a large indicator gauge began to move in a clockwise manner from the red all the way until it was in the green.

Gasparyan now pushed back the transparent plastic protector covering a large red button and he hovered his finger above it. 'This facility was built to test lightning insulation for military planes, amongst other things. For one hundred milliseconds this archaic yet beautiful machine can discharge the same amount of electrical power as all the generator facilities in the entire country. Two and a half million volts. Would you like to do the honours?'

Munroe jiggled the handcuffs binding his hands behind his back. 'I'm a little tied up at the moment,' he replied sarcastically, looking down at Pushkin who was still grappling with his handcuffs.

'Very well. Let's see what happens,' Gasparyan said giddily, and he slammed his finger down on the button.

In the blink of an eye a blue lightning bolt appeared from the top of the metal towers and hit Pushkin on the top of his head, coursing through his body before dispersing into the metal floor and beyond. The man's face instantaneously erupted into a scarring of black and red patches where the skin had burnt to the muscles. His shirt glinted in growing spots of crimson red, and the left side of his trousers burst into yellow flames that licked up to his waist. Oddly, the body remained stiff and upright, and although the man was obviously dead, Gasparyan hit the button again and again and again, sending multiple lightning bolts into the man until steam began billowing from him. It was only once the entire body was a smoking bloody mess of charred skin and muscle that Gasparyan administered a final zap and then stood back from the console as the corpse collapsed to the metal floor, both its arms coming free from their sockets, leaving two bloody stumps fused at one end to the melted handcuffs.

'Fascinating,' Gasparyan said, turning his attention back to Munroe, who looked sickened by the scene. 'I had expected him to really cook, char to a cinder or even blow up, but it was an unrealistic expectation. The body is sixty-five per cent water. Still, you don't see that every day.' He thought about it intensely before tapping his finger against Munroe's forehead. 'I do want you to do this job for us but, honestly, I really would love to see you on that monstrous contraption. I wonder if you'd burn quicker, perhaps start with a lower voltage and then turn it up slowly.'

However cruel and disgusting this show of intimidation was, it was just that... intimidation, and Munroe slowly nodded his head. 'I'll do the job.'

His acceptance was greeted by a laugh from Gasparyan. 'Of course you will, Ethan, but before I let you on your merry way I would feel a lot better if we had some insurance.'

'Assurance you mean.'

'No,' Gasparyan said, shaking his head, and one of the chaperones now opened a metal storage cupboard and pulled out a heavy-duty red case and placed it on top of the control table. 'I meant insurance.'

He unclicked the plastic locks and pulled open the lid to display a strange-looking gun. It was made from white plastic but with no place for a magazine to be inserted, and a glass piece was set into the base of the barrel just above the grip. Gasparyan slid back the barrel, like an automatic, and when it had clicked into place he reached into the red case with his free hand and picked up a transparent cylindrical cartridge, which he popped into the opening. He then pressed the release button, which sent the barrel clicking back into place; the 'gun' now loaded.

'Don't fight this,' Gasparyan said sternly, and he pressed the muzzle into Munroe's neck right where his carotid artery ran underneath his glands.

With a loud snapping sound Munroe felt a sharp pain and then Gasparyan pulled the gun away and dropped it back into the case, whereupon he picked up the other piece of hardware and dangled it between his fingers.

'You have a small microchip embedded just below the surface of your skin, attached to your carotid artery.'

He now pointed his finger at the dangling device. 'This display can read your temperature and heart rate as well as listen in to everything you say. I will be monitoring you throughout to ensure your compliance. My men will also be following you at a distance and any deviation from my instructions will result in a small charge being set off. Not big enough to kill you but just the right yield to blow a small hole in the aforementioned artery. Again, Ethan, this will not kill you, but the potent gram of poison the charge releases will. Rest assured you will be dead within minutes.'

Munroe swallowed hard and he was now glaring over at Gasparyan, who looked at the display and smiled. 'Your heart rate is rocketing. Had some worrying news, have you?'

Munroe's glare quickly faded, and he expelled a measured breath as Gasparyan glanced at the display again, this time looking surprised. 'And now it's back to normal. That's impressive. No wonder you're so good at what you do, and believe me, you'll need those skills where you're going... Are you paying attention to me?'

Munroe's gaze was now fixed on Gasparyan's chest and the small red dot that had appeared exactly where his heart was located. His host looked down, but he did not panic.

'Looks like your friend has caught up to us. Do yourself a favour and call him off, would you?' Munroe looked to the tree line on the edge of the facility's clearing and made out Drogan taking cover behind a tree, using his belt wrapped around the trunk to steady his rifle. Munroe stepped in front of Gasparyan so that the red laser spot was on his own chest and he slowly shook his head from side to side.

Moments later, the spot disappeared, and Gasparyan expelled a mildly relieved breath. 'Good, now that we're all friends let's head back downstairs, shall we?'

Munroe was bustled down the way they had come and, once back outside, and on Gasparyan's command, his restraints were uncuffed.

He rubbed his wrists and then raised his hand in Drogan's direction and clasped his fist tightly. His colleague quickly disappeared into the thick forest as Gasparyan took a moment to survey the charred and bloody body of Dimitri Pushkin. The man's face was barely recognisable and with no hair, bleeding gums and some of his teeth simply missing, blown apart by the charge, he looked like something one would find in a slaughter house's butcher bin.

'Can I get my gun back?' Munroe asked, and Gasparyan shook his head instantly. 'Not a chance, Ethan, I've seen your work. You'll need to get new equipment before you go in tonight.'

'Tonight!' Munroe said, stealing a glance at his Breitling watch. 'It'll be dark in two hours.'

'Then you'd better get to work, hadn't you? My friend here will give you the details,' Gasparyan replied, nodding to the nearest guard. 'And given your DSV connections there is nothing you can't achieve in such a short amount of time.'

Gasparyan gave a limp salute and along with the other suited blond he headed back towards the Mercedes Benz as Munroe called out after him, tired of this game already and rubbing the sharp pain in his neck where the micro-chip had been injected into his flesh. 'Where am I going anyway?'

'The Kremlin, Mr Munroe. You're breaking into the Kremlin.'

Chapter 9

'Hello, boys,' Sloan said, sliding into the back seat of the grey Lexus LS saloon. 'How's our grieving widow?' She leant forwards and delivered a hard but friendly slap on both men's shoulders as the one to her left lowered the Viper spotting scope from his eye and reached back with his palm open, instantly recognising her voice.

'Jax, it's good to see you. Welcome to Washington.'

Despite the genial Midwestern accent, Zeke Dalton was a formidable presence. With wide shoulders and thick arms, the red-haired, blue-eyed ex-Green Beret had come to DSV's attention through the special forces. His lingual skills were impressive – he spoke seven languages including Russian, Italian and Spanish – and his training in explosives and heavy weapons made him arguably the best DSV had. His infiltration of the formidable and dangerous Mexican cartel, Los Zetas, was legendary within the top echelons of the intelligence community, and his other undercover work had borne him far more experience than his twenty-eight years would suggest.

'It's a bitch about Sinclair,' Sloan said bluntly, shaking his hand firmly. Her words had the second man, to her right, sucking in a deep breath, his lips taught with anger.

'We didn't see it coming,' the man said as Dalton shook his head.

'Then you're in good company, Jack. Neither did we.'

Jack Talon was smaller than his teammate, but with a neck as thick as a bodybuilder's thigh. At thirty-one, his short, black hair was receding and his hazel brown eyes piercing. Like Dalton he had come to DSV through the military, but that was where the similarities ended. Recruitment in the navy had led to Talon becoming one of the youngest men to pass the BUD's training, and he subsequently became a member of the Navy Seals, Seals Team 3. Four years of operations later and he was scouted by the CIA to join the Special Operations Group, or SOG, where he thrived. At the paramilitary branch of the CIA, Talon had served in about every theatre of war imaginable, but his training and expertise as a case officer, or spy handler for the uninitiated, had seen him conduct clandestine human intelligence operations throughout the world. It was this particular skill that had gained him interest from DSV. Talon's ability to manage assets covertly was second to none and Sloan could see that not noticing the traitor, Sinclair, right under his nose was getting to him.

'So what's he been up to?' she asked.

'Take a look for yourself,' Dalton replied, passing her the spotting scope and then pointing to the grandiose white brick house off in the distance at the end of a lengthy driveway, snuggly positioned within a semicircle of white oak trees.

Sloan took a look and found herself staring directly into the large bay window of the house's front room, where a short, bald man with a moustache sat watching a large sixty-inch flat-screen TV. She had never met the man personally, but she recognised him from the photographs. 'So, that's Anne Sinclair's husband,' she said, in a formal tone, surprised that such a tall woman as the colonel would hitch her wagon to such a short, diminutive man. 'He doesn't look like much.'

'Yeah, but he's wealthy,' Talon said as Sloan continued to watch the man rubbing his temple. 'He's partnered at one of the biggest law firms in DC.'

'He looks more nervous than heartbroken,' she noted, passing the scope back to Dalton.

'Either way, he's been holed up there ever since he was denied travel to London.'

'How did we manage that?' Sloan asked, directing the question towards Talon as Dalton resumed his surveillance.

'Secretary of Defence Williamson has put him on the watch list. Told him his life could be in danger, and until confirmation he stays in the country. He's got a security detail of three men guarding the house.'

Secretary Williamson was one of the Three Kings of DSV and a good man... for a politician. He wouldn't have taken the measure personally but rather passed the order down through the chain of command but still, to bar a husband from travelling to see his wife's body, what little there was left, could only last for maybe another twenty-four hours.

'So he knows she's dead and that the media reports are bullshit?'

'Yep,' Dalton replied, taking a break and passing the scope over to Talon. 'He believes she was killed and has agreed to stay quiet to allow time to track the killers down. Unless...'

'Unless he's Daedalus as well and knows exactly what's happened,' Sloan interrupted, and Dalton glanced back at her with a nod.

'We've got his hard line and communications bugged, but so far the only people he's spoken to are family and a few close friends. It could be he had no idea who his wife really was. We're just waiting and seeing what he does.'

Talon lowered the scope from his eye and he looked over at Sloan and smiled. 'But I'm guessing that you being here suggests taking a different tack? What's the word from McCitrick and Remus?'

'The word is we hold off until midnight and then we rattle his cage and see what falls out. The story that Sinclair is still alive won't last past tomorrow morning. The US ambassador is demanding to see her and allowing her a night's rest is all the time we've got. After that the media will know she's dead and it'll make it that much more difficult to get to him... in private.'

Talon thought about it for a moment. 'OK, we could have the security detail pull back and then when he goes to bed we could go in with balaclavas and do the "we're Daedalus wanting answers" scenario. If that doesn't work, then we could induce the truth chemically.'

Sloan was looking agreeable, but it was Dalton who seemed uneasy at the prospect. 'If this guy is a civilian then we'll be doing him some serious damage. Are we sure this is the right route to take?'

All three of them sat silently for a moment and then both Sloan and Talon nodded.

'DSV is compromised, Bauer is out there in the ether, God knows where, and the facility at Cape Wrath is receiving serious media attention. The only lead we have is being chased by Munroe, and Mr Sinclair may be in the middle of it all. I don't see we have any other choice.'

Dalton looked at them both and without hesitation he nodded. 'Agreed. We go in once he's in bed, snug as a bug.'

Sloan and Talon barely had time to respond when at the end of the drive all the house's lights went off simultaneously.

'Hold on,' Dalton said, grabbing the scope back and focusing his attention towards the murky silhouette of the house as the drive lights began to black out, one by one, until the whole residence was plunged into the black of the night sky.

As Dalton and Sloan scanned the darkness for movement, Talon opened his laptop and scrolled through his tracking software. 'All the communication taps are down. The mains have been cut.'

Sloan and Dalton were already out of the car, followed closely by Talon, and with guns drawn they edged their way down the dark driveway, sticking to the edges of the tree line.

As the drive opened up into a parking area, Dalton held his fist in the air, bringing all three to a stop. He then unclipped a set of thin, compact night-vision goggles, which he passed over to Sloan, and then he and Talon slipped on their own. The process took no more than a few seconds and then they continued on towards the house.

As they approached the front entrance, Dalton flicked his finger to the left and Talon split off from the group and headed around the side of the house as Dalton and Sloan came to a stop either side of the entrance.

Sloan peaked in through the side window and saw the body of a woman in a black suit and white shirt lying face up on the wooden floor of the large hallway. The blood stain on her chest looked black through the night vision and her glassy eyes stared directly up at the ceiling.

Dalton had noticed the security guard's body as well, and after a glance at Sloan, he took the lead and entered, with Sloan tight on his six.

It was warm, the thermostat having been cranked up to the max, and Dalton knelt down next to the body, checking for a pulse, as Sloan quietly closed the door and headed to the base of the main staircase. She glanced back at Dalton who retrieved his hand from the guard's neck and shook his head before joining her.

'Clockwise, room by room. First floor's yours,' he instructed, and semi-crouched he manoeuvred his way into the room on the right as Sloan cautiously made her way up the carpeted stairs, keeping her feet to the step edges in an attempt not to make a noise as the staircase took her weight.

At the top of the stairs two passages led off in opposite directions and Sloan was about to head right when she heard a noise along the opposite landing. It was nothing more than a light scuffle, but it was enough to change her direction, and with her Glock firearm held to her chest but pointing forwards she headed down the left landing.

The landing itself, illuminated in the green glow of the goggles, was clear and as she reached the first room on the right she quietly nudged the door open and it swung back on its well-oiled hinges without a sound.

The bedroom was empty. After checking the corners she pulled back onto the landing and lightly stepped until she reached the next door, again on the right. With her barrel pointed towards the opening she reached out and placed her palm on the wooden surface of the door, and was about to push it open when from inside a light flicked on.

Sloan immediately closed her eyes, the light blinding through her goggles, and she pulled back her hand and slowly slipped the goggles off her head, hooking them onto her belt. Wincing, she now hugged the side of the door frame and once again reached forwards and gently pushed the door open.

The door swung back as silently as the last and Sloan found herself staring into the dull eyes of another of the guards, in a black suit and white shirt, legs sprawled out towards her and his upper torso propped up by the edge of a blue-cloth double sofa on the opposite side of the room. The single bullet hole to the back of his head was still oozing blood onto the sofa and a dark crimson patch was slowly spreading as the cloth absorbed the liquid.

On the right stood a bed made up in white French linen with an antique mahogany sideboard next to it, but it was what she saw on the left that had Sloan halting in her tracks.

Half the wall had been slid away to one side, revealing an opening into another room, a small panic room of sorts, but it wasn't the gun rack holding a Remington combat shotgun or the curved computer and keyboard sitting on top of a glass desk that made her freeze. It was the heavy-set man wearing a grey, Viper tactical vest and balaclava who was playing with one of the USB ports and retrieving a memory card.

Sloan instinctively made a snap decision to do things quietly. Taking out three security guards warranted more than just one invader and that meant the other could still be downstairs. A gunshot would alert them and place her team in a potentially vulnerable situation. That being said, the silenced pistol in the man's free hand was not to be taken lightly.

Glock raised, Sloan quietly, step by step, approached the man and she was about to tell him to not move an inch when in an instant her whole approach became academic.

The sound of a gunshot downstairs thundered through the house and the man in front of her spun around like greased lightning, catching her shoulder with his free arm and bringing the pistol to bear upon her. It wasn't fast enough though and Sloan got off a shot into the man's stomach, sending him reeling back into the panic room, against the desk and down onto his backside. Sloan dodged to one side as he raised his pistol again towards her and then placed a shot directly into the man's hand, sending the pistol to the floor and blood spraying across the computer screen.

Downstairs, there were another three shots from a Glock and another four from a dampened, silenced pistol.

Sloan advanced on the man and kicked the pistol away from the torn and bloody piece of meat that had once been a hand, and roughly pulled off the balaclava.

Ordinarily, the sight of blond hair and blue eyes would not have made a difference, but to Sloan it suggested one thing.

Daedalus.

The man was in his early twenties but his cold stare hinted at a seasoning that someone only gets from conflict experience. He was a professional killer, and the way he barely registered what must have been an agonising wound, his fingers hanging from the bone, told Sloan that this was a man of brutish will and the type of mental toughness one only finds in the battle hardened.

Downstairs, the sound of more dampened shots were then silenced by a single shot from a Glock and, apart from the heavy breathing of Sloan's wounded prisoner, the whole house fell into silence once more.

Her gun still aimed at the man's head, Sloan reached down and picked up the memory card that had fallen to the floor during the commotion. 'This must be important, to risk a breach where government security have been placed.'

The man said nothing, his nostrils flaring and beads of sweat forming into bullets that trickled down the side of his temple.

'I wonder, is this Colonel Sinclair's or her husband's?'

The man smiled through stiff lips as he fought the pain and Sloan's eyebrow raised upwards slightly. 'Well at least I know you speak English.'

'Clear,' Dalton shouted from somewhere below, and his voice was followed by the sound of footsteps hurriedly making their way up the staircase.

'I'm in here,' Sloan shouted, never taking her eyes off the wounded prisoner. With the barrel of her firearm aimed directly at his forehead she waited motionless, her eyes never blinking, until Dalton appeared at the open door.

'Well, what have we got here?' Dalton said, immediately moving past Sloan and pulling the wounded man from the floor by his hair. He then brought out a zip tie from his jacket pocket and bound the man's hand and stump together, causing him to groan loudly. 'Your friend downstairs didn't fare as well as you, but once we get you patched up,' he said, reaching over to the bed and dragging the top sheet off, wrapping it around the man's mangled hand to stem the bleeding, 'we'll really go to work on you.'

The wounded man only grunted in defiance as Dalton lassoed another zip tie around his ankles. Once tightened, Dalton used one last one to secure the man's ankles to the radiator pipe on the wall leaving him standing awkwardly and attempting to nurse his wounded hand.

'He was downloading something onto this,' Sloan said, holstering her gun and holding up the memory card. 'From that terminal.'

'I'll have someone from the tech department take a look.'

'Agreed. There's no way of telling if it's got booby traps on it. Could wipe the data.' Sloan tossed the memory card in the air and caught it. 'But this is worth looking at right now.'

There was no reply from Dalton who poked his head out of the door and yelled downstairs. 'Jack, we need your laptop.'

'On my way,' Talon called back. and they heard the front door swing open and closed as Dalton shot Sloan a look of concern.

'C'mon, you need to see this.' He headed out of the room as Sloan knelt and patted their prisoner down. Satisfied there were no knives or other weapons on his person she gave him a hard slap on his arse. 'Don't go anywhere, boy. We have a lot to talk about.'

If looks could kill then Sloan would have fallen to the floor dead there and then. She exited the room and headed down the gloomy landing to find Dalton waiting halfway down the stairs, holding a flashlight, which he clicked on, bathing the hallway below in a cone of light.

'There was only one other and the third security guard didn't make it,' Dalton said as he led her into the dining room off to the right and flashed his torchlight upon a suited guard with a thin garrotte wound running across his neck from ear to ear.

'Jesus, they moved fast,' Sloan noted, seeing the open back door the dead guard had had his back to. 'It only took us, what, forty-five seconds to reach the front door?'

'Impressive, even by our standards. I think they took this guy down before the electricity was cut and then boom, the guard in the hallway, up the stairs and boom, the guard in the bedroom.'

Dalton shook his head as they moved into the kitchen and saw the body of a man wearing a flak jacket and balaclava slumped beneath the main sink with a bullet in his temple. 'Still, goddamn fast.'

Sloan already knew where her colleague was taking her. The only loose end was Mr Sinclair and the lack of noise or complaints from the man whose house had just been invaded told her all she needed to know. It was confirmed as they entered the main sitting room.

Slouched on the sofa, wearing a paisley red and silver robe with blue silk pyjamas and leather slippers sat Colonel Sinclair's husband. His hands lay outstretched to either side, palms up as if he had tried to raise his arms in surrender. The waving of the white flag had not made any difference though and as Dalton hovered his flashlight over the man, Sloan could see the neat single bullet wound in the centre of his forehead. The shot had been close range, leaving blackish powder burns around the hole itself, and suffice to say that whatever his involvement with Daedalus, the death of his wife had made him nothing more than a loose end.

As they both took in the grisly sight, the whole house suddenly lit up as the power came back on. Behind them the flat-screen TV burst into life, bringing up the Sky

News channel, which displayed footage of the aftermath of the explosion at DSV's Cape Wrath facility.

'Jack must have got the power back on,' Dalton said, and they both turned to check out the news story that had the banner headline '*Unanswered questions at unacknowledged facility in Cape Wrath. MOD to give a statement within the hour*'.

'The kings need to get ahead of this or it's going to get out of control,' Dalton said, and Sloan nodded in agreement.

'So much for the news cycle moving on,' she replied as Talon appeared from the open doorway.

'How did you get the lights back on so quickly?' Dalton asked, but the question drew a blank from Talon.

'I thought that was you.'

All three of them looked at each other and Sloan rushed to the large sitting room window and peered out into the lit driveway.

'It's clear, we're the only ones here,' Talon assured her, and with a final look, Sloan strode over to him and passed him the memory card.

'It could be on a delay timer,' Dalton suggested, joining them at the laptop, which Talon placed on the coffee table. He plugged the memory card into the USB port. 'Lights go off, mission executed, lights go on. Unless anyone passed at just the right time, nothing would seem amiss.'

Sloan didn't look convinced as Talon began tapping away at the keyboard. 'They knew not to cut the computer hard-line in the panic room, so we know that's on a separate feed, but the sooner we get some techies over to take a look the better.'

'Already on their way. I called from the car,' Talon replied, his eyes widening as the memory card's files were accessed. 'There's no lock on this, it's a simple download and he copied the whole hard drive. It'll take a while to go through but...' Talon focused in on a file that was the only folder coloured red, the others all being the standard blue, and he clicked it open and watched as a mass of emails and documents all opened at the same time.

'There's a lot of information, but it appears to relate to the same project. Codename Steel Thunder.'

'Sounds like a TV show,' Dalton remarked. Sloan sat down beside Talon and scanned the documents for herself.

'Yeah, Goebbels would have been proud,' she replied and then something caught her eye. 'Can you pull this up, Jack?' she asked, tapping at a series of emails. 'The subject boxes all have the same date. Two days from now... a full gathering to discuss operation Steel Thunder.'

Talon glanced up at both Dalton and Sloan. The glint in their eyes said the same thing and a smile emerged across all their faces at the same time.

'They're meeting,' Sloan said, and both men nodded, the excitement building in them palpable. 'Daedalus are having a family meeting, all of them in one place. The entire fucking clan.'

The opportunity to take out the entire organisation in one swoop had never been considered. Hell, it had never even been discussed.

'Whatever this Steel Thunder is, it's incredibly important to them,' Talon commented, then realising he had understated the significance of an operation that would bring together the whole crooked little empire. 'They blew up the UK Parliament and that was done through back channels. Whatever this operation is we should put our focus on that. You both know the damage they're capable of.'

'Agreed. We need to find out what Steel Thunder is, but we need to confirm all this as best we can. Daedalus are slippery bastards and it could be a ruse. I wouldn't put it past Bauer, but if we can take them all into custody at once then...' Sloan paused as she considered what this could mean, and it was Dalton who finished her sentence.

'It would mean an end to over seventy years of cat and mouse, and the completion of a charter laid down by Churchill, Roosevelt and de Gaulle. The final hammer blow to the Nazis, and in reality... to the end of the war.'

Chapter 10

The blaring sound of the ambulance's sirens sent onlookers shifting either side of it as the vehicle rolled swiftly down the centre of the Red Square. At the far end, St Basil's Cathedral dominated the view with its tulip-shaped multicoloured spires raising upwards into the sky, each bulb corresponding to a different church. It was one of the most iconic buildings in Russia. And although a favourite of visiting tourists, and a testament to the lasting endurance of the Orthodox Church, it was barely registered by Yuri Drogan as he pulled up to the Spasskaya Tower entrance on the north-east side of the Kremlin's surrounding wall.

'We're approaching the entrance, enjoy it, boys. Only dignitaries and the president usually get to use this gate,' Drogan said calmly as he looked back at the two men wearing the same blue medic outfits as him.

The last-minute nature of the plan to break into the Kremlin had meant recruiting two of Drogan's colleagues that Drogan ordinarily would not have chosen. As part of the Russian mafia's Black Hand the two could be trusted to hold their nerve, and taking part in such an incursion was part of the attraction, but it had meant calling upon the less cerebral gang members. The smart ones would never have agreed. Why bring unnecessary heat on themselves? Drogan was counting on his threat of a bullet to their heads if either one of them lost their cool, but considering these men were violent gang members whose only skill was intimidation they made up the loosest link of the operation. Still, Munroe's job, so far as Drogan was concerned, was not only a way to clear a debt he owed but also to go down in mafia legend. To break into the Kremlin and steal government intel right from under their noses took the kind of balls that gained respect, and in his chosen life only two things mattered. Making money and gaining respect, and he was already a good earner.

'Ethan, you hear me?'

'Loud and clear,' Munroe replied, and Drogan subtly pushed his miniature receiver deeper into the canal of his ear to stop the buzzing sensation he felt. 'We're pulling up now.'

The ambulance came to a hasty stop and was greeted by a member of the Kremlin Regiment dressed in blue jacket and trousers, with a gold belt and pumped-up blue hat.

'Identification,' he demanded in Russian, and Drogan raised the ID clipped to his shirt with his forefinger.

The guard took a brief look as the towering wooden gates were already being pulled back and he nodded in urgency. 'It's the Senate building. Go straight and take a right at the Tsar Bell. Just follow the guards' instructions from there.'

Drogan gave a salute and then took off through the entrance, heading down along the brief two-hundred-metre piece of tarmac with the bright yellow painted walls of the Presidium of the Supreme Soviet on his right, an historic relic from the days of the CCCP. So much of the modern-day Kremlin was nothing more than a monument to the buried history of the Soviet era. As Drogan reached the turning, he saw another of the Kremlin Regiment's finest standing in front of the Tsar Bell, waving him down the right-hand road. The bell had been commissioned in the eighteenth century by Empress Anna Ivanovna, the niece of Peter the Great, but it had cracked after a fire had broken out and cold water had been thrown on it. Somehow it had become a treasured piece of history, but to Drogan it was just a big bell. Simple as that.

Having been born in St Petersburg, Drogan had been taught from an early age about the Kremlin, possibly the most famous place in the whole of Russia, but to this day, and even after the calling of organised crime had drawn him to Moscow, he had never seen inside it with his own eyes. Like in most cities around the globe that had world history on their doorsteps, it was only tourists that ever took the time to visit them.

Two more guards waved him into a free spot directly outside the Russian Senate building, which also served as the president's residence, and Drogan prayed the man was in. It would make the legend that much meatier.

'OK, you two. Get the gurney out and let me do the talking. Especially you, Krill,' Drogan said, staring at the larger of the two men who had a fleshy, brutish face not even a mother could love. 'No going *Battleship Potemkin* if we get problems. Just let me handle it. Do well on this and I'll bring you in on the diamond job I mentioned.'

Krill gave a heavy nod and the two men left through the rear of the ambulance and began sliding out the gurney as Drogan exited via the driver's side. Krill would do as he was told, and with a profitable job at the end of the day he'd be happy. Of course, there was no diamond job, not yet, but Drogan would sort something out to appease his mafia associates.

'This way, quickly,' the guard instructed and took off up the stairs to the Senate entrance, followed by the would-be medics and the gurney as two other guards waited by the ambulance.

They passed the checkpoint with a wave from the receptionist and went through the red-carpeted corridors of the Senate building. The arched white stonework was far more impressive than the exterior suggested, and the large grand paintings of Russia's heroes, and villains, hung majestically from the walls. The troop of medics were escorted to an elevator and once inside they began heading up to the first floor.

'We think it's a heart attack, but he's been unconscious since he dropped ten minutes ago. It's impressive how fast you got here.'

Drogan stared at the man and nodded. 'He's lucky, we were at the Metropol Hotel for a guest with a suspected cardiac arrest, but it turned out to be nothing more than a panic attack or we'd have been over twenty minutes away.'

The elevator opened into a large white plaster corridor with green carpets and black-and-white aerial shots of the Kremlin going back over fifty years lining the wall chronologically. The guard led them down it at a jog.

'Why hasn't anyone attended to him? This is the Kremlin!'

The guard looked somewhat embarrassed. 'We're still waiting on the Kremlin doctor but he's not here yet.'

'Well someone call him and tell him not to bother, but I hope he gets reprimanded for this delay. In an episode of cardiac arrest, minutes can mean the difference between life and death.'

'I can assure you he will be,' the guard replied as they turned a corner to find a group of people crowding an open door with the name Colonel Anatoly painted on it in gold lettering.

'Out of the way,' the guard barked, and like the parting of the Red Sea the spectators pulled back to the walls of the corridor, creating an opening, allowing Drogan and his two men pulling the gurney to enter.

The office walls were made up of cherrywood raised panels and the bright white plaster ceiling was in stark contrast to the dark navy carpet covering the floor below. There were glass and cherrywood cabinets with small halogen bulbs lighting up the rows of books contained upon their shelves, and at the far end an encased full-size Russian Federation flag hung above a large mahogany desk. At the side of it a comfy-looking brown leather chair had been overturned and two grey paper trays had been thrown to the floor, sending A4 files everywhere.

There on top of the desk lay the motionless Colonel Anatoly, his green military shirt unbuttoned and the silver crucifix around his neck dangling to one side as a man in a suit held his wrist, checking his pulse.

'Stop that right now,' Drogan ordered with his arm outstretched, his finger pointing directly at the pulse checker. 'And everyone outside now!'

The ex-Spetsnaz operative's tone and voice were commanding, and as he set to work checking the colonel's vitals, Krill quickly ushered everyone outside, including the guard who had brought them. 'No one comes in until we've stabilised this man,' Drogan yelled, and with that Krill slammed the door shut.

The three men looked at each other and with a nod of satisfaction Drogan leant over and whispered in Anatoly's ear, 'We're clear.'

One of the colonel's eyes popped open, looking around the room, and then the other opened and he sat up and rubbed at his face. 'Where is he?'

Drogan said nothing and instead looked back at the two other medics and snapped his fingers.

As one held the gurney, Krill now reached down and released clips at both ends, just underneath the foam bedding, and then pulled back the panel to reveal a secret compartment and Munroe lying flat within it.

'Colonel,' Munroe greeted him, slipping out of the tight space with a helping hand from Krill. He was dressed in a Russian army major's uniform. 'John McCitrick sends his thanks and says he owes you.'

Anatoly gave a forced smile and he shook Munroe's hand as Krill reached to the end of the secret compartment and retrieved the red-banded hat that he passed over to Munroe.

'You have ten minutes,' Drogan said, and both he and Munroe set their stop watches in time as Anatoly moved over to the overturned chair, placed it upright and stood on it, pulling the metal vent away.

'I unscrewed it before faking the heart attack. You know where you're going?'

Munroe nodded, and without another word he stood up on the chair and hauled himself into the cramped space as Anatoly resumed his position, flat out on the desk, and Krill placed the vent back in place behind Munroe.

The shaft space was as wide as the plans Munroe had studied showed it would be. Not big enough to crouch but spacious enough to slide comfortably and Munroe pressed his jacket to the sides so his shirt was in contact with the metal surface and began to slide along the shaft.

Shortly after getting the name of the target and details of the package he was to procure, Munroe had contacted McCitrick immediately by text message. Either Gasparyan was a sloppy organiser or not as smart as he made himself out to be and Munroe had noted the bad planning on the Nazi's behalf right away. Still, one man's mistake was another man's advantage, but even with the threat of the poisonous chip in his neck, his request to carry out Gasparyan's mission had initially been denied. McCitrick had deemed it to be politically dangerous, and he had not been willing to create a serious diplomatic incident if anything went wrong. He had been more concerned with getting the dangerous chip out of Munroe's neck as quickly as possible. The tone had quickly changed though after McCitrick received a report from Sloan during their text chatter. Apparently the incursion into Colonel Sinclair's home had unearthed two crucial pieces of information. First, details of a Daedalus project named Operation Steel Thunder, and, second, the fact that the organisation's upper echelon were meeting up in one place to finalise it personally. Add to this the mentioning of Gasparyan's direct link to the project in one of Sinclair's encoded emails and his mention of Steel Thunder to Munroe earlier and suddenly Munroe's mission to the Kremlin was made a highest priority. So much so that McCitrick had been willing to risk a double agent MI6 had within the Kremlin itself. Because what no one knew, except for a select few, was that Colonel Andrei Anatoly had been working as an MI6 asset for the past five years. Why the man had become a double agent for the British Munroe hadn't been told but in the intelligence world of subterfuge and betrayal Anatoly was considered as solid as they came.

Within an hour Munroe had met with a secretary from the British embassy in Moscow and the gurney with a secret compartment, and the Russian major's outfit, had been handed over. Drogan had also thrown in his considerable connections and within another hour an ambulance had arrived, care of Krill and his partner, and the Kremlin doctor on call had been snatched off the street whilst making his way to his shift for the night.

Munroe was as nauseated by organised crime as anyone else, but to give Drogan's criminal colleagues their dues, if someone needed tracking down and snatching they put even the intelligence services to shame. Despite Yuri's position with the Russian Mafia, Munroe trusted the ex-soldier more than most politicians he had met. The operation had been planned and organised in under three hours, but of course that had been the easy part. If Munroe was discovered then not only would an international incident take place but even more of a spotlight would be cast on DSV than the Cape Wrath incident had caused already. And even if he were successful it was doubtful that Gasparyan would not blow the small microchip in his neck. All in all, this was turning out to be a real turd of a day, but as Munroe approached the third vent along he pushed such thoughts from his mind and focused on the job at hand.

Munroe stared through the metal bars of the vent to see a small office space below. Apart from a chair, desk and HP monitor, the room was bare. More importantly, it was empty. He pulled out a small electric screwdriver with a rotating arm and carefully slid it through the grate, adjusting the angle until he felt the torque of the screw.

The first came out with ease, and after retrieving the screw using the magnetic tip of the screwdriver he then went in for another. Three screws later and Munroe pulled up the vent and exited through the narrow opening before lowering himself down onto the desk below. He then replaced the vent and after straightening his hat and uniform he made his way to the door, grasped the handle, and without pausing he strode outside and into the corridor. Now was not the time for hesitation and he exuded the confidence that a man of such rank would exhibit.

The corridor was empty, and as he strolled along it he recalled the image of the plans he had looked at earlier. Gasparyan's target's office was on this floor, just around the next corner.

Munroe kept walking and as he turned the corner he came face to face with a blue-jacketed regimental guard standing in front of the same room Munroe had come here to enter, and Munroe came to a halt, his expression never betraying his surprise. 'I have business with Secretary Volkov,' Munroe instructed in flawless Russian, his dialect reflecting a Moscow twinge.

The guard, noting his rank, snapped to attention. 'The secretary will be back shortly, sir.'

'Shortly won't do, comrade. I have an appointment with him and I expect him to be on time.'

Munroe's voice held a confidence that had the younger man looking uneasy, but he remained at attention with his chin held high.

'I'm sorry, sir. But he should be back within the next ten minutes.'

Munroe could see the young man was looking more nervous with each passing second and he seized upon the weakness with relish. 'Comrade, Colonel Anatoly is at this very minute fighting for his life having suffered a heart attack and it is essential that I get his last order, before he fell unconscious, to the secretary. Do you understand? Now get off your behind and go bring him here immediately.' Munroe leant forwards until he was within inches of the soldier's face and gritted his teeth. 'And if he dies before I get this message to Secretary Volkov then I will hold you personally responsible, and you don't want me as an enemy, son.'

The guard was already nodding before Munroe had even finished speaking and Munroe took a step backwards, allowing the young man to take off in a jog, disappearing around the same corner he had just come from. Munroe glanced from left to right and, once sure he was alone, he grabbed the doorknob and let himself into Secretary Volkov's office.

The table light was already on and Munroe found himself looking at a space that, for all intents and purposes, was near identical to Colonel Anatoly's. The only real difference was that the panels here were made of mahogany, and instead of glass cases stacked with books these were open, door-less cases lined with awards and family pictures.

Munroe scanned the room until he saw what he was looking for and he now stepped quickly over to a black metal safe with a circular combination lock in the corner of the room, behind the big mahogany desk.

Just where Gasparyan's man had said it would be.

Munroe knelt down and began to enter the number he'd been given.

20-67-92.

On the last number he heard the familiar clicking sound as the safe unlocked and the hefty front panel swung open to reveal Secretary Volkov's most treasured items. There were some bundles of US dollars, a red frilly g-string, perhaps belonging to his wife or girlfriend, Munroe hoped, and lastly what he had been sent here to collect.

Munroe reached in and picked up the brown folder with a red wax seal, a seal, Gasparyan's man had stated that, if broken, would determine Munroe's fate. He then closed the door and re-spun the combination lock, pulling out a handkerchief from his pocket and wiping down the handle along with the lock itself. He didn't know how deep in with Daedalus Volkov was, but if the man started screaming theft then Munroe wasn't about to get caught out by his fingerprints.

With the speedy wipe-down complete, Munroe pulled two black strips of Velcro from his trouser pocket and stuck them to the brown folder. He then pulled out the back of his shirt and slid the folder into his waistband connecting the Velcro with the opposite pieces already stitched to the inside of his belt.

Once it was secure, he tucked in his shirt and straightened his jacket before heading back to the office door. As he reached it, the door swung open and Secretary Volkov entered and came to a hurried stop as behind him the soldier Munroe had run into earlier peered over his shoulder.

'Is this the man?' Volkov demanded angrily, and the soldier acknowledged the question with a sharp nod.

'Yes, sir.'

'And who are you?' Volkov said grimly, noting the rank on Munroe's lapel. 'Major.'

Volkov cautiously took a step further into his office as behind him the soldier, his eyes tightening with mistrust, followed. 'Well, who are you?'

Munroe raised his hands briefly as a show of respect and then used his left to reach inside his jacket's breast pocket and pull out a credit-card-sized leather wallet, which he allowed to fall open, revealing his FSB security clearance. 'My name is Lipofsky and we need to talk, Mr Secretary.'

Whilst the soldier shrank back into the corridor immediately upon seeing the identification, Volkov remained defiant, obviously upset that anyone would barge their way into his office. Whoever they were.

'Secret Service? What do they want?'

Munroe placed the ID back in his pocket and, with a single step forwards, spoke in nothing more than a whisper so only the secretary could hear. 'Steel Thunder.'

Volkov let slip a light gasp and as Munroe now stared at him menacingly the secretary waved back at the soldier without ever breaking Munroe's glare. 'That will be all. I don't want to be disturbed.'

'Yes, sir,' the soldier replied, and then shut the door, leaving Munroe and Volkov alone in the office.

The two men stared at each other for a few seconds, each daring the other to speak first, and with a cough to clear his throat it was the secretary who succumbed to the uncomfortable silence.

'Where did you hear that?' he asked as Munroe motioned for him to take a seat behind the secretary's own desk.

'You should know, Mr Secretary,' Munroe stated intimidatingly as Volkov slumped down in his chair. At maybe fifty-something the man's plump waistline and red-speckled cheeks screamed of the wealthy life of rich food and expensive alcohol to be expected from one of the president's inner circle. But an oligarch in power, although wealthy by most standards, was a mere minnow in a circle of men that had become billionaires through political connections and the accumulation of the country's energy companies. Volkov was not your typical idealist, he was something of an enigma – which Munroe now wanted to crack open and solicit the truth from.

'You've been busy, comrade,' Munroe began, standing still at the opposite side of the desk. 'We've been keeping an eye on you, on the president's orders, and I can say safely that he will not be happy with what we have discovered.'

At this moment Munroe knew about as much of Volkov's affairs as the soldier outside did, and although the secretary sat there anxiously in his comfy-looking leather chair he said nothing, his right eye twitching slightly.

'Steel Thunder, Mr Secretary… are you insane?'

If Daedalus were involved then it had to be big and bold, and as Munroe mentioned the project's codename again his bluff paid off and Volkov licked his lips nervously.

'I'm just the middle man,' Volkov justified as Munroe reached to the inside rear of his trousers and pulled the brown folder away with the sound of cracking Velcro, dropping the package on the desk before him, but with the unbroken wax seal on the underside and out of sight. 'Come now, Secretary. You're far more than that. I will give you one last chance to explain your role in all this or by order of the president you will be taken somewhere that will help you to remember, and I can assure you that you will not see the light of day for the last few weeks of your pitiful life.'

Munroe smiled like a man with the guaranteed winning hand at a poker game and he craned his head towards the black safe against the wall. 'You'll never see that frilly red g-string again either, that's for sure.'

The mention of the underwear obtained a look of embarrassment from Volkov and then the chubby man rubbed his forehead, the stress he was under surprisingly obvious for a politician.

'Everything I did was for the protection and security of Mother Russia,' Volkov began as Munroe continued to stare down at him with the look of a sceptic. 'When the collapse of the Soviet Union happened, many of us believed it would afford us new opportunities, new space to breathe. There were also many who felt bitterness at the destruction of the life they had been born to believe in. They were wary, and with good reason, for as the so-called "iron curtain" dropped, another remained, and it has sought to corral us ever since, to keep us in our place.'

'NATO,' Munroe replied, and the word received a look of disgust from Volkov.

'NATO. The West's apparatus created for only one reason, to keep Russia from realising its global ambitions as the United States has done for decades. And then something happened that gave us time to plan and time to prepare.'

Munroe now kept quiet and stood there patiently as Volkov swallowed deeply, savouring his next sentence. '9/11, and with it the invasion of Iraq. A monumental disaster instigated by leaders who had no idea what they were setting loose. A global jihad that would keep them and the West occupied for over a decade. But one man's disaster is another's good fortune, and the focus was taken off Russia and placed onto terrorists. Almost overnight world focus shifted, and as I already said, it gave us the breathing room to further our ambitions as a nation, and rightly so.'

Volkov sat up in his chair and slid his open palms across the surface of his wooden desk, illustrating the country's expansion. 'We now control Europe's energy, the key to any power base. We forged closer ties with China and Iran, the very nations that have done so much damage to the US, and after all this our hands are clean. We even took back Crimea, but then and after everything that's happened, what did they do? Sanctions. Not easy, but in the long term survivable… and then the war on terror came to an end and once more focus shifted back to us. As we now know the iron curtain of NATO has once again been raised.'

Volkov tapped his finger on the desk and smiled defiantly. 'But soon, thanks to men such as me, men with the foresight and the sheer will to reshape the future as we see fit, the world's focus will once more be shifted, and Russia will acquire another few decades to cement its future. Once this happens, not even the West will be able to challenge us. We will be immoveable.'

Even though Volkov hadn't said it yet Munroe now realised what Steel Thunder was. The real question was how, and did Volkov know that Daedalus was pulling the strings?

'You're orchestrating a terrorist attack. Creating a new enemy of the West.' Munroe shook his head. 'You sanctimonious idiot, Volkov.'

Secretary Volkov looked furious and his lips curled into a snarl. 'It will be more than just a terrorist attack. It will make 9/11 look like a footnote in history. The mere precursor for the main show to come. And have no illusions, Agent Lipofsky, Russia will thrive and no one will be any the wiser of our involvement.'

'Spoken like any conspirator in history. They'll never know… until they do. And what then? This constitutes an act of war, Mr Secretary.'

Volkov stood up and slammed his fist onto the mahogany table. 'This constitutes an act of faith.'

'Someone always finds out,' Munroe replied, and he grabbed the secretary by his shirt collar, playing up the threat of violence perfectly. 'And when they do, we will all suffer.'

Volkov, although sweating slightly, shook his head. 'It's all been arranged, and when it's over there will only be one place for the blame to be heaped.'

Munroe tightened his grip on Volkov's collar and pulled him closer, but the man just kept smiling.

'Very soon one of the West's major cities will experience a nuclear detonation, and in its terrible aftermath it will be one of the West's most powerful countries that will be blamed. Friend will turn against friend. If there is to be another world war, Agent Lipofsky, then it will occur among the very allies who have spent decades trying to avoid it.'

Chapter 11

'Ethan. Can you hear me?'

Drogan's voice was distorted and Munroe struggled to hear as his earpiece faded in and out, all the while he still gripped Volkov by his collar.

'Ethan... we can't stay... we're getting... make your own way... meet you outside...'

'So what are you going to do?' Volkov asked, pulling at the tight grip around his neck. 'Steel Thunder is a done deal. It's too far gone to stop.'

'We'll see,' Munroe replied, and releasing his grip he pushed Volkov back into his seat.

'This operation leads all the way to the Senate and stops right outside the door of the president,' Volkov declared, standing back up defiantly. 'If the security services alert him to it he'll be in an impossible position. Our allies will never trust us again, and he can't stop it, which leaves him only one course of action: to let it play out. If that happens you can bet that I along with anyone else who knows the truth – that includes you, Agent Lipofsky – won't see past next week.'

Munroe pulled out the Walther PPK concealed in a hidden pocket between the fabric of his jacket's lining. Padding had been sewn in to hide the firearm's shape through his uniform and he retrieved a silencer from his trouser pocket and swiftly attached it onto the barrel.

'What the hell do you think you're doing?' Volkov demanded loudly and Munroe now moved towards him with his finger pressed against his lips, the barrel pointed squarely at the secretary's chest.

'Do you even know who you're working with? The people carrying out your shifting of world focus?'

Volkov had frozen, and he instinctively placed his hand in the air. 'They are men of courage, communists who haven't forgotten their pledge to the mother that bore them, and with the strength to carry out what needs to be done. They are heroes.'

Munroe stared at the chubby little man, now perspiring heavily but trying to look as proud as he could despite the large yellow marks of sweat staining the armpits of his white shirt, and he rolled his eyes. 'Well those *heroes* of yours are the same ones who asked me to put a bullet in your head once I had this folder. And they know you tried to take their plan and turn it to your own advantage. Does the name Dimitri Pushkin mean anything to you?'

The name had Volkov turning a light shade of grey. He said nothing at first and then, after a moment to gather himself, he attempted to sound confident. 'It is true I saw fit to bring Steel Thunder under the protection of the Russian authorities, but the men I have been working for are communists. Our goals are one and the same, but this way things will be safer, under my control. This project is far too dangerous to leave with some fledgling communist organisation and believe me, they will thank me for it eventually. They certainly don't have the spirit or will to want me dead. They need me and what I can provide.'

It was now becoming clear that Volkov had absolutely no idea who this 'communist organisation' he had partnered with actually was, and neither did he know that Dimitri Pushkin had been taken off the chess board.

Munroe slid the folder from off the desk, once again ensuring the unbroken seal was not in view, and with his gun still raised he slipped it back into place underneath his shirt. 'Pushkin's already dead, and anything he was working on is far from being in your hands.'

'Bullshit,' Volkov replied, but he was beginning to look even more nervous, if that were possible. 'He is in a safe place as we speak.'

'Really!' Munroe replied, wide eyed. 'Well, that's odd because I watched Dimitri Pushkin being electrocuted to a crisp earlier today. Oh, they want you dead all right. And there's something else you should know about your *partners*. They're not communists… they're fascists.'

That bit of information was as far as Munroe would go, but he enjoyed the look of confusion on Volkov's face as he hit the man with another revelatory punch to the gut. 'I'm not with the FSB. And I'm not going to kill you, Mr Secretary, although I am taking this folder.'

'If you're not FSB then who are you?'

Munroe slid the Walther back into his secret pocket, stepped back, and grabbed the door handle.

'Someone,' he said, reverting to English, 'who is going to have you lying awake at night asking yourself that very question.'

The change of language had the worry in Volkov's face turning to anger and in perfect English he replied, 'The moment you leave this office I'll have you arrested. You will never get out of the Kremlin.'

'No, you won't,' Munroe said, opening the door and motioning the soldier outside to move aside with a swish of his hand, which he did dutifully. 'Thank you for talking with me, Mr Secretary,' Munroe said politely in Russian, and he closed the door and began heading back down the corridor when a mild-mannered voice called out after him.

'You, Major.'

Munroe came to an abrupt halt and he noticed the soldier snap his heels to attention before turning around.

'Who are you?'

Munroe stood there for no more than a minor pause before raising his hand to his forehead and saluting. 'Mr President.'

Russian President Vladimir Belov slowly made his way towards Munroe and waved his hand away firmly. 'Forget the salute. Tell me who you are.'

Munroe stayed at attention and lowered his arm to his side. 'Major Vasiliy Lipofsky, sir.'

'I don't know your face, Major.'

'I only transferred here yesterday, Mr President. I had a message for Secretary Volkov.'

President Belov stared at Munroe for a moment as behind them the young soldier looked unsure, probably because he'd not mentioned his FSB credentials to the Russian leader.

'What was the message?' President Belov asked at the exact moment that Secretary Volkov swung open his door and marched outside, looking like a bulldog chewing on a wasp.

'Ivan. Do you know this man?'

Valkov halted abruptly, his expression holding, and for a moment Munroe thought he was toast but sure enough the secretary managed a smile and he nodded. 'Yes, the major here just told me that Colonel Anatoly has had a heart attack.'

President Belov looked genuinely concerned and he turned back to Munroe. 'How is he?'

'We're not sure, sir. I was just on my way back to check. The medics are moving him to an ambulance as we speak.'

President Belov patted Munroe on the shoulder and urged him to walk with him. 'Take me to him,' he said, glancing back at Secretary Valkov. 'I'll be back in ten minutes. We need to have a meeting.'

'Yes, Mr President,' Valkov replied with a smile that evaporated as soon as the president turned his back and Munroe winked at him and then joined the Russian leader's side.

'Colonel Anatoly is an old friend, but he never listens to my advice. I've told him many times to look after himself.'

'I believe the medics have managed to stabilise him,' Munroe replied, offering the president a reassuring update. 'But it goes without saying he needs hospital care, sir.'

President Belov nodded and the two men continued down the corridor to a wide staircase and then descended to the main entrance and past the armed security who all snapped to attention and saluted. Moments later and they were outside to find Krill and his colleague sliding the unconscious colonel into the back of the ambulance as Drogan watched on.

'Hold on,' President Belov ordered, and Drogan, along with the others turned around to see Munroe and the President of Russia approach them.

'Anatoly, my friend,' the president said, grasping the arm of the still unconscious colonel as Drogan shot Munroe a look of complete bewilderment. 'How is he?'

'It's difficult to say until we get him to the hospital, but he's stabilised for now.'

'Good, then get going,' President Belov ordered and as Drogan and the others scrambled inside the ambulance he turned to Munroe. 'Go with him, Major, and report to me directly.'

Munroe snapped to attention once again and saluted before making his way to the ambulance's passenger side.

'Welcome to the Kremlin, Major Lipofsky. Every day brings us something new,' President Belov stated, and Munroe pulled open the door and smiled cordially.

'If you're scared of wolves, don't go into the woods.'

The Russian saying drew a short smile from the president.

Within minutes they were back on Red Square, and Drogan erupted.

'What by the Holy Mary herself were you doing in there?'

The absolute astonishment in his voice had Munroe laughing hard and even Krill gave a deep, booming chuckle. 'You know how it is, you visit the Kremlin, see the sights and then hang out with the President of Russia.' Munroe looked over at Drogan and smiled with sarcastic smugness. 'You've never met him? He's a charming man.'

Again, Drogan and Krill burst into raucous laughter and Munroe followed suit as Krill placed his gigantic hand on top of the driver's seat. 'Charming!' the Russian boomed. 'He's a bigger crook than I am.'

Again, they all burst into laughter and as it died away into silence Munroe reached under the back of his shirt and pulled out the brown folder, the wax seal still unbroken. He then tapped a message on his phone and held it up to Drogan.

Drogan said nothing, pointing his finger into the back compartment at Krill, but as Munroe now turned the display of the phone to the large Russian, all he received was a shrug and a blank look.

'What package?' Krill replied gruffly, and his response had Munroe shaking his fist in anger and pressing his finger to his lips. If Gasparyan was keeping his word, and Munroe had no doubt he would, then he was still listening to everything that was being said, courtesy of the microchip in his neck.

'The package we're dropping off to Gasparyan.' Munroe said, making it sound as if they had been referring to the sealed folder. A sentence lost in communication.

Krill only now realised the angle and he, again, shrugged his shoulders.

Drogan looked apologetic. '*Shit, Ethan. I'm sorry,*' he mouthed silently as Munroe began scanning the passing buildings until he found what he was looking for, and he slapped his friend on the shoulder and pointed to a hardware store up ahead.

Without a word Drogan brought the ambulance to a stop by the side of the pavement as Munroe opened up the glove compartment and pulled out an empty envelope and a black biro before taking a minute to scribble down a list of items.

Copper wiring, any kind
Four Duracell batteries
Plastic calculator

Once completed, he passed the list over to Drogan and handed him a small stack of roubles.

'So, we drop the package off, meet with Gasparyan and get this microchip out of my neck. And he and we live to fight another day,' Munroe said, again pointing Drogan to the hardware store. 'Do you hear that, Gasparyan?' he shouted as Drogan flicked a salute and quietly exited the vehicle before heading inside, leaving the door resting against its lock.

'I've not opened the folder, but you already know I didn't kill Volkov. I never would have made it out, so it was either him or the package and I figure the package is worth more to you.'

Munroe knew that his alerting the secretary to his co-conspirators wanting to kill him would not go down well with the Daedalus agent but if everything went to plan then it wouldn't matter anyway. It was a gamble, but then everything he'd done that night had been a gamble and he only hoped his luck held out.

As he rotated his finger at Krill, who in turn responded by reliving the experience of having been close enough to the president to mug him, something one of his captains during SAS training had told him rolled through his mind.

'People say they're lucky but I say bullshit. The difference between being lucky and unlucky is preparation. Those that do and those that don't.'

Krill now kept the conversation going for Gasparyan's sake and began to dramatically explain how he could have, if the guards hadn't been there, strong-armed President Belov and relieved him of his wallet as Munroe continued to run the captain's advice through his mind.

Was luck merely preparation? Well tonight he was going to find out.

The white BMW 750 rolled slowly down the long dirt road of Elk Island National Park located on the outskirts of Moscow. Towering above and lining the road stood dozens of shaggy fir trees stretching as far as the eye could see, and the freezing cold temperature had left a coating of frost upon their spiny leaves, which glistened in the vehicle's front lights.

Munroe had been sent the coordinates soon after being dropped off at Drogan's car, and even though the ex-Spetsnaz soldier had offered to come with him, Munroe had refused. They had been very vocal about it, so Gasparyan was made aware, and the Russian had left with Krill to drop Colonel Anatoly at the nearest hospital where he would wake up after the drug wore off and the Kremlin could believe whatever they wanted.

Even so, Gasparyan would automatically assume that this was misdirection and his buddies had come along anyway. Munroe was going to have to play this one carefully.

With his iPhone on the seat between his legs, Munroe followed the directions for a further mile and a half, taking him deeper into the wilderness of the park. Twenty-eight thousand acres of forest wilderness on the edge of Moscow had confirmed its status as a green city, and it put Central Park to shame. That being said, you were more likely to be mugged in New York and survive than get mauled to death by a bear so in some respects it equalled out.

Munroe turned down the even tighter dirt road to his left as directed by the soothing female voice of his phone and another half a mile later she declared that the destination had been reached as he entered a clearing surrounded by thin aspens.

Munroe came to a stop upon seeing Gasparyan's black Mercedes Benz illuminated in his headlights. He left the lights on, but switched off the engine, dimming them slightly, and exited the car.

Standing in front of the vehicle, with his two goons on either side pointing their Glocks at Munroe, was Gasparyan, his hands crossed before him. He was wearing the same smug smile he had had on earlier and as Munroe crossed the twenty-metre gap between them the Daedalus agent raised his hand.

'That's far enough, Ethan,' Gasparyan said, craning his neck to one side in curiosity. 'You look good in the military uniform. You could have been poured into that thing. Now, where's the folder?'

'It's nearby,' Munroe replied, coming to a halt as he was ordered with his palms open.

'How near?'

'Near enough.'

Gasparyan lowered his hand and motioned to Munroe with a flick of his head. 'Throw your gun on the floor.'

'I don't have a gun.'

'Of course you have a damn gun, Ethan.' Gasparyan sighed, shaking his head in frustration as he reached into his own jacket pocket and pulled out the microchip activator he had shown Munroe back at the Marx generator. 'Now drop it on the floor very slowly. It only takes a slight push of this button to end your day with the most painful death imaginable.'

Munroe, slowly unbuttoned his jacket and pulled the Walther PPK from the hidden pocket, tossing it onto the grass in front of him. 'This is the only one I have.'

'Well forgive me if I don't trust you. Pull up your shirt and your trouser legs.'

Without complaint, Munroe pulled out the shirt ends from his waist and did a 360 before pulling up both his trouser legs to reveal nothing but his socks. 'Happy?'

'Almost, Ethan,' Gasparyan replied, and he nodded to one of his goons who marched over to Munroe, his Glock still aimed, and proceeded to pat him down before coming to a stop at the back of Munroe's trousers.

'Got it,' the goon said, roughly ripping the folder from its Velcro pads and then frog-marching Munroe to Gasparyan.

'If you want me to spare your life then you should show me the respect I deserve.'

The goon jammed his heel into the back of Munroe's leg, sending him to the floor on both knees.

'That's better. Now we can talk.' The goon passed the folder over to Gasparyan, who immediately checked to make sure the seal had not been tampered with. 'Good, you did as you were told. That warrants a reprieve, and I can now make my appointment with a man who will put what is in this folder you retrieved to practical use.'

From behind, the other goon produced the same injector that Munroe had been microchipped with earlier. He approached Munroe and pushed the barrel against his neck, but before he could do anything Gasparyan reached out and placed his palm on the weapon.

'There is, though, the matter of Secretary Volkov.'

Munroe looked up at the activator device dangling from Gasparyan's index finger tauntingly.

'That you left him alive complicates our plans, and you told him it was us who wanted him dead.' He wagged his finger from left to right. 'That won't do. That won't do at all.'

Gasparyan lifted up his foot and rested it against Munroe's chest, preparing to shove him backwards, but then he paused as Munroe did something that had him staring down in astonishment.

'Please… I don't want to die like this,' Munroe pleaded, grasping hold of Gasparyan's shoe to stop himself from falling backwards. 'I'm not afraid of dying, but not by poisoning. Make it quick. A bullet to the head.'

There were no tears in Munroe's eyes but the sense of sheer desperation in his voice had Gasparyan taking a moment to briefly push his free hand against his own groin. It was sickeningly apparent that the sensation of feeling power over another's life was intoxicating to the Daedalus agent, almost sexual, and Munroe now lost his grip around the shoe as he was thrust backwards to the ground.

'For men such as us, in our world, there is only one honourable death and a bullet to the head is all we can, or should, expect. It can take minutes of painful agony, writhing about on the ground, before the poison takes you.' Gasparyan took a step backwards along with the goons, creating a circle around Munroe. 'I would offer you the same respectful death I am sure you would offer me. So be it.'

The nearest goon raised the Glock to Munroe's head and in that moment his whole body braced as he heard the familiar click as the gun was cocked. But Gasparyan quickly raised his arm. 'On the other hand…' he said, and pressed the activator button.

Munroe clasped his hand to his neck and instinctively leapt to his feet as the three other men stepped further backwards. Within seconds his arms began to shake, starting at the tips of his fingers and then spreading to his chest and he began to run wildly as Gasparyan chased him at a distance, taunting him with every step.

'Can you feel the cyanide slithering down your throat and into your stomach?' he jeered, pure sadistic delight on his face. 'The bitter almond taste, the last meal you'll ever know.'

Munroe took a few more shaky steps before his legs gave out and he tumbled to the cold grass, ending up in the foetal position and clutching his stomach as forced moans were expelled from his mouth.

'How does it feel, knowing you're about to die, because of me, and there is nothing you can do about it. Such a feeling of helplessness as you give in to your own terror.'

Gasparyan kicked Munroe in the back, hard, enjoying the yelp that he heard, and now he got down on his haunches and placed his hands either side of the dying man's cheeks and held firmly. 'I do so love this process.' His pupils were so wide it made his eyes look black as he was overcome by an almost orgasmic sense of pleasure, spittle dribbling from his lips. 'I want to see your eyes fade, Ethan Munroe,' he continued as white foam began to pour from Munroe's mouth and down his chin, 'and I will be the last thing you ever see because then…' Gasparyan pulled Munroe's shaking face even closer so they were within inches of each other. 'You will be my spirit slave in the afterlife. And I will bring you great pain for eternity, as I will all the others.'

With these revolting words Munroe's eyes spasmed shut and his whole body went limp as Gasparyan dropped him to the floor like a person dropping a piece of rubbish into a bin, and he stood back up and sucked in a deep breath.

Nearby the two goons shot each other a worried look, but it dissolved instantly as Gasparyan strode back to the

Mercedes and climbed into the back seat like nothing had taken place.

'Let's go,' he yelled, and within moments the goons had joined him and the vehicle had sped back down the dirt road and out of sight, leaving the motionless body of Munroe lying curled up in a ball at the centre of the dark clearing, the BMW's lights illuminating a small portion at its centre.

The roar of the Mercedes engine trailed off in the distance as something broke the silence.

'That is one sick bastard.'

Munroe uncurled and got to his feet, spitting out the bitter remains of the Alka-Seltzer he had slipped into his mouth when tumbling to the ground. He then picked up his phone and tapped on the tracer app to bring up Gasparyan's location as a red dot appeared, heading out of the park, courtesy of the tiny bug he had stuck to the heel of the psycho's shoe before being thrust to the ground.

The satellite went black and an incoming call alert now appeared on the display.

'What do you think?' Munroe said, after pressing the answer button.

'I think you should get an Oscar,' Drogan replied and Munroe laughed out loud.

'Where are you?'

'Two hundred metres to your right. I have you directly in my cross hairs.'

Munroe turned in the general direction and waved. 'I thought he was going to shoot me at one point.'

'So did I, but you were right. That bastard needed to see you suffer.'

It hadn't taken a brain surgeon to figure out that Gasparyan was a complete sadist in the classic sense of the word. The man enjoyed inflicting pain on others, both physical and mental. The bloody electrocuted pulp of Dimitri Pushkin back at the Marx generator had proved that. But when his henchman had placed his Glock to Munroe's head, Munroe had a horrible moment of thinking that the sick Daedalus agent had summoned the last thread of empathy he might have had. Fortunately that was not the case, and a few further seconds of being threatened by the Glock would have meant Drogan putting holes in everyone.

They had dropped the colonel off at the entrance of Moscow's Gineco Clinic just around the corner from the Kremlin, and after saying goodbye to Krill, had taken Drogan's BMW and a hired Ford Focus separately. Upon approaching Elk Island, Munroe had taken ten minutes to put together something that McCitrick had sent over plans for. Something that at the time even Munroe had no idea was possible as it was so simple. But that was the main part of the deception. Take the circuit board from a disposable camera, a metal rod, wind it together with insulated copper wiring and a few other things and you have a miniature EMP device capable of knocking out a number of electrical devices: a CCTV camera, a laptop, but more importantly for Munroe, a microchip. Hold a battery-powered calculator while you emit the pulse and if it cuts out and stops working then you know the EMP worked. It had taken just ten minutes to put together, thanks to the plans provided by DSV techies, and now the only thing left to do was remove the microchip. Munroe had left it where it was so as not to draw attention to the fresh wound in his neck, but with basic medical instruments Drogan could do the honours, and unlike pulling out a bullet it would barely leave a scar.

'I need to get this thing out of me ASAP,' Munroe said, rubbing at the small bulge in his neck.

'Then meet me back on the road, I've got the knife and a local anaesthetic from the ambulance. Won't take long.'

Munroe began heading back to Drogan's BMW. 'Good, because if he checks those plans in the folder he'll realise we swapped them for a blank piece of paper and there's a good chance he'll run.'

'And if he doesn't?' Drogan asked as Munroe reached the car, opened the door and picked up the piece of blue planning paper beneath the seat.

'Then he should lead us to the bombmaker and we can stop that nuclear bomb before it's even been built.'

Drogan began to nod but then a puzzled expression appeared across his face. 'Hold on, Ethan, I'm confused. If this Pushkin guy was building a bomb for them then how did he manage it without the blueprints you're holding?'

Munroe looked over at his friend and smiled. 'So you *are* paying attention.'

Munroe was pretty sure his friend would be flicking him the middle finger from out there in the darkness right about now. 'The Russians have always had a habit of compartmentalising sensitive data, and it doesn't get more sensitive, or dangerous, than this. This is likely only half or maybe a third of the actual blueprint, and Pushkin took the project as far as possible, but with this piece they could complete it. No, Yuri, the real question is why did Gasparyan kill Pushkin? It could be to sever the link with the Russians for good. No Pushkin and no blueprint means a dead end, but it also means something more important.'

'It means Daedalus have someone else who can finish off the bomb.'

'Exactly,' Munroe replied warily, 'and like I said, Gasparyan is on his way to meet that bombmaker right now, and I'm going to follow him.'

There was silence and then Drogan came back on the line, his voice business-like. 'OK, I'll see you up on the road and then, after that, I'm gone. My debt has been repaid tenfold. Next time we get together, how about just a bite to eat?'

'Sounds good, Yuri.'

Munroe clicked off his phone and placed the actual blueprints on the hood of his car. The switch had been easier than he had imagined and the seal had been a waste of someone's time. With a fine scalpel Munroe had cut the opposite end of the folder, along the crease, and the plans inside had just slipped out. Some gentle restoration work with cardboard-brown glue and no one was the wiser. That is until the folder was opened proper.

Munroe took one last look at the plans and shook his head before getting back in the car and starting up the engine, what he'd seen in the plans completely occupying his thoughts. How the hell had Daedalus even become aware of this piece of Russian technology? If it ever got out it would propel terrorist attacks towards devastation on a global scale. It was a game changer and Munroe felt an uncomfortable gnawing sensation in his stomach. These plans marked a dark future for the security of the world and how they would counter it was unknown. There was only one thing he was sure of. When McCitrick found out about it he was going to be more than worried, he was going to be terrified.

Chapter 12

'Mr Bauer, how good it is to see you again, and free of any steel jewellery.' The bald-headed butler dressed in a tuxedo welcomed Bauer warmly, offering to take the visitor's jacket with outstretched arms.

Bauer snorted in amusement as he turned his back to the man and had his jacket slipped from his shoulders. 'Thank you, Mr Teston. It's a pleasure to see you too.'

As Mr Teston placed the clothing on a wooden coat hanger, and found a place for it within the cloakroom, Bauer took a step towards the stone handrails of the spacious veranda and gazed down at the small lake town of Hallstatt. Surrounded by mountains, the Austrian town had been a centre for salt mining since prehistoric times and the small community, built into the side of a mountain, was as scenic as it was isolated. This summer chalet, right on the water's edge, was built and paid for by the Daedalus hierarchy and served as a retreat, or sometimes gathering place, for the organisation... or by those that mattered externally. Out on the lake, expensive yachts sailed the calm waters, and one could almost taste the opulence and wealth in the air. It was this sensation that Bauer enjoyed most – being surrounded by both old and new money, all millionaires many times over, and yet it all meant nothing when compared to the power and affluence of the Daedalus core. There was something exhilarating about such power hiding in plain sight, and in knowing how little the lives of these pretenders meant in the grand scheme of things.

'They're ready for you, sir,' Mr Teston announced, and he waited patiently until Bauer had taken in his fill of the scenery before motioning towards the glass-panelled door leading deeper into the chalet.

The courteous manners of Mr Teston were of course just to show respect. Bauer had been here many times over the years and he waited for the door to be opened and then made his way inside as the butler followed closely behind.

'You should know, sir, that there has been some unpleasant talk surrounding your audacious escape.'

Bauer did not respond until he reached the set of double doors, from which the muffled sound of music was emanating. 'Let me guess. Sinclair.'

Mr Teston gave a gracious nod. 'Yes, sir. There are some who say the price was too high.'

'Ahh. Are they the ones with the foresight of a blind man?'

'Those would be the ones, sir. But suffice to say your standing remains strong with the reichführer.'

Bauer clicked his heels and gave a small bow of his head. 'Thank you, Mr Teston. You are my friend, always.'

Mr Teston smiled and then placed his white-gloved hand on the doorknob and with a twist swung the door open to reveal a single man with his back to the door, staring out of the full-length windows onto Halstätter See, swaying gently from side to side.

Next to the man, a turntable played the record of 'O mio babbino caro' from the opera by Gianni Schicchi, and as Bauer entered the room and began walking over to join him, the man raised his finger in the air, bringing Bauer to a halt. Without turning around, he lowered his hand, and there the two stood as the record played and the door behind them was closed.

Bauer watched as the thin red shawl around the man's shoulders slowly fanned from side to side in rhythm with the man's swaying, and his head moved with the music. The man lovingly cherished every note until after a few minutes it came to an end. The needle on the turntable lifted and swung back to one side, plunging the room into silence, save for the crackling of wood burning in the fireplace at the far side of the room.

'The last time I listened to that aria was back in 1981, on the day of the führer's death. In hindsight, perhaps it should have been Wagner, but this always seemed more fitting of our relationship.'

Reichführer Bormann slowly turned to face Bauer and his eyes glistened with tears. 'My father was the führer's most trusted confidant, and because of this he always treated me like a son, especially so after my father was executed by Israeli filth in '68.'

Bormann raised his hands up and glanced around the room. 'I believe that is why he passed the sceptre on to me, and I can proudly say that as of today we are within a hairsbreadth of validating the belief he held and the wisdom he bestowed upon me.'

Bormann made his way towards Bauer, his movement stiff and calculated, as a man's in his seventies usually is. 'And it is you, Hans, who have done more than any other of my people to see it done.'

The old man placed his wrinkled hand on Bauer's shoulder and squeezed. 'I am proud to know that under my leadership we will have reached the goal set out for us by the führer himself and, when my time comes, years from now, I want you to take my place. I want you to bring about and solidify the Fourth Reich that we have spent so many years planning for.'

Bauer's eyes widened and he stood proudly. 'Thank you, Reichführer. I had no idea.'

Bormann snorted and shook his head. 'Of course you did. Who else but the great grandson of Reinhard Heydrich, the man with the iron heart, could fill the shoes left by Adolf Hitler and Martin Bormann?'

Bormann drew back his hand and the smile evaporated as he took a step over to the nearest black-leather armchair and pointed to the other. 'Take a seat, Hans, and tell me, how goes Steel Thunder?'

Bauer sat down opposite Bormann and relaxed in his chair, interlocking his fingers in a stern pose. 'My time in DSV's prison was as one would expect, uneventful, but on the day – as planned – that I made my escape, as we agreed, Colonel Sinclair was served up as a sacrifice.'

The admission had Bormann waving his pasty finger in front of Bauer. 'No one else but us knows that. After this conversation, you must never speak of it again.'

Bauer nodded in agreement as Bormann withdrew his finger before continuing. 'The others believe it was you, and you alone, who took it upon yourself to decide Sinclair's fate, and it must stay this way for the sake of unity. You have my support, always, and that is all that matters. When Steel Thunder bears fruit and they see what we have done for them, they will kiss your boots in praise. This is the final hurdle, and with DSV making so much noise over the past six months there are many who fear they will be next. Of course, no one would dare admit it but fear breeds insecurity, and that insecurity can quickly turn to betrayal. No, only you and I must take the burden of this final push on our own shoulders. When it is done it won't matter what they think. Daedalus will be victorious, and a new world will be born.'

The sheer excitement at the thought had Bormann's whole body quivering, but while the old man was fixated on completing the seventy-year undertaking laid out for him, Bauer could only imagine the spoils of a world in servitude, and the power he would hold, more than any man had ever had in the history of humankind.

'I understand, Reichführer, and have organised the gathering of Daedalus as you requested. It will signify the culmination of all our hard work.'

'Good, good.' Bormann's quivering beginning to dissipate. 'How long will it take now that the plans from the Kremlin have been retrieved?'

'Oh, not long. And all the loose ends are being nicely tied up.'

'And Sinclair's husband, has that been taken care of?'

For the first time Bauer looked unsure and this was jumped on immediately by Bormann. 'Hans?'

'There were some complications, and we lost a few men, but the husband was taken care of.'

'Lost to who?'

'I'm not sure exactly. Possibly DSV or CIA, but his computer was scrubbed. I had someone check once it had all died down.'

Bormann still looked concerned and Bauer raised his hand in an appeasing manner. 'There is no need to worry. I assure you.'

The old man stared at him sceptically but the look soon faded and he nodded. 'And Munroe?'

'Dead. A sad end for someone who could have been a valued ally.'

'It's a shame it had to end that way. I would have enjoyed taking him apart myself when Steel Thunder has concluded.'

'As would I,' Bauer stated coldly, and then he shrugged his shoulders. 'I was told his death was a painful one though.'

'Really?' Bormann said, getting to his feet. 'Then why don't you make your führer happy and tell me all about it over lunch. Every tender and excruciating detail.'

Bauer got to his feet and took the old man's arm. 'Nothing would give me greater pleasure, Reichführer.'

Chapter 13

'You're breaking up again, Secretary,' McCitrick replied, doing his best to articulate each word above the phone line's poor connection. 'Hello, hello, hello? Secretary Jankins, are you there?'

'Yes, John, I can hear you now.'

John McCitrick stood behind his desk at the Ministry of Defence. The secretary needed to know what McCitrick had just heard from Munroe as soon as possible, but the man was at thirty-three thousand feet somewhere above the Atlantic Ocean on his way to a meeting, and this was not making things easy. Normally the phone lines to the on-board telephone were clear, crystal even, but today, whether it be an oncoming storm or simply due to hardware issues, the line was terrible.

'I'm going to bring Captain Munroe onto the call, Secretary, and let him tell you what he just told me.'

McCitrick reached over and pressed the button that was flashing red and, unexpectedly, the connection cleared up considerably. 'Ethan, you're on with the secretary. Would you walk him through what you just told me?'

'Mr Secretary, it's a pleasure to meet you, finally,' Munroe's voice crackled over the intercom speaker, his tone professional. 'I hoped it would have been face to face but events have overtaken that timetable.'

'As would have I, Captain. It's good to speak with you though. I have been reading your reports on Daedalus and even though I am not a great supporter of the secrecy your department brings with it, I do appreciate it is warranted… to a degree.'

The secretary sounded exactly how Munroe had imagined, a straight shooter to the point of misfiring, but what he was going to hear would determine if the politician had any flexibility within that backbone of his.

'I understand completely, Mr Secretary,' Munroe began, not wanting to waste time defending DSV's unique position within the realms of British Intelligence. 'If you'll forgive me for getting straight to the point, but events demand it. I was tasked with contacting one of Colonel Sinclair's Daedalus assets in the guise of her replacement, and what I've uncovered is a serious concern for national and world security alike. I was able to recover the plans that Daedalus were attempting to acquire, sir. They are plans for a nuclear weapon, unlike any we've seen before.'

There was a brief pause, and then Jankins spoke, his voice wavering slightly. 'Are we talking about an increased yield?'

'No, sir. In fact, it's a relatively small yield by today's standards, just under one kiloton. About the same size as Trinity, the first atomic bomb ever exploded during the Manhattan Project…'

Munroe's voice continued to crackle, the interference coming in waves, and he was already beginning his next sentence when Jankins interrupted. 'If it's a small yield then what's your concern, Captain? Technology surpassed that size of technology decades ago.'

'If you'll just let me finish, Mr Secretary. It's not the size of the yield... it's the size of the bomb itself. It's small enough to fit inside a briefcase.'

There was silence on the line and McCitrick gave Jankins a few moments to digest the information before speaking up. 'We've long suspected that the Russians had the designs for such a device during the Cold War, but no one has ever seen them. There were intelligence reports when the Soviet Union fell in 1990 that dozens were made and held by KGB operatives in East Berlin, to be detonated if the West ever invaded, but we've never had any concrete proof... until now.'

There was still more silence from the secretary and Munroe's voice now came back on the line as he resumed his report. 'All nuclear bombs take up a lot of space, Secretary. Our security in part is based around that fact, but a bomb like this could be delivered anywhere, with little to no detection. Hell, it could even be posted through the mail, special delivery. From what I can tell, the original specs have been refined over the years and even the weight of it has been brought down significantly. This bomb has the potential to penetrate the most secure places on the planet, sir. And Daedalus is prepared to use it.'

'It signals an endgame, Mr Secretary,' McCitrick stated bluntly. 'We saw how brazen Daedalus were in bombing the Houses of Parliament – killing hundreds... but this escalation would suggest they are willing to kill hundreds of thousands. Perhaps millions.'

McCitrick heard the sound of a heavy sigh coming from the other end of the line and, unsure that the secretary was truly understanding the threat, he prepared to spell it out, but Munroe's voice emerged from the static of the other line and beat him to it.

'Sir, DSV have been combating Daedalus for decades and in that time, as I am sure the reports you've read have shown you, there is no operation they have ever carried out, or attempted, that has not been attacked from multiple angles.'

'Meaning?'

'*Meaning* that something of this magnitude would not be left to a single operation. If a secretary of the Russian Senate was able to get his hands on these plans then there must be others stored away, and I have no doubt that Daedalus would have been chasing those at the same time they were chasing the one I have in my hands right now. It would have been a contingency plan for just this type of setback.'

'Hold on, Captain. Where exactly did you get these plans?' Jankins demanded, sounding, worryingly, more concerned with the *how* than the *why*. 'Well, Captain?'

'We took them from inside the Kremlin,' Munroe replied, his voice calm and his words to the point.

The silence from Jankins was not a good sign. From everything McCitrick had told him Munroe knew the man was more of a career politician, and though an honest, straight-arrow type, Munroe was unsure of how much personal conviction there was in his heart.

'You conducted a covert operation on behalf of Her Majesty's government to steal military technology from inside the Kremlin?'

'When you put it like that, sir, it does sound like we were playing it loose,' McCitrick interrupted, attempting to sound as reasonable as possible, 'but it was acquired from Secretary Volkov himself who had plans to pass it into the hands of Daedalus. Just as concerning was that the secretary believed he was passing it on to a communist organisation whose purpose was to use the detonation to turn Western allies against one another and crack NATO in the process.'

The sound of a few heavy breaths could be heard on the line and when Jankins came back on he sounded as if he were holding back his anger, each word emphasised to the letter.

'Does anyone in the Russian government know you were there? Can what could reasonably be construed as an act of war be traced back to us?'

'Well, I did run into President Belov, sir.'

'You *ran in* to the Russian president! So he knows what you look like,' Jankins stated, his voice now wavering as McCitrick attempted to bring the conversation down a notch.

'Michael, I think we're missing the point. And anyway, if the Russian president finds out about this then he'll be glad we intervened. His secretary's actions could have started a war.'

'Which is exactly what *you* may have done,' Jankins shouted. 'This was my biggest concern when I was first briefed on DSV and its total lack of accountability. I was shocked and dismayed that such an organisation has been operating outside of the law for decades, without even the prime minister or the US president ever knowing about it. And before you lecture me again, John, on the seriousness of Daedalus and the very real danger they represent, let me tell you what I keep telling you. The continuation and fanaticism of Nazism and its enduring legacy is, I agree, one of the most dangerous problems facing a free world. I was shocked to learn how much influence and power they have cultivated and passed on from generation to generation. It's frankly terrifying, but what happens when the very sword forged to stop them becomes just as dangerous as they themselves?'

'Oh, that is just bullshit and you know it,' McCitrick growled, having had enough of the secretary's lack of confidence in the very organisation he was there to protect and help. 'If it wasn't for DSV the world would be a very different place.'

'Yes, and that's the problem. Because of your people, John, we may find ourselves in a war with Russia, the result of which may mean no world left to save. You don't—'

'Gentlemen, would the pair of you SHUT UP.'

Both men went quiet as Munroe erupted back down the line. 'The only thing that matters at this moment is negating any possibility that Daedalus gains access to this technology, but we must act as if they already have it, which may be closer to the truth than we would like to admit. I am, right as we speak, chasing the only lead – Gasparyan – to a destination that may bring me in contact with whoever they are getting to build this thing. And if I can be frank, I'm in the middle of an airport covertly tracking this bastard and you're not making it any easier.'

Munroe's statement was met with silence and after a pause he came back on the line with confidence in his voice. 'I also believe that Captain Sloan and DSV's American counterparts are on the verge of taking down the whole of the Daedalus hierarchy in one fell swoop, so all in all I would say we're doing one hell of a job. What we need now, more than ever, is the support and guidance of our commanders... which is you two. So, what shall we do? Fight amongst ourselves over differences of opinion, or do we destroy Daedalus and allow DSV's seventy-year mission to be accomplished once and for all?'

The other two connecting lines remained silent, so Munroe pushed a little further. 'And I've got about a minute for you to make up your minds, gentlemen, because I'm about to go dark. My target is on the move.'

McCitrick stood at his desk, staring at the speaker phone, and a smile spread across his face. 'Captain Munroe's assessment is correct, sir. We can argue out our differences after this is over and if the next twenty-four hours prove successful we might not have any differences to argue about.'

There was a muffled sigh from the speaker and then Jankins came back on the line, now fully composed.

'Agreed. Captain Munroe, I want you to get as much intel as possible and then have Gasparyan and all those connected taken into custody. You'll have anything or anyone you need when it comes time to make the arrests.'

'Thank you, sir,' Munroe replied curtly, and then his line went dead, leaving only Jankins and McCitrick.

'I suggest we begin sending this along the grapevine, sir. To MI6 and the CIA.'

Jankins took a moment to mull over the proposition and then he came back with a stern tone in his voice. 'Not yet. I'm meeting with the other heads of DSV tomorrow morning. I will inform them then and they can pass it down the pipeline.'

McCitrick was surprised by the announcement. 'I wasn't told about this,' he replied, concern in his voice.

'It was last minute. We're meeting to discuss the problem of Cape Wrath. The media are still holding the story in the news cycle.'

'It will die down, sir. It always does.'

'Well, from a political standpoint we all want to be on the same page and quash anything before it becomes an issue, no matter how likely. The human rights lawyers would have a field day if they found out, and that is the kind of attention that once out of the box would be impossible to cram back in. No, I'll speak with them and then you can pass it on to MI6. The threat isn't imminent and besides, if you and Captain Munroe are on the money then by this time tomorrow there won't be any Daedalus to worry about. You'll be out of a job, John.'

It was a notion that in all McCitrick's time with DSV he had never actually entertained, and he chuckled to himself. 'This is one time I would be happy to be made redundant, sir.'

'Good,' Jankins replied as his voice began to fade into static, the line becoming faint, 'you and me both.'

Chapter 14

Munroe checked his mobile was on silent and then placed it down on the table before picking up his coffee and taking a sip. He allowed his eyes to settle momentarily on Gasparyan and his two goons, sitting patiently on the other side of the concourse lounge. There was maybe thirty metres between the coffee shop he was sitting in and the small group, but the dense stream of passengers flowing past enabled him to stay anonymous and blend in with all the other travellers either waiting or heading for their flights.

Back in Russia, Drogan had dropped Munroe off at Sheremetyevo International Airport after removing the microchip, which he had managed with the skill of a licensed surgeon. Such experience had likely been gained through extracting bullets from either himself or his criminal cohorts at some time or other. It was experience that Munroe was glad of, and after two stiches and a large plaster to cover what any authority figures would find curious he ended up back at the airport he had started from. Except this time Gasparyan was in his sights and upon seeing the man buying a ticket direct to JFK Airport, New York, he had done the same, using a different airline. Travelling on a separate flight had added a modicum of risk, but given the eleven-hour flight time, taking the same plane would have made it more likely that Gasparyan and his men would run into Munroe and make him. The long flight meant passengers stretching their legs, and a walk down to the end of the aircraft and back was too common an occurrence to take a chance. Anyway, the man had a tracker attached to the sole of his shoe, so he wasn't going anywhere without Munroe knowing about it.

The length of the flight had been a cause for concern, because if Gasparyan was the type of person to kick off his shoes and put on the airline slippers provided then the tracker might be discovered. Fortunately, this hadn't appeared to be the case, and as Munroe took a sip of his coffee, and stole another glance at Gasparyan, the group of three stood up and were greeted by a new arrival. The slim, well-dressed woman wearing a black suit and tie, with her red hair tied back in a ponytail, shook Gasparyan's hand and smiled courteously. He passed over his briefcase to her, whereupon she took a few steps back-wards, allowing the three men to speak privately amongst themselves. They spoke for a few moments and one of the goons nodded and began to walk away, but he was called back loudly by Gasparyan, and Munroe could just make out the name above the chaotic buzz of the concourse.

'Orlov, wait.' The big Russian bruiser stopped and came back to the group where his boss laid out a couple more directives, his finger wagging back and forth, after which Gasparyan took off following the woman, who Munroe presumed was a driver, along with one of the goons, leaving Orlov to sit back down on his seat.

Who was he waiting for?

Munroe pulled up his tracking app, just to make sure it was still operating, and then waited as the red blip began to move further away. In a normal operation of this type he would have already been out of his chair and following his target at a distance, but with the tracker in place he waited to see what Orlov would do next, but after another two minutes of nothing he decided to make a move.

Munroe drained the last dregs of his coffee and stood up, pulling the navy-blue NY Yankees baseball cap he had bought upon arrival down over his eyes. Not so much that it looked suspicious, but enough to keep part of his face hidden when viewed from the right angle, and he made his way out of the coffee shop with the empty black backpack he had purchased along with the cap thrown over his shoulder.

Every surveillance operation Munroe had ever conducted during his service had gone to plan. There were always unavoidable hurdles thrown in along the way, such as a pedestrian bumping into you and drawing unwanted attention, or getting caught up in a traffic jam when following a vehicle, but so long as the rules of training were followed it usually went smoothly. There were other times, however, although rare, when coincidences dropped you right in the middle of it. And as Munroe passed by just metres away from the still seated Orlov, concealed by the crowds of people passing between them, that's exactly what happened.

Drawing level with the henchman, a gap appeared in the crowd of people at the exact same moment Orlov looked over – his and Munroe's eyes locked on to each other. It took just a few more steps for the man's eyebrows to raise in astonishment at finding Munroe there, and he stood up and pulled something small and dark from his pocket.

In one move Munroe threw his empty backpack into Orlov's face and using the momentum of his throw leapt through the space in the crowd. In one long stride he reached the man and grabbed his hand with the object in.

It was a phone, and it was already dialling.

Munroe managed to jam his finger onto the end-call icon, but the move allowed Orlov the opportunity to drive his knee hard into Munroe's groin, dropping him to the floor as the Russian took off running down the concourse.

By sheer luck the blow had missed the intended targets and caught Munroe on the pubic bone. Although it was painful, he was up and chasing within seconds.

Orlov had no more than a ten-metre head start, but as Munroe followed the thick bald head bobbing up and down in the crowd he caught a glimpse of him jabbing at the mobile in his hand.

If Gasparyan knew that Munroe was not only alive but following them then the killer would make a run for it. Where to, Munroe had no idea, but anywhere other than the location of the bombmaker and it would be only a short time before Gasparyan realised how he was being tracked and searched every inch of his clothes and body.

The ten metres between them now looked like a thousand miles and as Munroe noticed a group of young men approaching up ahead he did the only thing he could.

'Hey,' Munroe hollered at the top of his voice, pointing towards Orlov, 'the big bald guy just tried to rape my wife, stop him!'

When in a crowd, people tend to regress to a herd mentality, and it takes a lot to pull them out of it. Shout 'stop that man' and no one will do a thing except stare. Shout 'stop that man, he's a murderer' and most people will get out of the way, not wanting to get killed themselves. Shout 'stop the rapist' though and nine out of ten times a man will pile in and give it a go. And as Munroe had hoped one of the young men, wearing a Metallica T-shirt and black shorts, from the group up ahead heard the call. He charged Orlov with a shoulder barge that landed with a heavy thud. It did little to slow the Russian down, the impact instead launching the young man off to the side in a series of directionless pirouettes, knocking him out cold before he even hit the floor.

The brave if not embarrassing attempt may not have gotten the result Munroe had hoped for but the blow did knock the mobile out of Orlov's hand, and it disappeared into the crowd of people, many of whom were just trying to get out of the way. The movement caused some onlookers to begin panicking and Munroe found himself fighting to push through the crowd.

Orlov paused briefly, glancing behind him for the phone before continuing to run, never breaking his stride. Munroe slid through the crowd and as it began to thin out he took off once again as Orlov's bald head glinted in the sunlight further down the concourse.

By the time he dashed through the main airport entrance into the hot summer air, Orlov had already made it past the two thick traffic lanes outside and athletically hopped the metal barrier of the nearest car park with grace that was impressive for a man of that size.

Munroe followed, and was halfway across the first lane when he caught sight of Orlov piling into a red Jeep Cherokee and he immediately skidded to a halt and ran back towards the pavement and the line of yellow taxi cabs waiting for fares. Munroe pulled open the driver's door of a yellow Nissan NV200 with the engine already running, flung the driver to the tarmac and took off in it at high speed. He caught a glimpse of the furious taxi driver in the rear-view mirror, and much to his surprise it appeared the other drivers hadn't taken off after him. He'd almost expected it; taxi drivers usually protected their own… but not today.

Munroe accelerated around the long semicircle that linked onto the Van Wyck expressway, Route 678, but not before connecting to the entrance of the airport car park. And as he came around the bend he saw the red Cherokee smash through the barrier and slide onto the expressway in a cloud of burning rubber, fifty metres ahead.

It was impossible to tell if Orlov had seen him enter a vehicle, but given his aggressive driving as he flew past a station wagon, almost clipping the wing mirror, Orlov wasn't taking any chances. Munroe ground his boot to the accelerator and darted past the traffic towards the Jeep. There were two possibilities that ran through Munroe's mind as he approached the red Cherokee at high speed. He had no idea where Orlov had come from before the meeting at the Marx generator. Did he fly in with Gasparyan from New York? If he had then the Cherokee could be his own car, waiting for him on arrival. If that were the case then could he have another phone hooked up inside? On the other hand, if he had just hotwired and stolen it, then there would be no phone he could access. If the former were true, then every second counted until Munroe could get control of this guy and with this at the forefront of his mind he revved up behind Orlov's Jeep and slammed into the boot. The blow sent the vehicle swerving from side to side as Orlov struggled to keep control and Munroe pulled out to the right and accelerated up to him until they were level.

The good news was that there was no phone in the car that Munroe could see, and as Orlov shouted some slur in broken Russian, his face red with anger, he returned the favour and ploughed into the yellow taxi. The jolt sent Munroe across the expressway to the outermost lane where he collided with the steel guardrail, shattering his side window and sending a trail of sparks down the right side of the taxi before he wrestled with the steering wheel and swung back towards the Jeep.

The collision had done something to the taxi's front right wheel and Munroe could feel the weight of something pressing against the tyre. As he attempted to shake it free by weaving back and forth sharply, Orlov seized the advantage and began to put some distance between them.

Munroe continued the back and forth motion for a few more seconds and then he heard a cracking sound and felt the pressure on his steering wheel release. He had back control of the car. He glanced back instinctively, looking for whatever had caused the problem, but instead saw a man with a moustache driving a Lexus with his window down, screaming out something about Munroe's mother being a hooker. He offered a quick smile and then hit the accelerator, the taxi's engine roaring in response as he locked onto the red Cherokee that was already hurtling down the ramp of the next turn-off. The road led upwards to a junction that then crossed over the expressway into South Ozone Park and Munroe watched as Orlov slammed up onto the kerb to miss the cars waiting at the traffic light and screeched around to the right and over the bridge.

It was here that Munroe lost sight of him, and as he approached the lights he had to slam down hard on the brake as some idiot in a Chevy 4x4, not to be outdone by the red Cherokee, did the same thing and drove up onto the kerb, but this time turning right. Munroe didn't bother with his horn, it probably would have the idiot getting out of his car looking for a fight, and he crossed over the kerb and stamped on the accelerator, skidding around the corner at speed and just missing the silver people carrier coming the other way. He cleared the corner in time to see Orlov's car turning down a residential side road, but by the time he had reached it, the Jeep was nowhere to be found.

Munroe entered the road and kept driving as he considered the possibilities. The roads, as across most of America, were built on a grid system, cutting buildings into rectangular areas, hence the name 'blocks'. As he approached the first junction and looked both ways he caught no sign of Orlov. It would be relying on sheer luck to guess which way Orlov had gone, but the man needed a telephone fast, which meant finding a public telephone and these were only found on main streets, the nearest being the one he just turned off, not residential roads.

But which way?

A smart person would have turned right and right again to backtrack to the main road, leaving the pursuer to keep going in the opposite direction.

Orlov may look like a dumb thug, but to be Gasparyan's protection he would have needed some brains, and with this educated guess in mind Munroe turned right and when he reached the next junction turned right again before coming to a stop at the main street. He scanned the road to his left and then to the right, and to his relief he caught sight of the red Jeep Cherokee parked up on the side of the road a short way up. Orlov had just exited the car and was picking up the payphone receiver next to it.

Munroe slammed the accelerator down to the floor and took off towards the Jeep. He now, for the first time, clicked in his safety belt, glancing down at the steering wheel and the writing stylised into the rubber, confirming what he already suspected to be the case.

AIR BAG.

The taxi topped out at forty miles an hour as Munroe slammed into the front edge of the Cherokee, sending it flipping off to one side as the payphone was knocked out of its stand and ended up trapped beneath the vehicle. At the same moment, the air bag deployed, slapping into Munroe's face as he was thrown forwards by the force of the collision. The Cherokee's horn, damaged during the impact, blared away loudly.

A few moments passed as Munroe gently sat back in his seat and steadied himself before he opened the taxi door and exited. He felt no balance issues as he stood up and although his nose hurt it wasn't broken. His hearing was a little muffled. All in all, he felt OK, and as he looked over the front of the taxi's crumpled bonnet he found Orlov unscathed except for a cut on his forehead, already scrambling to his feet, his eyes wide in shock.

'You crazy bastard,' he howled as passers-by were already beginning to congregate around the wreck.

'You're coming with me, Orlov,' Munroe replied in a finite tone, but the big Russian was already having none of it, and he turned and began to run back down into the residential area with Munroe giving chase.

For a man carrying the weight of heavy muscles, Orlov was surprisingly light-footed and he made it a hundred metres down the road before cutting down the side of a house, jumping over the bordering fence into the next-door yard.

Munroe followed and after quickly vaulting the fence he picked up a metal garden sprinkler from off the lawn, unplugged the hose and hurled it at Orlov, catching him square in the back of the head with such force that the Russian was knocked to the floor. 'That's enough. I've already wasted enough time on you,' Munroe said, taking a deep breath to compose himself as he approached.

'How are you here?' Orlov said, getting back to his feet. 'I saw you die.'

'No, you saw a man giving you an acting class with a couple of Alka-Seltzer in his mouth. And a word to the unwise, when you want to kill someone… always check for a pulse afterwards.'

Orlov expelled a deep grunt and swung his fist forwards, but the attempt was sluggish and Munroe ducked down onto one knee and delivered a solid punch to his ribcage, feeling a rib or two crack under the force.

The Russian stumbled backwards, his face wincing in pain, and then he clenched his fists and raised them protectively in front of his chin. 'Vostok boxing champ, 2015,' Orlov said with a menacing smile and he began to move in a semicircle around Munroe who stood motionless. 'But since working for Gasparyan, I've broken more bones than you've had hot showers… men, women, children. It makes no difference to me. I'm going to beat you to within an inch of your life and then break your neck.'

'Following orders just like a good Daedalus boy should,' Munroe said, standing motionless as Orlov looked at him in puzzlement.

'Daeda-who?'

Just hired muscle, Munroe thought. How many of Gasparyan's or Bauer's lapdogs knew who, or what, they were really working for? And if they did, would it have mattered? There is no honour amongst thieves, as the saying went, but when you threw the Nazi's into the mix

168

it was surprising how many crooks suddenly found their morality.

'Broken bones, huh?' Munroe said, taking off his jacket and gently placing it on the floor to one side before slowly raising his fists. 'Then you'll know there are two hundred and six bones in the human body, some more important than others.' He pointed at Orlov's chest. 'There's the ribs and then there's the collarbone.'

Before Orlov could react, Munroe struck his fist hard into the top of the man's chest, feeling the collarbone crack, which produced a guttural groan from the Russian, his left arm now hanging unnaturally to his waist.

Instinctively, Orlov thrust forwards with his right arm and Munroe caught it and swivelled around with it in his grip, his back now to the Russian.

'Then there's the wrist,' he said and with a quick flip he broke Orlov's hand, hearing the metacarpals crack. Releasing the man's arm he stood back as Orlov grimaced at the pain. 'And you can't forget the patella.'

Munroe jammed his boot into the side of Orlov's knee and the Russian sunk to his knees, yelling out in pain as Munroe finished off his lesson in anatomy.

'And finally, the old reliable, the jaw.'

He swung his forearm across the side of Orlov's face and with one last crack the big Russian fell to the floor, still conscious but only just as Munroe stood over him, angry but in control.

'Women and children, huh?' was all he said before swinging his boot, like a footballer taking a penalty, across Orlov's face, knocking him out cold.

Munroe sucked in a deep breath and then pulled out his mobile and dialled a number from his contact list. 'This is Agent Munroe. I have an immediate pick up from my satellite location. Backyard. Name Orlov, works for Gasparyan. Daedalus Priority but not associated. I won't be on site, but I need pick-up and equipment. Standard gear. Mobile location is open for meeting place.'

He could hear the sound of a keyboard tapping away and then a voice came on the line.

'Thank you, Agent Munroe. Dispatching immediately, ETA five minutes. A car will be with you in the same time.'

Munroe hung up and slipped the mobile back into his trouser pocket and picked up his jacket from the floor and put it back on. DSV would have contacted the nearest police station, and under the banner of a terror suspect Orlov would be picked up and given hospital treatment – which he was going to need – and then detained until pick-up and taken to the US version of Cape Wrath. That he wasn't a member of Daedalus, if that were true, would afford him many more judicial entitlements, but that was not for Munroe to decide. He checked the tracker app on his phone and noted the unmoving red blip on the screen. Wherever Gasparyan was heading he appeared to have arrived and it was only a short drive from his location.

Munroe glanced over at the green garden hose, then down at Orlov and decided it was pointless to tie the man up. They would be here in minutes and, besides, it would be a few months before the Russian was walking again.

Munroe made his way back to the street to see a large crowd had gathered around the crashed taxi and Cherokee, so he walked in the opposite direction, killing time and distance before his pick-up arrived. He should have been excited by the prospect of taking the Daedalus hierarchy down in one swoop, and Gasparyan and the bombmaker would tie things up nicely, but still something was troubling him. After everything that had happened over the past six months, he had imagined that he would be there when it all finally came crashing down. But it would be Jax who got to be the one. Of course, he was glad that their global mission spanning over seven decades was being brought to a successful conclusion and that he had played his part in it, but still it was gnawing at him.

Munroe shook the feeling from his mind and concentrated on what would come next. All he wanted now was to see the look on Gasparyan's face when he saw Ethan Munroe, back from the dead.

Chapter 15

'This is Uptown One in position. Zero tangos, I repeat, zero tangos at entry point.'

Zeke Dalton trained his AR-15 semi-automatic rifle on the rusting metal back door of the building and awaited a response. Clothed in an all-black SWAT outfit with no identifying patches and wearing a black combat helmet with a small camera attached at the side, Dalton had been in position since arriving on the scene two minutes ago. The building's exit that he was scoping out opened onto a bland rear car park where three black limousines were parked up in the bays.

'Uptown One, this is Downtown Two. Approaching from your right and preparing to breach. Wait for my mark.'

To his right, on the far side of the car park, Captain Jaqueline Sloan approached using the next-door building's side wall for cover, which blocked the line of sight from the windows above. Behind her, Jack Talon and another man brought up the rear, all outfitted in the same gear as Dalton.

'Hold,' Sloan ordered, raising her palm and making a fist. 'Jean, you ready to get us in?'

At five foot eight inches and with short wiry blond hair, Jean Barbeau didn't exactly stand out from the crowd. The Frenchman was well built with thick shoulders and blue eyes, and a relaxed demeanour that exuded a mysterious quality, a certain *je ne sais quoi*. It was these traits that served him well within the intelligence world by automatically putting people at ease, but this miscalculation in underestimating the man was met with disastrous consequences. At sixteen he faked his age with a forged passport and was accepted into the French Foreign Legion. Most of the recruits of the world-renowned regiment saw it as a place to begin again, to start over anew. Barbeau on the other hand had seen it as a place from which to begin. After four years of multiple deployments, from Afghanistan to off-the-books operations in the Ivory Coast and Iraq, the seasoned twenty-year-old had been reassigned to the newly formed DGSI, the French General Directorate for Internal Security, focusing on counterterrorism and espionage. That successful stint had seen him recruited to the DRSD, Directorate of Intelligence and Security of Defence, largely working undercover operations, and it was here he was noticed by the Minister for Armed Forces. Soon after, DSV had come knocking. Excelling in undercover work and speaking five languages without any hint of his French accent, the man was able to blend in to almost any operation. His knowledge of small and medium firearms was beyond reproach and his ability to use them was even more impressive. Barbeau had once made a sniper shot from just under four thousand metres, putting him at the top of the longest shots ever made – although unacknowledged. He was a strong asset for DSV, even if he regularly clashed with his sector chief, Colonel Jacques Remus – but over petty stuff. Either way, the grief he caused was worth the skills he brought to the table, and his loyalty to DSV was as solid as his abilities.

Barbeau pulled out his single-tubed scope and examined the lock on the rusty metal back door. 'Should take no more than twelve seconds,' he replied confidently, returning the scope to his pocket. 'Any problems though and I can blast through in eight.'

The alternative already had Sloan shaking her head. 'No charges unless it's absolutely necessary. We need to take them by stealth. These bastards have an escape plan for every eventuality. We need to catch them with their pants down.'

'They'll be butt naked by the time we roll up on them,' Barbeau replied as Sloan turned her attention to Talon.

'You and I are in first, followed by Dalton and Barbeau. This is a classic breach scenario, flash bangs and lethal force is authorised but only as a last resort or for self-preservation, understand? Just as we planned.'

The two men gave a single nod in unison as Sloan finished off her run-through of the plan.

'The only one we have a face for is Hans Bauer. The rest of the Daedalus hierarchy are just names pinned on a board. It's most likely that the only ones armed are the security, but even so, shoot to incapacitate unless you deem it unavoidable... Ready?'

Both men tapped their helmets lightly and readied their AR-15s as Sloan pressed at the round microphone strapped around her throat. 'Uptown One, prepare to breach on my command.'

On the other side of the car park, Dalton looked over and nodded as Sloan raised her hand in the air and with it, like turning a switch, any trepidation she had been feeling about finally taking down Daedalus evaporated.

'Commence breach.'

Followed closely by Barbeau, Sloan took off from the covering wall and with her knees bent and AR-15 firmly aimed forwards she made her way to the door. The moment they broke cover, both Dalton and Talon covered the windows for any sign of movement, and as Sloan came to a kneeling position just next to the door, Barbeau let his rifle fall to his side on the sling around his shoulder, pulled out a lockpick and immediately went to work.

Ten seconds later they heard the sound of a metallic spring giving way and Sloan flicked two fingers in the air summoning Dalton and Talon, who quickly joined them. They lined up in a row and placed their free hands on the shoulder in front. With a tap from Sloan, Dalton turned the knob and swung the door back as the four entered, one after the other. Upon finding the ground floor empty, Barbeau and Talon took defensive positions at either side of the room as Sloan and Dalton pushed forwards. There were large plastic bags of fertiliser and soil propped up against the walls and on the right side a wooden staircase led up to the next floor.

With Barbeau and Talon covering the rear, Sloan took point, and she and Dalton pressed up the stairs as quietly as possible, scanning the level above.

Again the floor was empty of life, but two doors led off to separate rooms and another staircase, this one with red carpet. The kitchen was decked out in brand-new equipment, with a shiny silver oven and two large refrigerators next to it, and on the other side of a steel preparation table in the middle of the room a large white freezer hummed away quietly against the wall.

Sloan and Dalton cleared the first room as Barbeau and Talon took point on the second, but on finding nothing but stored food the two teams retreated and met back in the central room.

'These rooms are too narrow,' Barbeau whispered, motioning to the farthest wall. 'This building must be separated by a central wall running up its middle. It'll mean more rooms to clear.'

'We clear our way up and then back down on the other side,' she murmured softly and made her way to the next set of stairs with the other three lined up behind her.

The stairs opened up onto a main landing with light-coloured wood laminate tiles running its length, and the walls were covered with expensive blue Petrouchka wallpaper with hanging brass wall lamps upon them, lighting the windowless interior. There were only two access points, a door on the left and a white elevator at the far end.

Sloan flicked her hand towards the entrance on the left and Barbeau and Talon quietly made their way to the doorway, each footstep carefully placed, and then entered, with Talon poking the barrel of his suppresser inside at first as opposed to a noisy, swift breach.

The luxurious bedroom was empty, and the spotless white basin and French cotton sheets looked unused. The two men moved back onto the landing and with a shake of Talon's head they joined Sloan and Dalton either side of the door to the elevator. She glanced over at Dalton and then pressed the button and immediately the doors slid open revealing it to be empty.

There was a moment of hesitation from Sloan. The idea of getting caught like fish in a barrel was unsettling and the plans had made no mention of an elevator, but given the height of the building it had been considered.

Sloan entered as the other three followed and Barbeau and Talon got down on one knee facing the opening as a first line of defence, as Sloan and Dalton stood behind them. There was only a single button and having already committed to entering the elevator Sloan glanced over at her teammates, and following a series of nods in reply to her look, she gently pressed the button, causing the doors to close. With a jerk they began to ascend.

The elevator was sluggish and hot and as they rose higher, floor by floor, each of the team tempered the adrenalin that pushed with every passing second to send their muscles into action. The urge expressed itself through a shuffling of their grips on the firearms they were holding and even Sloan found herself sucking in a deep breath as she controlled her own body.

From above, the faint sound of classical music rang out and the higher they went the louder it got. By the time the elevator car lurched to a halt, the small fireteam were more than ready to face whatever was about to be thrown at them. For each of them it was like flicking on a switch and going into auto-pilot, and with their guns still raised, expecting the worst, the whole car fell into silence.

The doors slid back to reveal... nothing. They exited, taking up defensive positions against the walls of what looked like a business reception area. An oak desk sat upon light grey carpets, and cracked white marble panels covered the walls, adding a formal, glossy look to the room. On the desk was a computer terminal and from the walls hung various motivational posters with images of waves and mountains being the central theme.

Past the desk to the left was a dark varnished door and the music, which was loud almost to the point of distraction, was coming from the other side.

Without need of direction from Sloan the group took their positions either side of the doorway, their footsteps easily concealed by the tones of a Wagner opera, and waited for the order.

Sloan had already pulled out a flash grenade. She glanced up at the three men who readied their weapons and, with a nod, prepared to make the final breach.

The room ahead of them rang with the sound of music and the mumbling of voices, which were impossible to make out. There was no way to discern how many people were there, but at a guess it was three or four at least.

Sloan now mouthed a countdown from three.

Three.

Two.

One.

Sloan pushed open the door no more than a couple of inches and threw in her flash grenade before closing it again. She did it so precisely that even though it all happened within a microsecond the swift closing of the door barely made a sound.

There was an almighty bang as the grenade exploded. Immediately, Sloan kicked open the door as the three men dashed inside and came to a sudden stop. Sloan entered last and she stared around the room as swirls of smoke and the sparks from the flash grenade burnt out. There was a moment of calm as they all stood still, their AR-15s pointing towards the centre of the room.

Sloan took a single step forwards and then halted in her tracks, her eyes widening in shock as she took in the scene.

She lowered her firearm slightly, her face scrunched up in astonishment.

'What the fuck is going on?'

Chapter 16

Munroe pulled the silver Ford Mondeo up next to the kerb and cut the engine, one hundred metres from the red blip on his tracker app. After being picked up within five minutes of his call and leaving the delivery driver to make his own way back, Munroe had driven at high speed, only just missing two speed traps along the way, over the Williamsburg bridge into downtown Manhattan. Gasparyan's red blip had remained static during his trip and fortunately Orlov's diversion had made no difference.

Munroe had skirted Chinatown and due to heavy road-works had entered the district of Tribeca before crossing Canal Street and coming to a stop on the edge of Soho. Gasparyan had arrived at this location fifteen minutes before. Munroe looked up at the office block; he was eager to get in there. He unclipped the 9mm Beretta that had been left for him in the glove compartment and leant forwards in his seat before slipping the gun into his back holster. He then exited the vehicle and quickstepped over to the main entrance and then calmly walked past the large front windows, peeking a glance inside as he did so. There was a small reception with a rent-a-cop dressed in a grey buttoned shirt sitting behind a desk and no sign of any further security, such as metal detectors or bag X-ray conveyers.

His gaze eventually settled on a black public bin on the edge of the pavement. He walked over and pulled out a small cardboard box, which he placed under his arm before heading inside.

The reception area was cool as the conditioners in the ceiling blew cold air downwards from their vents, and Munroe walked up to the front desk and rested his elbow on the counter. It took a few seconds for the security guard to tear himself away from his mobile phone. He looked up lazily and raised his eyebrows.

'Yes?'

'I've got a delivery for the third floor,' Munroe replied, in a flawless Brooklyn accent, raising his left shoulder and the box nestled under his arm.

The guard could not have looked less interested if he'd tried. 'You can leave it with me.'

'Sorry, pal, but I need a signature.'

The guard wasn't about to put up a fight and he passed over a clipboard. 'Sign here.'

Munroe took the biro attached by a piece of string and signed a fake name and then he pushed back the clipboard and walked past the guard to the elevators behind.

'Hold up. Who are you dropping it off for?' the guard asked, and Munroe paused and turned back to face the man. He had no idea and he thought up a name on the spot.

'Jones,' he replied, making it look like he was scratching his back but actually edging toward his holster. The guard wasn't armed but if need be a light pistol whip would do the job.

The guard flipped over the clipboard to a printed list underneath and trailed his finger down the pages. As he made his way to the third page Munroe was already wrapping his hand around the Beretta's grip.

'Got it, Jones,' the guard said, his finger coming to a stop, and Munroe pulled back his hand. 'But he's on the eighth floor, not third.'

'Thanks,' Munroe replied, and he walked over to the elevator, pressed the button and once the doors opened he stepped inside and pulled out his mobile. The red blip was pinging from a height of ninety-three metres and Munroe made a calculated guess as to the floor.

Say a little over three metres per floor so somewhere around the thirtieth floor.

Munroe pushed the button and the doors slid shut. As the elevator began to rise he searched for any cameras and upon finding none, he dropped the box to one side, pulled out his Beretta and cocked back the slide, loading the first bullet. He then put it back in the holster and watched the red digital readout above the doors.

He had expected much tougher security downstairs with this building being Daedalus connected. If Gasparyan was meeting their bombmaker then the floor they were on could be the assembly room, and as such security would be paramount. Where were the surveillance cameras tracking every inch of floorspace inside the building?

There were a lot of assumptions within this rationalisation; this building could be nothing more than a meeting place. Or an exchange point that could lead to a more secure assembly building.

Munroe cleared his mind. He'd not been able to sleep on the flight over and he was now running on over forty-eight hours without a wink of sleep. Although he was fine and energised enough, he tended to overthink things after such a time period. As the elevator approached the thirtieth floor, Munroe's forced focus kicked in and he checked the tracker app and the red blip, which showed he was now at the same height.

Munroe side-stepped to the edge of the elevator as the doors slid back and surveyed the open-plan office space before him. The edges were lined with cubicles, one after another with a second closer in towards the middle of the room, and at the centre a large board table was secured to the floor and surrounded by office chairs. Whatever took place here, it was not a Daedalus meeting point. It was too open plan and secrecy was always a top priority with the group. Munroe exited the elevator and with his Beretta drawn he ventured further into the room.

On his left was a block of toilets, and further along he came across a small open kitchen with a sink, green plastic kettle and rows of cupboards. On his right, wall length windows offered a fantastic view of Upper Manhattan and in the distance he could just make out a narrow strip of green, which had to be Central Park.

Munroe paused and reached over to tap the kettle's surface – it was cold, so he pulled back and continued onwards, wanting to check out the far side of the office space.

He was greeted by more cubicles, all of which were empty but new and ready to be occupied. But he then noticed a single pinewood door, easily missed from a distance as the rows of strip lights above it were switched off.

Munroe approached it, his firearm at his side, and took a look at his phone. Gasparyan's blip was less than ten metres away. Munroe carefully pressed his ear against the door, listening to the muffled sound of voices from the other side. There was anger, or maybe frustration in the tone of one of them and although he couldn't make out the words, the door being too thick, he knew he recognised one of the voices. Munroe focused his attention on that one voice and as it got louder he realised who it was.

Hans Bauer.

Munroe pulled back and, with his gun aimed at the doorway but held close to his chest, he reached down and grasped the handle. Then with his shoulder he bashed into it, sending the door flying open. He rushed inside, his finger already on the trigger and clearing his corners with the barrel.

'Hello again, Han—' was all he managed before he came to an abrupt halt, staring wide-eyed in surprise at the people before him, who stared back in mirrored astonishment. 'What the hell are you doing here?'

Captain Jaqueline Sloan gave no reply and instead motioned over to the eighty-inch, 4K flat screen attached to the opposite wall, and the large face upon it – which was smiling with sheer arrogance.

'Hello, Ethan. Welcome to my party.'

Munroe lowered his gun as the oversized image of Hans Bauer gave him a limp wristed salute.

'It's a rare thing to see you looking surprised, and I must say I'm enjoying it.'

Munroe glanced over at Sloan and her team before his eyes darted around the room. Bauer wagged his oversized finger in front of him.

'Calm down, Ethan, and let me explain your predicament as I did to Captain Sloan and her band of idiots a few minutes ago. Firstly, do not attempt to leave this room. There are charges placed throughout this entire floor and if you try anything I will detonate them, killing you all.' Bauer held up a black box with a red switch on it and tapped it with his finger. 'I also have the room signal sealed, so don't bother trying to make any calls.'

Sloan motioned to the corner of the room and the wiring disappearing into the white ceiling tiles. 'We've already looked. The place is wired and ready to go.' She almost appeared apologetic at the fact as Munroe lowered his gun and shot a glance at the three other men.

'Lads.'

'Munroe,' came the response from Talon on behalf of all three of them as Bauer began to speak again, the obnoxious playfulness fading from his voice and becoming more intense.

'Let me first say how genuinely happy I am to see you, Ethan. Until you burst in through that door I was under the impression that Gasparyan had killed you. I don't know exactly how you managed to escape, but with your background in subterfuge and doctorate in bullshit it doesn't surprise me, and I am already enjoying tormenting Gasparyan for his failure. I mean it, you know, when I say I'm glad you're alive, because what is the point of successfully deceiving those you most despise if they aren't around to witness it?'

'It's more than I can say.' A familiar voice could be heard off screen and then a pissed-off Gasparyan appeared next to Bauer. 'You put on a good show for me, Ethan, and I have to admit I got a little sucked into the moment. Watching you die so slowly was a treat, and even though it was a ruse, I suppose I can forgive you. It just means I get to see you die again, for real at some point. Nevertheless, great acting on you part.'

Munroe watched as in the background, just over the top of Bauer's head, he caught a glimpse of the red-headed woman who had met Gasparyan back at JFK. She offered a smile, and seeing her only further confirmed for Munroe the length and scope of the set-up that had been manufactured in order to bring him and DSV to this place.

'Yes, yes,' Bauer interrupted, motioning Gasparyan away from the screen with his hand, visibly unhappy his voice wasn't the one being heard. 'You did well to get Ethan here, but let us not forget who the true hero of this story is.'

'Forgo the bullshit, Hans, and get to the point,' Munroe growled, and even though he was standing on a pile of explosives ready to ignite on the whims of a madman, he could do without listening to the droning narcissistic ramblings of the bastard. Plus, if Bauer wanted them dead, they would be. This was about something far bigger.

'Easy, Ethan. You sound just like Captain Sloan. She was very upset in not finding a meeting between the top echelons of Daedalus. Very angry indeed. We will of course be having such a meeting to discuss the future, and very soon, but this, I'm afraid, is not it.'

Sloan simply raised her eyebrow and then turned back to face the screen as Bauer continued.

'We've been at each other's throats for decades, the Disavowed and Daedalus. Engaged in this game of cat and mouse since long before any of us here were even born. Certainly long before we cared to create you, Ethan. And where has it got us? I'll tell you... nowhere. Back and forth we go like a pendulum. We penetrate DSV with one of our agents, you take one of our pawns off the table.'

'Like the late Colonel Sinclair, you mean?' Sloan said, with a look of mild satisfaction.

'Exactly. Although that was hardly *your* doing, was it? If I'd not given her up you would still be none the wiser.'

Bauer shook his head, appearing genuinely frustrated by his conundrum. 'No, we've been doing this too long and it was perhaps that a fresh set of eyes were needed. Ones not formed on past experiences. A new pair. *My* eyes.'

All five members of DSV remained quiet. This was Bauer's show and for the time being he had them at a serious disadvantage, so they listened attentively and it drew a smile to the Nazi's lips.

'It's quite simple really, even if the solution was not. How to rid ourselves of the only obstacle in our way because, aside from you and your motley crew of political cronies, the world has no idea we even exist, and who would believe it anyway? How can a world whose people have lost all sense of conviction truly appreciate the absolute dedication it takes to keep an organisation such as Daedalus thriving and surviving, generation to generation?'

'I think you mean obsession,' Barbeau stated bluntly, and Bauer shrugged his shoulders at the light dig.

'Maybe, my little froggie friend, but regardless; DSV must disappear, once and for all.'

'You have most of us in this room, which is filled with explosives,' Sloan said calmly. 'So why not just push that switch of yours?'

The goading had Munroe trying to catch her eye and get her to take it easy, but Sloan's full attention was on Bauer.

'Very true, Jax. I could press this switch and end you all right now before going after the stragglers, but the politicians, your Three Wise Kings, would be a tough ask. If we didn't take them out all at once along with McCitrick and Remus then the baton would be passed to

another generation and the cycle begins all over again...
No, something far shrewder is needed.'

It was typical of the man to drag out what most people could deliver in a couple of paragraphs and Munroe put his Beretta back in its holster and crossed his arms. Bauer didn't want to kill them. The explosives were to keep them in the room listening instead of trying to find him. All detonators had a limited working distance, which meant he had to be close. Bauer wanted to make them suffer. 'So it's a stalemate, Hans. You've got your freedom, but without the blueprints for the nuclear briefcase, which we have in our possession, whatever you had planned is over before it started.'

Bauer looked surprised by the mention of the blueprints and his mouth dropped open slightly.

'You don't know yet, do you? I swapped the blueprints back in Russia and replaced them with a few pieces of Kremlin-headed paper. Your man Gasparyan has a unique souvenir, but I think he was hoping for a lot more.'

Bauer continued to stare at him blankly and Munroe carried on, but carefully and politely. The last thing he wanted was Bauer breaking into a rage and blowing them all to hell.

'I'm sorry, Hans. But technology like that could, almost certainly would, be the prelude to World War Three. And that would do neither of us any good. DSV or Daedalus. There's no point in ruling a world that's in ashes.'

Bauer sat back in his seat, allowing for a better view of his surroundings, and Munroe could see the island city of New York off in the distance through the window of whatever office he was sitting in. The position of it suggested he was somewhere in New Jersey.

Bauer sat there for a few moments and then he leant forwards and placed the tips of his fingers together. 'Unless we already had the plans.'

Munroe felt a pang of unease as Bauer sat there motionless, his expression blank.

'If that were the case then we would have to breakdown a new scenario, wouldn't we?'

Sloan shot Munroe a look of worry as Bauer calmly began to explain.

'Let's say, for argument's sake, that the blueprints for the nuclear briefcase that you have in your possession were not the only ones the Russians had. The ability to strike at an enemy from within their own borders with no alert time for a retaliation and also the anonymity of being able to make a plausible full denial – do you think that a weapon of such potential would be stored in just one place, one set of blueprints at the mercy of a natural disaster or even a rogue accident? It's possible, but I doubt it. And let us say Daedalus were able to get hold of these additional plans, a year ago perhaps, then it would be enough time to build, maybe even perfect that weapon. And with the resources of a private military contractor that had a world-class research and developmental sector... oh, I don't know, maybe like the Daedalus-owned Blackstar... it would be even more realistic to imagine that it could be built, and not just one.'

DSV's assault on Blackstar six months earlier began to run through Munroe's mind. Bauer's pride at providing state-of-the-art military equipment for the most powerful countries in the world including China, USA... Russia.

Bauer seemed to sense what was on Munroe's mind and he addressed it immediately, his expression and demeanour lacking any of his usual smugness.

'DSV's interference with Blackstar could very well have caused some problems, but not if the weapon had already been built. Besides, the measure of a winner is not in his lack of losses but in how he picks himself back up and rolls with the punches. The turning of a negative into a positive, and as you know, Daedalus is very good at that. Very good indeed.'

There was a palpable unease in the air as Bauer continued with his 'fictional' hypothesis.

'But it doesn't sound like a very good idea, does it? I think we can all agree that if someone set off a nuclear bomb like that, for whatever reason, then the entire planet would come after the perpetrators. Such a brazen terrorist attack like this, on a scale never seen in the history of the world, is going to come at a price. They would never get away with it, and the governments of the West would make them pay...'

For the first time the beginnings of a smile flickered across Bauer's lips. 'Unless someone else was blamed for it. Either a terrorist organisation, or maybe even a group of people that no one in the world knew about except for a select few within the corridors of power. A secretive group chasing an enemy only they knew about. A group with tremendous, unaccountable power at their finger-tips. A group that, maybe, so far as anyone knew, had completed their mission many decades ago and had simply become corrupt and gone rogue. A group that decided to use their clandestine power to forge foreign policy and shape world events as they saw fit. Perhaps even to bring about a new Cold War, and all of this under the noses of the democratically elected, who never even knew they existed in the first place.'

Bauer settled back in to his seat and tapped his finger against his lips thoughtfully. 'Now that would be a flaw-less plan, but how could a group like that be made to look guilty? It would take some serious sleight of hand to make "the good guys",' Bauer said, flicking his fingers in inverted commas, 'look like the bad guys. You'd have to uncover, I don't know, a secret prison where they kept the people who were persecuted by them, or maybe those who discovered their plans and wanted to tell the world. Maybe someone like me, the CEO of a private military contractor, who has an exemplary business reputation working with governments around the world. But for that to work you would have to draw the media's attention to it, like perhaps by an explosion during a breakout, the good guys fighting back against their secretive oppressors. And imagine if one of this group's agents was caught on camera breaking into the Kremlin and stealing the blue-prints for a terribly dangerous weapon, like the nuclear briefcase. Now that would look bad. But, still, you would need more.'

Bauer was smiling like the Cheshire Cat, and as Munroe and Sloan stared at the devious madman, they knew already that this was no fairy tale. The knots in both their stomachs continued to tighten with every word that was uttered.

'I've got it,' Bauer said, putting his finger up in the air, 'what if one of the heads of this group had a change of heart when she discovered their diabolical plan and was about to turn whistle-blower but was then killed for it? Again, the group's agents are caught on film shortly before her death and, even worse, can you imagine if her husband was then murdered to tie up loose ends? But of course, for that to work you would need a video or pictures of say, I don't know, the three agents standing over the body in his living room and holding the guns they used to kill him. Now that would be fairly conclusive.'

As Bauer smiled ominously, Sloan shook her head. She appeared to realise something, her eyes squinting together tightly. 'Back at Sinclair's house, when the lights came on in the front room. That was you. Getting us all together for a group picture.'

Bauer offered a small grin as he now shook his head and made a clicking sound with his tongue, quickly moving on to the next part of his story excitedly. 'Still, what if there were politicians, perhaps the political wing of this group, who could get the truth out and tell the world that this group weren't the rogue terrorists everyone believed them to be? What about them?'

Bauer's face now disappeared from the screen and it was replaced with colour footage from a surveillance camera looking down on a busy reception area with people passing through X-ray machines and metal detectors. The view quickly shifted to a shot of a conference room as a man in a white shirt entered and placed a metal plate filled with assorted sandwiches down next to a coffee jug. He then left, and the surveillance footage began to switch cameras, following him as he made his way down a long corridor with multiple pinewood doors on either side. The flat screen now flickered off and when it came back on it was a split screen, with the surveillance footage on the left, still tracking the man, and Bauer on the right who dialled a number into his phone and placed it to his ear.

'Anyone recognise the place?' Dalton asked, but Munroe along with the others just shook their heads as the man in the surveillance footage came to a stop, reaching into his pocket and pulling out his phone, which he then answered.

'Hello?'

The sound of the man's voice came from Bauer's phone, which was being transmitted through the flat screen, and he smiled pleasantly and began to talk.

'Hello, is that Jamie Porter?'

'Yes.'

'Hi, Jamie, I was given your number by reception and I'm hoping you can help me with something extremely urgent. I'm the head of security for Mr Harold Grieves. He was attending a meeting in conference room two and we think he might have left some papers by mistake. Papers that are highly confidential. I need you to take a look, please, as I said it's extremely urgent we find them.'

Munroe watched the footage to see Porter already nodding his head. 'I can have a look for you, Mr...?'

'It's Mr McCitrick.'

'Well, Mr McCitrick, if I'm not mistaken there is a conference beginning in the next twenty minutes, but I can take a look.' Porter was already heading for a set of stairs.

'Thank you, Jamie. I'll stay on the line.'

Munroe and the others watched helplessly as Porter made his way across the reception area and flashed his ID card to the nearest security guard who let him past an access point, avoiding the small line of people having their bags X-rayed. Then the camera shifted again, and they found themselves looking at a large hall with maybe two hundred chairs positioned around a central lectern. Porter appeared from the top of the screen and began making his way towards the front.

'It might be under the lectern where Mr Grieves was giving a speech. Take a look, would you?'

Porter now approached the glossy wooden lectern and ducked down, reappearing with an average-sized briefcase.

'Were the papers in a brown briefcase?' Porter asked.

'Yes. That's it. Tell me, Jamie, is anyone else still in the room?'

Porter looked around and then focused on something off screen. 'There's three people still in here.'

'Good, they may be from our party. Is there a Mr Jankins? And if there is, could you put him on and ask if he could check the papers for me? No peeking now, Jamie. As I said they are highly confidential.'

The live footage shifted to another angle, showing Porter approaching three men deep in conversation, and as one of them turned around Munroe felt a wave of desperation roll over him as Secretary of Defence Michael Jankins spoke to Porter briefly before taking the briefcase from him.

'Where was Jankins' meeting today?' Munroe demanded and Sloan motioned out of the window, horrified.

'The United Nations headquarters, three miles away.'

'Jesus Christ,' Munroe muttered, and then asked a question he had already guessed the answer to. 'Who's he meeting?'

Sloan looked crushed as the words trickled from her mouth. 'The US Secretary of Defence and the French Minister for the Armed Forces. The Three Wise Kings... all in one place.'

'Oh my god,' Barbeau uttered in barely more than a whisper as they watched Jankins place the briefcase on the table and slide back the flip locks, before putting the mobile Porter had passed him to one ear.

'What is this John?' The surveillance camera zoomed in on the case just as Jankins flipped open the briefcase lid. He froze at the sight of an oversized red digital timer counting down the final few seconds.

Three.

'It's Hans Bauer...'

Two.

'...and checkmate.'

One...

Chapter 17

'Down!' Munroe yelled, tackling Sloan to the ground. Even as he buried his head in her shoulders, his eyes tightly shut, the darkness was lit up by a blinding white flash, the light feeling almost tangible as if forcing its way through every pore in his skin. It was followed near instantly by a shock wave that hit them like a concrete wall, slamming through his body mercilessly and lifting both him and Sloan off the ground, hurling them back against the wall as the whole building rippled around them like paper in the wind as the tremendous force of the shock wave penetrated it. They were both still off the ground as the sound of the windows all shattering at once was overtaken by a deafening boom, like twenty cracks of thunder localised in the small office space at the same time.

Munroe could feel debris and glass shards hitting his body. The impact with the wall alone had knocked him unconscious for a moment, and he came to having collapsed to the floor as tiles and metal casings dropped from above, covering them both in the wreckage of what had once been the ceiling.

As they both lay there clinging to each other the sweeping sound of air being sucked from the room could be heard, and all around the deep, pervasive rumbling of the explosion's aftermath hung in their ears.

Munroe lay there for another few seconds and then, with the darkness having receded from his vision, he slowly opened his eyes and carefully lifted his head away from the black fabric of Sloan's shoulder and surveyed the room.

His first sense was that he was hovering in mid-air, but as he looked down he found they had landed on one of the desks that had been blown back against the far wall during the blast and he now slowly scanned the area. His senses were dulled, and his head felt as if it were wrapped in cotton wool, no doubt a result of the concussion he had received, and like on awaking after fainting, the world around him felt surreal and disjointed. It took a few more moments for him to get his bearings as nearby a pile of ceiling rubble began to shift and he saw Dalton clamber out of it and stumble to his feet. The sight of it brought some focus to his mind and he slid off the table and onto his feet, both legs shaking as he did so. Slowly, he turned and looked out of the opening that had moments earlier been a line of windows.

A few miles away, on the east side of Manhattan, a thick stalk of what looked like shifting brown dirt rose high above the surrounding buildings. At its top the familiar cap of a mushroom cloud expanded upwards and outwards, casting a shadowy symbol of chaos upon the East Side below. It was impossible to tell how much damage had been done, the choking base of smoke and dust still being sucked upwards, but outside of the visible dust bowl almost everything within a mile and a half had been levelled. And even though some of the buildings had survived the blast, their blackened shells now constituted nothing more than gigantic tombstones to the dead within them. It was impossible to be sure, but the death toll must have been in the tens of thousands, and along with them the Three Wise Kings who had been the intended target all along.

Munroe looked over at Dalton, who looked pretty much as he felt, and Munroe pointed his quivering finger to the back of a SWAT jacket obscured by debris as the sound of someone stirring behind him caught his attention.

As Dalton stumbled over towards the mound, Munroe turned around to see Sloan, her eyes open, staring at the hard concrete of the ceiling above.

'Jax,' Munroe called out, his throat dry, his voice croaking. 'You're safe. We're alive.' He gently took her hand in his. There was some blood coming from her nose and her SWAT jacket was ripped in places and covered in white dust, but she did not appear to have sustained any serious wounds.

She craned her head towards him and although her pupils were dilated and she was clearly in shock, she smiled. 'You look terrible, Ethan.' She ran her fingers across Munroe's cheek before looking down at his chest, and then she winced.

Munroe followed her gaze to see a shard of glass sticking out just above his waist. The surrounding blood had been absorbed by his white T-shirt. The sight had him suddenly feeling the pain of it and although it looked bad he could tell by the minimal amount of blood it was likely just a flesh wound.

Sloan sat up and took a moment to gain her balance before instinctively reaching into one of her clip-buttoned pockets and producing a small folded piece of white triage bandage. As Munroe slipped off his jacket, Dalton was pulling Barbeau from the wreckage. His loud groaning was a good sign.

Munroe remained silent as Sloan ripped away his T-shirt, but she paused as, with her head beginning to clear, her focus switched; she and Barbeau gazed fixedly at the towering mushroom cloud hanging above the East Side. Despite the obvious tragedy and all the people who had died and would die yet due to radiation poisoning, it was a sight to behold.

As Dalton found the top of Talon's leg, he called back to them, 'Jean, help me.'

As Barbeau joined Dalton and began pulling the debris off Talon it was Sloan who turned back and attended to Munroe. She unzipped her jacket and then wrapped it around her left hand, preparing the bandage in her right.

'You don't see that every day,' she commented flatly, clearly still dazed and working on instinct more than anything else. She motioned in the direction of the destruction. 'Is that a helicopter?'

The moment Munroe turned to see no helicopter in sight, Sloan pulled out the glass shard quickly and then pushed in a piece of bandage to soak up the blood that was squirting out.

'Thanks for that,' Munroe groaned as she held a pad to his wound and began wrapping a bandage around his mid-section, as on the far side of the room Talon was dragged to his feet. Although conscious, his leg was bent unnaturally. It was clear he had received a compound fracture during the blast.

'Hang in there, Jack. It's nothing a few months of R and R can't fix.'

Talon managed a grunt but the pain he was in was obvious and as Barbeau looked around for a temporary splint Dalton pulled out a small cardboard box and retrieved the plastic morphine injection within it.

'No,' Talon spat, his teeth clenched together due to the pain, 'no drugs until we're out of here.'

Dalton paused and then he nodded and packed away the syringe. Meanwhile Barbeau used a desk leg as a splint as Sloan finished Munroe's bandage and once done he offered her an appreciative nod and then slipped his jacket back on gently.

'We have to get out of here. Now.'

The other three nodded their reply, but Sloan was quiet and Munroe gently pulled her off the table and slid off her jacket as he checked her torso and legs for wounds.

'There's nothing we can do here, and even though it looks like the wind's blowing north, if it changes then we've got radiation fallout to think of.' Sloan was still looking resistive and Munroe knew what she was thinking. She was not a woman who considered retreat easily, and even though they had no other choice but to regroup, the heavy knock to her head during the blast was having an effect. 'Look, Jax, DSV is totally compromised and we need to make contact with McCitrick and Remus before we do anything else.'

The mention of McCitrick caused her demeanour to lighten and she looked up at him and nodded.

Munroe nodded back at her and finished checking her body for wounds. Seeing that she was clear, he passed back her jacket before retrieving his mobile, only now noting its smashed display. 'Shit, does anyone have a working phone?'

Barbeau stopped wrapping the splint to Talon's leg and checked his pockets, throwing his phone over to Munroe before resuming his work.

'I'm not getting any signal,' he said, pocketing the phone as Barbeau finished his emergency first aid and with the help of Dalton got Talon back on his feet. 'I've got a four-door downstairs, we can take the Brooklyn Bridge off the island.'

'Hold on,' Sloan said, moving her finger to the ceiling, 'the explosives.'

Dalton now drew everyone's attention to the explosive charges they had seen upon entering the room and one of the boxes had ripped open in the blast revealing nothing but red sand inside. 'We couldn't have known without dismantling it. The casing is standard military issue.'

'Jesus, Bauer planned this thing perfectly,' Munroe said, but Sloan just shrugged it off.

'Like you said: first, we regroup. And then we repay in kind. Now let's go,' she said, starting to shake off the effects of her concussion, and with that they headed through the door, Talon being helped at the rear.

The office next door had weathered the blast as badly as the other room. The cubicles nearest the windows had been blown apart and the others had been shredded by the incoming glass. Bauer had chosen the right building to host his big reveal. Two or three blocks closer and the blast could have collapsed the tall building block, and any farther and they would not have experienced the windows shattering. The Daedalus captain had planned it perfectly, and as they approached the elevator Munroe promised himself that whatever it took, no matter the cost, he would see him pay for what he had done. And seeing as Bauer had just become guilty of genocide with the simple press of his finger, the man had a lot to pay for.

The button for the elevator was still lit up and upon pushing, the doors opened.

'Thank God,' Dalton remarked, even though they all looked at it warily. The blast could have damaged the suspension wires. After a glance back at the group Munroe picked up a nearby chair, placed it inside and popped open the maintenance hatch. So far as he could tell the mechanism looked unaffected, and he came back down and threw the chair out into the office. 'Looks OK.'

It was all the assurance anyone needed. Talon was helped inside, followed by Sloan and Munroe. Within seconds they were back at the reception area on the ground floor.

'Hold on,' Munroe instructed, and he pulled out his Beretta and skirted the wall before poking the barrel towards the reception desk, but the only thing there was an upturned desk and shattered glass.

'Security guard's gone. Probably took off the moment I got in the elevator.' Bauer had not left anything to chance so far which is why the guard had to have been a plant. He wouldn't have known he was working for Daedalus and, who knew, he may even have been caught in the blast.

'I'll bring the car over.'

Munroe jogged to the entrance, stepped over the glass and through the broken door onto the street and came to a brief stop as groups of people ran past him, all with fear in their eyes. At this distance from the blast, the damage was minimal and it appeared that only the windows facing the direction of the bomb had been destroyed, but a strange odour hung in the air that assaulted his nose with the potency of a public toilet. It was a nauseating smell, like the aftermath of napalm mixed with burnt meat and chemicals. Although revolting in its own right it was not the reason people were running around chaotically. It was the sight above them.

Munroe looked up and even from down on the ground, surrounded by buildings, the brown smoking dome of the mushroom cloud could be seen high above the rooftops. It was an image that was universally well known, universally feared.

Munroe raced to the silver Mondeo and then parked it up outside the entrance as Sloan got into the front seat whilst the other two put down the back seats and laid Talon inside. Once they were all in, Munroe sped off, and by the time they were approaching the Brooklyn Bridge the roads were beginning to clog as many of Manhattan's residents had the same idea.

Get the hell off the island.

'Jax, call McCitrick,' Munroe said, noticing Barbeau's phone had finally got a signal back. It must have been the blast affecting the mobile networks because the closer they got to the bridge the stronger the signal became. Jax was about to dial the number when the phone began to ring from an incoming call, the display reading 'unknown number'.

Sloan glanced over at the others and then answered it, putting it on loudspeaker.

'Well it's good to see you five alive and well,' Bauer stated, his tone sounding genuine. 'Although I see Mr Talon is a bit worse for wear.'

Munroe motioned to the phone and Sloan immediately covered the camera with her thumb. Bauer seemed to have everything at his fingertips and seeing them at their weakest was not going to be a pleasure he would get to enjoy for long.

'Oh, come on. Don't be such sore losers...' The line went silent for a time and, after realising they weren't going to allow him to see them, Bauer spoke once more.

His playful tone had been replaced by a more business-like one. 'Very well, if you're going to be like that then allow me to do the speaking because I will only say this once and it is something you need to hear. I don't intend to gloat because I must admit you have been worthy opponents, but everything comes to an end eventually. You've had a good run but you can't stop progress, and Daedalus *is* that progress. So let me tell you what is going to happen. You have four hours' head start and then, on the dot, two agents within MI6 and CIA will receive intel through tried and trusted sources. Intel concerning the secret little agency of yours. These two agents will then corroborate their information with each other and after that a detailed picture will emerge of DSV and their rogue intentions. There is no one of worth, since about twenty minutes ago, who can clear your name and by the end of tonight I expect your names and faces to be number one on the most wanted terrorist lists throughout the Western world. I doubt there will be any mention to the media because your disloyalty will be an unacceptable disgrace to the three countries that make up DSV. How could they admit it was their own people, using tax payers' dollars, that caused such a devastating attack and cost the lives of thousands? I mean really, can you imagine any politician worth their salt admitting to being so incompetent – and that includes all the intelligence services – as to fund an organisation that did so much damage without even knowing about them in the first place?' Bauer let out a chuckle. 'There has to be a movie in there somewhere. Anyway, the answer is *no*. The full weight of the Western judicial system, covert and overt, is about to come down on you, ladies and gentlemen, and they are going to squeeze you. They're going to chase you. They're going to hound you and eventually they are going to catch you. And if you're not killed in the process I am willing to bet you end up in one of those secret military courts you, for many decades, have reserved for the likes of me and my family. Today you have become worthy of your name. Because as of today you truly are disavowed. Rogue angels fallen from grace. Now you can understand what the project Steel Thunder was for. The total annihilation of DSV. So run away and hide, my little rats. Find cover in some dark, dingy cave somewhere because by the time the world is finished with you, that shitty hole is going to feel like a sanctuary. Scurry away now, and pray I don't come after you myself... You've already got enough enemies to contend with.'

No one in the car said a thing as the call cut out. There was nothing to say. Munroe had considered a parting insult, but he thought better of it. Why give the man the satisfaction? But if Bauer thought they were going to lay down and die then he didn't yet realise who he was dealing with. This wasn't over yet, not by a longshot, and by the time this was finished he would see Bauer and all his sick family behind bars, for real this time, and he would be the one to throw away the key.

As they made it onto the Brooklyn Bridge, Munroe turned back and eyed each member of DSV before settling on Sloan who, along with everyone else, was looking defeated.

'You know a poet once said "I never saw a wild thing look sorry for itself",' he said and it immediately got a smile from Sloan. 'C'mon, lads, you're not going to get domesticated on me now, are you?'

Chapter 18

John McCitrick flopped back in his executive work chair and cradled his head in his hands before rubbing his temple firmly at the images of destruction being shown on Sky News. In the thirty minutes since the initial report the story had gone from a gas explosion to a missile strike and now a terrorist attack. And although there had been no official confirmation, the images of a mushroom cloud spiralling upwards to the sky above Manhattan had left no one in any doubt that the explosion had been nuclear. McCitrick, though, knew what had happened, and unlike anyone else in the Ministry of Defence he knew who was responsible. They had to be. Daedalus had just made their sickest and boldest move yet.

Outside his office room the whole department was in a state of organised chaos as anyone and everyone attempted to gain a handle on what just happened, and as McCitrick caught the sight of a woman running past the glass windows of his office he shouted out to her. 'Janice, get in here.'

The woman, wearing a light grey cashmere top and brown leather trousers, opened his door halfway and leant inside, bringing with her the sounds of feverish activity.

'Where's my phone call?' he asked furiously, but she held her hands up in the air apologetically.

'I'm waiting for the secretary of defence to call back and I can't even get through to the prime minister. He's been in a Cobra meeting since it happened.'

'Fuck. OK, Janice, you tell whoever's taking calls at Number Ten that if they want to be the person who held back the intel on who committed this attack then it's on their head. If not, then you tell them to get off their arses and get a message to the prime minister saying that I'm the man to talk to.'

'Understood, boss,' Janice replied, and she closed the door and headed out of sight as McCitrick turned back to the TV screen and ran his hand roughly through his hair. In all the years that DSV had been in operation there had never been something like this and if ever there was a time that the secret organisation and knowledge of Daedalus was to come out in the open, it was now. All he knew so far was that all of the Three Wise Kings were at the United Nations HQ, which was now nothing more than a radioactive hole in the ground. Worse still, two DSV members, American and French, had been conducting security for them. And if those losses weren't terrible enough, he'd had no word from Sloan and her team who had also been in New York at the time. And where the hell was Munroe!

'Jesus Christ.' McCitrick looked out of his office window down at Victoria Embankment and then up at the London Eye on the other side of the Thames. Thousands of tourists and citizens all enjoying their day out and most still blissfully unaware of the horrific tragedy the city of New York had just experienced. They had no idea yet how many had been lost, but it would be in the tens of thousands, and with the radioactive cloud drifting north-west towards the east coast how many more would die in the months and years to come? It was a catastrophe like no other and would take years, decades even, for New York to get back to the way it had been, if that was even possible. So many analysts and intelligence agencies had contemplated a nuclear terrorist attack on Western soil and for seventy-odd years it had been held at bay. There had been some close calls during that period, but it had never happened. Now it had, the world would never be the same again.

The sound of his mobile vibrating drew McCitrick away from such thoughts and he swung around on his chair and plucked it from off the desk. It was an unknown number, but he accepted it and pressed it to his ear.

'McCitrick.'

'John, it's Munroe.'

McCitrick sat up in his chair and hunched over the mouthpiece. 'Ethan, where the hell have you—'

'Shut up and listen. We're short on time.' Munroe's voice crackled over the line's poor reception. 'I'm with Sloan and the team. We're OK and heading out of New York but you need to hear this. It was a set-up, John, by Bauer and Daedalus. His breakout, Sinclair's death, my infiltration of the Kremlin, the nuclear explosion taking out the Three Kings, it was all orchestrated for one reason. To take DSV out of the picture and make us look responsible for today's attack.'

A cold chill ran down McCitrick's spine. 'What are you talking about, Ethan? I'm waiting for a call from the PM. I'm about to disclose the existence of DSV and Daedalus.'

'It's too late for that. Daedalus has been planning this for the last year and in under four hours' time a piece of intel is going to drop into the laps of MI6 and the CIA accusing us of being a rogue agency that no one even knew existed. And with the Three Kings gone we've no way to prove the truth… because no one knows.'

McCitrick looked out of his office to the space outside, his eyes darting amongst the dozens of Ministry staff, all of whom were busy working away. 'Is Sloan there?'

'Yes, sir. You're on speaker phone and I can confirm everything Captain Munroe is saying. The Daedalus meeting was total bullshit. A ruse to get us in the same place at the same time. The only person we saw was Bauer via conference call. He told us everything just before setting off the bomb.'

McCitrick shook his head and swallowed deeply. 'I'll head to Downing Street right now. Force my way in if I have to. I can get this cleared up. Give me—'

'John. It's too late for that,' Munroe interrupted loudly, coming back on the line. 'If I know Bauer, and I do, he dropped the intel on us the moment after the bomb went off. Hell, maybe even before. Don't you get it? DSV has fallen and the police are probably on their way to arrest you even as we speak. You have to get out of there, now.'

At the far end of the office, a group of four policemen appeared in the doorway and began trying to get the attention of anyone nearby. 'Hold on a moment,' McCitrick replied and he immediately grabbed his jacket and opened his drawer, picking up the memory stick inside and slipping out of his office towards the fire exit. 'You're right, I'm compromised. I'm heading outside.'

McCitrick pressed open the safety latch but before he had even made it onto the outside stairwell the fire alarms began ringing. He looked back inside and caught a glimpse of the policemen who were now running in his direction and as the door closed fully he took off and began leaping down the steps. 'Ethan, they're on me so here's the plan. It's a Code Zulu. Split up and make your way to the designated safe house. If you can't remember where it is then Sloan can fill you in.'

McCitrick jumped down the last flight as the sound of heavy boots on metal rang out from above. 'I'll join you all once I get out of the country. I authorise you, Captain Sloan, to access and transfer all DSV funds to a new account. Run it through one of the dummy corporations.'

McCitrick was now running across the Ministry's front lawn to the car park and he unlocked his metallic blue Jaguar F-type with the remote and hurled himself inside as the four police officers made it off the ladder and began running over towards him, shouting for him to stop as they went. McCitrick jammed the gear into reverse and sped backwards, and then into first and out onto Victoria Embankment, sending the car park's white stone shingle into the faces of the policemen as his wheels spun.

'You still there?'

'We're here,' Munroe replied as McCitrick drove up onto the pavement and past the traffic, honking his horn and causing pedestrians to dive out of the way. It was a tight fit, but his driving skills were exemplary. 'Captain Sloan, I need you to do something else for me. I need you to remote access my computer after I hang up and download all my files before wiping it clean. There's a programme within my files named "Dishwasher". Once you've downloaded my files then unleash this, please. It will rinse my hard drive permanently.'

'Sir, I can't access the Ministry of Defence's system remotely. It's a closed system.'

'Oh ye of little faith, Captain. The Ministry's system is closed but my computer is separate from it. A security measure I had installed and one I hoped not to use. I'll send you the portal web address and the code. Should be easy for a woman of your talents. Hold on a moment.'

McCitrick smiled to himself as he approached the Houses of Parliament and he came screeching to a halt and grabbed a black log book from the glove compartment and exited the car. 'Anyone want my Jaguar? It's not stolen and all the payments have been made.'

Most of the people around him remained silent but a young man in his early twenties raised his hand.

'I'll take it.' McCitrick handed him the keys and a piece of paper. 'Here's the V5C and all the certificates. I've already signed it, so enjoy. It is now legally yours,' he said, heading towards the entrance of Westminster tube station, glancing back briefly. 'Oh, and she likes premium.'

McCitrick quickly descended the steps, placing the mobile back to his ear. 'Use whatever funds you need to get you all to the safe house and I will meet you there as soon as I can.'

'Thank you, sir,' Munroe said respectfully, impressed at the section head's preparation given he had found out he was having to go on the lam no more than four minutes ago.

McCitrick came to a stop at the tube station turnstiles and he pulled out a ticket and fed it into the opening. As the barriers flipped open he headed towards a staff entrance and knocked on the door. 'And, ladies and gentlemen, we will be OK. I don't know how yet, but once we meet up I will have formulated a plan. You've all done well, and I make this promise to you. We will come out of this mess smelling like daisies and with Daedalus in the ground… permanently. Now, just get yourselves to the safe house and I will see you there.'

McCitrick hung up just as the staff room door opened and he was greeted by an old man with slicked-back hair, wearing a boiler suit.

'John,' the man said with a beaming smile, his eyes widening. 'Nice to see you.'

'Good to see you too, Gerald. Can I get my bag, please?'

Gerald welcomed his visitor inside and closed the door behind him. 'In a rush as always, John.' Without pause he unlocked one of the metal lockers on the wall of the staff room and pulled out a big blue duffle bag. 'All safe, as promised,' Gerald added, and he passed it over to McCitrick who slipped a key into the zip's padlock and unlocked it.

'Of that I had no doubt, my friend. And did you get this month's cheque?'

'I did, John, and thanks for the bonus. It was a welcomed surprise. I'm taking the wife on a cruise,' Gerald said as McCitrick pulled out a heavy-looking overcoat, T-shirt and jeans and checked the plastic bag underneath containing passports and a stack of money.

'Good, she'll enjoy it, and it's well deserved. I don't know what I'd do without you.'

Gerald nodded his head and smiled. 'Do you need anything else?'

McCitrick placed the clothes on a hook on the wall and began taking off his tie. 'Maybe just a little privacy.'

'Of course.' Gerald opened the door and headed out as McCitrick called after him.

'And, Gerald, I may be away for some time. But if you don't hear from me I promise I'll square up with you on my return. I will be back.'

'I look forward to it, John.'

Within an hour the section head was on a plane to Ukraine, and from there an international flight to the Americas under the name of Herbert Roth. For John McCitrick, subterfuge and spy work wasn't just a job, it was a way of life, and he was about to use his considerable talents to take apart Bauer and his cronies. No more performing the dance that DSV and Daedalus had performed for so many years. Keeping them in check whilst never exposing the secret war to the world. DSV had been founded on a remit of secrecy to never allow a fascist flame to raise its head and attract those who would seek to follow it, but after what had happened in New York that remit was dead. It was now an all-out war.

As McCitrick gazed down on the glimmering waters of the Atlantic he found himself faced with many unknowns. If he was honest with himself, he had no real idea how this was all going to turn out. He couldn't know how many, if any, friends would still be there for him and his team in the coming weeks. But of one thing he was sure. These new-age Nazis were about to learn a lesson they appeared not to have learnt. No one fucked with his people, except him, and those that did would live to regret it.

Chapter 19

'Who's with him at the moment?' GCHQ Director James Bremen demanded, glancing towards the closed door on the other side of the reception desk.

'Same as it was ten minutes ago, James.'

Bremen sighed deeply in frustration and tapped his knuckles on the desk. 'Get me in next, Lori. It's important.'

'Always is, James,' Lori Benedict replied, raising her eyebrow at him and then her shoulders sagged as he served up the most pleading expression possible. 'I'll try and get you in when he finishes, but no promises. He's got a phone call from the president within the hour.'

'That's why I need to speak with him beforehand.'

Lori nodded as the internal phone on her desk rang. 'Yes, sir... No change. Still scheduled for four o'clock... I will. And, sir,' she now looked up at him, 'I have James Bremen here to see you. He says it's important and concerns your call with the president.'

There was a long pause and then she nodded her head. 'Of course. I'll send him in.'

She replaced the receiver and smiled up at Bremen. 'He's just finished, you can go in.'

'Thanks, Lori,' Bremen replied, and he pointed over to the man stood in the hallway trying not to look out of place. 'I may need him in there. Could you get him a drink while he waits?'

Lori nodded and waved the man over as Bremen made his way to the door briskly and after knocking went inside.

Prime Minister Andrew Previn sat behind his desk looking like a deeply troubled man, his face etched with worries and concerns as he intently poured over the many documents before him.

'Hi, James, what do you need?'

Everyone had noticed that Prime Minister Previn's physical demeanour had withered since the attack on New York two weeks earlier. At first his acts of solidarity with America had strengthened his political capital, but since learning the attack had been carried out by members of his own intelligence service his usual energy and strength had deserted him. Even though it was a fate shared by the US and France equally, it was Previn who appeared to have taken it the worst. It might have been due to his own experience of military service, which the other leaders did not have. Or it might have been his close bond, since childhood, to Defence Secretary Michael Jankins, and the revelation that his friend had colluded with the homegrown terrorists only to get bitten by them, a miscalculation that had cost him his life, and the lives of so many others, which at the last count totalled eighty-seven thousand. But to Bremen, it was their decision not to tell the media and the people who the real culprits were – this rogue agency DSV. The world was now demanding to know who had committed this atrocity, and Previn was being attacked personally for what many saw as an ineptitude of leadership and a failure of the intelligence services.

'Thank you for the time, Prime Minister, I know your schedule's busy.'

'Forget the pleasantries, James, I don't have time for it. What's up?'

Bremen's demeanour relaxed and he slid one hand into his pocket. 'It's been two weeks and we're no closer to finding out where any of this group are. They've gone underground, and with their training, contacts and funding it's possible they could go undetected for as long as they want.'

Prime Minister Previn looked up from his desk and stared at his visitor angrily. 'You're not telling me anything I don't already know, James.'

'I know,' Bremen replied, holding his hands up agreeably, 'so perhaps it's time to release everything we have on them.'

The idea had Previn shaking his head, but Bremen now sought to bolster his case.

'I know there would be some political fallout—'

'Some!' Previn laughed humourlessly as Bremen continued.

'I know, but we've got nothing, and plastering their pictures all over the media will back them into a corner. They'll be more likely to make a mistake and that's when we will get them.'

Previn stayed silent and Bremen now took his hand out of his pocket and approached the table.

'If we have to keep tracking them covertly then, with their knowledge and abilities, it could go on forever, or until they make a mistake. And from everything I've learnt about DSV in the past few weeks they are not likely to make mistakes. I mean Christ, Andrew, these people have continued operating under Her Majesty's government, the

French and the Americans for over seventy years without anyone knowing. Chasing a ghost of an enemy that hasn't existed since the Second World War. Whatever enemies Churchill and Truman had to set this above their top-secret layers of intelligence have been and gone for a long time. Who knows what shit they've been up to: drugs, manipulating foreign policy through false flags. These bastards are like Teflon.'

Previn stood up from the table and wagged his finger. 'They had political cover, that's how they managed it, and that cover is now gone. Anyway, the decision's already been made by myself, President Rosalyn and President Toussaint. The damage it would do to our countries, our allies, is considered too high. No, we find them and then end it there and then. No court hearings, no media frenzy. They die as ex-military, homegrown terrorists. It will leave the public with a bitter taste in their mouths, one of unfinished business, but it's better than the alternative.'

Bremen waited patiently as Prime Minister Previn made his way around to the other side of the desk and sat down in his chair, eyeing the workload in front of him.

'Now if that's all you wanted then I have a country to run, and I suggest you get back to work.'

Bremen moved over to the side of his desk and tapped his finger lightly on its surface. 'In that case, sir, I may have an idea that could help us, if you would allow me.'

Previn looked up curiously and he nodded. 'I'm willing to entertain anything at this moment in time.'

'I'm glad you feel that way,' he said, picking up the telephone off the prime minister's desk. 'May I?'

'Very well,' Previn replied, and Bremen began to speak into the receiver.

'Lori, could you send in my guest, please?'

Bremen put the phone down as Prime Minister Previn eyed him warily.

'Who is it?'

'Someone I think could help with the situation. He is already aware of DSV's existence and his information has already been placed under the Official Secrets Act.'

The two men watched as the door opened and in walked a man wearing a dark-green tweed suit and light-blue tie. Alongside the Cartier cufflinks and Omega watch his ensemble whispered extreme wealth. He approached the desk as Bremen made the introductions.

'Prime Minister, I would like to introduce you to someone I believe could be of help to us during this difficult time.'

Prime Minister Previn got up from his chair and shook the already waiting hand as the man smiled politely. 'It is a pleasure to meet you, Prime Minister. My name is Bauer, Hans Bauer, and I hope I might be of some help in bringing resolution to this terrible tragedy.'

'Mr Bauer is the CEO of one of the largest private military contractors in the world, Blackstar. He was also held illegally in the Cape Wrath internment camp for five months by DSV after refusing to help them.'

Previn looked unsure but he smiled courteously. 'I'm very sorry to hear that, Mr Bauer.'

'Please, sir. Call me Hans,' Bauer asked, his tone sincere and respectful, and Previn offered a small nod.

'I'm sorry to hear that, Hans. And what exactly did you refuse?'

'I refused a man you know as John McCitrick who demanded I use our considerable resources at Blackstar to acquire an amount of Uranium-235. He also demanded that we provide him with access to certain prototype machinery and vehicles from our research and development department.'

'As you probably already know, sir, Blackstar has government contracts with many Western countries,' Bremen added, and Bauer immediately sought to clarify his position.

'We are a private firm and as such are not bound by the chains of share prices. I am a patriot, sir, to the capitalist worldview and as such we only accept contracts from members of NATO. Significantly, the United States, the United Kingdom and France among other European allies, which is one of the multitude of reasons I refused Mr McCitrick's demand. As a result, I and most of my family and business partners were detained illegally in DSV's underground prison at Cape Wrath, and Blackstar was taken over for a short time, legally, I might add, by the US government on suspicion of aiding and abetting terrorists. Of course I use the term "legally" very loosely now I know exactly what and who they are.'

'The stealth helicopter used in the escape of the serial killer known as Icarus, who we suspect was actually a DSV agent, belonged to Blackstar, sir. And as we now know the attack on Parliament was orchestrated by DSV, but what we didn't know was that they used Blackstar technology.'

Prime Minister Previn was looking uneasy at the open mention of such things that had been classified at the highest level, and he raised his chin upwards questioningly. 'And how is it you know of this group, this DSV, when so many of us in government did not?'

Bauer looked at the Prime Minister sympathetically. 'Once I was detained my interrogators were extremely open about who they were. They had hoped I and Blackstar would willingly accept being absorbed into their fold.

Their method was to convince me that they were fighting an underground organisation of fascists, Nazis actually, left over from the war, if you can believe that.' Bauer chuckled at the notion, but it was a laugh of disappointment and disbelief. 'They told me that Churchill himself had personally created the agency, and although I never believed the fascist enemy was real, in the modern age anyway, I did see for myself the governmental power they wielded. Without it they never would have been able to take control of Blackstar so successfully, or in such a clandestine manner.'

Prime Minister Previn said nothing, taking in all the information, and Bremen and Bauer waited silently until the obvious question was asked.

'Well, I am extremely sorry for what both you and your family have been through. But what is it that you're offering?'

The question was directed towards Bremen as well, and it was he who answered.

'Given the sensitive nature of the hunt for DSV members, I believe that Blackstar could be in a unique position to help us.'

'How so?' Previn asked, leaning against the edge of his desk, his arms folded.

'Their contractors, with direction from GCHQ and MI6, could approach the search with far less scrutiny than us.'

'And, Prime Minister,' Bauer added, leaning his head to one side, 'the true identity of who we are looking for would be held by me and only me. I already know who they are and am bound by the Official Secrets Act. We would be contracted as investigators only and once we track them down the information would be passed on to Mr Bremen. The important part though, sir, is that everything would be handled in a private capacity. Our media footprint, and those of the people within the government, would be kept to a minimum.'

Previn stared at Bauer blankly, and it was impossible to tell how he felt about the idea. 'Mr Bauer, Hans, would you please give us a few minutes.'

Bauer offered a small bow and turned and left the room, leaving the two men alone in the prime minister's office.

'What would be the legalities of such a course?' Previn asked, unfolding his arms.

'Well, legally, we can offer a contract for investigative services, and it would keep all intel on DSV to a minimum, which is half the battle. And as he said himself, he already knows about DSV and has agreed not to bring a lawsuit concerning his internment. That goes for all the other Blackstar partners and family, who you should know were never told about DSV and the true nature of their kidnapping. As head of the company, Bauer was the only one they told, and *as* head of a private company he holds autonomy over his staff, guided by us of course, that a public company would not. But I would suggest one thing.'

'And that is?'

'Blackstar is a US company, so it would draw less attention coming from the Americans. That is so long as a tight circle of those in the know can be maintained. Plus they will want to be in on the ground floor, so I say, let them. We all lose equally if this ever gets out, but that is something to discuss with the president on your call.'

Previn considered it and he was beginning to agree. The three nations had already agreed to keep this out of direct sunlight and the intentions of it were pure and honest. 'How about the French?'

'They'll want to be in the loop on equal terms with us, and putting the US at the head of it does just that. I'm sure they will be onboard with that aspect of it.'

The prime minister's eyelids drooped as they always did when in deep contemplation and he stood there, leaning against the side of the desk, Bremen waiting patiently. Finally, he looked up wide eyed and gave a nod. 'I need to speak to the presidents then. Get Mr Bauer back in, could you, James?'

Previn pushed himself off the desk and waited as Bremen disappeared for a moment and then returned with Hans Bauer in tow.

'I'm going to consider your generous offer, Hans. We find ourselves in a very difficult situation and must seek to bring those who are guilty of these crimes to justice, but also ensure that the Western countries and NATO are protected from the nefarious truth. I also want to say that I greatly respect your willingness to let go of the crimes DSV committed against you. To be caged against your will, having your company abused in such a way, would be intolerable to some, who, I suspect, would allow revenge to get in the way of what is best for all the nations involved. You have my gratitude and my thanks.'

Hans Bauer smiled graciously but shook his head. 'No, Mr Prime Minister, it is I who should be thanking you for your leadership and foresight. Thanking you for the opportunity, should it be agreed upon, of serving and upholding the Western ideals I hold so dear. As a patriot of the West I only hope we can find these traitors, these purveyors of hate, and that I can be the one to help bring them to justice.'

Chapter 20

Munroe pushed open the wooden storm shutter and gazed out across the forest landscape, as overhead the blazing sun shone down mercilessly. He allowed the humidity to wash over him and sucked in a deep, refreshing breath, the earthy smell of the air filling his lungs. It reminded him of his operational days with the SAS and weeks of jungle training as he and his team acclimatised to the conditions. Climate was like any other type of training so far as Munroe was concerned, and once you got the feel for it you never forgot how to deal with it. Humidity though was, to him, the most unforgiving. The stifling feeling of dense water vapour surrounding your body could make some people quite claustrophobic. But he'd spent enough time sweating and surviving in air you could almost swim through, and all with one hundred pounds of gear and weapons strapped to his back.

'Ethan.'

Munroe looked down from his second-floor window to see Sloan in khaki shorts, trainers and a blue sleeveless T-shirt waving at him. 'He's arrived.'

Munroe energetically made his way back to his bed and slipped on a blue shirt with sleeves, not bothering to button it up because even with the air conditioning the house acted like an oven. At night the walls took hours to cool down. Munroe slipped on his black trainers and headed out of the door and down the terracotta-tiled staircase.

It had been two weeks since their escape from New York and the journey so far had been grim and not just because they were on the run but because of the destruction they had witnessed. They had headed to a safe house in Queens, west of Manhattan, with the looming mushroom cloud in their rear-view mirror all the way. Eventually it had dispersed, becoming a thick black oil slick in the sky, running north-west and up the coast as the slow wind pulled it along with the breeze. Talon had slept most of the way under the effects of the morphine, and even though their vehicle had broken windows and was caked in dust no one had batted an eyelid. Most people were staying home for fear of radiation and the streets were largely vacant. The only cars they had come across were police cars and ambulances heading in the opposite direction, towards the blast.

At the safe house, a small condo with surrounding hedges providing privacy, they had spent the next hour taking care of Talon's leg, and with the medical equipment and supplies stored inside, Dayton and Sloan had managed to re-set the bone and cast it in plaster. Munroe and Barbeau had used the time to take showers and begin making plans for their exit out of the country. They organised three separate routes. In such a situation they were meant to all travel separately, but given Talon's injury that wasn't possible and a splitting up of the group into three had been decided. Dalton would travel with Talon, Barbeau on his own, and Munroe and Sloan would go as husband and wife, as their passports stated. It was standard procedure to have multiple passports stored in safe houses in countries around the world. In America they had access to over fifty passports, each with different aliases and each located in a different state. For the British team the passports had been made as husband and wife to work for Munroe and Sloan. If only one was needed, then it didn't matter, but if they were together then both were covered. In DSV all eventualities were prepared for as standard and identification was no different.

Within four hours of arriving at the safe house they were all ready to go, and despite the attack, the majority of airports were still open for business. They expected heavy traffic within the terminals but it turned out to be fairly quiet. The TV announcements and emergency channels had been broadcasting that most people should stay in their homes. The areas of expected fallout had been evacuated as best they could, given the millions of households in the path of the smoky, black trail of the radioactive cloud. People were scared and waiting, in fear of another attack, but it didn't stop them from being glued to their TV screens and watching the updates and footage of the destruction the blast had left behind. Direct control of the situation had been passed over to FEMA and within only a few hours there were emergency services wearing yellow hazmat suits working on the peripherals of the blast crater, as close as humanly possible without suffering a hot dose of radiation. There were already remarkable stories of luck and tragedy, but most of all it was the terrible loss of life that dominated the news updates. By the time Munroe and the others had departed for JFK Airport it had to be said that even though everything that could be done was being done, it was all just a drop in the ocean compared to the destruction and chaos the bomb had created. It was the thoughts of payback in the minds of the DSV agents, if payback were even possible, that guided them onwards.

Even though security had been increased at the airport there was a laxness in the security personnel's duties that was noticed by all and expected by none. Many of the guards were either on their phones trying to get hold of their loved ones or glued to the TV screens dotted around the terminals. There was something about the very nature of an atomic bomb attack that most people appeared to react to on a subconscious level, as if a new precedent had been set in the world – one that would change its path forever. Like a nightmare thing that had been released from Pandora's Box, its consequences just the precursor to a new world to come.

It was here they had split up, with Dalton and Talon heading straight for the overseas safe house, whereas Munroe, Sloan and Barbeau had taken the long trip around on connecting flights with a wait over. Barbeau, it turned out, had not had a problem, but for Munroe and Sloan, changing flights in the Bahamas had proven more difficult. When their flight had been ordered off the runway, away from a terminal gate, they were sure that Bauer had once again gotten the drop on them, but it had turned out to be due to fear of radiation. It made little sense but the authorities had decided to take extreme care when dealing with all flights coming in from New York. The idea was that these flights could be seeping radiation caused by the fallout and that for fear of contamination they had to be checked before anyone was allowed anywhere near the gate. Four people in hazmat suits and two Geiger counters later and they'd been allowed into the country.

The two-hour delay had meant Munroe and Sloan missing their connection, so they had checked into a motel for the night and caught the first flight out, landing at Augusto C. Sandino International Airport on the west coast of Nicaragua. From here the trip had been uneventful and four taxi journeys later, each change of vehicle making it more difficult for anyone who may try and trace their steps at a later date, they arrived.

Located in the El Diablo Nature Reserve, the residence was one of DSV's most isolated safe houses, set within a thousand square acres of tropical cloud forest and mountain ranges. The safe house was made up of two buildings, with the smallest containing an underground bunker filled with food, a weapons store and high-tech communications equipment. The larger one, a chalet, contained a main kitchen, eight bedrooms and a communal lounge where since arriving Munroe had spent most of his time, watching the updates on the satellite TV. It was chaos in New York as the emergency services began to organise and every news channel was focused on nothing else. It was already being labelled as the worst terrorist attack the world had ever seen. There was also much talk of a realignment of the world in the twenty-first century, and how this was the catalyst that would set the global change, which would reshape the next hundred years. Of course, much of it was said in the moment, the anger and raw emotions on display on every reporter and news anchor, but there was something more to it than that. As Munroe and the others had watched there was a genuine sense that this event would be recognised in the future as the moment the world changed dramatically forever. 9/11 had changed the world for a generation but the overall impression this nuclear attack gave was that the world had changed for good. The dawn of nuclear terrorism had arrived and with it no longer the fear of thousands dying, but cities of millions being wiped off the map in the blink of an eye.

Two days after they arrived, McCitrick turned up. His evacuation from the Ministry of Defence and then the country was flawless and well organised, but the grounding of all flights for twenty-four hours in France following the attack had delayed him. Unfortunately all he had brought with him were his commiserations and the promise that DSV wasn't out of the game, but there would be a period of waiting to see how the dust settled, figuratively and literally.

After two weeks and no sign of their mugshots appearing anywhere it seemed that Bauer had guessed correctly concerning the handling of DSV by their own governments. Officially the attack had not been blamed on anyone, and although multiple media outlets had suspicions, the world was in the dark. The destruction in New York and FEMA's response in saving lives from the fallout had been the focus of the media's narrative, but after two weeks things were beginning to change. The total damage and loss of life would take months, if not years, to be fully realised, and even the death count of the initial blast was educated guesswork. So massive was its scale, in a city like New York, that it was reasonable to assume many of the casualties would go unknown forever.

After two weeks of scrambling, with the emergency services now having brought some defined order to the situation, the media's focus was fully trained on the 'who' and 'how'. Middle Eastern terrorist groups had been in the fray since the start, but the sophistication of such an attack had fostered many conspiracy theories.

To add to all this there had been no word from Remus or Lavigne, the other French DSV agent, and Barbeau along with McCitrick had spent weeks attempting to track them down. Munroe had only met Lavigne once, but he had a solid record and a similar military career to the others. The two men could be accounted for up until a day after the attack, both in Paris, but since then, nothing. It was for this reason that McCitrick had made the risky decision to take leave of the safe house and catch a flight over to France and make contact with an asset of his. It was dangerous, so much so that Barbeau had proposed going with him, but the section head had refused the offer. It was bad enough one of them poking their heads above the parapet, and besides, McCitrick worked best alone.

He had taken off three days ago in the hopes of not only getting info on the two Frenchmen but a line on what the intelligence agencies on both sides of the Atlantic were up to and how bad it was for DSV.

Munroe exited the front door of the chalet to see Sloan, Dalton and Barbeau already in deep conversation with McCitrick, who had arrived moments earlier in a silver Ford Sedan rental car. He approached, offering a welcoming nod.

'How's Talon?' McCitrick was asking as Dalton reassured him.

'He's back on his feet. That man has the healing abilities of a lizard. Another few days and he'll be off the crutches.'

'That's good because we're going to need him,' McCitrick informed the four of them as they fell silent, everyone waiting to hear what he knew. 'OK, there's good news and bad news so let's get the bad over with. MI6 and CIA believe we are responsible for New York. Just as Bauer said, a source dropped fake intel along with a narrative exposing the existence of DSV. That no one had ever heard of us, including the heads of state, has only compounded the lie that we're behind this. They believe we're a corrupt and rogue agency that's been abusing the system for years with the official anonymity of the allied charter Winston Churchill provided us.'

McCitrick looked less disappointed and instead angry at the idea, and who could blame him? After all the sacrifices DSV had made over the years, to now be tagged as the enemy was a bitter pill to swallow. 'They know nothing about Daedalus, and as far as everyone is concerned, the creation of DSV should only have been a temporary measure after the war. It should have been disbanded when it was realised that the enemy of its mission never existed.'

Everyone, including Munroe, looked more than a little disheartened at the notion as McCitrick continued, his anger mounting.

'There was never any security precaution made for a situation like this. Losing the Three Kings like that... I'm certain it was Colonel Sinclair who gave them our operating procedures and security measures and all they had to do was find a weakness... and they did. Cape Wrath has been seen as an illegal internment camp for anyone who crossed us, and there's also talk that we could have been behind other terrorist attacks in the past when we guided foreign policy to our advantage. They think we make billions as gun runners, and that's in part why we shut down Blackstar.'

'What a crock of shit,' Dalton snarled and McCitrick offered a sympathetic nod.

'Of course it is, but they believe it, and the intel that was dropped in their laps makes for compelling reading. Any way you cut it, we are officially fucked.'

They all looked around at each other uneasily as Munroe expelled a deep sigh. 'So what's the good news?'

'Hold on. I'm not finished with the bad yet,' McCitrick replied with a grimace. 'Remus and Lavigne have been taken into custody, off the books, by the CIA. I haven't been able to locate them yet, but word is they're going to be executed for treason in the same classified military courts that had been reserved for Daedalus.'

'Jesus,' Barbeau said, massaging his forehead.

'I know. And that's the reason we've not seen our faces in the media. We're a major embarrassment and they just want us to disappear,' McCitrick said apprehensively as he approached the reality of what this meant. 'All in all, if we want to make it through to the other side we have one option left to us.'

'Expose Daedalus,' Munroe said and McCitrick nodded, the anger in his face evaporating to be replaced by the look of a professional who doesn't entertain emotion.

'It's the only way. And even then it's going to be a hard sell. We have to show our own people, unequivocally, what Daedalus are and what they've done. This is all or nothing, ladies and gentlemen, and we are going to have to do it with targets on our backs.'

'Sounds about normal to me,' Barbeau stated casually, and his delivery of the line received smiles from the group as McCitrick used the upturn in morale to give some good news.

'It's the way they're approaching this that gives us an edge. By keeping this out of the media we have a much better ability to move around without attention. Then there is the arrogance of Daedalus. They think we're broken and as such they will never expect us to come after them so brazenly. We can use it to our advantage.'

Some of McCitrick's points warranted encouragement, but there was still the most obvious problem and Munroe addressed it right away. 'To expose Daedalus we would need to infiltrate the hierarchy as a start and that means more than just Bauer. We need *everyone*, and even when we had the resources we never penetrated the core, which means one of two things, John. You're either giving us a pep talk with no real plan, or,' Munroe looked around the group and he smiled, 'you've already found a way in.'

McCitrick stared at him blankly, and then slowly returned the smile.

'As a matter of fact, I think I have. It's a long shot, but it's a solid long shot.'

The contradiction wasn't lost on anyone, but in their line of work long shots were the gold standard in desperate times such as these.

McCitrick paused, waiting for someone to say something, but when nothing came he now looked directly at Munroe as everyone else's attention remained fixed on him. 'When you brought in Howard Getz, the Daedalus banker you and Sloan did a spot of skydiving with, the computer records on his laptop revealed some interesting information. It was still being analysed when the whole Sinclair situation went down and, well, as you know, we've been on a different line of enquiry ever since. But it was part of the intel I took with me when I had to make my quick exit from the Ministry of Defence.'

McCitrick held up a memory stick between his fingers and gave it a gentle shake. 'There are multimillion transfers from Daedalus, through dummy corporations to numerous entities and organisations, many of which are less than reputable.'

'So what did little Howard come up with?' Sloan asked as McCitrick dropped the memory stick back in his pocket.

'Quite a lot, actually, but there is one in particular, a Mexican *corporation*, if you will, that hundreds of millions was paid to, I'm guessing for a certain type of product. On top of everything else, Daedalus either had a side business in drugs or were possibly paying for services rendered.'

'Are we talking about the Mexican cartel?' Munroe asked. They were arguably the most dangerous drug suppliers, killers and extortionists in the world, and McCitrick was now looking deadly serious.

'Los Zetas.'

The name drew silence from the group and as McCitrick let the name hang in the air it was Barbeau who finally spoke up.

'Are we talking about the breakaway faction, the ones the original Los Zetas considered too wild? Because I did some undercover work with that group before I joined DSV. They're maniacs.'

McCitrick nodded and then he smiled. 'MI6 caught a conversation between their *tenientes*, or lieutenant, and Howard Getz where the Mexican demanded a meeting with his boss, or top guy as he put it, a man he referred to as Dr Loathlife. He was given the meeting and from what I can tell a line of communication was set up with subsequent meetings.'

'Dr Loathlife – charming,' Sloan noted, shaking her head. 'What kind of name is that?'

'It's not,' Munroe replied, mixing the letters in his head. 'It's an alias, an anagram of the person Daedalus hold so dear to their hearts… Adolf Hitler.'

'Exactly,' McCitrick replied, pointing his finger at Munroe. 'I think that they had dealings with the head of Daedalus, the person Hans Bauer reports to, and as the last communication was only a month ago, we have a way of tracking this Dr Loathlife.'

Everyone once again went silent as they all mulled over the possibility and the potential success of such an operation. McCitrick was right when he said it was a long shot, but it was one that did, at least, exist. A way to the heart of Daedalus, but an extremely dangerous one and Munroe knew it.

'Are you suggesting we conduct an operation to kidnap the top lieutenant of the Mexican cartel, probably the most dangerous and violent mafia group on the planet, and squeeze him for information?'

'No! I'm not suggesting that at all,' McCitrick replied, looking appalled by the idea. 'I'm suggesting we make a deal with them.'

'A deal?'

'Yes, a deal,' McCitrick replied and he looked around at everyone with the expression of a sly old fox. 'A deal with the Devil himself.'

Chapter 21

The Nissan 4x4 drove up the dusty road towards the small housing complex just outside the Mexican town of Los Ramones in Nuevo León, with Munroe at the wheel and McCitrick riding shotgun. The private plane from Nicaragua had provided anonymity for the two men and had proved the easiest part of the endeavour so far. Getting a meeting with Los Zetas' top lieutenant, a young man in his twenties by the name of Francisco Estrada, had been the tough part. An audience with such a powerful man was usually only granted when proposing a high-level drug deal or by being brought there to meet your maker. They wanted neither.

McCitrick's contact turned out to be a captain in the local police force who balanced the fine line between the corrupter and the corrupted, which was common within Mexican law enforcement. These men were not natural criminals, but given the power and reach of the drug cartels it was more about survival in a country that was only a few levels away from becoming a full-blown narco state. And within the chaotic and violent world of such a nation, Los Zetas was perhaps the most dangerous.

The story of this cartel's rise to power was as legendary as it was mysterious, and would lead to Mexico becoming one of the most violent places on earth. Their inception came from a battalion of Mexico's special forces, an army unit that had not only been trained by the US special forces but also the Israeli Defence Force in counter insurgence. These elite soldiers were tasked with taking down rebels and narcos who ravaged the country, and their expertise brought about a fearsome reputation, enjoying success after success. And then, one night, just like that, the whole unit disappeared.

They soon reappeared, having sold their skills to the highest bidder, one of the biggest cartels, and so Los Zetas was born. Their military training and tactics punched holes in their criminal rivals, and then when their boss was arrested they did what had been their plan from the start. They took over the cartel.

What followed were the most violent and bloodthirsty chapters in Mexico's history with whole police divisions and villages being wiped out. Flayings, castrations and beheadings became the tools of the fear tactics they were taught, and piles of bodies were left to rot in the streets as Los Zetas carved out their bloody criminal empire mercilessly. Within a few years the unit had become the most powerful cartel in Mexico.

In recent years, and with many of the original members killed or in prison, Los Zetas' push for power had stagnated, but to underestimate such a group would be foolish, and as Munroe pulled up into a row of buildings, he knew their endeavour could go sideways at any moment.

The story of Los Zetas' rise to power had been embellished over the years but the basic story was accurate. And even though the younger recruits that had filled the vacuum over time may not have had the same elite training that was once standard within the group, the tactics, violence and ongoing military-style training was very much alive.

Munroe now came to a stop as ahead three military jeeps supporting 50mm machine guns blocked their path and three men with AK47s exited one of the vehicles and walked slowly over to them. With black bandanas covering the lower parts of their faces they approached the driver's side window and one pointed the barrel of his gun inside.

'Weapons,' the man said in Spanish, and both Munroe and McCitrick held up their palms.

'We have none,' Munroe replied, his accent strong, and it received a nod from the man.

'Get out,' was all he said and Munroe, followed by McCitrick, slowly exited the vehicle and allowed the other two men to pat them down. Once satisfied they were clean, the first man nudged the AK47's barrel in Munroe's back. 'Follow me.'

The row of connected houses they were guided towards was part of a much larger estate, with maybe a hundred houses built in small communities divided by roads and circular driveways in the middle. Beyond that there was nothing but dry, arid desert with strips of farming land amongst the landscape. But given the heat and obvious lack of rainfall it didn't seem a place that could cultivate much produce.

'Get moving,' the man ordered, pointing his weapon to the open doorway of the first house. As they entered they were met by another man, also wearing a black bandana, who led them inside the living room and to an opening that had been cut into the floor. He then descended down a wooden ladder and waved at them to follow as they were shadowed from behind by the others.

The gloomy square tunnel was cold and musty with wooden braces along the walls to stop any collapse, and its length was lit by yellow industrial LED lights with protective steel bird cages around the bulbs.

'Down there,' their chaperone ordered, and both Munroe and McCitrick did as they were instructed, heading deeper into what turned out to be a network of passageways, each with entrances to the separate houses above. It was nothing new to Munroe who had seen such tunnels first-hand, a favourite of drug cartels in Mexico, but this was different and more expansive. They must have travelled over three hundred metres, and every twenty the tunnel opened up into a rectangular waiting area where two armed men stood guard, so all sections of the tunnels could be defended from any uninvited guests.

By the time they reached the designated exit, Munroe's white cotton shirt and blue jeans were peppered heavily with dust, and as they were both guided up the short wooden ladder he figured they must have walked to the other side of the estate.

They exited right into a kitchen and were met by a man who held two black plastic zip ties in his hand, and two more men with AK47s held the barrels to Munroe and McCitrick's heads as they put out their hands and allowed themselves to be restrained.

All this was to be expected, although the feeling of being completely at someone's mercy was not pleasant. It was an emotion that both men had learnt to deal with many years earlier, however, and they calmly allowed themselves to be led into the main sitting room.

The room was spotless and had the odour of recent construction. The thick grey carpet and white leather sofas that sat upon it looked like they had just been taken out of their wrapping, and an expensive jagged white marble coffee table stood before them, all in contrast to the generic printed paintings hanging on the walls. Around the edges of the room were six men in black military attire, not unlike riot gear with helmets, each armed with M4 automatic rifles. They stood protectively over a man wearing a dark floral shirt, tan chinos and slip-on red leather shoes who sat in the centre of the sofa and eyed them both with black dilated pupils.

At twenty-nine years old, Francisco Estrada was no ordinary cartel leader. His intelligence and ability, as well as the notorious sixth sense he was said to possess, had allowed him to evade authorities time and time again and had gained him the nickname the Desert Fox.

Munroe gazed at the motionless Los Zetas lieutenant with neither contempt nor respect as he ran through what he had learned about the man. Born into a family in complete poverty, the young Estrada had learnt from an early age the meaning of violence. One of three children, he was the only one to live past the age of ten, the other two beaten to death by their father whose propensity for violence was well known. So much so that the man was jailed for life after being convicted of the murder of two young girls. This was most likely the reason the young Estrada survived, and given talk of his father being guilty of many more murders he was never charged with, there was genuine belief that his old man had been a serial killer.

By the age of ten Estrada was acting as a drug mule for the local cartel. By twelve he had committed his first murder, and by thirteen he had allegedly been involved in the torturous flaying of a rival dealer. The skinless man actually survived for a few weeks afterwards until infection set in, but he never gave up the name of his attackers.

Even at this young age Estrada was a person to be feared. And he steadily rose up the ranks before being recruited into Los Zetas aged seventeen. His ability to stay on the right side of power during internal wars within the cartel – along with his instincts, propensity for sheer violence and loyalty to the boss – had seen him become a lieutenant by the age of twenty-four. All in all, there was not much to work with to make a connection with the man, and Munroe and McCitrick had settled on the one thing that could define him, and in doing so create a measure of control, no matter how small.

His loyalty.

'Mr Estrada,' McCitrick began, but he was shut down immediately by a swift wagging of the lieutenant's finger and the room fell into silence once again as Estrada stared at his visitors. He tilted his head from side to side inquisitively before, after what seemed like minutes, he pointed at Munroe. 'You, Mr Munroe. Do I look like a man who helps his enemies?'

Munroe gave a slow shake of his head. 'No, Mr Estrada. You do not.'

'And you, Mr McKitrish,' he said, mispronouncing McCitrick's name, 'do I look like someone who would let you bend me over and screw me in the ass?'

'No, Mr Estrada. You do not,' McCitrick replied, mimicking Munroe's answer as Estrada sat up, holding his hands together.

'Then why are you trying to?'

The questions were perplexing, but Munroe was already realising what he was getting at and it sent a small ripple of apprehension through his body, because if he was right then coming here had been a terrible idea. 'I'm not sure what you've heard, Mr Estrada, and as we stand here, bound and surrounded by you and your men, there are many things I am unsure of. But wanting to cause you problems is not one of them.'

Munroe watched as Estrada stared at him with soulless eyes, and he noticed the man's jaw muscle begin to tighten, forcing him to add, 'But there's a lot of shit being slung around at the moment. If you allow me to explain, I hope you will see we bring nothing but good intentions.'

The jaw muscle began to relax and Estrada sat back in his sofa. 'By shit slinging, I assume you mean the rumours that you and a few others are responsible for the big bang in New York.'

'That's the one,' Munroe replied as Estrada scratched an itch on his cheek before speaking again.

'Because whoever set off that bomb has caused my business a lot of problems. The raised security level means I'm losing double the shipments to the US. And if that was down to you then I would feel bound to return the trouble.'

Estrada clicked his fingers and hard blows to the back of their legs brought both men down onto their knees and another man flipped out a switch blade and held it under Munroe's eye as Estrada spoke again. 'And the return would have to be severe and long lasting. Perhaps we could begin with forcing you to screw your friend, and then we could...' Estrada turned to the nearest guard. 'What's the dog, you know, the biter?'

'Chupo?'

'Yes, that's it, perhaps we let the Alsatian Chupo screw you, then we could skin your arms and legs, cover you with salt and then begin all over again.'

Estrada appeared not to be taking any joy in the sexual aspects of his torture methods but rather the sheer pain that they would bring, and he sat forwards again and once more placed his hands together. 'That is if "the shit that was slung" is correct.'

McCitrick attempted to speak, but he received a firm finger pointing from Estrada. 'Not you. I want Mr Munroe to answer.'

With the knife still poking into his skin, just below his eye, Munroe looked composed and unrattled and, with his breathing measured, he replied. 'Mr Estrada, if you think we would come here and offer ourselves up after causing you so many problems then, with respect, the remarkable tales of the sixth sense they say you possess are complete bullshit.'

You could sense the atmosphere change in the room as all the men in there, except for Estrada, stiffened, but Munroe continued, his demeanour still calm and collected.

'It is the very people who slung that shit at us who were responsible, and we want them dead. We also believe you know how to contact them, and for this we offer something that we hope you will accept. Your boss is in Apodaca prison serving a life sentence. The military protection and security are impenetrable, without going to war with the government, and the people in place there are incorruptible. But my team and I have certain abilities and resources that mean we can get him out for you, and in a way that will have them wondering if he's still even alive. Which, I should add, will give him free rein for a while to come.'

Estrada didn't move but continued to hold his hands together, the only tell he was considering it was that his forefinger began to tap against the top of his other hand as Munroe motioned to the window.

'And if you don't find that convincing enough then perhaps our skills and tactics will persuade you we're as good as we say we are.'

A red laser dot appeared on the coffee table, but as the armed men began to move, it was Estrada who held his fist in the air. 'Everyone hold.'

Munroe looked over at the dot and nodded. 'This building is being laser painted by our team for the drone circling overhead, and the load it carries would take out most of this estate.'

Estrada looked angry at first but then he calmed and slowly lowered his fist. 'You'd die as well.'

'I never had any intention of blowing us up. Only to show you what we're capable of and reassure you we can get your boss out of prison. But...' Munroe pushed the knife away with his cheek and got to his feet, 'we want the actual people who dropped the bomb in New York. And I'm guessing you might even already know it was them, but after I tell you who and what they are I can assure you, Mr Estrada, you'll want them dead as much as we do.'

Francisco Estrada returned his gaze to the red dot on the coffee table, which now disappeared, and he then sat back in the sofa and crossed his legs. He stared at Munroe, his eyes tightening, gauging Munroe before sucking in a deep breath and getting to his feet. 'Untie them. And then we can sort out the details,' he said, and McCitrick was pulled to his feet and his zip tie cut, but when one of the men tried to cut off Munroe's he pulled his hands away. He then slid his wrists in opposite directions around 360 degrees and the pressure on the zip tie broke under the force, releasing him.

'Never bind a man with zip ties with his hands in front of him. Use handcuffs.'

For the first time Estrada smiled, and although it was more of a grimace he shook Munroe's and McCitrick's hands in an overfriendly manner, which somehow made the man even more creepy than he had already appeared to be.

'Come. There is a restaurant I own nearby. Let me show you some hospitality.'

Estrada headed towards the tunnel and was followed by almost all the armed guards except for one, the same one who had greeted them earlier, as Munroe and McCitrick began speaking in English.

'Can you take us back to our vehicle?' McCitrick asked, but the Los Zetas guard only shrugged his shoulders, and so McCitrick asked again, in Spanish this time, as Munroe made his way over to the window and tapped his miniature earpiece with his fingers. 'Everyone stand down. For now.' He then turned around as the guard ushered them back to the kitchen and the long walk back to their vehicle.

'Amazing what you can do with a laser pen,' McCitrick said. 'Still, you do know they're going to skin us and then kill us after this is all over, don't you?'

'Oh, yes,' Munroe replied with a smirk as they followed the guard's lead. 'Without question.'

Chapter 22

The white converted Ford F-150 pick-up truck approached the main gates of Apodaca prison, its darkened windows making it impossible to see the occupants, and the brand-new, gleaming vehicle stood out against the rusty and battered cars on the road. At midday the Mexican heat was stifling and the rippling waves off the tarmac's surface distorted the vehicle's image. The glinting mirage caught the eyes of the three armed security guards sitting in their concrete cubicle at the front gate post.

The sight of the truck had two of the guards tightening their grips on their CZ 805 BREN assault rifles as the third picked up the telephone and made a call.

There were no scheduled arrivals at that time of day and the two armed guards left the cubicle and exited the tight pedestrian doorway of the main gate and waited as the vehicle came to a stop.

The guard nearest the window rotated his finger in a circular motion and immediately the dark-tinted window rolled down on its electric motors.

'What's your business?' the guard asked gruffly in Spanish and as the man behind the wheel took off his sunglasses the other guard glanced down at the licence plate and called out to his colleague.

'Americans.'

The guard, still holding his rifle tightly, leant in closer to the open window and once again spoke, in English this time, 'State your business.'

Munroe placed his glasses down on the dashboard and passed over a brown A5 envelope to the guard who let his rifle hang from around his neck and opened it.

'I'm with the American consulate and have permission from Governor Garcia to interview one of your inmates,' he stated in a Californian accent. Munroe then held a laminated consulate pass in front of the guard as the envelope was opened and the contents read. It was a few moments before the guard raised his finger and headed back to the entrance cubicle to confer with his colleague on the phone.

As they waited, the remaining guard tapped on the passenger-side window, which was rolled down to reveal Munroe as the only occupant.

'No security?' the guard asked, sounding almost disappointed.

'No attention needed,' Munroe replied, and the guard stepped back as the other returned from the cubicle and approached the driver's window.

'There are no scheduled visits today. You'll have to clear it with the warden,' he said, passing back the envelope. 'Straight ahead. A guard will take you to meet him.'

Munroe took the envelope and placed it back in his inside jacket pocket and then put on his sunglasses and nodded in appreciation as the sturdy metal gates slid back on their runners, allowing the vehicle entry.

Apodaca prison was renowned for just two things, the housing of some of the most dangerous cartel members, and the violence that came with it. A few years back a prison riot had broken out and after the deaths of over thirty inmates, and suspected complicity by some of the guards, it had climaxed in over thirty top-level cartel members walking out of the front gate.

Since then the prison, which was built to hold one and a half thousand inmates but held over three thousand, had seen fires, more escapes and regular murders to keep the media interested, and it was always a matter of when, not if, the next violent outburst would occur. It did not help matters that across the road from the main prison sat two tarmacked runways, an ex-international airport that had since become a flight school, providing an easy escape for those with the money and power to make it happen.

Munroe drove slowly up the main prison entrance road before coming to a stop at a green Jeep that sat across the road and then parked up to one side where the waiting guard was pointing. He switched off the engine and exited the vehicle and made his way around to the Jeep, keeping his palms open, but not dramatically. The guards here had a right to be extremely cautious when dealing with new arrivals, and as Munroe came to a stop in front of the guard he noted the man scanning his person for any tell-tale bumps of concealed weapons.

'Señor Killean,' the guard said, holding his hand out for Munroe's papers, which Munroe provided along with his consulate identification tag. The guard took a look and then with a flick of his finger he motioned for Munroe to follow him and they headed inside a plain-looking concrete building off to the left.

Even during his early days of special operations it had always surprised Munroe how much trust people put into an identification card or uniform. These things could be faked so easily with the right training. How can someone just flip a badge and instantly be entitled to a degree of respect or obedience, irrespective of who they are? Of course, there was no other way to do it until it became standard to have biochips implanted, or retina scans in standard use across the world, but it was still remarkable how far a bit of knowledge and the balls to use it could go.

'This way,' the guard instructed, and Munroe was led past a steel-grilled reception desk and waiting area to a room at the far end of the corridor with a black sign reading Warden G. Hernandez. The guard knocked on the door and waited for a reply before swinging it open and announcing his guest.

'Señor Michael Killean from the US consulate to speak with you, sir.'

Sat behind a weathered wooden desk, Warden Gabriel Hernandez made no attempt to get up out of his chair and instead nodded and then waited for Munroe to enter the cramped office and for the guard to leave, closing the door behind him. He then pointed at the only other chair in front of the desk and grunted as Munroe sat down and placed the envelope, along with his ID card, onto the desk.

The office was as grimy as Munroe had expected the prison cells to be, with cracked lilac-coloured plaster covering the walls and a picture of Governor Garcia hanging behind him over a double window that looked out onto one of the fenced prison yards. It was no surprise the warden looked as unaccommodating as he did.

'I'm sorry for the inconvenience, Mr Killean, but your request to see Manuel Ortega has been denied.'

It wasn't a positive way to start the conversation and Munroe calmly plucked the paperwork from the envelope and laid it out before the unamused warden. 'I was under the impression that the governor had already spoken with you.'

Warden Hernandez leant forwards and pushed the piece of paper back across the table and then slouched in his seat. 'He did, but we've already had two serious fights today amongst the inmates and the last thing I need is Ortega getting a special visit from a US official.'

Munroe looked puzzled by the response. 'And why would that be a problem, Warden?'

Hernandez swung his chair and thrust his thumb towards the window and the prison buildings beyond. 'We have two warring factions in here, Los Zetas and the Gulf Cartel. Each group as violent as the other, and keeping them from trying to kill each other is a daily task. Prison life, Mr Killean, is like high school, but with deadly consequences. The smallest, petty, childish gripes and divisions are all it takes to set off a prison riot, and with tensions already high I'm not about to get them all riled up by having you here.'

'Riled up by having me here?' Munroe replied, playing his part perfectly, and Hernandez now swivelled back to face him and leant both his elbows on the table.

'This prison has had two serious riots in the past year. Lot of deaths go with such a riot and we've had many cartel members walk out of those front gates, never to be seen again. It's the reason I was brought in as the new warden, Mr Killean. This prison can never again have cartel members escape, and I was chosen, with my military background, to make sure it never happens. I have completely ramped up the security at Apodaca prison and I am proud to say only two types of inmate ever exit through these gates. Those that have served their time, and those that are dead.' Hernandez leant forwards with flared nostrils. 'And those are the only fucking options. If they riot and try to break out then they get shot, all of them, and the repercussions of such an event would be very bad for the communities of Mexico. So, as I said,' Hernandez continued, settling back into his seat, 'I won't tempt a riot, and your being here does just that. If you go in and speak with the boss of Los Zetas then the Gulf Cartel are going to think he's either making some kind of deal or will get jealous he's getting special treatment somehow. None of these inmates get visits from the US consulate. The truth of it doesn't matter to these people, only the perception, and they will perceive that Manuel Ortega is up to something, which is enough to set them upon each other. It's high school rules, Mr Killean, and I have enough to worry about without setting off a riot today. So, as I said, I'm sorry you wasted the trip.'

Munroe stared at the warden silently and he could see there was little if no negotiation to be had, not without a push, and he reached into his pocket, pulled out his iPhone and dialled a number.

'There's no point in calling the governor. I have the final say here. I might take some shit for my decision but it's better than a full-scale riot.'

'Hello, it's Michael Killean from the US consulate. Could I speak with Governor Garcia, please… yes, I spoke with her earlier today… thank you.'

Munroe waited for a few moments and then he smiled as the call was put through. 'Thank you for taking my call, Governor. I'm with Warden Hernandez but he's not allowing me access. I wondered if you could speak with him.'

Munroe listened in silence and then he passed over the mobile and, with a deep sigh, Hernandez took it and placed it to his ear.

'I'm sorry, Governor, but the prison is at a tier three and it would be dangerous…'

It was interesting to watch Hernandez go through such a range of emotions in such a short space of time, and Munroe observed the man switch from defiance, to outrage, to reasoned respect and, finally, compliance.

'Yes, Governor, I wasn't aware of the situation, but if we have an event at Apodaca I cannot be held responsible… Yes. Very well, I will. Thank you.'

The call ended and Hernandez passed the phone back to Munroe who dropped it into his pocket. 'I had no idea what it was about. If you'd told me I would have been more understanding.'

'Not at all, Warden. It is I who understand your concerns and although I'm not at liberty to go into details, I hope you can see why I must speak with Manuel Ortega.'

As Hernandez picked up the green telephone off his desk and began to make the necessary arrangements, Munroe held his poker face. If the man knew that it was John McCitrick using a voice modulator to mimic Governor Garcia's voice then he would have ended up inside one of those cells himself in less time than it took to make the call. Hernandez had just been told that the head of Los Zetas, Manuel Ortega, had knowledge that could lead to the capture of the individuals who set off the nuclear bomb in New York the previous month. It had also been suggested that another such bomb was in play at that very moment, and the information the cartel boss could provide may end up saving millions of people's lives… unless the warden did not allow it.

Munroe watched as Hernandez gave his orders, looking nervous. It wasn't every day you're told that your decision could place the weight of millions of lives on your shoulders.

Hernandez put down the telephone and got to his feet along with Munroe before picking up the paperwork and passing it over. 'There's a room at the end of his pod you can use. I'll have a guard take you over to him now.'

'Thank you, Warden, you're doing a lot of good,' Munroe replied, and Hernandez nodded stiffly as the door opened and the same guard that had greeted Munroe initially appeared.

'You've already met Officer Lopez. He will take you over there… and do exactly as he tells you. I wasn't exaggerating about the tension in here today.'

'Thank you for this,' Munroe said, and he shook the warden's hand and followed Officer Lopez out of the door.

The walk over to the cells was short and involved crossing over a tight, fenced bridge to the other side of the complex. It was here that Munroe got his first look at the prison layout. There were four main structures, each shaped in an X-formation with a central hub. Nearby lay the exercise yards, which were already filled with inmates, and further past that a football field containing the only grass in the entire prison. Munroe was taken past three security gates and as they made it along the long path with fenced yards on either side the inmates began to collect up against them, curious to see who was coming into their part of the world.

'We would usually give VIPs a stab-proof vest but you didn't want to draw attention to yourself,' Officer Lopez said, nodding at the gathering crowds of mean-looking faces they were passing by. 'The men in here are from the Gulf Cartel and we keep them segregated from the Zetas.'

The very mention of the Zetas had some of the men spitting on the ground and holding up gang signs with their fingers as the rumble of discontent grew ever louder. There wasn't a single person not covered in jail-house tattoos and many whose bald heads and faces were emblazoned with them. Munroe kept his expression respectful, but with no sign of weakness, and as they approached the entrance for the cell block a large man with a black goatee and a gold, sleeveless Los Angeles Lakers top called out to him.

'Hey, Lopez. Who's the American?'

'Just a lawyer,' Lopez replied, but the man, who now was grasping the chain links above his head, revealing a sweaty bush of armpit hair, grimaced and his lips tightened.

'Yeah, then where's his briefcase?'

Munroe wagged the A5 envelope in his fingers. 'Just a delivery boy,' he said as the inmate tutted in disbelief.

'Yeah, gringo? How about I deliver my dick in your ass.'

The growing crowd around him laughed gruffly as Lopez raised his hand, and he smiled as they reached the entrance and unlocked the door with the set of keys hanging from his belt on a sturdy retractable key ring. 'That's Ricardo Soto, one of the Gulf Cartel's lieutenants,' he said, glancing back at the man with the Lakers shirt. 'They're all right once you get to know them, but if you want to survive working in this place you never turn your back on them.'

Munroe noted the inmate who was still staring at him and menacingly blew him a kiss. 'Believe me, that's the last guy I would turn my back on.'

The smell inside assaulted Munroe's nose like smelling salts. It was a mix of sweat, body odour and farts that hung in the air like a noxious poisonous cloud. His nose wrinkled as he took in the interior, the place so many of these inmates would call home for life. 'I can see why they riot.'

'You get used to it, and don't use that word,' Lopez said as he made his way over to the central observation booth. The booth itself was mounted fifteen foot in the air upon a thick cylinder of concrete and allowed a 360-degree view of the four rows of housing that led away from it. Each row had thick steel-bar doors leading inside, allowing for a closed common room that surrounded the observation booth in the middle.

'We house over seven hundred inmates in each of these buildings and given it's only built for a third of that things can get a little tense.'

Lopez unlocked one of the metal side doors, allowing the key chain to zip back into its casing. 'What did you say to the warden, anyway? It's unusual for him to change his mind.'

'That it could mean life or death if I didn't see Ortega,' Munroe replied as he was ushered into another corridor. The comment had Lopez chuckling.

'Everything that happens in this place is life and death. It's nothing new.'

'Yeah, well, in this case it could mean a lot more than a few thousand deaths.' Lopez looked like he was going to ask another question but seemed to think better of it and with a simple nod he led Munroe through another series of locked gates before opening the final door into a room that contained nothing but a table and two plastic chairs. 'Wait here. I'll get him.'

Munroe took a seat before scanning every inch of the room for any hint of recording equipment. Satisfied there were no microphones, he placed his finger to his ear. 'Did you catch all that?'

'We got it,' Sloan's voice chimed in. The microphone receivers were state of the art and could be positioned deep within the ear canal and extracted by magnet when needed, making them impossible to be seen with the naked eye. The vibration though was highly irritating, and Munroe rubbed his ear gently and waited for the sound of footsteps to return. The plan was relatively simple. Upon meeting with Ortega he was to be given a specialised pill, one that had been used before by DSV during extraction operations. The pill would induce a controlled coma that would slow his heart down to a shallow rate that even knowledgeable and experienced medics could easily miss. With almost no readable pulse and zero reaction to stimuli the person could remain in the state for over two hours. Then, with the right cocktail of drugs, the initial conditions could be reversed and the individual revived with no side effects. The only issue to be overcome was that in the event of death the body would be handled by the prison mortuary, with a stayover of at least twenty-four hours until confirmation could be made officially. This of course was a problem, but one they would overcome by way of Ortega's powerful position. For fear of igniting a violent backlash from the cartel, the governor, played by McCitrick, would demand that Ortega be taken to the main hospital in nearby Monterrey to show that everything had been done to save the man, rather than let him die in the prison hospital. The prison hospitals in Mexico were not known for their high-end equipment, and to rely on such mediocre treatment could easily be seen by many as deliberate, potentially resulting in violent repercussions for the authorities. So Dalton and Talon, both having the darker skin to pass as Mexican nationals, would pick up the body in an ambulance along with Munroe, or Michael Killean, before heading back to the consulate. Case closed, until someone realised what had happened.

This approach did though require control over the phone lines, just in case Warden Hernandez decided to call the governor back for any reason, or to alert any of the cartels. Bribery in this part of the world was a necessary way of life, and so Sloan would be monitoring and directing any outgoing calls while laying down a dampening field to create mobile interference. Again, thanks to the technology DSV had acquired from Daedalus some months back. It was a sound plan but it all had to run like clockwork, because any deviation could cause either the death of Ortega or get the real authorities attending.

Like many of DSV's operations concerning Daedalus, deception and subterfuge was essential and the team had gotten extremely good at it. As Munroe now heard the sounds of footsteps approaching from outside the door, he and the others prepared to put all those skills to the test.

The door opened and Lopez respectfully moved to one side as behind him a man in his mid-thirties appeared, wearing an expensive blue silk shirt, ironed grey trousers and slip-on leather shoes. He wore no shackles or restraints, and he paused at the open doorway and ran his gold ringed fingers through his shiny black hair. 'Mr Killean?'

Manuel Ortega, the boss of Los Zetas, had a boyish look to him, his skin tanned, his eyebrows plucked and his lips having a healthy shine. As Munroe got up to greet him he couldn't help but think the cartel boss looked more preened now than in the photos he'd seen of him before his arrest.

'It's nice to meet you, Mr Ortega,' Munroe said, shaking the man's hand, 'and thank you for talking with me.'

Ortega did not smile but he nodded and then raised his finger in the air and without looking back he barked an order to Officer Lopez. 'Leave us.'

Lopez did as he was told, his eyes to the floor, and Munroe pointed to the seat opposite and smiled. 'Please, take a seat.'

Ortega didn't move for a moment, but then he expelled a deep breath and sat down, clearly only because *he* chose to. 'So you're the ones being blamed for New York?'

Munroe nodded slowly, his every mannerism and expression being scrutinised by Ortega like a hawk. The cartel boss stared at him through those hypnotic amber eyes of his, which appeared to command respect or fear equally, a trait the boss of Los Zetas was well known for.

'Wrongly, Mr Ortega. But my friends and I very much want to catch those who are responsible, which is why I'm here today.'

Ortega still hadn't blinked since entering and he continued to stare, his head tilting just slightly to one side. 'I'm sure my lieutenant, Estrada, told you of the disruption it has caused us?'

'He did,' Munroe said, retrieving a pen from his pocket and unscrewing the top end to reveal a secret compartment and the special pill inside, which he dropped onto the table. 'Once we get you outside of this place we hope that Mr Estrada will provide us with information that will see those who have caused you so many problems taken care of.' Munroe screwed on the pen top and placed it back in his pocket. 'Mr Estrada told me you approve of our plan.'

Ortega nodded and then glanced down at the pill lying on the surface of the table and then back up at Munroe. 'Your plan involves a great deal of trust on my part. How do I know I won't take it and wake up in an American jail?'

'Because then we would never get hold of the people who committed the attack on New York and clear our names. Both our survival is intertwined at this moment in time, so you will either have to trust me or not. I can't make you.'

Ortega stopped tilting his head and he leant his hands against the edge of the table. 'No, you can't, and whether I trust you or not... well, that is what I'm contemplating.'

From everything Munroe had read on the man he was devious, totally lacking in empathy, except when it came to his own family, and had not only ordered but carried out personally the killings of not just police and politicians, but also their entire families whilst making his way to the top of the cartel. At thirty-five he was considered learned and wise in a business that rarely saw members make it past their late forties, and his inflated ego and narcissism meant that disagreement to anything he said was seldom heard. But it was this that Munroe now attempted to play into. To a man who was never told no it was possible that, given the circumstances, he might appreciate some level-headed honesty.

'We don't have much time to spare, Mr Ortega, or may I call you Manuel?'

Ortega didn't reply, but continued to stare at him, his face void of expression.

'OK then, Manuel. I know who you are but let me tell you who I am and who my friends are. We are the organisation that the government call upon when their intelligence agencies can't get something done. We are the only agency in the Western world who answers to no one, and has access to everyone and everything. We don't operate inside of the law… we decide which laws apply to us. The CIA, MI6, the Israeli Defence Force, who I believe taught your original members all they know – we tower above them. In the spy world where shades of grey are the theatre of expertise our own operations are colour-blind, because we have licence to do whatever we want. Christ, even the President of the United States has neither the access nor ability to tell us what or what not to do.'

'Take it easy, Ethan,' Sloan whispered in his earpiece as Munroe continued.

'Let me tell you who those associates of *yours* are. Those individuals whose information we want from your Lieutenant Estrada. They're Nazis. Remnants of the Second World War who over the past seventy years have festered into an organisation that has more money, power and connections than all the cartels and organised crime syndicates around the world combined. They are the real bogeyman, and they don't bother killing thousands of people, like Los Zetas have. They can kill hundreds of millions in just a day, and New York was purely an appetiser – shit, not even that. It was a single peanut from the restaurant bar before even sitting down for the meal. This group has the ability to do what no other person in history has managed to achieve. Caesar, Genghis Khan, Napoleon. They're fucking amateurs compared to this group. They want to rule the world and everything in it... and they could, too.'

Ortega now began to wince, his expression not angry but focused as Munroe capped off his speech.

'Now you know who they are... then who are we?' Munroe leant into the table, his demeanour calm, his stare intense. 'We're the people that they fear. We're *their* bogeyman.'

He allowed a short silence for the atmosphere to settle and then he sat back in his seat and grasped his hands together. 'So how do you know you can trust us? Well that's simple. Because if you couldn't... you'd already be dead.'

Munroe watched as Ortega sat back and raised his chin upwards thoughtfully. Munroe had laid it on pretty thick, but it wasn't without forethought. The cartel boss did know that whoever they were, the governments of the most powerful nations on earth were all after them, Lieutenant Estrada had let slip that bit of information during their lunch. They knew that Bauer – or whoever they thought Daedalus was – saw DSV as a threat, so much so that they had committed the worst terrorist attack of all time as a way to take them down. Ortega didn't know everything, not by a long shot, but he did know that the group Munroe was with were legit and everyone was either terrified or desperate to stop them. Put all that together and it equalled a group with a shitload of power and influence, and as Munroe watched the man deliberate, he wondered if it would be enough to get them what they wanted. Daedalus.

'The only people that have spoken to me like that before, Mr Killean, have ended up flayed and decapitated in one of our "kitchens". And as for this Nazi thing, I have no idea. Seems like bullshit, I don't know, but I do think you can do what you say you can do.' Ortega scooped the pill off the table and held it up to his lips. 'And for that, and that alone, you may have my trust. This one time.'

Ortega gave a dry smile and raised the pill. But at that very moment the muffled sound of a shotgun blast echoed from down the hallway, and they both turned to the door, momentarily stunned.

Munroe leapt to his feet and over to the door as another blast, closer this time, rang out and the edge of the door exploded into splinters of wood and dust, sending them both down to the floor for protection. Munroe was already back on his feet and going for the other side of the entrance so as to grab whoever came in, but he was stopped dead in his tracks as the door was flung open and a shotgun was shoved in his face.

'Here he is, the delivery boy.'

Ricardo Soto, lieutenant of the Gulf Cartel, still wearing his Lakers shirt, jammed the barrel of his shotgun into Munroe's chest, driving him back a few feet before turning it on Ortega, who was looking shocked but unafraid.

'Ortega, you piece of shit. If you think you're going to break out of here and leave the rest of us behind, then think again.'

Munroe looked out to the corridor and saw not only all the security doors open, but that the common room beyond was complete mayhem with inmates running riot, and he caught a glance of Lopez being thrown to the ground and then dragged off out of sight.

'So you've got one of two options, Ortega. Either we all get out of here, or you get wasted right now.' Soto spat before turning the barrel towards Munroe. 'What's the plan, *puto*? Or do I unload this shotgun into you right here and now?'

Chapter 23

'You're making a big mistake, Ricardo,' Manuel Ortega warned from his position on the floor and Ricardo Soto now turned the shotgun away from Munroe and aimed it directly at the Los Zetas boss's groin.

'You're the one making the mistake, thinking you can make a run for it solo. Think again. Now what's the plan, or do I feminise you with this shotgun?'

Ortega looked unfazed by the shotgun and he motioned towards Munroe with his chin. 'Ask him, it was his plan.'

Soto shifted the shotgun back towards Munroe again. 'So, gringo. Who are you and how were you going to get this prick out of here?'

As Munroe considered his answer there was one burning question at the forefront of his mind.

How the hell did Soto know the Los Zetas boss was about to be broken out of jail?

Munroe had already decided on the answer when he heard Sloan through his earpiece confirm his choice.

'Tell him the truth, Ethan.'

'Well, I'm not from the US consulate. We're mercenaries hired by Francisco Estrada. I was going to fake his death.' He pointed to the pill lying on the floor next to Ortega. 'That will put a person into a coma and simulate death.'

Soto's eyebrow raised, and he took a step away from Munroe with his shotgun now pointed on Ortega. He slowly knelt down and with his free hand picked up the pill. 'Nice. Estrada always was a slippery one.' He eyed the pill briefly before dropping it into his breast pocket, gripping the shotgun tightly once more. 'How were you going to get his body out?'

'We've got a lock-on phone system and the ability to fake the governor's voice. Then a crew of my men were going to pick us up in an ambulance.'

Munroe's plan received a wide-eyed, childlike look of astonishment from Soto who then grinned his approval. 'Very nice. That's some top-grade shit.'

'I appreciate that,' Munroe replied, and with his hands raised he slowly got to his feet as Soto took a step back, ensuring there was enough distance, 'but it will only work for one person.'

Soto thought about it for a moment and then he frowned awkwardly. 'Then you better come up with a new plan.'

Munroe glanced over at Ortega who shrugged his shoulders. 'Well, I could take you instead of him.'

'Asshole,' Ortega spat, but Munroe could tell it was an act, just as his offer was, but it was a long shot that hit way off the mark. Soto wasn't that stupid.

'You take me for an idiot, *puto*,' Soto growled, and he spat on the floor in Munroe's direction. 'So you can kill me when I'm out cold… no, you better come up with something else. Have your crew break in here with their vehicle.'

Maybe Soto wasn't that bright after all!

'They'd never make it past the front gates, there are too many guards and weapons. They'd be shot to hell before they could even reach the cell blocks.'

From behind Soto the scraping sound of fast approaching footsteps could be heard above the chaos going on in the common area and three men in prison outfits came to a stop at the doorway, one tapping Soto on the shoulder.

'Ricardo, the goons are grouping.'

The news had Soto gritting his teeth and Munroe guessed the 'goons' or *seguir* was prison slang for the guards. Every second that passed meant there was less chance that he and Ortega were going to make it out.

'Do you have keys for the gates?' he asked and Soto glanced back at one of the inmates and he received a nod.

'We've got three of the guards. Their keys will get us to the warden's office.'

'And how many guns?'

'*Nada*, just the shotgun from the observation guard.'

This was the first bit of good news Munroe had heard since the Gulf lieutenant had burst in. 'OK, we've got two choices. There's already a riot going on and you have the keys so we make a mad dash, the whole cell block moving in a crowd, but how many will make it is the question.'

The make or break approach received about as much support as Munroe had expected.

'Or?' Soto demanded, and Munroe pointed over at Ortega who was still sat up on the floor.

'Or, I leave Ortega,' he said and now motioned to the three inmates still standing in the doorway, 'and with that pill get your boss out of here instead… but I expect to be paid generously by the Gulf Cartel.'

'You backstabbing son of a bitch,' Ortega yelled and he received a hard punch to his face for his complaint by the nearest inmate.

Soto turned to his cartel partners. 'You boys have short sentences. I get out and you have my word on blood that we'll get you out later.'

Whether it was a testament to the fear and loyalty Ricardo Soto inspired or that they believed his promise was impossible to say, but it only took a few moments for all three inmates to nod sternly and Soto now turned back to face Munroe. 'Deal, but you cross me and you and your friends' mercenary asses will be dead, your families dead. There's nowhere you'll be able to hide.'

Munroe looked unfazed by the threat. 'This is just a job for us. You pay and we won't have a problem.'

Soto nodded and then lowered his shotgun as Munroe pointed past them and down the corridor. 'And I need one of the officers, Lopez. Make it look official.'

'What do you mean *official*?'

'Because, Ricardo, running towards a bunch of armed prison guards with you thrown over my shoulder is likely to get me shot. With the guard out front and you looking dead or dying we've got a better shot of getting out of here alive. Once you're in the ambulance it won't matter what they realise.'

'And how about Lopez, he'll squeal the moment we get to the entrance,' Soto continued to complain but it had Munroe shaking his head.

'Not if he already thinks you're dead or dying.' Munroe looked over at the closest inmate. 'Get Lopez on his feet and keep him in the common room. We'll come to you.'

The inmates all looked over at Soto and with a nod from him they headed back down the corridor as Munroe closed the door behind them.

'It's my lucky day, huh, Manuel, you slippery piece of shit,' Soto said, pointing the shotgun towards Ortega's head. 'Not so lucky for you though. Wait until the boss hears I cut off the head of Los Zetas.'

Soto was already applying pressure to the trigger when Munroe called over to him. 'Hey, how did you know I was breaking him out?'

Soto turned back and with the one arm supporting the shotgun he used his free hand to pull a mobile out of his pocket. 'I got a call warning me when you arrived.'

'From who?' Munroe asked, feigning a look of complete surprise.

'I have no idea, but they don't like Manuel, that's for sure.'

'Well how about that,' Munroe grunted, and without warning he landed a solid headbutt at the base of Soto's nose. In one fluid movement he grabbed the shotgun and brought his boot down against the back of the man's leg, sending him awkwardly to the floor. Munroe then slammed the butt of the shotgun into Soto's face, dropping him to the floor in a heap. 'OK, Mr Ortega,' Munroe said, leaning down and retrieving the pill from Soto's breast pocket, 'let's do this, shall we?'

Despite a bloody cut on his cheek from where the inmate had punched him, Ortega began to grin and he plucked the pill from Munroe's fingers. 'I could tell you were bullshitting,' the cartel boss said and he kicked Soto hard in the head and then attempted to grab the shotgun but Munroe moved it out of reach.

'That son of a bitch needs to die.'

The venom in Ortega's eyes was unyielding but Munroe pumped out the cartridges one by one and threw the shotgun to the floor. 'Then you'll have to do it another time. The sound of the shotgun will only complicate things with Officer Lopez.'

Ortega considered it and then slowly nodded before sliding his arms around Soto's neck and swivelling his grasp swiftly to one side until the sound of his neck snapping echoed around the room. 'Good advice,' Ortega replied, and he allowed Soto's body to drop to the floor as Munroe stood there motionless, taking a few moments before explaining his plan further. Besides, what could he say to the cartel boss? A snapped neck was, by this killer's standards, a pleasant way to go. 'Now, hopefully with the riot that's going on his colleagues will be too occupied to notice you over my shoulder.'

Ortega looked less than convinced. 'This is dangerous, Mr Munroe.'

Munroe gave a simple nod and passed over the pill. 'Breaking a cartel boss out of jail usually is, but I meant what I said. I'll get you out of here.'

Ortega paused and held the pill to his lips and stared at Munroe menacingly. 'You'd better or you'll find yourself—'

'Yeah, yeah. Flayed alive. I get it,' Munroe said dismissively, tired of the threats. 'Now put the pill in your mouth, crush it up and swallow.'

Ortega stared at him furiously and then a smile crept across his lips. 'I like you, Munroe. I'll see you on the other side.'

With that the Los Zetas boss popped the pill into his mouth and crushed it as he was told to before swallowing.

Munroe instructed him to sit down on one of the plastic chairs.

'It works fast, so sit down. I don't want you collapsing and cracking your head.'

Ortega did as directed, and within thirty seconds his eyes started to flutter. After a minute and a half both shoulders sagged and his body went limp and Munroe slid him onto the floor. He then pressed his two fingers against his neck and waited as he felt the pulse begin to fade. Another few minutes and it would be undetectable altogether. Munroe put his fingers to his ear. 'Did you get all that?'

'We got it,' Sloan replied, her tone sounding formal.

'You've been pretty quiet, Jax. I wasn't sure you were still there.'

'Didn't want to disturb you. And good job. The ambulance is on its way.'

'Roger that,' Munroe replied, and he stepped over Ortega and opened the door. 'Now let's see how well this goes.'

Where the corridor met the common area, Munroe could see the three inmates detaining Officer Lopez and although he looked the worse for wear, his shirt ripped and a few bruises to his cheeks, he was alive.

Munroe shot them a glance and the inmates, without a word, left his side and joined in with the numerous fights playing out over by the jail cells.

'Lopez,' Munroe yelled, and it got the officer's attention. He looked over and immediately stumbled towards Munroe. 'Where the hell have you been?'

'Where do you think, there's a fucking riot going on,' Lopez replied as Munroe opened the door fully and the knelt down over Ortega's body.

'Soto attacked him. I managed to knock him out,' Munroe said, nodding towards Soto's motionless body, 'but I think he's had a heart attack. We need to get him out of here.'

Lopez reached down and touched his fingers to Ortega's neck, withdrawing them with a panicked look. 'He's barely got a pulse.'

'That's why we need to get him out of here, to a hospital,' he pushed, but Lopez was looking unsure and Munroe now grabbed the officer by his ripped lapels. 'I need information from this man. If he dies, so does my lead. Now let's *go!*'

The battering Lopez had received at the hands of the rioters had definitely left the man shaken, perhaps even with a mild concussion, and Munroe released his grip and grasped his shoulder comfortingly. 'Can you imagine what will happen to us if the Los Zetas inmates catch us with their dead boss? It'll make that beating you got look like a love tap.'

The notion of something far worse to come had Lopez nodding and he shook himself out of it as Munroe pointed down at Ortega.

'You carry him, and I'll clear a path for us.'

Lopez offered a shaky nod of his head as Munroe pulled Ortega to his feet, and with Lopez's help slumped him over the officer's shoulder. He then grabbed the shotgun and reloaded the shells he had expelled in front of Soto before heading to the door and opening it a crack.

The corridor was clear, and even though he could see inmates passing back and forth there was no sight of Soto's colleagues. 'OK, here we go. Don't look at anyone directly and if we get attacked just keep moving towards the cell block entrance, I'll take care of it… OK?'

Officer Lopez was now looking relatively composed and he nodded as Munroe opened the door and took the lead. 'Let's go.'

They made their way along the empty corridor with ease, Munroe a few feet ahead of Lopez with the shotgun held firmly against his hip, and as they approached the open gate at the end they came to a stop and surveyed the common room.

The scene was bloody chaos with all the cell blocks having been opened up, and although they were filled with inmates fighting one another, all taking the opportunity to unleash some good old-fashioned gang rivalry, there were around twenty or so in the common room. At the far end, the main exit door was wide open and the bright sunshine outside illuminated the entrance like some golden-gated exit from the hell they were in.

It was only a thirty-metre walk and Munroe began heading toward it, glancing back a few times to see Lopez sticking to him like glue. They had made it about halfway when a group of three inmates, mercilessly beating some unlucky prisoner, paused and all looked over at Munroe in unison. If the situation hadn't been so dire it could have been comical, and as their victim lay groaning on the floor Munroe realised that it was the same three friends of Soto's. They weren't looking at him but at the man draped over Lopez's shoulder.

Munroe offered no expression and just kept moving towards the door as the nearest inmate, obviously recognising that their unconscious passenger wasn't their boss, Soto, yelled at them.

'What the fuck!' he shouted, seemingly oblivious of the shotgun Munroe was pointing at them. 'Where's Soto?'

As the three men surrounded them the gun in Munroe's hands suddenly felt like far more of a hindrance than a help. Sure, he could kill all three of them on the spot, but then what? The noise would most likely have hundreds of prisoners heading towards them to see what was going on, and seeing three prisoners with shotgun blasts to the chest would set them all off. The funny thing about prisoners was many of them would kill each other, given the chance, but offer them a figure of authority such as himself and Lopez and all was forgiven. At least until they were both beaten to death before then resuming their own tribal conflicts, and so with only seven cartridges in the pump-action Munroe opted for the more delicate approach.

His first swing hit the nearest prisoner square in the nose with the gun's butt, and he used the momentum to jam his boot into another's chest, sending him flying backwards to the floor. The double move was swift, but not enough to prepare for the third prisoner's fist that caught Munroe in the jaw, slamming him against the wall as the two men tussled for control of the shotgun. To his credit, Lopez continued moving towards the exit as Munroe thrust the shotgun's metal receiver directly against his attacker's nose, which gave way under the blow, flattening with a squelch as the cartilage crumpled. Munroe then drove his knee into the man's chin with a loud cracking sound, flicking the unconscious man backwards as the second prisoner, recovered from the boot to the chest, tackled him at the waist, sending them both sliding across the floor.

The heavy blow had flung the shotgun from Munroe's grip, sliding it over to the other side of the common room. He leapt back up to his feet, the final prisoner attempting to grapple him as he rose. The loose grip had the man slipping back onto his knees and as Munroe raised his boot, preparing to land a knockout kick, he caught a glance of the shotgun being picked up by a bald-headed inmate with tattoos covering most of his face.

Munroe dropped his boot to the floor and brought his fist down into the kneeling man's cheek, rendering him near unconscious. Pulling him to his feet by the scruff of his collar, he flung the prisoner with all his strength towards the tattooed inmate who was by now raising the barrel of the pump-action in Munroe's direction. The two inmates collided, forcing the pump-action's barrel to one side, but it went off, peppering the concrete wall opposite as Munroe now dashed towards Lopez, who had already reached the open exit. Another shot sprayed the wall just inches behind him, exploding in a cloud of dust, and with only a few metres to daylight Munroe leapt forwards as yet another shot hit the wall close behind him.

Lopez and the limp, snoozing body of Ortega collapsed to the dusty floor outside with Munroe on top of them both, multiple groans issuing from the officer at the bottom of the pile. The sunlight was blinding after the gloom of the cell block and as Lopez began pushing Ortega off of him, Munroe kicked his boot against the metal door, flinging it backwards, hitting something solid, and he heard someone collapse as the top of the bald head of the tattooed inmate suddenly appeared out of the doorway. The head began to move. Munroe jammed his boot into the door once more and it hit with a thud.

'Get up,' Munroe ordered, pulling Lopez to his feet and then helping him pick up Ortega. They steadied themselves as the full scale of the prison riot now became evident.

Part of the yard's fencing had collapsed and all around them hundreds of inmates were fighting in pockets, sending plumes of dust up into the air. At the far end, the prison guards, already clothed in riot gear, were in lines, one row behind the other, guarding the fenced bridge connecting the prison yard to the administration buildings.

'Move,' Munroe shouted over the cacophony of squeals and yelling as some inmates dealt out the pain whilst others received it. 'Quickly.'

With Munroe in the lead again the convoy of three men made their way up towards the gated bridge with little interference, most of the inmates far more interested in each other than the armed guards watching it all take place. With raised hands Munroe approached the gate and allowed Lopez to move to his side, his face not obscured, and as they reached it Munroe felt a wave of relief as he saw Warden Hernandez behind the second row.

'Let them through,' he ordered, and one of the riot guards immediately walked over to the gate, unlocked it and allowed the three of them through before locking it securely once more.

'I warned you, Mr Killean,' Warden Hernandez chastised, his tone unforgiving. 'I've already had to call the nearby military base for additional men.'

Munroe now slid Ortega off Lopez's shoulder and onto his own as Hernandez grasped the unconscious inmate and raised his head for a better look.

'Ortega! Why did you bring him out?'

'He's had a heart attack, sir,' Lopez said, unwittingly cementing Munroe's story. 'We need to get him to a hospital.'

The news had Hernandez turning white and his mouth dropped like a drawbridge. 'Is he dead?'

Munroe shook his head. 'He will be without medical attention. Did the ambulance arrive?'

'That was you? Yes, it's in the car park.'

Munroe was already making his way towards the main buildings with Ortega slumped over his shoulder. 'I called the cell block, because if he dies—'

'If he dies there will be bloodshed on the streets of Mexico, Mr Killean,' Hernandez interrupted, and he grabbed Ortega's other arm and placed his around the unconscious man's neck as both he and Munroe headed towards the car park, leaving Lopez resting against the wall to catch his breath.

'If he dies there could be a lot more than just blood in the streets, Warden,' Munroe replied as up ahead he saw Talon and Barbeau dressed in paramedic uniforms.

'Hey, over here,' Hernandez yelled, and the two medics rushed over and took the motionless body of Ortega and placed it on a gurney before sliding him into the back of the ambulance as Dalton began working on the man. 'Which hospital?' Hernandez yelled after them.

'San Jose,' Talon yelled back and then jumped in the driver's side and the ambulance took off at high speed.

'I'm heading over there as well,' Munroe said, retrieving the car keys from his pocket. 'I need to be there the moment he wakes up.'

'You mean if he wakes up,' Hernandez said, and he wiped the beads of sweat from his brow with his shirt sleeve, leaving a long dark smear along it. 'I'll have a military escort sent over to San Jose immediately while we get all this under control.'

Munroe took a step towards his pick-up and then he paused and turned back to face the warden, who was now staring at him like he was a turd that wouldn't flush. 'I am sorry, Warden. But what you've done here today may end up saving millions of lives, that is if Ortega makes it... Oh, and you should know they have the observation guard's pump-action.'

The extra piece of information had Hernandez expelling a heavy sigh and without another word he headed back to his men and the thunderous sound of yelling and screaming, leaving Munroe alone in the car park. He headed to his truck, unlocked the door and slid into the driver's seat before slamming it shut and lightly pressing his finger to his ear. 'Sloan, did you get all that?'

'I did,' came her single reply and Munroe placed the key into the ignition and started up the engine.

'I'm on my way.'

Chapter 24

To remain within the state of Nuevo León after breaking one of Mexico's most powerful cartel bosses out of its central prison was asking for trouble, but Francisco Estrada had insisted upon it. The meeting point was over a hundred miles south of Apodaca prison, in the desert, but the news of the escape was on every news channel this side of the border.

Munroe drove the white pick-up speedily across the sands of the dust road and towards the cluster of shack buildings a mile in front of them, breaking the landscape like an approaching messenger of doom. In the passenger seat McCitrick sat silently, taking the last few minutes to load the first bullet into the chamber of his 9mm Glock. They would not allow themselves to be patted down this time and the handover would be done at a distance of their choosing, but as McCitrick slid the firearm into his side holster he knew this would only go simply if they did it on their terms. Los Zetas was not known for leaving loose ends and that went for men within their own ranks, never mind a couple of gringos who the entire community of global intelligence agencies were looking for. No, this would not be a simple transfer.

'You do the talking. He likes you,' McCitrick said, receiving a raised eyebrow from Munroe.

'Maybe so, but I've got a bad feeling about this, John. They're not going to let us walk out of here. And God knows who Estrada might have contacted.'

'We know this already,' McCitrick replied flippantly, slipping his Glock into its shoulder holster, 'but our backs are against the wall on this one, Ethan. We've taken all the precautions we can, so now we don't have any a choice but to follow through.'

'Enter the lion's den, as it were,' Munroe stated, his analogy receiving a smile from McCitrick.

'Exactly. We've done it before and, anyway, I may have a last resort still up my sleeve.'

The reply from his boss was more mysterious than Munroe was used to, and he glanced over with a questioning look in his eyes to be met only by a wide smile.

'Just focus on the job at hand, Ethan. It's all going to work out just fine.'

There was genuine confidence in his voice, and although unsure exactly what they were talking about, Munroe turned his attention back to the dusty road before them. He trusted McCitrick enough to take his word for it and besides, knowing one was walking into a trap was half the battle.

'OK, here we go.' Munroe slowed the pick-up to ten miles an hour as they entered the main high street of what had been an old mining town in the late nineteenth century, left to rot in the unforgiving haze of Nuevo León's desert. The wooden buildings were still standing, the craftmanship a testament to their longevity, and although there was not even an electric grid this far out, two yellow generators had been set up at the far end, lighting up their welcome party with dazzling LED bulbs.

'I count fifteen,' McCitrick said as Munroe brought the Jeep to a stop twenty metres from two black Range Rovers parked across the road, and a red Toyota truck with a mounted fifty-calibre machine gun aim directly at their windscreen.

'Twenty-four,' Munroe corrected, nodding to the gunmen on the roofs above them, either side of the street.

'A full deck,' McCitrick replied, and he shot Munroe a confirming glance. With that, both men exited the Jeep and took their positions either side of the bonnet as Francisco Estrada appeared from the Range Rover with a security crew of three.

'Ahh, *bien hecho*,' Estrada called out and although visibly pleased with the outcome there was something about his tone that Munroe couldn't put his finger on. Like a distaste for having to say the actual words of congratulations. 'You did exactly what you said you would do. Now, where is he?'

Estrada craned his neck from side to side trying to get a glimpse of his recently freed boss, but when he could not see him he began to stare at them with suspicion. 'Well?'

'He's safe and ready to be picked up,' Munroe said, and he waved Estrada over to their Jeep, 'so if you'll come over to us we can discuss how this is going to work.'

It was clear that Estrada wasn't keen on their terms. 'Why don't you,' he said, pointing his finger at them, 'come over here.'

'Guns make me nervous, Francisco, and that's a lot of firepower behind you.' Munroe nodded towards the fifty-calibre machine gun. 'Come to us and let's conclude our business.'

The remark had Estrada laughing out loud. 'Guns make you nervous? OK! I'll come to you.'

The Los Zetas lieutenant had only made it a few paces when Munroe raised his hand in the air.

'Not you, boys,' he said to the three armed guards moving with him. 'Just you.'

Estrada thought about it for a moment and then he nodded overdramatically. 'OK, stay here,' he commanded and then walked over the twenty-metre gap to greet them. 'Cautious, I respect that.'

McCitrick pulled out a photograph and passed it over. 'He's nearby.'

Estrada took the polaroid and inspected the picture of Manuel Ortega, awake and wide-eyed, holding a copy of the local newspaper and sitting on a toilet wearing handcuffs.

'You give us the information as agreed and we leave,' Munroe stated, jabbing his finger at the picture. 'You'll get a phone call within ten minutes with the location of Manuel Ortega. He's a bit drowsy, but apart from that he's in fighting shape.'

Not a man to be given orders, Estrada looked less than happy but his expression of dissatisfaction quickly turned into a smile and he nodded his head. 'Very well, but nothing foolish. Just a straight swap. Anything else would not be good for your health.'

'Oh, I can imagine,' Munroe replied, figuring the flaying of his skin would be a mere appetiser to the psychopath. 'We'll keep our side of the bargain.'

Estrada slipped the polaroid into his pocket and rubbed his palms together. 'The Dr Loathlife you seek – I never met him personally. There was always a buffer, a middle man, but you get him and it will lead you to the man… or woman… you so desperately want.'

Munroe silently cursed the additional lead they would have to track. It wasn't what they had agreed, but with the barrel of the fifty-calibre aimed at them it would have to do. 'OK, what's the name.'

'Herman Creasey, based in South Beach, Miami. He's got a small law firm there. Just google it, he hides in plain sight. He may seem low level, but I assure you he's got all the connections as well as a gift for laundering money, that's how we met initially. Then his boss, Dr Loathlife, got in touch through him, which resulted in some large shipment deals.' Estrada shook his head and chuckled. 'Dr Loathlife! If you're going to use an alias then at least make it believable, heh? Anyway, that's your man. Get him and you get what you want.'

Munroe and McCitrick glanced over at each other and then returned Estrada's gaze and nodded. 'OK. Give us ten minutes to check out the information and if its solid then I'll call you with Mr Ortega's location.'

Estrada looked as if he was about to threaten them again but his demeanour relaxed and he nodded in agreement. 'Very well. Our business is concluded.' He began heading back towards his men. 'I have to admit I was doubtful you could pull it off, but he said you would do it.'

The final comment had Munroe stiffening and he called out to Estrada in alarm. 'Who said we could pull it off?'

'Don't worry, it's fine. I got a call from one of Creasey's associates. He knew you'd been sniffing around Los Zetas, so I just said we were providing you with passports and a whole lot of money for you to disappear in exchange for Manuel Ortega.'

The sobering admission made in such a cavalier way had both Munroe and McCitrick momentarily stunned and Estrada raised his hands up pacifyingly. 'I said don't worry, they have no idea why you're really doing it, for the information, and besides, my money is on them killing you before you ever get near them, and we'll be doing business long after you depart this world.'

Estrada kept his raised arms in the air and smiled smugly. 'Business is business.'

Munroe watched as the top half of Estrada's forehead exploded into a bloody pulp, followed by those of his three security guards and the fifty-calibre gunner, who all hit the floor dead at almost the same time, blood gushing from their wounds.

'Sniper,' Munroe yelled as shooters on the roof began letting off rounds indiscriminately into the night, not knowing where the shots were coming from. McCitrick made it to cover behind a building on the left side of the street while Munroe made it to the opposite side as the sound of automatic gunfire shattered the night air from all directions.

Munroe pulled out his Glock and hugged the safety of the building, pressing his finger to his ear. 'I need eyes,' he shouted, and the voice of Zeke Dalton came on the line.

'This is Downtown, I've got multiple incoming.'

'Uptown, I count at least twenty,' Barbeau now cut in as another Los Zetas shooter got clipped and tumbled off the roof, crashing to the ground just in front of the Jeep.

'They're approaching from all sides, and I've got eyes on six, no seven armoured Humvees approaching from the south, east and west,' Dalton confirmed. 'What's the order?'

'Hold fire,' McCitrick ordered over the earpiece as another two roof shooters were fatally hit. 'Downtown and Easttown, can you cut a path for us south-east?'

'Downtown, negative. You've got three Humvees blocking,' Dalton replied as Sloan now added confirmation.

'Easttown, negative. Another two Humvees with turret guns blocking.'

For anyone unfamiliar with the jargon being used it could have sounded like garbled mayhem, but for Munroe it painted a perfect picture of what lay out there in the dark around them. It was basic terminology. Before driving to the meet the others had taken up sniper positions that covered all angles of the deserted town. Uptown was north, Downtown was south and so on, and as Talon now came on the line Munroe realised how bad it was.

'Westtown has eyes on four turreted Humvees, fifty metres to your west, taking up defensive positions.'

They were surrounded, and up ahead as the last two Los Zetas gunmen collapsed to the ground with neat headshots the firing came to an abrupt stop and an eerie silence fell upon the deserted town. Munroe looked across the road at McCitrick, who like him was attempting to formulate a plan when the sharp sound of a loudspeaker's electronic squeak pierced the air and with it a familiar voice calmly called out to them.

'You're surrounded, gentlemen, so I suggest you ask those pesky snipers of yours to take their fingers off the triggers so we can have a little talk.'

The smug voice of Hans Bauer had Munroe's stomach turning and with a nod from McCitrick he pressed his finger to his ear. 'Hold your fire. Repeat, everyone hold fire.'

There was a pause and then Bauer came back on the loudspeaker. 'I can't hear any gun fire so will have to take that as a yes… I knew we'd be seeing you again, Ethan, but I hadn't expected the gang all together in one place.'

Bauer's voice echoed down the street as Dalton came back on the earpiece. 'I've got Bauer, he's hanging out of a Humvee to the north using the vehicles speaker. Do I take the shot?'

'No, everyone stand down. He's playing with us so let's see what his game is,' McCitrick answered as Bauer continued speaking via the Humvee's loudspeaker.

'Your jail break was impressive but also pointless. Money from the cartel? You should know by now there is no escape for any of you. The only place you'll be escaping to is the afterlife, and it won't be me who does it but your own people. The leaders of the free world have a real hard-on for you lot, and disappearing off into the sun with new identities is not going to be possible, I'm afraid.'

The fact that Bauer didn't know that the cartel had given them information on Daedalus was at that moment the only thing they had going for them, and although useless for the time being, it did give Munroe a sliver of hope.

'I want one of your snipers to focus their sights on what I'm holding up. I'm in one of the Humvees to the north, though I wouldn't recommend taking a shot or you will all die here and now, that I promise you.'

Munroe waited in silence. After a few seconds Barbeau came through on the earpiece. 'You are not going to believe this… he's holding what I think is a CIA iden-tification card in the air.'

A few more moments passed and then Bauer came back on the loudspeaker. 'So as you can see my being here is completely legal, and the men who have you surrounded are Blackstar employees. We are here at the direct request of the British, American and French governments.' The arrogance in his voice was so thick you could have cut it with a knife, and Munroe shot McCitrick a murderous glare.

'Oh, how the tables have turned, and although we could end this right here, right now, I want to grant you mercy. The longer you're on the run and a threat to the peace-loving people of this world, the more time I can use to cement the trust I have already gained with your old bosses, so, with that in mind, I am willing to grant you temporary clemency. But it does come at a cost. I need to take one of you into custody as a token of the good work we at Blackstar are doing. Now, I can't guarantee if the chosen one will live or die because your governments have seen fit to put dead, rather than alive, on the wanted poster, which makes things tricky. But it will buy you some time to find a new hiding hole to crawl into, and some time to think about what a mess you've made of things, how I completely screwed you in an operation that you have to admit was far beyond anything you could have conceived, let alone carried out. So, lady and gentlemen, I give you sixty seconds to send out your martyr or you all die. And for all four snipers out there, you should know we already have your positions and you will fall quicker than Ethan and John, who are at this moment cowering behind the two buildings just past their Jeep... So, make your choice, the clock is ticking.'

There was radio silence as Munroe stared over at McCitrick, who was looking blank faced. Again Bauer had played it flawlessly and to Munroe there were only two options left to them.

One, they made this abandoned town their last stand, giving Daedalus the keys to the future of the Fourth

Reich. Or two, one of them offered themselves up for certain death, allowing the others one last chance to reach and take down the Daedalus hierarchy, and possibly clear their names. The latter was a long shot, but at least it was a shot, and with Bauer not knowing that they knew about Herman Creasey it gave them a small but potent edge.

'Forty seconds left,' Bauer informed them with a light chuckle. 'It's now or never.'

'I say we scrap it out,' Sloan said, her voice holding firm. 'Some of us could make it and carry on the fight.'

'No,' Munroe replied, still looking over at McCitrick. 'I'll go. The bastard hates me the most, so why not? Just promise me that whatever happens you take down Daedalus. No matter whether DSV clears their name or not. That's why we're the Disavowed, isn't it? We're expendable, isn't that what you told me once, John? We're the collateral for ensuring the just cause is fulfilled. And stopping the enslavement of the world from a Fourth Reich is the most just cause I can think of. I'll do it.'

'Twenty seconds,' Bauer called out and Munroe raised his hands and prepared to come out.

'You win, Bauer.'

The loud reply had Munroe halting where he was, and he looked over to the other side of the street to see McCitrick appear from the shadows with his hands held up in the air.

'I'm coming out.'

Munroe was shocked as voices of complaints rumbled over the earpiece, but McCitrick silenced them.

'Everyone, shut up. If I was twenty years younger then I would have sent one of you out,' he said with a grin that only Munroe could see, 'but it has to be me, and it's the last resort.'

Munroe looked stunned. 'This was what you had up your sleeve? To give yourself up to these psychopaths!'

'I'm not giving up, Ethan. I'm saving your lives.' McCitrick's face was just visible from the shadows and even though Munroe didn't like it, he understood it. 'And it's not being done in vain. Your final orders are to use any and all intel, equipment and actions to destroy Daedalus and reveal them to the world for what they are. That's your primary goal. Do that and DSV will be cleared as well. Your licence to kill remains active and it's now your decisions and yours alone that will guide you, so do what you must, even if it means being guided by the ends justifying the means, understood? Whatever it takes… good luck to you. I'm proud of you all. You are without a doubt the most capable soldiers I have ever had the fortune to work with. As importantly, you're my friends, so go and do what you swore to do, protect the free world from Nazi infiltration. Use all your abilities and I promise that you will not fail. I have every confidence. I'll keep the earpiece in for as long as I can… Good luck.'

With his hands in the air, McCitrick gave Munroe a stern nod and then he walked out into the middle of the street as Bauer's voice bellowed once again.

'John McCitrick, good job. Walk towards me. Ethan, you may take the Jeep and leave the area. No one will attempt to stop you.'

Munroe holstered his Glock and stepped out onto the street and headed slowly for the vehicle as McCitrick continued towards Estrada's dead body and then beyond, past the Range Rovers, until he disappeared into the darkness. Munroe watched until the last moment and then he pulled open the driver's door and paused as the sound of Bauer's voice once more boomed down the street.

'Nice to see you in the flesh, Ethan, and don't worry about McCitrick. He'll be well taken care of.'

Munroe stared towards the darkness and raised his hand and flipped the bird.

'That's the spirit, Ethan, but I wouldn't waste your time on silly gestures because you've not only got the governments of the free world chasing after you but Los Zetas as well. I'm sure that getting the blame for killing the top lieutenant of Los Zetas and his men will get you no favours from that bunch of sadistic drug peddlers. I suggest you all run as fast as your little legs will carry you, because the chase is on, the bloodhounds have your scent, and they will rip you apart when they catch you. So run, you fools, run.'

Munroe slid into the Jeep and turned the car around before heading back down the dirt road, passing the numerous silhouettes of Humvees and armed men on either side. He pressed his finger to his ear. 'Everybody head back to the rendezvous. We've got work to do. And, John, if you can still hear me… Hang in there, we're coming to get you.'

Chapter 25

'Everyone is seated, Madame Schneider. They are ready to begin.'

Ursula Schneider made a final small change to her speech with the flick of her pen and nodded at the young man in the blue Armani suit, sending him scuttling over to the wall phone and making confirmation.

'We're ready,' he said, before hanging up the receiver and darting back to be at Schneider's side, readjusting his light-blue tie as he did so.

In her late forties, Ursula Schneider was an imposing woman, not because of her physique, which was slim and petite, but due to her presence and steely gaze, which was now focused on the set of light wood doors that had opened up before her. With the elegance and poise of a movie star walking the red carpet, she glided through the doorway and past the rows of seated attendees who stood up and warmly applauded her. With a loving smile she sauntered past them all, offering gentle nods as she went and then, upon reaching the central stage, she rose up the steps and made her way to the wooden podium. Behind her a row of men and women also stood up and clapped politely as she placed her speech on the wooden surface and then grasped either side of the stand lightly.

She continued to offer smiles and nods of gratitude until the applause began to fade, and the attendees all took to their seats and a silence fell upon the large assembly hall, which had every one of its two thousand seats occupied.

Schneider straightened the piece of paper containing her speech, and then held her hands together and began to speak.

'Ladies and gentlemen, leaders of the world,' she glanced back at the row of people behind her, 'members of my government. Thank you all for being in attendance. I would like to begin by making a special thanks to the American president for being here during such a challenging time following the horrific attack on the city of New York.'

Schneider now offered a small bow to the president sitting in the front row, and it was returned in kind. 'We are here today to show our support and send a message to any of those that seek to destroy the peaceful world we have created, that we stand united, shoulder to shoulder, and together we will find and make pay those that are responsible.'

Schneider allowed the gentle applause to subside and then she took in a deep breath and expelled it in a way that had her looking somewhat ashamed. 'When I was elected as German chancellor three years ago it was a proud day for both myself and my administration, but it was accompanied with a deep moment of reflection on the events of the last century that inflamed the world, and the role Germany took in them. The shame of such a destructive time in human history, and the pride of knowing every aspect of it has been stamped out by future generations, bringing us to the point we are at now. I am proud to say that Germany and its citizens have evolved into a country that has played its part, along with other great nations, in bringing Europe together and binding it in friendship and the common goals that the EU stands for. It is not perfect, I believe we can all attest to that, but I believe it is the foundation of a long-lasting peace that will continue to evolve with the generations that come after us.'

Chancellor Schneider looked down at the podium for a few moments, her hands still clasped together, and then she looked up across the thousands of people watching her and she smiled. 'It has always brought comfort to know that out of something so horrific as the Second World War has evolved a general world peace, with technology that binds us ever closer, and it is with this in mind that I offer you my humble proposal that has brought you all here today. For like the phoenix that arose from the ashes of war, creating a new world order of peace and civility, I hope that the terrible destruction in New York may bring about a new rising star that will shine upon every nation, and every one of the seven billion people that call Earth their home.'

There was a light applause, which only intensified once the American president added to the clapping, and Schneider stood there and took a moment to clap as well before continuing.

'It was here in Geneva that the first world organisation was formed, with the central mission of laying the foundation for a truly interconnected world. As you know its name was the League of Nations, and as you also know it failed because it had no army to ensure peace. So it evolved, and in this very room the first meeting of the United Nations took place.' Schneider now held her hand back to the large gold United Nations symbol on the wall behind her. 'And it too has evolved, not only bringing together one hundred and ninety-three countries under the banner of respect, peace and cooperation, but with a unified army to ensure peace around the globe... But this too has not been without its difficulties. And so I suggest that at the dawn of nuclear terrorism, which we have staved off for so long, we now should see this peaceful organisation evolve once more and this time into the guiding light it was always meant to be. An organisation with not only a new army, but a new political structure that represents all its nations and their collective wishes equally. An organisation that respects and preserves individual cultures and diversity but also binds us together in a new society of minds, because after all is said and done, do we not all share the same goals? To see our families thrive, to live a peaceful life where opportunity is for all, and hopes and dreams can become reality for all the children who dream them.'

Out among the delegates there was silence. It wasn't the silence of difference but more of curiosity at a plan so bold. A collective yearning for the possibility, if only they could be convinced of turning it into a reality, and with this rapt atmosphere Schneider continued to persuade them.

'With the recent breakthroughs in practical nuclear fusion happening around the world, is it not time we invested in and supported these technologies with national funds, the likes of which were seen at the dawn of the industrial revolution? Ladies and gentlemen, science fiction is quickly becoming science fact. We are at the precipice of a world with free, almost unlimited, clean energy. Could this not be one of the cornerstones of a new evolving global organisation to build upon what the League of Nations and then the United Nations have already achieved, finally creating the global, interconnected world we all wish for?'

Chancellor Schneider placed her hands on either side of the podium. 'I want to be blunt and honest with everyone here. It won't be easy to begin with, there are many hurdles to overcome, many old grudges to reconcile, but then nothing good has every come easily. We could lay the foundations of what in a few generations could truly evolve into world peace, a unity of humanity that has only ever been dreamt about, never achieved. All I suggest, all I ask, is that we begin this very day in setting about the talks, the conversations that will bring about the action to see if such a new organisation can succeed, and just as the modern age was born from the darkness of the Second World War, so a new, peaceful and enlightened age may emerge out of the utter destruction that has fallen upon New York City. And if we can achieve what so many have attempted before us, can we not say that we were truly worthy of our positions, and that we have transcended the petty human traits that have always held us back from becoming a united world?'

Chancellor Schneider stood back from the podium looking strong, confident yet humble, and faced the two thousand faces all looking up at her in silence. She waited, the lack of a response not affecting her demeanour, for what seemed like an age and just as she was about to approach the podium again and thank everyone for their time, a single person began to clap. She looked down to the front row to see the US president offering his applause and then quickly the appreciation began to grow as more delegates joined in. Within a few more seconds the entire assembly hall was alive with the sounds of clapping. It wasn't a standing ovation, but it was loud and inclusive, a solid starting point, and she approached the lectern and began clapping herself. This amount of support could mean they had a real shot at beginning the conversation, and as the applause continued she looked out across the assembly hall and wondered, taking a mental snapshot of the scene.

Could this be the moment in history where it all began? The true beginning of a new world?

Chapter 26

Herman Creasey downed the double measure of tequila and then slammed his shot glass onto the wooden bar top with a grimace. 'And another.'

The barman stopped restocking the shelves with alcopops and grasped the golden bottle of San Jose before pouring another double from high above the glass, not spilling a drop. Creasey slid a ten dollar note across the counter, which was snatched up and swiftly deposited in the till, the sound of a ringing bell confirming the sale as Creasey picked up the shot and turned to face the commotion with his back leaning against the bar. Dozens of people were dancing on the outdoor dance floor and some more than others were getting their groove on and grinding to the Latino beat.

Ahh, there was nothing like Miami South Beach on a beautiful clear night and he loved nothing more than trawling the clubs until he got lucky.

Creasey sipped the tequila this time and allowed his inhibitions to desert him as his hips began to wobble left and right. At forty-two years old, balding and with a weight that 'technically' was labelled obese, he rocked back and forth with his rolls of fat jigging up and down rhythmically. He knew he wasn't much to look at, but with the money to impress he managed to attract surprisingly good-looking women, and across the dance floor a curvy young Latino girl caught his eye, wearing a tight red miniskirt and a pink backless crop top.

Creasey continued to stare, coolly nodding his head from side to side and then for an instant the girl looked over at him before quickly turning away, her long black hair flicking over her shoulder. He downed the rest of his tequila, slamming the glass on the bar top, and wiggling his whole body like a plate of jelly in time with the speakers pumping 'Rhythm is Gonna Get You' by Gloria Estefan, he gently pelvic-thrusted his way across the dance floor.

His target still had her back to him and as he jerked the last few metres her friends noticed him with a look of alarm, which in his drunken state he mistook for approval.

Yeah, baby, I'm unstoppable.

Creasey stopped the pelvic thrusts and now just stood gyrating, eyeing the back of the girl's head as one of her friends motioned to the overweight bald guy who appeared to be in the throes of an orgasm, his eyes fluttering wildly, and so the girl now turned around and gave an obligatory smile.

'Hey, baby,' Creasey slurred, and he held his fingers like guns and pointed them towards her whilst rotating them clockwise in time with the beat. 'Is the rhythm gonna get you? Because if not, perhaps I can get *you a* drink?'

The girl stifled a smirk as her friends began to giggle behind her and she raised her glass. 'I've got one, thanks.'

Creasey continued to rotate his gun fingers campily and he glanced down at his chest. 'It may not look like it, but I've got it going on.'

The girl lowered her glass and winced. 'Oh yeah, and what's that… a heart condition?'

Her friends all laughed out loud, but to Creasey's credit his 'attempt' at a cool exterior never faltered, and he instead began to pelvic thrust backwards, his gun fingers still doing their thing, and melted away into the dancing crowd as quickly as he had appeared.

He was still committed to his seizure-like shuffle when someone bumped into him from behind and he felt a hand slip into his trouser pocket and slide out with his wallet. Creasey dropped the act and spun around to catch a glimpse of a red-headed woman in a white dress just ahead of him, making her way to the bar's entrance, and he immediately gave chase.

Pushing past the mass of customers, he made it out onto the sidewalk of Ocean Drive and scanned the beach on the other side before looking over to his left and catching the redhead further up the road.

Creasey took after her as best he could, and as the woman glanced back at him and saw him in pursuit she upped her pace to a gentle jog and disappeared around the corner. By the time he reached it, he came to a juddering halt as he saw the woman now leaning against a lamppost next to a black transit van with tinted windows.

The set-up was obvious and as she gave him a little wave and held his wallet out in her hand, Creasey took a step backwards and pulled his phone from his pocket. He managed to dial in 9-1-1 before he felt a sharp pain in his neck and a pair of strong hands grabbed him, either side of his arms. The two men behind him were wearing black balaclavas and as he struggled to free himself a piece of duct tape was slapped over his mouth and his wrists were forced behind him and bound by a zip tie.

With muffled screams Creasey was dragged roughly towards the transit van as the redhead was tossed a small roll of notes and she began walking away. The transit van's side door slid open and he was greeted by another balaclava-clad man before being tossed inside.

The other two men joined him and with the door now shut the engine started up. As the vehicle began to pull away, Creasey could feel his senses begin to dull as the heavy curtain of sleep was draped over his entire body.

Above him one of the men pulled off his balaclava and a pair of brown piercing eyes stared down at him, the man's black hair sagging to one side with the weight of sweat.

'We need to have a talk with you,' the man said, tapping his gloved finger against Creasey's forehead. 'So, go to sleep, Mr Creasey, and we will see you later.'

—

The sound of thrashing water woke Creasey from his slumber and he forced open his eyes and groggily looked down at the set of gnashing white teeth as they slammed shut inches from his face. He jerked his head backwards as foamy dark-brown water splashed across his cheeks.

'What the fuck!' he shouted, his throat dry and his voice raspy as his blurred vision focused upon the shiny white row of teeth that again snapped shut mere inches from his nose. 'Get me out of here, please.'

The sound of laughter filled the air as Creasey now made out the thing beneath him and he felt a warm sensation spread around his groin as he pissed himself.

He was in a shack or a boathouse, with wooden walkways running around its edges creating a rectangular opening to the dirty brown water below, and two pairs of eyes poked up above its surface surrounded by swirls of foam. Creasey had been strapped with duct tape to an old armchair and, with leather gloves on his hands, a man was tipping him towards the water. As the set of jaws broke the water's surface again, the hard tip of its nose bumped against his, sending him into a panic as he struggled against his bindings.

Below him the two crocodiles settled back in the water as the armchair was pulled upright again and the man took a few steps along the walkway until he was face to face with Creasey, noting the wet patch that had appeared around his groin.

'Somebody's had an accident,' the man said, amused.

'What do you expect,' Creasey replied, his attention fixed on the dark green, plate-armoured animals below him, 'those are the biggest fucking alligators I've ever seen.'

The man wagged his finger in the air. 'They're not alligators, they're crocodiles. Crocodiles are far more aggressive. They should rip you apart in minutes, porkchop.'

Creasey was already shaking his head from side to side. 'Enough of the scare tactics. Who are you?'

The man slowly removed his black leather gloves and slapped them both against his palm before placing them on a piece of wood jutting out from the side of the shack's wall. 'My name is Ethan Munroe. You may or may not have heard of me, but suffice to say we know you and we need to know some things, Herman, some very secret things. Daedalus things.'

A smile of realisation quickly spread across Creasey's lips and he chuckled. 'DSV. Rogue agents. Nuclear terrorists. I never expected to see you.' He looked up at Dalton and Barbeau, who were holding his chair, and his smile grew even bigger, his eyes tightening as he attempted to recall the faces above him. 'Zeke Dalton and

Jean Barbeau, we know you all well. And where is John McCitrick? Skulking back there in the shadows no doubt.'

'I'm afraid not. We left him out of the loop for this one.'

Munroe was counting on the Daedalus agent not knowing yet that McCitrick was as of that moment at the mercy of Hans Bauer and his reply confirmed it.

'That is a shame, I would have liked to have seen his face one last time before your own people take you down. It must be eating you up inside to know that every intelligence agency in the West is after you, with us in the driving seat.'

Creasey obviously knew what they had only just learnt – that Bauer was working with the government. 'Perturbing to say the least.'

'Perturbing! That's an understatement,' Creasey said with a bellowing laugh. 'The very people DSV was set up to contain are taking you down on behalf of your own governments. You have to admit, it is a stroke of sheer genius. The knives are out for you, boys, and it's just a matter of time before you all get sliced and diced. You can't run forever.'

Munroe was in no mood for the arrogant attitude and he quickly moved on to the reason they were here. 'The knives are out indeed. I like the way you think, Mr Creasey. Tell me, how do your legs feel?'

The question had Creasey's smug expression evaporate and he now looked down at his bound body and something suddenly occurred to him. He attempted to struggle against the silver duct tape holding his arms and legs to the armchair, but apart from his large belly wobbling a bit nothing moved. 'What have you done? Why can't I feel my limbs?'

Munroe took a step closer and folded his arms. 'We took the liberty of giving you a few local anaesthetics, in the right areas. It'll wear off in an hour or so, but it should give us more than enough time.'

A look of apprehension crept across Creasey's face, but it was quickly replaced with a knowing smile. 'Firstly, DSV would never condone torture. Of course you're all capable of such an act but you're recruited for your high morals and you would never stoop so low. You forget, Mr Munroe, we know far more about your little troop, in part thanks to Colonel Sinclair's infiltration, than you know about us. Torture isn't what you do. Secondly, if you want to cause pain then it helps if the victim can actually feel it, and besides,' Creasey's eyes rolled, completely disbelieving of what was being threatened, 'I thought you were going to feed me to the reptiles over there?'

Munroe continued to stare at the smug man and then he clicked his fingers and Dalton and Barbeau picked up the armchair and walked it back through the open doorway behind them. The room was dark and as they dropped the armchair down onto the floor with a thud, Munroe appeared at the doorway and flicked the switch next to him.

A single lightbulb above them, stained brown, lit up the room in nothing more than a gloomy haze but it was enough for Creasey to see the shelves on the wall opposite and more importantly what was on them. As he nervously scanned over the numerous instruments his gaze came to a stop on the glinting steel machete that was resting against a small yellow chainsaw, and Creasey looked up at Munroe and rolled his eyes again sarcastically, but Munroe raised his finger briefly to his lips.

'*Firstly*, Mr Creasey, thanks to Daedalus we no longer work for our respective governments and as such our capabilities have changed. DSV and our boss McCitrick could and would never condone torture, which is why he's not here. Truth is he doesn't even know where we are at the moment, let alone what we're about to do. Secondly,' Munroe continued, walking over to the nearest shelf, from which he picked up the chainsaw and ran his finger across the rugged blade, 'you can't feel your extremities because I want you to talk and not die from the pain I am about to inflict. And, thirdly, we don't plan to feed you to the crocodiles… only parts of you.'

Munroe rested the chainsaw against his gloved hand. 'I'm not a fan of chainsaws, personally. You always get pieces of meat all over your clothes, but I need to make it quick and not have you bleed to death. Mr Dalton, would you ready the tourniquets, please?'

With a nod Dalton slipped a thick zip tie just above Creasey's kneecap and tightened it, the plastic cord digging deep into his trousers, and it was now that the Daedalus agent began to look nervous.

'Look, whatever it is you want, I'm sure we can come to some arrangement.'

'Well that's good. Because we want to know just two things. Who is the head of Daedalus, and where are you supposed to be meeting him and his cronies, and before you say they're not meeting together, don't. Hans Bauer already told us they are, so don't waste my time, and we know you're invited. We were surprised to discover you are much higher up the totem pole than we had previously thought, and the key finance man for Daedalus. It's an important position.'

Some of the intel was just educated guessing, but Bauer's one weakness was his narcissism and Munroe had believed him completely when he said that Daedalus would be meeting up. The question was where and when, and judging by Herman's expression he had hit the nail on the head.

Creasey's eyes widened and although he was now sweating heavily he shook his head slightly with gritted teeth. 'I'm not telling you a thing, and anyway, I don't believe you. This is scare tactics 101, that's all, and you've failed… miserably.'

In response, Barbeau tossed over a plastic face mask, which Munroe slipped on with one hand as the others now took a step backwards and also slid their own masks on.

'Wrong answer, Mr Creasey.'

Munroe grabbed the plastic pull handle and firmly tugged it towards him as the blades of the chainsaw began to spin, the high-pitched buzz of the engine filling the room. He then held it in front of him and revved the throttle, sending a flurry of black smoke from the side exhaust and began to lower the blade towards Creasey's leg, just below the kneecap.

It wasn't until the blade was within a millimetre of his leg and the blades already catching the fluff of his trousers that Creasey began to yell. 'I don't know anything.'

Munroe shot him a look and then, with a nod, he drove the chainsaw downwards into Creasey's leg as blood spurted onto his face mask and the man began to scream. The high-pitched whine lowered as it sawed through solid bone and then resumed its pitch as it passed through and sliced the soft muscle on the other side, sending blood and flesh cascading to the floor.

Munroe pulled back the chainsaw and placed it on the ground next to him, the motor humming away, and then picked up the detached limb and headed back to the shack. He glanced back as Dalton applied another tourniquet to Creasey's other leg, and threw the bloody piece of meat into the water.

'He did warn you,' Dalton said blankly. Creasey's screams descended into near sobbing as he looked down at the bloody stump. 'Just be glad you can't feel it.'

Munroe now walked back over and wiped the blood from his visor with a rag as Creasey yelled at him, spittle hurtling from his lips.

'You fucking bastard. Animal. I hope I get to see them kill the fucking lot of you.'

'Again, wrong answer,' Munroe replied and he picked up the chainsaw and before Creasey could even plead for mercy he throttled up and sawed through his other leg, again just below the kneecap, spewing more blood in a plume of mist into the air and sending the limb to the floor with a thud.

'Jesus Christ,' Creasey wailed as Munroe picked up the booted foot and this time threw it into the water from where he was standing before turning back. Dalton now placed a tourniquet around Creasey's right arm, just above the elbow.

Blood was absolutely everywhere. Creasey, who was now outwardly sobbing, tears streaming down his cheeks, began begging even before Dalton had secured the zip tie around his arm.

'I'll tell you everything. Please, no more.'

Munroe paused, and he looked at Dalton, who nodded. 'He's had enough, Ethan. But it's up to you. We're with you either way.'

With a nod he placed the chainsaw back on the floor and cut the engine. He then slid off his face protector and knelt down before leaning in closely to Creasey. 'You killed thousands in that nuclear blast, you son of a bitch. How many women, children, families, all gone in the blink of an eye, and for what? So you pricks can play being the master race.'

Munroe looked furious and now Creasey nodded, his face covered in blood spatter. 'We should have turned to these kinds of methods a long time ago, Herman. Fight fire with fire, an eye for an eye, because if we had then maybe all those people in New York would still be alive… Now, who runs Daedalus? Who is Dr Loathlife?'

'Reichführer Bormann, the son of Martin Bormann.' Creasey actually seemed happy to be given the opportunity to tell Munroe. 'He's been the head of Daedalus since the sixties and he controls the Families of the Three.'

'Families of the Three?' Barbeau asked, also slipping off his mask and kneeling down next to the man.

'The bloodlines of the founding fathers: Bormann, Muller and… the Führer Adolf Hitler.'

'Wait, Herman, Hitler didn't have any children.'

Creasey was now looking pale and both Dalton and Barbeau set to work in stopping the bleeding as he continued. 'Yes, he did, but they were pushed out of the top position and the reichführer took command, but they are still on the council.'

And just like that a huge piece of the puzzle dropped into place, and as Creasey appeared to weaken, Munroe pushed for the location and time of Daedalus's meeting place.

'Tell me where they are meeting and I promise you'll live.'

'They have a chalet in the Keys, in Key West. 1604 Longshore Street, just off Duval. They'll be there over the next couple of days to celebrate and strategise for the future.'

'Thank you, Herman. Now it's time for you to go to sleep,' Munroe said. Dalton stuck a syringe into the man's neck and his eyes fluttered and then he was out, his body totally limp.

Barbeau now stopped dressing the bloody stump and they all stood back up as Dalton released a large sigh of relief. 'We did it. Nice job, Ethan.'

'Thanks. Same to you, boys.' He turned to the far door and called out, 'Sloan, Talon. It's over.'

The door opened and both Sloan and Talon entered the room, surveying the bloody aftermath of what had just taken place.

'Jesus, lads, don't expect me to clean up,' Sloan said, wrinkling her nose at the sight but Munroe ignored the quip and instead motioned to Dalton.

'OK, let's get him out of here.'

Dalton nodded and then he reached down and pressed a release button which unclicked the base of the sofa, and it fell open to reveal Creasey's two real legs, which had been placed through holes in the armchair's seat. The false legs had then been glued on, just below his knees.

'What the hell did you use, Jean?' Sloan asked and Barbeau gave a smirk. 'Pigs' legs, which I wrapped in a pork joint and glued to his shoes. Looked good, no?'

'You're not kidding, it felt as if I was doing it for real,' Munroe said as Dalton and Talon pulled Creasy out of the sofa.

'Too much blood though, Jean. What is that stuff?' Dalton asked as they placed the sedated Creasey in a wheelchair that Sloan had brought over to them.

'Just corn syrup and dye,' the Frenchman replied, almost taking offence at the observation. 'You said you wanted dramatic, and I gave you dramatic.'

'It was perfect,' Munroe said with appreciation, and they all now stood over the sleeping Herman Creasey.

'When he realises he got duped he is going to be pissed,' Talon said, but Barbeau was already shaking his head.

'When he wakes up back at his apartment with both his legs he'll be ecstatic, trust me.'

The comment had all five of them nodding in agreement before Munroe slapped his hands together. 'Now, let's get a shower and then we go and get McCitrick back,' he said, heading towards the door as Sloan began pushing Creasey's wheelchair after him and he raised his finger in the air. 'C'mon, lads, we've got a party to crash and we don't want to be late.'

Chapter 27

The blazing sun was coming to a rest over the island town of Key West as on the pier groups of people gathered to watch the sunset disappear beneath the clear blue ocean. Further inland, the shops on Duval Street were already flipping the closed signs in their windows, and the restaurants and bars prepared for the usual busy trade the hot night would bring.

With forty-two bridges crossing four separate water masses, including the Atlantic Ocean and the Gulf of Mexico, the overseas highway, or Route 1 as it was officially known, linked the islands of the Florida Keys with a one-hundred-and-thirteen-mile stretch of road between Miami and the city of Key West at the United States' southernmost tip. With views and weather matching any of the classic pirate tales of old, the city had long since been a beautiful hideaway for those that knew about it. It had gained a notoriety during the nineties when the AIDS epidemic was at its height, and with no cure on the horizon many ill people had travelled to spend their last days in as much comfort as possible. Such was the allure that the writer Ernest Hemingway had settled here, and still to this day his house remained preserved, owned by the unique five-toed cats he had left it to in his last will and testament. It was from inside the writer's famous haunt, Sloppy Joe's Bar, that Munroe sat quietly and watched his mark from the table in the darkest corner of the room as he took another sip of his drink. Sloan ran facial recognition on the picture he had taken of the woman earlier, revealing her as Miss Brianna Bauer. Aside from the name there were a number of notable facial features she shared with her brother. Munroe had watched her leave the address provided by Creasey, and with the others watching over the residence he had opted to follow her and see where she went. The endeavour had proved fruitless, though, and apart from being in the top echelons of a future Fourth Reich she appeared to enjoy the same pleasures as anyone else.

As Munroe watched her sip down her second strawberry daiquiri he couldn't help but think how truly twisted people could look so normal on the outside. He could imagine, without too much difficulty, Hans Bauer and his sister drinking the blood of dying babies for fun, or any other depraved act the imagination could conjure. But when they were observed just doing what they did in everyday life they appeared as normal and insignificant as any other person on the planet. After receiving a call on her mobile she drained her drink and slipped on a pair of black Gucci sunglasses. She then plucked her Louis Vuitton handbag off the seat next to her and walked out of the bar, heading up Duval Street with Munroe shadowing her.

'We're heading in your direction,' Munroe said, keeping his distance as Miss Bauer trundled along the sidewalk with self-entitled poise.

'I've got her,' Sloan confirmed, and Munroe looked over the street to see his teammate wearing a navy baseball cap, sleeveless grey tank top and tanned cargo pants hanging around a trinket stall, 'and we have movement outside the residence.'

Munroe watched as Miss Bauer turned off Duval Street and headed down to a crossroads where, after a few more course changes, she reached a white-front beach house with a security guard in green khakis and a blue aertex shirt protecting it. With a nod she headed inside as a black Porsche Cayenne SUV drove towards them and pulled up outside.

'This might be it,' Munroe whispered, and he watched as the grey-suited driver got out and opened the back passenger door and pulled out a man who was still dressed in the same clothes he had been wearing the last time they had seen him.

'I've got eyes on McCitrick,' Munroe said as John McCitrick, looking none the worse for wear, was frog-marched up the small path and inside the beach house.

'Waiting for orders,' Dalton's voice crackled over Munroe's earpiece and he waited for a few seconds and then replied with one word.

'Execute.'

Apart for the two security guards out front the road was empty, with most tourists and a few residents out on the docks enjoying the beautiful sunset. From the far end, Dalton appeared in shorts and a sweatshirt. He was jogging at a slow pace as Barbeau appeared around the opposite corner, both men making their way towards the beach house.

Barbeau was walking and as the beach house was closer to him they reached it at the same time. Dalton tripped to the floor, getting the guard's attention, and at the same moment Barbeau grabbed the man around the throat and squeezed as Dalton leapt up and grabbed the guard's hands, which were already reaching for the gun in his side holster.

Within ten seconds the guard was out, and both men picked up the body and placed it underneath the sprawl of bushy hedges running along the property's dividing fence just off from the path. They then headed to the opposite side of the building and waited as Munroe and Sloan briskly approached the beach house and made their way up the path.

When Herman Creasey had said that security would be at a minimum he wasn't kidding, and in the three hours they had been surveying the property they had only counted one guard at the front entrance and no surveillance cameras on the property. Daedalus felt comfortable here, and that was just fine with Munroe. The 'master race' in their natural habitat.

Sloan moved to the left side of the door and with Munroe taking the right they pulled out their Walther PPKs and swiftly screwed on the silencers. Sloan then grasped the door handle and with a nod she opened it, allowing Munroe to enter, with her bringing up the rear.

The air was cool inside, and the hum of the air conditioner overhead muffled the voices coming from above them on the first floor. The interior was open-plan with white walls and grey, marbled tiles covering the hallway. A few seaside paintings with gold-painted wooden frames hung from the walls. Straight ahead was a single staircase where the tiles met green carpet, glossed wooden bannisters running its length. On the left sat a lounge area with a TV and couch and on the right stood an office, each room door-less, opening the front of the house into one large room.

Munroe was already approaching the staircase when he heard the sound of footsteps above and he manoeuvred to the left as Sloan went to the right, both concealing themselves behind opposite walls.

'Possible exiting of new arrivals,' Munroe uttered in nothing more than a whisper as just one of the security guards who had delivered McCitrick strolled down the stairs and then exited by the front door. Munroe now moved back to the hallway and watched as Dalton and Barbeau grabbed him from behind in a neck lock, rendering the man unconscious within seconds.

Munroe now headed to the stairs with Sloan close behind him, as the guard on the front lawn was dragged towards the same bushy hedge line as before and quickly dumped out of sight.

At the stairs Munroe came to a stop were the white wooden steps ascended upwards with no carpet covering, and so he gently manoeuvred upwards placing his boots at either side of the boarding in an effort not to have any creak under his weight. Sloan followed in kind and as they approached the landing above, the sound of mumbled conversation could be heard being carried down the corridor to where they were positioned.

They both paused for a moment to gauge their surroundings, and as Munroe scoped out the landing of the first floor he was surprised at the lack of pretentious flaunting of their wealth. It appeared to be just a nice beachside property that fit in with the neighbourhood, but isn't that exactly what one would want from a safe house and meeting point? Nothing that would draw attention.

Munroe pointed to the only closed door on the landing, from where the sounds of conversation were coming, and Sloan took point with him in tow, both staying low, their firearms at the ready.

About halfway down the landing Sloan motioned to the room next to the closed door and Munroe automatically followed her inside to a room with a central dining table and chairs. Apart from these furnishings it appeared unused and empty of any decorations. Whoever owned this house, it seemed rarely occupied.

The voices were now clear as crystal and Munroe noted an opening in the wall, a hatchway with bottles placed along its frame allowing for drinks to be passed through from one room to the next.

Munroe and Sloan now moved either side of it and peered inside to see ten people sat on sofas and chairs, all focused on an old man sitting behind a sturdy-looking mahogany desk. The right wall Munroe could see held Perspex display cases with a custom 1851 Navy revolver, a lacquered case next to it holding six brass shells, and further along hung the American flag, the stars and stripes encased in a glass display with the German flag next to it. Behind the desk two single wall-length windows looked out onto the nearby shipping docks and, beyond, the clear blue sea stretched out all the way to the horizon.

They watched through the gaps between the bottles and listened as the old man continued his address to the small group of people before him, including Brianna Bauer who was sat at the end of a green leather sofa that was positioned furthest from a wooden bar counter attached to the opposite side of the wall and filled with a good collection of fine spirits, few of which Munroe recognised.

'And so it goes without saying that some of you are feeling sidelined but I hope after today we can all come together and celebrate in what we have all managed to achieve. Never in the seventy years of our undertaking have all the pieces been so perfectly aligned. In all that time we have never been so well positioned to accomplish our goals and before I go any further I want to explain exactly what has been going on and why it was kept from you. I can put it into a few simple words: accountability and deniability. This applies to some more than others. But before we get to that I want to tell you a story, a true story, which began when you all nominated me to take my place as reichführer ten years ago.'

Reichführer Bormann slowly got to his feet and stood before them as he folded his arms and gazed down sternly at his seated audience. 'I had wanted to wait until our friend Mr Gasparyan could join us. He has been instrumental in our work but as usual he is running late so I will have him explain his part when he arrives.'

Bormann surveyed the attendees like a high-school lecturer and once satisfied all the attention was fully on him he began. 'For too long we have played a game of cat and mouse with the governments of the world and their unelected guardians the Disavowed, or DSV as they call themselves. They have been a thorn in our side for far too long, and like a game of tic-tac-toe there has never been a winner, only stalemate after stalemate. It is this that has seen us all grow old, with no end in sight for the roles we were born to inherit, and I decided this could go on no longer.'

Bormann pointed over to the Perspex case holding the Navy revolver and he grunted. 'Ideas are no different than technology. If they cease to evolve they become redundant and our plans and ideals are no different. It is with this in mind that I, your reichführer, decided to act and evolve the rules of the game so we may realise what our founding fathers set in stone, but failed to accomplish, with a thousand-year Reich. A glorious age where the world is guided by the rules of nature. Where only the strong survive and flourish and the weak and undesirable are made to serve or perish. The Nazi Reich came so close to realising that dream—' Bormann held up his thumb and forefinger just a few millimetres apart and his nose wrinkled in frustration at the lost opportunity '—and it is *I* that have now ensured that this dream is realised.'

Bormann had a look of confidence and supreme authority, and he held his chin up slightly as he revealed the truth.

'It was we who were responsible for the nuclear detonation in New York.'

Until that moment, Munroe had assumed that the actions of Daedalus had always been a collective decision, but as he listened it became obvious that this group, just like the Nazis before them, were nothing but a dictatorship. One person's desires to be carried out, no matter the cost, and as he watched the others looking horrified, Munroe's focus rested solely on Bormann, the true drive behind everything that had happened.

'Why?' one of people exclaimed, as others shook their heads, and they were all met with a look of sheer contempt from Bormann.

'So many of you have become weak and corrupted by your lavish lifestyles and the money that affords it. Your will has faltered over the decades as you have surrounded yourselves with sycophants and expensive things. You all disgust me, and if our fathers could see what has become of you all they would only find relief in the knowledge that I am in control, and now let me tell you why.'

A familiar voice now rose above Bormann's and Munroe slowly shifted his position to see Hans Bauer standing up from his seat and taking a few steps towards the old man.

'Our reichführer has plans to have us all murdered,' Bauer said, turning to face the small crowd of people, 'and he tasked me with the job.'

The accusation had Bormann looking shell-shocked, as if he'd been struck in the face with a brick, and his mouth dropped open as Bauer continued in a menacing tone.

'I thought it prudent to wait until this meeting so I would have the opportunity to address you all in person.'

'Hans, what are you doing?' Bormann yelled, and Bauer strode over and punched the old man in the face, sending him back into his seat with a heavy thud. As the reichführer yelled in pain, cradling his nose, another man came into view wearing what could only be described as a butler's tuxedo and holding two black plastic zip ties in his hand.

'Mr Teston, if you would be so good as to bind and gag this treacherous old fool, please.'

Teston gave a polite nod and then slipped the restraints around the old man's wrists, binding him to the chair he was sitting in and then tightening them as hard as he could.

As Bormann began to yell at him in rage, blood dripping down his broken nose, Teston produced a red piece of cloth and proceeded to gag the old man roughly before standing back and eyeing their leader with disgust.

Some of the audience were now getting to their feet in anger but Bauer raised his hands and appealed for calm as Teston stood by the still huffing Bormann and folded his arms respectfully.

'My brothers and sisters, please allow me to explain, and if I do not have your support afterwards I will give myself up and let you do with me as you will, but there is much more going on here than you could imagine, and I must share it with you.'

Bauer clicked his fingers and there was a sound of shuffling as the landing door opened, and footsteps could be heard heading off to one of the other rooms. A few moments later they returned and Munroe watched as John McCitrick was hauled into the room, his hands now bound behind his back, a section of black tape covering his mouth.

'Allow me to introduce someone you have only seen in photographs. One of the heads of DSV, and the reason I have been able to turn to our advantage the absolute mess Reichführer Bormann has made.'

The plea was made with such humble emotion, an Oscar-worthy performance, because anyone who knew Bauer also knew the man didn't have a humble bone in his body. Munroe glanced over at Sloan as she goaded him to make a move, but instead he raised his hand. He wanted to know exactly what was going on before charging in.

From the chair Bormann was now furiously screaming behind his gag and Bauer took a moment to deliver a hard punch to the old man's jaw, knocking him out in one blow. 'Shut up, you treacherous wretch.'

Strangely the crowd showed no emotion to the punch and they remained seated and quiet as Bauer now addressed them in the most courteous and respectful way imaginable.

'Our great leader has lost faith in all of us for some time, I'm afraid. You heard the disgust he has for us from his very lips. And it is true he wanted me to murder you all this very day for, as he sees it, our unified failing of character. He confided in me that he wished for Daedalus to start afresh, but this time bound by only two families. His, the bloodline of Martin Bormann, and mine, of Reinhard Heydrich. His wish was to consolidate all our wealth and power under one roof.'

Bauer looked to his sister and raised his hand towards her. 'I am sorry I did not tell you, sister, but I feared for your safety.'

Brianna Bauer appeared dismayed and she looked out over the others with an expression of anger. 'You should have told us what was going on, Hans. If we do not have each other's trust then we have nothing. We have all the bloodlines here.' Miss Bauer now began pointing to the various couples around the room. 'The bloodlines of so many great leaders, and even the führer himself.'

Both Munroe and Sloan eagerly tried to see who she was pointing to, but it was impossible from their position, so instead they glanced over at one another and then returned their attention to Miss Bauer, who was still looking mightily upset.

'How could you take such an action as nuclear terrorism and not involve us? We are all accountable, are we not?'

Given the extreme events she was taking about there was a strange distancing in her demeanour and Munroe noted it immediately. Like someone who cared little for the tragedy, as if the nuclear bomb going off in New York was as important or unimportant as denting one's car. The woman appeared to have no sense of connection to such a loss of life and instead was only upset at the problems it caused for her personally.

'You are as beautiful as you are wise, sister, and I only ask that you and everyone here allow me to explain.'

It didn't take long for Brianna Bauer to nod politely in agreement, and it was now that Bauer turned his attention back to the crowd at large and continued, his voice soft yet firm. 'It is true that our reichführer ordered the nuclear detonation in New York, and with my help, but we did it for very different reasons. The bomb itself was of Russian design, and he, in his insane reasoning, believed it would lead to a nuclear exchange between America and Russia, and in doing so set the world ablaze. He honestly believed that Daedalus would rise from the apocalypse to create a new world order. It was why he tasked me with releasing the Russians' blueprints to the American intelligence services after the bomb had gone off.'

Bauer now raised his finger in the air and grimaced. 'Had I done so I doubt any of us would be sitting here today. So instead I turned his foolish idea to our advantage, and had not only the political wing of DSV killed in the blast, but I also had them blamed for it.'

There were looks on many faces of relief and perhaps the beginnings of admiration as Bauer explained further what the elites of Daedalus had been kept in the dark about.

'As of this moment what is left of our adversaries, DSV, are being blamed and hunted by the very governments they have always so blindly served. Furthermore, Blackstar has been contracted to hunt them down, and I am a trusted adviser to the British prime minister himself.'

There was a murmuring of gasps and shock and Bauer waved his hands, appealing for silence. 'There is more. I have also ensured, with the decapitation of DSV's political wing, that no one even knows Daedalus exists and it is this which brings me to my final offering for your respect.'

Bauer reached over and picked up the plain silver control from off Bormann's desk. He pressed one of the buttons and from the opposite wall a panel slid back, revealing a flat monitor. He then pushed another button and the screen flashed into life, displaying the Sky News channel and a conference taking place. It showed the chancellor of Germany sat at the middle of a large table at the UN building in Geneva, giving a press conference to waiting journalists. On either side of her sat the leaders of the main countries of NATO, with the British prime minister on her left and the president of the United States on her right. The sound was off but the banner headline read, 'Talks begin with unanimous participation of NATO.'

Bauer was now smiling confidently, and he gestured towards the screen. 'Daedalus has always kept its associates and political members secret from most of us, it was the decree of Reichführer Bormann. Only two of us ever knew the true extent of our reach. He and I dealt with the political wing whereas you were tasked with the financial side. And you have done a remarkable job and although unfortunately I had word that Mr Creasey could not join us for this meeting, it is with his financial mind, in part, that we have all flourished. Of the millions we were left with at the end of the Second World War, you, through all our holdings and subsidiaries, have turned it into billions, and it is with that money we will now forge ahead to our true destiny. I will now do what our reichführer would never do because of the mistrust and contempt he had for you all. I will involve everyone here in the political aspiration we now find ourselves capable of. Nothing brings people together like a tragedy and it is the tragedy in New York that will set the stage for a new milestone. As of this moment these politicians are discussing the proposal of a new world order. A world where every country is bound by a new organisation, a global attempt at what the EU managed for only European countries. An organisation to replace the United Nations where the political and military are fused together in the attempt to create a lasting peace for all the people of the world.'

The crowd looked on as Bauer stood there and humbly held his hands out to the Daedalus core. He smiled. 'You are witnessing the beginnings, that under our guidance will become the foundation for something so many have dreamed about but never achieved… a one-world government.'

The faces of the crowd members were ones of awe and surprise but before they could ask questions Bauer took a few steps closer to the monitor and he tapped the German chancellor in the middle of the screen.

'And what no one except us in this room realises is that the woman at the heart of it all is one of us… born into Daedalus.'

There was now silence as Bauer stood back from the screen, crossed his hands and waited to see what reaction he would receive. And it was almost ten seconds of stunned silence before the Daedalus elite began to clap. Slowly at first and then louder and louder, their appreciation obvious.

Munroe looked over at Sloan and stared at her as blankly as she was staring back at him. He had no idea if what Bauer was saying could work, but that Daedalus had their dirty fingers at the centre of so much political power was extremely worrying, to say the least, and he now prepared his firearm as Munroe did the same.

'We've got it. Send them in,' he whispered quietly as they both retreated back onto the landing and positioned themselves either side of the doorway leading directly into the meeting room.

'They're on their way in,' Talon replied over Munroe's earpiece. With a nod Munroe kicked open the door and as Sloan entered she slammed her gun down over the single security guard's head, sending him to the floor. Munroe now aimed his Glock at Bauer and Teston, who was already looking decidedly nervous and standing motion-less in the far corner of the room.

'Nobody move,' Munroe shouted as Sloan focused on crowd control and screams and yells burst from many of their lips. The bizarre thing was that these dozen or so men and women looked like nobodies. There were no people of monstrous appearance with blood dripping from their lips but instead only a shocked bunch of pampered elites who looked offended that their day was being inter-rupted. The face of true entitlement.

Downstairs, they could hear doors crashing open, followed by the sound of hurried and heavy footsteps as a squad of three men rushed into the room and aimed their assault rifles at the small crowd of people. Two of the men wore black tactical uniforms with hoods and the third pointed his revolver at Bauer. 'Well, well, well.'

GCHQ chief and intelligence adviser to the British prime minister James Bremen snarled at Bauer, who was now looking completely shocked, and as his two men edged their way further into the room, Munroe holstered his gun and pulled off the strip of tape from McCitrick's lips as Sloan cut his binds.

'Did you hear it all?' Munroe asked, and Bremen nodded.

'I did, loud and clear, just as you said I would.'

'What the hell is going on?' Bauer yelled as Bremen barked orders to his two men, ignoring Bauer for the time being.

'Would you ladies and gentlemen go with these agents, please, they will have some questions for you.'

The crowd all looked at Bauer, who gave them a nod. 'Don't say a word,' he ordered, and like a bunch of mute cattle the group did as they were told, with the exception of Brianna Bauer who approached Bremen and slapped him across the face before then being guided sternly by Bremen's agents, who led the group downstairs and outside as McCitrick turned to Sloan. 'Well done, Captain. Go with them, would you, and keep an eye on them.'

Sloan shot him a smile. 'Yes, sir,' she said, and headed back downstairs as McCitrick turned to face Bremen.

'It's good to see you, James, but I do have one question. What is the head of GCHQ doing here?'

Bremen looked confused as Munroe now headed over and pushed Bauer against the wall. 'Your man here got in contact with me and managed to convince me that he could prove DSV's innocence while at the same time capturing the real culprit.' Bremen looked over at Munroe and raised his eyebrow. 'Looks like he was right.'

McCitrick managed a smile as Munroe patted Bauer down and then pushed him towards the two men and pressed his finger to his ear to check in on his other teammates.

'Talon, it's time to come in. How are we looking?'

There was silence over the earpiece and Munroe paused and looked out of the window towards the shipping yard in the distance. 'Talon. Come in.'

There was still silence, and then from the corner of his eye Munroe saw the barrel of a gun pointing directly at him.

'Honestly, John, I'm surprised your boys made it so far,' James Bremen said, taking a step back and moving his gun between both Munroe and McCitrick. 'Let go of him, Ethan.'

Munroe considered his options for a second and then let go of Bauer, who immediately went for Bormann's desk drawer, pulling out an automatic .45 Colt and pointing it towards Munroe.

'Sorry, John,' Bremen said coldly, 'but you're on the wrong side here.'

Chapter 28

McCitrick looked uncharacteristically shocked, and he stared at Bremen venomously as Bauer motioned Munroe back against the window with a wave of his hand. 'You're Daedalus? Since when?'

'Since always,' Bremen replied, and he nodded for McCitrick to join Munroe by the window as a deep grin appeared on Bauer's face. 'You're born into this life and with a lot of help and time it has allowed me to position myself exactly where I need to be.'

Munroe felt like he'd just been dealt a hefty blow to the stomach and McCitrick didn't look much better. With everything that had taken place over the past weeks it had to be said that this bunch of inbred, Nazi-loving despots had well and truly played a blinder and it sickened Munroe to his core.

Bremen almost looked sorry to be dumping this on McCitrick, perhaps a degree of professional courtesy on his part, but for Bauer it was the opposite and he appeared to be enjoying… no absolutely revelling in his serpent-like success.

'It's a game of chess that you idiots at DSV could never fathom,' Bauer said, continuing to take great pleasure in this final betrayal, 'that's why you could never hope to stop us, because the pieces were already in place before you even came to the table. The game was stacked against you before you ever sat down to play. That is our strength and always has been.'

'You're like a disease,' McCitrick said with distaste on his lips, 'and you infect everything around you.'

Bauer took a moment to slam the butt of his gun into Bormann's face once more – the old man was beginning to make groaning sounds – and then he approached McCitrick, all the while maintaining a sensible distance. 'Do you know how one infiltrates from the beginning?'

Both McCitrick and Munroe remained quiet, neither caring to add in any way to Bauer's gloating.

'No? Then let me tell you how. You make sure you're *there* at the beginning, idiots. The end of the Second World War signalled the beginning of a new world order. From that moment the beginnings of a true global community sprang into place. Everything of political worth on a global scale began then, and everything in the modern world today has capitalised on the back of it. Hell, there were Nazis everywhere after the war ended, they merely took off their uniforms.'

Bauer attempted a smile, but it manifested on his lips as a grimace. 'The Reich was able to recognise it and utilise those who were still willing, that's all. The incredible foresight is second nature to the true master race.'

Bremen was now smiling too, and he craned his head respectfully to Bauer. 'I apologise for the unexpected entrance, but after Munroe called me I didn't want any intercepted lines of communication to spoil the surprise.'

'Not at all, James, so long as you get the job done. But this does cause me some bother,' Bauer stated, now leaning on the desk's edge. 'Having these imbeciles on the run was a good way of ingratiating myself with Prime Minister Previn.'

Bremen looked over at McCitrick and his nostrils flared. 'Yes, I enjoyed making the introduction, but I'm sure we can spin it some other way. The position of the chief of GCHQ does not come without weight.'

The blatant ripping apart of everything McCitrick held dear had him looking venomous and as he and Munroe looked on Bauer rolled his eyes. 'I couldn't agree more.'

Bremen's forehead exploded in a puff of red mist, sending the man's brains splattering against the wall as both Munroe and McCitrick jolted backwards looking for the gunman until they settled their focus in unison on the barrel of Bauer's Colt 45.

Bremen continued to stand upright for a moment, the smug smile still etched on his face, and then his shoulders twitched and his knees began to buckle before he dropped to the floor in a heap, his hand still clutching the revolver.

'I can't have this game ending just yet,' Bauer said, enjoying the power difference between them. Then, as Teston gained the confidence to pull a Glock from his waistband and cover the two DSV agents, he moved over to the still unconscious Bormann and without pause put a bullet in his head as well, spraying the window behind him in crimson red. 'So, let's recap,' Bauer began, turning the Colt back on Munroe, 'you've not only killed GCHQ Chief James Bremen but one of Blackstar's board of directors. My, my. DSV have been causing mayhem recently.'

Bauer now flicked the edge of his barrel towards the door. 'I don't care how many of you survive just as long as there are a few for the world to hunt... and we *will* hunt you. To the ends of the earth.'

Bauer turned to Munroe with a genuine look of affection. 'Despite you being a do-gooder and a merciless prick, I like you, Ethan. I think chasing you would pose a challenge, though with the insurmountable force of nations that descend upon you it will probably be more akin to shooting fish in a barrel. I think, though, we can say goodbye to McCitrick here. He's old and unimportant.'

Munroe instinctively moved between the barrel of Bauer's gun and McCitrick and he stared at the new Daedalus reichführer with a furious glare. 'He goes, I go.'

Bauer's gun fell limply to one side and then it flicked back up and aimed directly at Munroe's chest. 'So be it. Goodbye, Ethan Munroe. I will enjoy chasing the others. Sloan especially, I think I could have some fun with her. She has spirit... I will enjoy breaking it.'

No sooner had he finished speaking than the window shattered and Munroe heard Talon's voice over his earpiece.

'Jump.'

As another bullet hit the mahogany desk, dropping Bauer to the floor in a defensive position, Munroe latched on to McCitrick and pulled him through the shattered window sending them falling down onto the roof below as another shot rang out overhead. Another push from Munroe sent both men tumbling off the roof and down to the back lawn, where they landed with a heavy thump.

'Let's move,' Munroe shouted and he dragged McCitrick to his feet and lugged the DSV section chief to the wall before calling out over his earpiece.

'Talk to me? Where are Sloan and Barbeau?'

'He picked her up when the shooting started.'

It was a relief and Munroe now focused on getting himself and McCitrick to safety. 'Somebody talk to me.'

'Two aggressors with automatics heading through the front door. Move.'

The voice was Dalton's this time, and with McCitrick now at his side they headed around the building with Munroe in the lead. 'Talon, you're clear. Fall back.'

'Already gone,' came the reply, and Munroe paused at the edge of the building and peered around to the front lawn.

'You're clear as well, Ethan. I'd take the Range Rover,' Dalton directed and without pause Munroe and McCitrick headed past the bushy hedge line concealing the two guards' bodies and leapt into the Range Rover parked up against the kerb. Munroe was already checking the ignition as McCitrick slammed the door shut and pressed the lock.

'Shit, no keys,' Munroe gasped as shots began slamming against the window and he looked up to see the two security guards exiting the beach house's entrance and firing at them. Each dull-sounding impact created a circular shatter mark and as the Range Rover's bulletproof glass took the damage Munroe prepared to exit from the driver's side as the sound of a sniper shot sent one of the guards flipping back onto the lawn. It was followed quickly by a second shot, which hit the other guard right between the eyes, dropping him to the grass in a heap. 'Thank you, Zeke,' Munroe shouted, and then he exited the vehicle and ran over to the two bodies and began searching their pockets. He found the keys on the first try and after grabbing one of the carbines next to the nearest guard he jumped back in the car and tossed the automatic weapon over to McCitrick before firing up the engine.

'There's two more Range Rovers approaching from the west,' Dalton informed them, and Munroe slammed the automatic into gear and took off in reverse down the street as the two oncoming vehicles began closing in on them.

'Get to the rendezvous, Zeke,' Munroe yelled as more bullets struck the windshield and as Munroe reached the end of the road he skidded the vehicle ninety degrees backwards and then took off at high speed with the other vehicles giving chase.

The roads were still busy despite the sun being near to setting behind them and Munroe weaved back and forth, angry pedestrians yelling insults as they hurtled past at high speed.

'I hope you've got a way out,' McCitrick said. Behind them automatic fire turned the back window into a splintered mess, but not penetrating; the bulletproof glass doing its job.

'Wouldn't be much good if we didn't, sir,' Munroe replied calmly and it garnered a smile from McCitrick, who wound down his window and began letting off rounds in short bursts at the cars behind.

Munroe careered up on the pavement and over the oncoming cross section, just missing an obese man wearing a shirt which read 'Fat Guys Do It Better', and as he glanced in his rear-view mirror he caught sight of the closest 4x4 ploughing into the man head on. The collision brought the vehicle to a brief stop before it revved up its engine and began chasing them once more as onlookers screamed and yelled out after the bloodstained car.

'Jesus,' Munroe yelled as McCitrick continued to lay down fire, his aim never landing a bullet anywhere else but the vehicle behind.

Sensing an opportunity to put some distance between them and their pursuers, Munroe dropped a gear and tore off at high speed and as he felt the first sliver of relief it ended when a white SUV appeared from the oncoming side road and slammed up against them, as even more bullets impacted on the driver's side window.

It was getting difficult to see due to the window damage but as Munroe fought against the steering wheel, being pulled to one side with every knock from the SUV, he caught sight of the man driving the car.

Gasparyan glared at him, his teeth gritted tightly shut as he slammed the SUV into the side of Munroe's Range Rover, and again Munroe dropped down a gear and returned the favour, slamming into the SUV at his side. Unfortunately it didn't have the effect he wanted and with Gasparyan screaming something from behind the steering wheel a man in a flak jacket appeared from the passenger side and began unloading his carbine over the top of the SUV's roof. Once again Gasparyan slammed back into them as automatic fire continued to rain down.

Their car's exterior was taking a beating, but the engine was still running strong and as Munroe looked up ahead he caught sight of a large yellow skip outside one of the upcoming shops. There was scaffolding surrounding the building where work was being carried out on the front entrance and Munroe jammed down the accelerator and headed straight for it. 'Hold on,' he shouted and McCitrick pulled his carbine back inside the vehicle and braced himself as Munroe swerved wide and tapped the brake, sending Gasparyan's SUV past them until they were level. Then one final time he slammed into its side, sending it careering off towards the skip. Munroe caught one final look of panic on the psychopath's face before the SUV collided with the skip, bringing the 4x4 to a crunching halt in a haze of twisted metal and dust.

Munroe now sped off down the road with the other two Range Rovers in pursuit.

'Couldn't have happened to a nicer guy,' he growled as McCitrick resumed his position at the passenger window and unleashed the last few bullets in his clip.

'I'm out,' he shouted.

Munroe called out over the earpiece. 'We're on Flagler Avenue—' was all Munroe managed before he was shunted from behind by the nearest Range Rover, sending them up onto the pavement and crashing through a row of white picket fences before skidding back onto the road. 'And we're coming in hot.'

With no more use for the carbine, McCitrick hurled it into the back seat, and for the first time clipped in his seat belt and attempted to close his passenger window, but the electrics had already given out. 'I don't want to sound ungrateful, Ethan, but I would like to get out of here in one piece.'

The comment drew a chuckle from Munroe as he dodged back and forth across the road attempting to stop the nearest Range Rover from getting up beside them. 'Doing my best, sir,' he uttered as they approached a level crossing with a group of children running across to the pavement in a panic, the three speeding vehicles hurtling towards them.

'Shit,' Munroe uttered under his breath and he tapped his brakes, allowing the last child to make it up onto the pavement before they sped past. Unfortunately the move cost him momentum, and from his side one of the Range Rovers pulled up next to him and began shooting once more into the driver's side window.

By this point the window had taken all it was going to handle and glass exploded onto his chest as the first hole appeared.

It's just a matter of time before the whole integrity of the frame gives way.

Munroe again rammed into the side of the vehicle and through the small hole he saw the barrel of a carbine raised up towards him, directly at his chest and with little else he could do in that moment he just waited for the shot to be taken when a powerful collision sent their car over to one side. At the same time, the Range Rover spun out and slid off the road, coming to a juddering stop in the hedge line of someone's front yard.

Munroe looked through the hole to see Barbeau's face in the driver's seat of a black Porsche Cayenne, with Sloan in the passenger side, and with a nod of appreciation he turned his attention to the Range Rover on his right that was already pulling up beside them. Munroe rammed his bonnet hard into the vehicle's front side, catching it just right and sending it hurtling into the side of a Red Lobster restaurant, where it crumpled in a cloud of smoke and debris.

'Thanks, Jean,' Munroe called out, and he received a cocky wink from the Frenchman who now took the lead, and with no one else following them, they sped away in a convoy for a few more minutes until they reached a small dirt road. Without slowing down Barbeau crashed through a small steel fence, followed by Munroe, bringing the two cars slamming onto the tarmac runway of Key West International Airport.

They both came to a tyre-burning stop next to a Cessna Citation X jet, whose engines were already rotating, and all four of them hopped out of their destroyed 4x4s and ran towards it as Dalton poked his head out of the open hatch and let down the unfolding steps.

'I wasn't sure you were going to get here,' he shouted as all four DSV agents piled in through the hatch. Dalton headed back to the cockpit where he was joined by Munroe who quickly slid into the pilot's seat.

Behind him the sound of the hatch locking into place had him grasping the throttle in preparation, but he paused as Dalton slapped him on the shoulder and pointed down to something further up the runway.

'Jesus Christ,' Munroe muttered heavily as he caught sight of the three police cars racing towards them from the furthest end of the runway. 'Is there anyone *not* after us?'

Without hesitation, Munroe pushed the throttles, sending the Cessna lurching forwards and it quickly began to gather speed.

'Everyone, brace yourselves,' Munroe yelled as the three police cars, lights flashing brightly, approached ever closer. Munroe was not about to swerve first. They needed at least five thousand feet of runway, and as the police cars continued to accelerate closer he knew it would be tight.

'This is going to be close,' Dalton said as Munroe was already attempting to lift them into the air as police cars bore down on them, neither willing to swerve.

In his head Munroe counted off the metres.

Seven hundred.

Five hundred.

Three hundred…

Munroe wrenched the yoke towards him, feeling the wheels just pull off the ground as all three police cars came screeching to a halt. The Cessna lifted off into the air, missing the middle car by only a few metres.

'Fucking hell,' Dalton shouted in relief and then he burst into laughter. 'That was some game of chicken.'

Munroe said nothing but shot his teammate a smile and continued to climb, leaving Key West far down below, and then flew onwards, out into the shiny blue waters of the Atlantic Ocean.

For the first five minutes no one said a thing, they only looked around at one another with smiles of appreciation, and it wasn't until Munroe announced over the intercom that they were now in international waters that they all began to relax. He passed over the controls to Dalton. 'Great shooting back there, Zeke. I owe you.'

Dalton shot him a smile and nodded. 'By the time this is all over I've got a feeling you'll be repaying me in kind.'

Munroe smiled and with a congratulatory slap on Dalton's shoulder he headed back to the cabin and the relieved-looking faces of the DSV team. He took a seat next to Sloan.

'I don't say this very often, but thank you,' McCitrick said loudly, and he glanced down the cabin at Dalton who waved his hand in the air. 'That was quite a rescue attempt.'

'Well I wanted to leave you,' Barbeau said with a smile, 'but Sloan just insisted.'

There were a few laughs but then an intense calm descended upon the cabin as McCitrick continued to speak his mind. It was the first time they had all been together since Mexico. 'We're going to have to drop off the map for a while... until we figure out what we're going to do. Good news is we have the finances and resources to stay one step ahead, but now our own governments are after us and with that asshole Bauer at the helm we'll have to play it careful. We may hate Daedalus, but we have to recognise that they have played us well and we need to learn from that.'

Sloan nodded solemnly as did Talon and Barbeau, but it was Munroe who was looking upbeat. 'Maybe so. But it's our turn next time. And I don't intend to get taken for a ride next time around.'

There was a mutual consensus in the air, and as McCitrick nodded he rubbed his fingers against his lips thoughtfully. 'So, before we go dark is there any unfinished business? We may not be able to resurface for a while. Not until everything settles down and we get an opening and the opportunity to repay the kindness they've shown us.'

They all looked at each other, but it was Munroe who spoke for them all.

'Well, sir. There is one last end to tie up.'

McCitrick's eyebrows raised upwards and he looked around to see that whatever it was they had all already agreed upon it. 'OK, so what's the loose end?'

Munroe could see his boss was already looking concerned, and he immediately sought to allay any fears. 'Don't worry, sir. I think you'll approve.'

Chapter 29

'Get up there,' Detective Rand ordered and roughly pushed the prisoner in the yellow jumpsuit up the steps of the Leer Jet 75. He glanced back at the three police cars that had cordoned off that part of the runway at Bordeaux Airport and gave the nearest officer a salute. 'Thanks for your help, we'll take it from here.'

The officer replied with a nod and then waved his hand in the air as the other armed officers got back in their vehicles and watched the detective head inside the plane. The pilot poked his head out of the hatch and the steps were pulled up.

'Sit,' Rand grunted, and he pushed the prisoner down into the grey leather seat and undid one side of the man's handcuffs, chaining it to the armrest. He then took a seat opposite and glanced over at the younger officer who was already on board.

'It's over an hour's trip so feel free to take a nap.'

The offer was said sarcastically at the younger man who shook his head and tightened the buckle on his seat belt. 'Not tired, sir. Appreciate the offer though.'

The engines of the jet powered up and began rolling towards the main runway, and it was only now that the armed escort began to make its way slowly off the tarmac. The younger officer watched the small motorcade and shook his head, looking up at Detective Rand. 'That's a lot of fire power for just one man,' he said, referring to the M4 automatic rifles the police unit had been carrying.

'Depends on the man, doesn't it, Officer…?'

'Talbot, sir. I only received this assignment this morning. Something about wanting an escort with no prior knowledge of the prisoner because of security concerns.'

Rand gave an uncaring nod and he glanced over at the prisoner who had a black canvas blindfold around his head and a pair of earmuffs over his ears. 'Good job too, the man's a category one. Do you know what that means?'

Talbot attempted not to look unknowledgeable and he shrugged his shoulders. 'I know it means he's dangerous.'

'How very astute of you, Officer Talbot. All you need to know is that this man is on a one-way trip and he's responsible for a lot of deaths.'

The vague description had Talbot now looking curious, and he leant forwards and whispered, 'Is he a serial killer?'

'No,' Rand replied, wincing, and he leant forwards as well and whispered back, 'and you don't have to whisper, you idiot, he's got ear muffs on. He can't hear a thing.'

Talbot wasn't amused, and he grunted and sat back in his seat. From the cockpit one of the pilots appeared and approached their seats. 'There's a nasty headwind,' the pilot stated, and he looked back at the small service galley, 'could add fifty minutes on to our trip, but don't worry, there's more than a few airports between here and Paris if we get into any trouble. Can I get you gentlemen a drink?'

'I'll have a coffee,' Rand replied as Talbot nodded and motioned to the detective.

'I'll have a coffee as well, please.'

'Of course,' the pilot said politely, and he headed back to the galley and began brewing two cups of coffee as Rand stared over at the still curious officer. He raised his finger and arched it towards him. 'You want to know who he is?'

Talbot leant forwards once more and looked over Rand's shoulder. Satisfied the pilot wasn't eavesdropping, he turned his attention back to the detective who had a distasteful look on his face. 'He's a terrorist. The most wanted man in the world. One of two we have in custody. The other's in a holding cell already in Paris, some guy called Lavigne, and our friend here is going to join him today.'

Talbot looked over at the prisoner and eyed him up and down. There was no further explanation needed and when he returned Rand's gaze he appeared angry, his lips curling upwards in disgust. 'New York?'

Rand sat back in his seat and slowly nodded his head. 'One of the masterminds behind the attack, apparently. I'm not meant to know but one of the agents transferring him into my custody let it slip. Yep,' both Rand and Talbot now stared over at the tall man chained to his seat, unaware he was being spoken about, 'that man sitting less than two feet away is responsible for the death of tens of thousands.'

The pilot now walked over and placed the steaming hot drinks on the cabin table before them as the two men sat back in their seats, eyeing each other knowingly.

'Would your passenger like anything, gentlemen?' the pilot asked. It appeared as if Rand was about to shake his head, but he paused and seemed to think better of it. 'Why not. He may not be getting another hot drink for a long time where he's going.'

Rand glanced over at the younger officer and motioned towards the prisoner. 'Why don't you do the honours. I doubt you'll see him in person again. Just pull his blindfold up and slip off his ear muffs. Don't worry, he won't bite.'

Talbot appeared excited by the prospect and unbuckled his seat belt and then bent over the prisoner as Rand took a sip of his coffee. The young officer did as he was told and cautiously slipped off the ear muffs and rested them against the seat before gripping the edges of the blindfold and slipping it up onto the prisoner's forehead.

Colonel Jacques Remus blinked his eyes and winced at the brightness of the cabin lights overhead. He then turned his attention to Talbot, who took a moment to study his features, staring at him like he was an animal in a cage.

'Drink?' was all the officer said, and Remus's eyelids tightened again as he acclimatised to his surroundings.

'What?' he replied, and now it was the pilot who leant closer to him and asked the question.

'Would you like a drink, sir?'

Colonel Remus stared into the eyes of Ethan Munroe, who was dressed up in a pilot's uniform, and he let slip a smile. 'A coffee would be lovely. Thank you... and what a nice outfit you're wearing.'

Munroe looked over at the police officers and gave a look as if he was creeped out by the comment before returning his gaze back to Remus. 'Thank you, sir. I'm becoming rather fond of it myself.'

Munroe pulled away and headed back to the galley before glancing back at Remus. 'How do you take it, sir?'

'Black,' Remus replied, now smiling at Talbot, 'and very hot.'

The security van escorted by four police cars sped down the taxi lane of Charles de Gaulle Airport towards the waiting Leer Jet as, inside, one of the armed officers cursed loudly. They were supposed to meet the aircraft on the other side of the runway in a hangar, and already an hour late the last-minute change of plans was unacceptable. 'Whoever screwed this up is going to get a boot so far up his arse,' Officer Yellis bellowed as they approached the jet, and now the sight of the open hatch had him really worrying. 'Shit,' he said, and pointed to the flip-down stairs hanging from the aircraft's exit. 'Pull up here.'

The security van skidded to a halt and Yellis was the first out, rushing over to the plane and pulling his Glock from its holster. As he got close he slowed his pace and behind him the other officers rushed to join him.

'Show yourself,' he yelled, holding still as the other officers took up positions around the open hatchway, pointing their weapons in preparation for anything.

'Whoever is in the Leer Jet, show yourself and do it slowly,' Yellis ordered again gruffly but there was no movement, and he glanced back at the other men and was about to take a step forwards when a muffled groan came from inside the aircraft. Yellis once more glanced back at the other armed officers and with a nod he approached the hatchway slowly until he reached the stairs and poked his head into the nearest window. What he saw had him lowering his gun in disbelief. 'What the hell?'

He was met by the face of a man with a gag stuffed in his mouth, who stared over at him with bleary eyes.

Manuel Ortega, boss of the Los Zetas cartel, attempted to say something but it was unintelligible, and Yellis now looked over to see two men passed out on their seats with coffee cups discarded on the floor next to them.

Yellis raised his hand in the air and holstered his gun as the other officers moved over to his position, and as they did so his attention turned to the piece of A4 paper that had been pinned to Ortega's shirt, a single sentence written in thick black marker.

Handle with care... You're welcome.

Chapter 30

Lori Benedict knocked on the door of the prime minister's personal office and waited. The death of GCHQ Director James Bremen had hit those at Number 10 who knew him very hard, particularly Prime Minister Previn, who was showing an unusual nervousness that she had not seen before. The confident and straight-speaking British leader had become closed-off and far more private than in all his previous years as prime minister. Even though his demeanour in public had not changed, behind closed doors and to those that knew him, the change had been obvious.

'Come,' the muffled voice called out and Benedict pushed open the door and poked her head inside.

'Hans Bauer on line one, sir.'

'Ah, good. Thank you, Lori.'

Prime Minister Andrew Previn picked up the green receiver off his desk and placed it to his ear as he turned and looked into the garden at the back of Number 10. 'Hans, thank you for the Blackstar report you provided… as you can imagine we're all very upset. James Bremen was a good man and someone I've known since before taking this office.'

'I know, Mr Prime Minister, it was a tragedy. He was a young man with so much talent and to see it happen in front of me, well… I've been having nightmares, if I'm honest.'

'That must have been horrible, to see it.'

'It was, but it has only spurred me on to do what I can to bring these DSV thugs to justice. I won't go into the unsightly details, but I will say that the complete lack of humanity shown when the trigger was pulled was something I would have expected from a movie drug lord.'

'Yes, as I said, I read your report and it was confirmed by MI6. John McCitrick and his men have close ties with the Los Zetas cartel. It's no surprise they share such disregard for human life. If one sleeps with dogs they will catch fleas.'

'I agree, Mr Prime Minister. I only wish we could have arrested them there and then.'

There was a pause, and when Previn came back on the line his tone had lowered and his voice was serious, almost raspy. 'It is imperative that these people are brought to justice. I would like to involve Blackstar more at this stage. As a private contractor, with the reputation you have of dealing with many Western governments, I know we can count on not only your transparency but your discretion, and until these people are arrested we will need much of both.'

'I very much appreciate the trust you're placing in me and my organisation, and we are at your disposal, Prime Minister. I consider this a duty, and given the lives these people have destroyed I will do anything and everything in my power to help.'

'That's good to hear, Hans, because I would like you to liaise personally with the new secretary of defence. I will have his direct number sent over to you and would like you to get in touch with him. He will be expecting your call.'

'Of course, Prime Minister. I will contact him the moment we're finished.'

There was now another pause, longer this time. Previn lightly rapped his knuckles on the desktop and held the receiver closer. 'I've decided that these people are a clear and present danger to not only British national security, but the West as a whole.'

'So what are you saying, Mr Prime Minister?'

'I'm saying we're going to war with these people, Hans. Whatever it takes.'

There was a short silence, and when Bauer came back on there was a coldness to his voice that could have frosted the receiver. 'Then war it is, Mr Prime Minister. And I will make you this one single promise, on my life, that by the time I'm through with them, the remaining members of DSV will wish they had never been born.'

Acknowledgements

To Kit Nevile, my editor, for all the hours, advice and help to make this book all I hoped it would be. Get ready for the next one.

To Alex Shah for his knowledge and guidance of firearms and the judiciary system.

To Tamsyn Curry for her automotive advice throughout the book.

To Michael, Iain, Nick and everyone at Canelo Publishing.

To Elinor at Canelo for all her help with *Project Icarus*. Much appreciated.

And as always Alison and Charlotte.